the MISMATCH

a novel

SARA JAFARI

DELL

NEW YORK

A Dell Trade Paperback Original

Copyright © 2021 by Sara Jafari
Book club guide copyright © 2021 by
Penguin Random House LLC

All rights reserved.

Published in the United States by Dell,
an imprint of Random House, a division of
Penguin Random House LLC, New York.

Originally published in the United Kingdom by Arrow, an imprint of Cornerstone, in 2021. Cornerstone is part of the Penguin Random House group of companies.

Dell and the House colophon are registered trademarks of Penguin Random House LLC.

ISBN 978-0-5933-5717-0
Ebook ISBN 978-0-5933-5718-7

Printed in the United States of America on acid-free paper

randomhousebooks.com
randomhousebookclub.com

2 4 6 8 9 7 5 3 1

Book design by Alexis Capitini

the
MISMATCH

To my best friend, the greatest mother,
and the strongest, smartest woman I know:
Touran Soltanifard-Razlighi

the
MISMATCH

PROLOGUE

Brighton, 1999

Neda wondered whether other people noticed when their families fell apart or if, like her, it caught them by surprise. Time and time again, after everything they had been through, and just when she felt able to exhale, loosen her shoulders, a new problem would arise, the ground shifting beneath her once more.

Her daughter's words echoed in her ears.

The cars ahead of her blurred into one. She pulled over to the side of the road, without indicating and without checking her mirrors, car tires screeching in the process. They jolted forward when she slammed on the brakes.

Laleh had spoken and there was no going back now.

"How could this have happened?" Neda said through gritted teeth.

"I don't . . ." Laleh whispered before breathing out unsteadily, tears running down her face.

A bus honked at them for stopping in the bus lane.

"You don't *know?*" Neda's tone was mocking.

"Do you hate me?"

"You're a stupid, stupid girl." Neda's head was in her hands as she came to terms with her own worst childhood fear being realized by her daughter. The mood in the car shifted from hostile to fearful. "What do we do?" Neda said to herself.

Laleh kept her head bowed while Neda turned and stared at her. She was ashamed of her daughter, of course, but that did not mean she wanted anything bad to happen to her. Thinking of how Hossein would react made Neda turn pale. What an Iranian man would do upon finding out his seventeen-year-old daughter had transgressed to such a degree . . .

"How could you?" Neda whispered. She gripped her daughter by the shoulders, fingernails digging into her flesh.

They were unaware of the cars still whizzing past them. Some drivers shouted profanities. It was all background noise. Inconsequential in comparison to what was to come.

Neda removed her hands from Laleh and folded them on top of each other in her lap.

"What should I do?" her daughter asked.

Neda had always provided her children with guidance, but how could she help Laleh now?

She made a promise to herself that she would do better for the others. But for her eldest daughter it was too late.

"You must never tell your dad." Neda spoke sharply then softened her tone. "He would kill you."

"So what do I do?"

"You have to leave."

Part
ONE

Chapter 1

SORAYA

London, 2014

When people asked Soraya how many people she had slept with the number varied depending on her mood.

Ten.

Six.

Three.

Twelve.

Or sometimes she might say nothing at all, instead suggesting she didn't want to talk about it, which made them think the number was at the higher end. Such inquiries focused on her level of experience, worked on the assumption that she must have some, so she didn't feel bad about lying. She knew she couldn't expose the extent of her inexperience; to be different was to be noticed. She didn't want to be noticed. Not in that way.

Soraya Nazari was twenty-one years old and had never been kissed.

At school and sixth form it was clear she was a virgin; everyone knew she wasn't allowed a boyfriend; her family's strictness was recognized. She wore unflattering clothes that showed no skin, revealed no curve, her shape left to the imagination, though she doubted anyone bothered to imagine it. She didn't go to parties, or the final year prom. She wasn't allowed.

At university, away from home, in London, no one knew her past. The only exception was her closest friend, Oliver. But his predicament was akin to hers, their mutual understanding unspoken and concrete.

Perhaps suspecting moving away from home would lead to haram acts, a week before Soraya left, three years ago now, her mum took her for a walk on Worthing Beach.

There was only an elderly couple walking along the seafront at a distance. The wind was lashing hard enough almost to blow her mum's silk hijab away. Despite the wind though, the sky was clear.

"I need to talk to you about something, and you need to take what I say seriously," her mum said.

Soraya could already feel the weight of what her mum wanted to say, and longed to escape such a conversation.

"Boys will try and get you alone when you go away. They may try and do *things* with you." Despite her mum's grave tone, Soraya rolled her eyes. "Don't let them do that. They only have one thing on their mind. Doing it would ruin your life. And remember"—she paused for dramatic effect—"God is watching."

"I know," Soraya said. "Nothing will happen. I'm smart enough, don't worry."

At least she hadn't lied to her mother: nothing did happen at university.

Soraya carefully considered everything she did; she thought and rethought the consequences of her actions. It was not as simple as once she moved away from home to university, all of the teachings from her younger years about the importance of morals and purity were discarded. She was gradual in her approach; gradual in doing the things she'd longed to do when she was growing up.

In first year, she drank for the first time, took drugs, and went to parties.

In second year, she wore short skirts and dresses without tights.

In third year, she attempted to talk to boys. But unlike the other rules she broke, this one was difficult to do with reckless abandon. Muslim guilt was a funny thing. It came when she least expected it.

It was impossible to disentangle her guilt at disobeying God from the guilt of disobeying her parents. The weight of it sat limp and heavy inside her.

Because she was a girl the rules enforced upon her all related to her sexuality, specifically with the aim of preserving her virginity. Going to parties and drinking alcohol led to a loosening of inhibitions (supposedly), which would (supposedly) then lead to premarital sex, known as zina. *A shameful deed, an evil, which leads to other evils.*

But with more and more time spent away from home, she wondered why sex was so evil. Why disobeying her family was so abhorrent. Why so much focus in her family's preaching was on controlling her, rather than on her being a good and just person.

She longed to think freely, and not overanalyze her every decision.

Such thoughts, while troubling in the dead of night when she was unable to sleep, were unimportant now. It was a week before her graduation, and she had to either find a job or move back home with her parents. While she was once, three years ago, like a rabbit released into the wild, there was now the imminent threat of having to return to the same small hutch. A hutch she had outgrown.

"Why do you want to work for Purple B? Why marketing? Why data protection?"

It was Soraya's first graduate job interview, but she was fairly certain they were meant to ask only one question at a time.

She laughed nervously to buy herself some time. She looked around the bland meeting room, hoping inspiration would spark, but with its glass walls it was sterile apart from the rectangular table and the chairs surrounding it.

"Um, well, I have a keen interest in social media, and I know how to use all the channels really well. You're a company that prides yourself on keeping people and companies safe, and data protection is incredibly important, especially today, with all the scandals in the news . . ." She wasn't actually sure if there were any scandals in the news currently but gave them a "you know" look as though this was obvious.

The two interviewers nodded slightly. The younger of them

was a portly man who gave her a reassuring smile, while the bald-headed, older man was impassive.

Their team was small, contained within one medium-size office, and the meeting room she was in was akin to a fish tank. She didn't dare look at the workers outside for fear that they were looking in.

"How do you think you can get people to subscribe? There's so much free content online everywhere these days, how can *you* encourage paid subscribers?" the older man asked.

Well, Soraya thought, *aren't you meant to teach me that?* Somehow this was not a question her English literature degree had prepared her for.

She knew how painful it was to attempt to read *Ulysses* in just one week, about the layers of symbolism in *A Doll's House,* could compare the different portrayals of misers in seventeenth-century literature, even knew Ronald Knox's ten commandments of detective fiction by heart. But all of that was useless to her here.

"Through social media . . ." Soraya began but wasn't quite sure how to finish. They looked at her, waiting. "And online engagement . . ." These buzzwords meant nothing to her.

After four more similarly painful interactions, they thanked her and said they would be in touch in the coming weeks.

"Before you go, I have to ask," the portly man began, "where are you from?"

Her smile faltered for just a second.

"Oh, I'm from Brighton," she said.

"Really?" he said, leaning forward. The other man was gathering papers, ignoring the conversation around him.

"Well, some people say I have a bit of a Northern accent because my family used to live in Liverpool, so I guess I might have a Northern twang . . ."

"I meant more your name. Soraya Nazari." He said it with the emphasis on the wrong letters, putting his Western spin on it. "It's different, rather . . . exotic."

There was a short silence.

How many times in recent years had Soraya been called "exotic"? Too many. And yet, she couldn't remember anyone calling her that back home when she was younger. She remembered frequently being called a "Paki" however.

At first, she didn't mind the term "exotic," preferred it to racial slurs anyway. But it was only when she told her friend Priya this and Priya's immediate reaction was to spit out "We're not fucking fruit!" that Soraya realized it wasn't a good thing, but rather an act of othering.

A dictionary definition of "exotic" is

1. Introduced from another country: not native to the place where found.
2. Foreign, alien.
3. Strikingly, excitingly, or mysteriously different or unusual.
4. Of or relating to striptease.

So, with this definition in mind, it stung to be called "exotic." But she was desperate; this was the first graduate interview she had been invited to, and she had applied for jobs all summer, so she pretended to be unbothered by his comment.

"Ah, yes, my family came over from Iran," she said. "But I've only been a few times."

"Anyway," the older man said, standing, perhaps saving his colleague from making any further remarks. "Thank you, Soraya, for coming in."

She shook their hands in turn, remembering to use a firm grasp as though they'd hire her based on her above-par handshake despite the interview being a flop.

As she waited for the lift—an awkward experience in which she pretended she couldn't see everyone working around her as there was no corridor, the office being just one room—she felt an unfounded sense of hope. Maybe she didn't do so badly, she thought. Perhaps it was like in exams when she thought she did terribly, but in reality got a respectable B.

When the lift eventually arrived Soraya quickly walked in and pressed the close button. She looked at herself in the mirror, straightening her Zara trouser suit. She had red lipstick smudged on her front teeth, which she wiped off quickly with her clammy forefinger, hoping they hadn't noticed.

Exiting the building onto Old Street, she was met by an onslaught of workers rushing back to their offices post-lunch. As she walked towards the station, she became increasingly irritated: by the strappy kitten heels she'd decided to wear, by London's uneven pavements, by the people hovering behind her, trying to get around her. In London, you couldn't just walk at your own pace to your destination. The streets were too overcrowded and you were either slowed down by those in front or, like now, bothered by the people breathing down your neck. There was no space simply to enjoy a leisurely walk. She felt the urge to stop, quite suddenly, and create a human domino effect of people piling into each other and toppling over.

Ultimately, though, she was irritated because she had nowhere to be, no purpose, and she had never had this feeling before. Education had always been at the forefront of her mind, and there was always something she should be doing—an essay to be written, a book to be read, notes to be revised.

Now her future lay ahead of her, with no plan, no time line of what was to come, and she was falling face-first, ungracefully, into adulthood.

Chapter 2

SORAYA

London, 2014

The Richard Hoggart Building stood tall and not quite proud. The building was newly renovated, its exterior now featuring a gleaming white entryway with gold accents. By the front was no longer a shabby car park but instead landscaped grounds with benches, the perfect place for pregraduation photos. Families stood with their phones out, encouraging their soon-to-be graduates to pose by the grand university building. It was strange, Soraya thought, that people she had once seen snort MD and pee out of open windows (girls included) were now in suits and heels with their families. Everyone looked older since their final exams in May, three months ago now. Many stayed in their London houses over the summer, but she had seen only a handful of people from her course since university had ended.

The sun shone down oppressively onto her dark hair, causing her to perspire under her heavy gown. In pictures the day would look special, glamorous even. But the sound of traffic roaring down New Cross Road, and car horns in the distance, somewhat dampened the effect.

She stood down the side of the building, away from everyone else, by the large rectangular rubbish bins.

She rang her sister Parvin for the third time.

"Soraya?"

"Yes, it's me." She forced herself to speak slowly. "Where are you guys? The ceremony starts in ten minutes."

"We're nearly there. The traffic has been so bad. Can you believe it's taken us nearly two hours!"

Count to ten.

At four, she said, "I told you it would take that long. I checked Google Maps, remember?"

"Yeah, well, Amir didn't want to leave that early. Anyway it's done now. We'll be there in five minutes, honestly, just relax. Bye!"

Parvin hung up.

Soraya began to pull at the skin around her nails, becoming aware of what she was doing only when she looked down to see her maroon nail varnish was chipped. Her index finger bled. She pressed it against her black gown.

She composed herself and went to rejoin her friends in front of the building.

"I can smell it on you," she heard a male voice saying from around the corner. His Yorkshire accent was deep, elongating the last word. "You can't even walk straight. It's ten A.M., Dad . . ."

"It's my son's graduation—can't a man have a drink on his only son's graduation day? Jesus Christ!" another male voice said, though this one sounded older.

"Paul, I think what Magnus means is, we're a bit worried about—"

The woman's voice was cut off.

"Oh, you're both too bloody dramatic. Always fucking worrying. Be quiet, the pair of you. I'm off to the gates for a fag, or are you going to tell me off for that too? Maybe I should just go home while I'm at it. Wouldn't want me to embarrass either of you, would you, eh?"

Before anyone was given the chance to respond there was the sound of retreating steps and then a small sigh.

"He'd been doing so well," the woman said softly.

"Well, he's pissed now. What if he does something in the ceremony? In front of everyone I know. God, he's just . . ."

"I'm sorry, love. I'll go and check he's OK. See you inside? Don't worry, I'll make sure he behaves."

There was a long silence. As Soraya stood away from the wall,

Magnus Evans rounded the corner. Without looking at her, perhaps not even realizing she was there, he punched the brick building hard.

"Fuck!" he said, grasping his hand, as though surprised it would hurt.

Soraya stood very still, wondering, *What am I even doing?*

"Are you OK?" she asked him.

He looked towards her then, his head jerking in surprise. "Oh," he said.

Magnus's unkempt, curly hair seemed to have lightened in the sun over the summer; it was nearly blond now.

They had been in some seminars and lectures together during their three years at Goldsmiths, but had never spoken directly to each other before. All she really knew of him was that more often than not he was the only person in their seminars who had read the assigned books, and that he was something of a ladies' man, even though she hated that expression.

She couldn't help but notice now how broad his shoulders were under the graduation gown and wondered, not for the first time, if the way his broken nose had been set bothered him. It bent ever so slightly to the left, and was crooked in a different way from hers. She imagined this quirk only made him more attractive to girls, gave a bit of an edge to his otherwise perfect physique. She was reminded of Angela Carter's Mr. Lyon, how his broken nose was described as akin to that of a handsome retired boxer, and thought it an apt description of Magnus too.

She looked at his hand. "You're bleeding."

He shook it.

"It fucking hurts too." He laughed then. The sound rang hollow. He locked his gaze with hers for a moment, and in the sunlight his eyes looked deep brown, striking. "I feel like a knob, I didn't know anyone was here."

The compulsion to tell him she understood was overwhelming. Because she did. She knew all about disappointing parents. Knew how even though you expected them to let you down, it still felt like your insides were being shoveled out when they did. You should

never let yourself hope when it came to a parent like that, but
sometimes it was unavoidable.

"You didn't hear any of that, did you?"

"No," she said, and pressed her lips together to stop herself
from saying anything else.

"I'm not the only one that's bleeding." He looked at her finger,
where a bright red streak was oozing from her fingernail.

She hadn't noticed she'd pulled it again. During her time at
university, when her anxiety worsened, she had learnt to accept
that the skin around her nails would always be sore. That washing
her hands would have to hurt due to the damage she was unconsciously inflicting on them.

Unlike for her friends and peers, studying English literature did
not come naturally to Soraya. She enjoyed it; her own life was so
staid at times, so rowdy at others, that being transported into detective stories, happily-ever-after romances, intense literary fiction,
and epic historical novels was more of a need for her than a pastime. Their love of romances was one of the few things she and her
mum had in common. But none of this meant Soraya was academically gifted. She had to work twice as hard to get worse grades than
students who wrote their essays in one stint the night before. For
this if for no other reason, she was glad university was over.

She shrugged. "Weird."

"What's your name again?" he asked, even though she knew
he already knew. They were Facebook friends; he had occasionally
liked her photos, which she found odd. He was a popular rugby
player, and she was a quiet nobody, who admittedly dressed very
well. He knew, but was doing the typical male thing of pretending
he didn't. She might never have had a boyfriend before, but she
knew what guys were like.

"Soraya, and you're . . . ?"

He narrowed his eyes at her, still cradling his hand. Up this
close, she noticed his dark eyebrows almost met in the middle. She
thought if anyone else had let their hair grow in this way it might
look unattractive, but perhaps it was the fact that this was a deliberate move that made it work for him.

"Magnus," he said. "We had seminars together."

"I thought you didn't know who I was?"

He shook his head and a glimmer of a smile traced his lips, but it was obvious he was distracted, his mind on other concerns. "I guess I did."

There was a short silence, in which neither of them made any move to leave.

He cleared his throat before asking, "You had a good summer, then?"

She had spent it between London and Brighton, and on the whole it had been unremarkable, though her sleep pattern had been worrying. Most days she woke at 1:00 or 2:00 P.M. and spent the afternoon applying for jobs in between Netflix TV show marathons.

"It was OK. Didn't do much, to be honest. How about you?"

"I started a new job a few months ago, so have been working all summer. Anything to not move back home." He shuddered at the thought, and she laughed.

"Yeah, I really don't want to go back home for good."

They looked at each other for a moment, and despite the fact that they were both now joking, smiles on their faces, she noticed that the sadness in his eyes remained. She wondered if he was seeing the same thing in her eyes that she saw in his. She thought so, because he gave her a smaller, soft smile, as though in acknowledgment.

Her phone pinged.

PARVIN: *We're walking up now.*

"Oh, my family are here. I've got to go. See you later, I guess."

She turned away and rounded the corner to see her mum, brother, and sister making their slow way towards her. She power walked over to them, getting away from Magnus to prevent any meeting of the two worlds she had endeavored for so long to keep separate: her university life and her home life.

The first thing she noticed was Parvin's figure-hugging dress.

It was calf-length, so didn't show any flesh that could be deemed incriminating by the men in their family, but it still outdid Soraya's. Not because the dress was particularly nice but because Parvin was Parvin. She was blessed with a flat stomach, big bottom, and tiny waist—a Betty Boop body type only she could be gifted with. Today, her long bleached-brown hair was curled into beachy waves, and Soraya noticed boys and girls checking out her sister.

Despite being twins, Parvin and Amir looked starkly different, which was exactly what Parvin wanted. Amir's thick, shiny almost-black hair was slicked back, which served to emphasize his slightly receding hairline. His beard was sharp and well groomed, giving his face a chiseled quality.

Her mum resembled a mother hen, standing between her unruly children, her hijab sharp and floral-patterned, matching her yellow A-line coat.

"Where's Dad?" Soraya asked, noticing an absence in the group. In actual fact there were two absences, but only one was spoken about.

The front of the building had quietened down, with just one family apart from Soraya's remaining.

"Everyone with a ticket needs to go in now. The ceremony is about to start!" an administrator called. The woman walked towards Soraya. "You too, come on."

And with that she was escorted away, her question left unanswered.

The ceremony was both anxiety-inducing and dull.

It seemed like everyone was competing to receive the loudest applause.

When her name was called, Soraya heard some weak clapping, and what she was sure was her best friend, Oliver, giving her a "woo." There was also a large booming yelp. It definitely did not come from her family but arose from a classmate.

As she was handed her certificate, she concentrated on not tripping over or drawing more attention to herself than was necessary while onstage. Once down the stairs and out of view, she looked towards the students who were sitting down. Magnus was looking over at her with a broad grin on his face.

He was known to be a flirt, but he'd never directed his attention towards her before.

A marquee reception on the college green followed the ceremony, with waiters dressed in tuxes serving elegant-looking canapés. The students were released onto the green first, and then parents and family members joined them shortly afterwards. The air there was fresh, a welcome change from the suffocating hall.

Soraya could see Magnus in the distance with a group, clearly his rugby friends. They were built. And they were loud. Full-bodied laughter came from them. It made Soraya want to cover her ears and escape. She hated the pack mentality lads had when they were together. They reminded her of the boys who'd laughed at her all those years ago at school, the ones who had commented on the dark hair on her fingers, on how different she supposedly was. Despite her school days being so long ago, their words stuck with her, pervading her thoughts unhelpfully.

She distinctly remembered a picture of Magnus on Facebook after a varsity match, his shorts riding up to expose his strong, muscly legs, with a group of cheerleaders around him. He was covered in mud, and Soraya got the impression at the time that he, and the girls around him, thought he looked handsome.

Rugby players at Goldsmiths, like at most universities, were a special breed; loved by some, hated by others. Soraya's friends fell into the latter category. Rumors went around that some of the previous year's had date-raped girls. They could often be found together in the student union, or the local pub, after a game, rowdy and excitable. Yet from seminars she knew Magnus was intelligent, even quiet sometimes. In many ways, she wasn't sure he fitted in with his crowd.

In one of their third-year seminars she remembered they had been studying a text which explored a dysfunctional romantic relationship. The class was quiet, as was often the case when people hadn't done the reading. The seminar tutor began to pick on people to get their opinions in an attempt to spark some kind of debate.

Most of the people who were selected to speak gave generic observations, commenting on the style of the writing, or the time period in which the text was written and how that affected it. However, what Magnus said when he was chosen to speak remained in Soraya's memory.

"I think it's a commentary against marriage, against the idea of belonging to another someone, which was a bold move in the nineteenth century. Even now, it would be a bold comment to make, but one I ultimately think is true. You can't belong to another person. It's no wonder marriage often ends in divorce—or worse, people sticking together when they can't stand each other. And is it even really right for human beings to be attached to another person for life?" He gave a small laugh after saying this, lightening what would otherwise be a bleak look at society.

She remembered him saying this for many reasons, one of them being that while he provoked a heated debate in the class about marriage on the whole, she noticed how pink the tops of his ears were after, as though he had accidentally revealed his opinion, despite his cool, controlled tone.

He was clearly speaking from the point of view of someone who disliked relationships, perhaps because he preferred more casual affairs. But still, she was surprised by how strong his feelings about it were.

It was difficult to judge Magnus's character, though, because she had never seen what he was really like outside the university classrooms and lecture halls. They did not go to the same parties. She, quite unlike Magnus, had spent the last three years with a select few individuals, who spent most of their days flicking through fashion magazines or talking about books they had read, preferring to spend their student loans on clothes rather than nights at the pub. Soraya's and Oliver's favorite pastime was spending hours in Selfridges looking at designer garments they could never afford.

Oliver appeared next to her then carrying two tall glasses of clear liquid. He wore a navy blue cord suit with a maroon bow tie and had grown out his afro, parting it to the side, a new look he had developed over the summer. It flattered his face nicely.

"Gin and tonic," he announced, taking a sip.

She downed hers in one, which was quite an effort.

"OK, then," Oliver said slowly, giving her side-eye.

"I can't drink in front of my family, remember?" Soraya quickly discarded the glass.

"Well, by all means then, down away." Oliver's dryness was something Soraya had acquired an understanding of a few weeks into their friendship, three years ago. He often spoke in a monotone, and when they'd first met, in freshers' week, she worried that she bored him. She soon realized that this was his tone with everyone, and that actually he quite liked her.

Despite coming from a different background, Oliver was the only close friend she had who truly understood her.

"I heard Margaret cheering for you," he said, lips pursed as he looked down at her.

"Margaret?" Soraya found herself smiling.

"Yes, Margaret Evans."

"Why are you calling him Margaret?"

"Because it's funny."

Despite smiling, she did not find it particularly funny.

"Since when were you two friends?" he asked.

"We're not."

"Maybe he *likes* you," Oliver said, amusement on his face, as though such a thought had to be humorous. She tried not to be offended.

"I mean . . ." She mock-shuddered.

She wouldn't tell Oliver what she'd overheard; some things were not gossip-worthy.

"Well, be careful, you know he's a player," Oliver said. "Damn, though, his ass looks good even with that robe on."

Soraya narrowed her eyes at him, opened her mouth to say something, then shook her head. "I have nothing to say to that."

When the families were let in, Oliver was swept away as his five siblings, parents, grandparents, and two cousins clustered around him. They had arrived even later than Soraya's family, despite him giving them directions all morning.

"I knew you should have worn your father's suit," Soraya heard his mother say.

"And why do you have your hair like that? Couldn't you have trimmed it for graduation?" his father added. "You could at least have made an effort, Oliver."

His family put exceptional pressure on him to be perfect. He said he thought it was because his parents were unhappy with their own lives, with what they hadn't achieved, that they were now attempting to live through their children. The plan they put in place for him, before he was even born, did not include him studying English at an arts university, or being gay. Therefore, of course, they did not accept either.

Soraya did not have long to dwell on Oliver's family because her own were walking towards her. Despite their distinctly different styles, they all had dark, well-defined eyebrows, large hazel eyes, and light olive skin.

Her mum was petite with strong cheekbones, tattooed black eyebrows, thin lips, and a cluster of freckles across her nose. Her hijab was moderately tight on her head, and she had a gold pin under her chin to fasten the silk fabric in place. She wore a thin trace of eyeliner—something she did only on special occasions. Parvin no doubt had drawn it on her. Her mum was hopeless at doing her own makeup.

As Parvin walked she swished her hips, keeping her head low while she typed on her phone. Soraya had spent all of the night before prepping her hair and skin for graduation, and two hours on her hair and makeup in the morning, but looking at her sister now she still didn't feel like it was enough. She resisted the urge to check whether Magnus was looking at Parvin.

Amir towered over them, somehow having dodged the Nazari family's small gene. He was grinning at Soraya, dimples prominent in his cheeks, which seemed impossible considering he had a beard. Perhaps she was only imagining his dimples from when he was younger. Despite his constant criticism of his sisters it was clear Amir was proud of them, which made it difficult, but not impossible, for them to resent his frequent sexist comments.

"Congratulations," they all said, in semi-unison.

"Thanks," Soraya said, before she saw her mum's gaze. She followed it to the waiter, who was holding a tray of canapés. The Nazari family's greatest pleasure in life was food. They didn't all, bar Parvin, have rounded bellies for no reason. As a result the family often attempted various diets to lose their stomach fat. Soraya herself had gained and lost the same five pounds for the last six years—yo-yo dieting was nothing if not normal in their household.

"Where's Dad?" Soraya asked her mum.

"He was tired so he stayed at home." Her mum looked to Amir for help but it was Parvin who spoke next.

"You have us here. Anyway you'd only moan if he came." Soraya felt a twitch of irritation. Nothing was ever a big deal unless it affected Parvin.

She wasn't even sure why she had gotten it into her head that he would show up. As she had wanted to say to Magnus before: she knew all too well what it was like to have a disappointing parent.

Chapter 3

NEDA

Tehran, 1973

Ever since she was a child, Neda was sure of one thing: she wanted to do more. More than her school friends were doing, what her mother did, and what was expected of her. She didn't want to stop learning, or stop working, once she married. She couldn't fathom the idea of no longer expanding her brain academically—because, after all, weren't human beings meant to challenge themselves?

She soaked up information, would become obsessed with subjects at school until she mastered them. And yet, secretly, she was intrigued by romance, though she didn't dare approach it. That was something she knew she needed real-life experience of in order to begin to truly understand it. While her dad was liberal enough to drink red wine in the evening, this liberalism did not extend to approving of his daughters talking to the opposite sex. And even if he did let her, she wasn't sure she would want to talk to boys. Learning from books was safe, risk-free. Talking to boys, men, was not.

Her academic success was not something her mother applauded. Maman wanted her to "act more like a girl," beginning by encouraging her to wear makeup. This was reinforced by Reza Shah calling for women to wear shorter skirts, be liberated, be his version of free. But Neda thought the whole point of freedom was to have choice. What was the point of freedom if it meant you were uncomfortable and not allowed to be quite yourself? How was that freedom?

It was clear to Neda that she was a disappointment to Maman;

their relationship had always been strained. Neda had tried to gain her mother's affection as every nonfavorite child does, but she had nine siblings to compete with. Maman disagreed with birth control and had babies right until her menopause hit. People in the neighborhood often made fun of her, saying she had a "large appetite." And in being one of her eldest, Neda was forced into maturity—or at least nanny duties—at a very early age, which meant Maman often saw her more as the help than as her daughter.

Days after Neda's seventeenth birthday, she put her hair in rollers the night before, shakily lined her eyes with black kohl, and made her cheeks a rosy pink. She resembled a doll. It was a stark contrast to her normally plain look. But Maman was too busy to notice this change, focusing on her younger children, ordering Neda around without looking at her.

"Don't you think I look different?" Neda asked.

Maman looked at her face, briefly; it was only a flash of a look, but it was enough. "What have you done to yourself? You look like a clown." She laughed, a raucous, infuriating sound. So, not quite the doll Neda had envisaged herself as.

Tears stung her eyes, and she wiped them away before they ran down her freshly blushed cheeks. In the process she smudged her eyeliner.

Rather than draw any further attention to herself, Neda retreated to the bathroom. She heard Maman call her name, feebly, before giving up and forgetting about the incident entirely.

Neda washed her face with a bar of soap and cold water, allowing the suds to get into her eyes, relishing the sting, until she had to press her fingers against her closed lids to bring herself momentary relief.

It was then that she finally learnt she couldn't force Maman to appreciate her, to like her, rather than love her out of obligation. Sometimes, obligatory love had to be enough. But Neda knew that when she married, she would make sure it was a love match. She needed to break the cycle she was born into, of being misunderstood and lonely. So at night she dreamt of her perfect match, and wondered if he was dreaming of her too.

Chapter 4

SORAYA

London, 2014

"Ten pounds for a burger *without* chips?" her mum muttered, taking her reading glasses off her face, no longer wishing to see the menu or the prices.

Instead she inspected the glass of tap water that had been handed to her, and Soraya could see her gaze settle on the faint lipstick mark on the rim. She hadn't taken a sip yet. She was often vocal about not understanding independent cafés and restaurants that were intentionally laid-back; her main qualm was that they looked, and often were, dirty. Dining out with her mum made Soraya hyperaware of her surroundings. Like how the waiter put the cutlery down in a heap, with no napkin underneath, expecting them to set their places themselves. And in such cases, she could almost hear her mother thinking, *When did they last disinfect the table?*

As the family had sat down, Soraya had felt a lingering, indescribable pang about getting a table for four and not five. And then she remembered that if things were different there would actually have been six of them at her graduation lunch.

Guilt overwhelmed her then; she had been so focused on herself she had almost forgotten about Laleh.

They were squeezed together in a raised dining booth, with Soraya and her mum on one side, and Parvin and Amir on the other. Amir spread himself sideways, meaning Parvin was on the edge of the banquette, and opposite him, Soraya had to tuck her feet under her seat. With any other man, she might have made a point of spreading herself too, but she let it slide with her brother. She had learnt it wasn't worth the argument.

Parvin distributed the knives and forks while Amir tore one of the napkins into little pieces. Soraya had no appetite but wanted the food to hurry up.

"Take a picture of me and my graduate daughter," her mum said, passing her phone to Parvin.

Soraya's mouth was aching from fake smiling all day. She tilted her head to the side slightly, and her mum put an arm around her, her own chin high with pride.

"One, two, three, smile!" Parvin said. "Oh, Mum!" Parvin came and adjusted her mum's hijab. "OK, one more time. C'mon, Soraya, smile a bit more, it's your graduation!"

"Beautiful," her mum said when she saw the picture, before sending the photos from the day to the family WhatsApp group.

Her dad replied promptly: *O I see Your all going for food without me.*

Soraya's mouth twitched. Parvin and Amir said nothing.

"I shouldn't have sent them to the group," her mum said. "It looks like I'm showing off."

"Well, he could have come!" Soraya blurted.

"I know, darling," her mum said. "He gets jealous, though."

The whole situation was baffling—but why was Soraya even surprised?

"It's my graduation. He should have come; he has no right to be jealous. He went to Parvin and Amir's graduation—why not mine?"

"It's probably better he didn't come. He would have made us leave early because he was tired," her mum said.

"And he would have ordered the most expensive thing on the menu. Remember when he did that at mine," Parvin said.

"And then say he doesn't like it after one bite." Amir chuckled. "Poor man, I wish he was here."

Soraya did too; despite all the pain he perpetually caused, he should have been here. It was clear her siblings enjoyed his company; they brightened up around him. She wondered why she didn't, why she held so much resentment towards him that it felt like a burning coal deep in her core. He had always been an absent parent, so she had nothing to compare his behavior to, and yet he was the person who had put so much pressure on her to do well in school. When she got into Goldsmiths with AAB in her A levels, his first response was not "Congratulations" but instead, "Why not three A's?"

All she wanted was for him to show he cared. And she hated herself for that.

"He chose not to be here, he's not a 'poor man,' " Soraya said.

"He's not well," Amir said.

Soraya sighed. It was at moments like these that she was most aware she was the only person in the family who didn't make excuses for their dad. Despite her and Parvin being close in some respects, she was reminded that Amir and Parvin were twins and would always band together. If things had been different, maybe she would have had a sister on her side in such arguments.

"You know, we wouldn't even be here if it wasn't for him." This was the pathetic card Amir always dealt.

"It's hardly impressive to have sperm . . ." Soraya muttered, very, very quietly.

"What?"

"Nothing."

Parvin was now on her phone while her mum watched her fighting children, her hands linked together on the tabletop, a small frown on her face.

"See, it *is* better that it's just us," she said.

Soraya, in a way, agreed, but it was the principle of the thing.

"Who was that English boy cheering for you anyway?" Amir asked.

There was a short silence.

"Someone from my course," she said. She could almost feel Parvin imploring her to think of a good excuse. "He's gay, you do know that, right?" She panicked and said it too quickly.

Her mum visibly relaxed. "Is he? He didn't look it."

"Well, he is."

"He's definitely not gay," Amir said.

"Do you want to bet? He's going out with Oliver," Soraya said.

Amir smiled, almost laughing. "Seriously?"

"Yes, that's why he cheered for me, Oliver asked him to."

Despite Soraya's cool tone, she felt herself sweating. Under the table, she picked at the cuticle by her forefinger.

Why *had* Magnus cheered for her? She had tried not to think about it, but now, with him mentioned again by her family, she couldn't help but admit to herself that she wanted to know. Before she might have thought he was being sarcastic, a typical lad move, but now she wondered whether he was doing it out of kindness. But, with it being the end of university, she might never see him again to find out. This fact was surprisingly disappointing to her. She had spent three years around this person, but now she would no longer see him again if she wished she could.

She wondered if he was having lunch with his family too. Had his dad sobered up? She hoped so. Thinking about his comments about marriage being wrong, now that she had heard his parents speaking, she wondered if perhaps he was talking about his parents, rather than his own entanglements. It would make sense.

She loved love, but thinking back to what the women in her family had lost for it, she wondered if some part of her too naturally shied away from the idea of belonging to another. Maybe this was why she was hesitant to become romantically involved with anyone. Maybe she did see Magnus's point after all.

She felt a bit of hard skin by her nail, ready to be pulled. She circled it with her middle finger, waiting.

The problem with keeping secrets from her family was that the thing she was trying to hide from them often ended up being masked by a web of lies that were difficult to keep up with.

Her dad messaged again: *Bring me food theres nothing in house.*

Her mum called the waitress over.

Soraya yanked the skin off and felt the familiar sting.

Chapter 5

SORAYA

London, 2014

The scent of cannabis was everywhere.

Soraya wrinkled her nose ever so slightly. In the damp room, one of many in the Victorian ten-bedroom house, there were at least a dozen people clustered together chatting. The room was sparsely furnished, containing only a double bed, a rectangular mirror, a wooden desk, and a tall wardrobe. They were all in different shades of brown veneer that clashed with the threadbare gray carpet. In one corner was an orange traffic cone.

The people who lived in the house had mere days left on their tenancy agreement, hence the large scale of the party. It appeared people from her university planned to either renew the contracts for their London flats and houses, with the hope of finding a job in the city, if, like Soraya, they hadn't already, or move back home. Some, with money she couldn't fathom having, were soon to leave London to travel the world.

Each room had been set up to play different music. In some, people smoked weed, while in others people danced to techno.

She had never been to such a large party before, and until now had never seen some of her classmates outside of seminars either. Different groups mixed together, popular artsy people talked to the sports lads, and those she considered more reclusive and enigmatic grouped together in a corner drinking wine straight from the bottle.

Soraya sat in one of the more chilled rooms, both atmospherically and in temperature. The bed she perched on was lumpy and she had been stranded with a girl she didn't know well—and whose name she didn't remember. She had hoped it would come up in conversation.

It hadn't.

The girl was white with blond dreadlocks, a fact that Soraya repeatedly tried to move past.

"I just don't want to start the real world. I'm not ready to be an adult, you know," the girl was saying. She spoke slowly, her lips curled into a lazy smile.

Soraya had opened her mouth to respond when something caught her eye. In the mirror on the wall opposite her, she could see Magnus entering the room, and he was staring at her. Not straight at her but through the mirror. She quickly directed her attention back to the unknown girl and muttered noncommittally.

"I know, right."

"It's like, I studied anthropology because I just care *so* much," the girl was saying. "You know? I want to learn, make a difference, go to other countries, really experience life. *Help people.* So I guess I do want to start the real world, but not right now."

"Yeah, I totally know what you mean."

Soraya turned her body towards Magnus, but he was no longer looking at her, now engaged in conversation with his friends.

Magnus wore a three-button T-shirt in an ugly shade of green. His muscles strained against the fabric, his skin smooth and hard-looking. She could understand why people would find muscles like that attractive, but it was the cockiness that attached itself to athletic men that ruined everything.

The boys looked like they all played rugby with him, and the girls were white and slender, dressed in crop tops and tight-fitting jeans. They lapped up all the jokes the boys made—Magnus's in particular—giggling and flicking their hair, and she noticed one of the girls leaning closer to him, touching his arm while she laughed at something he'd said. It was as if the girls were houseplants in desperate need of light, and the boys were the sun.

She shook her head, wishing to rid herself of the tragic scene she was witnessing.

"Urgh, *they're* here," the girl said.

"They . . . ?" Soraya began, before turning to find her companion's gaze fixed on Magnus. "Oh, what do you mean?"

"Nothing. I fucked one of their housemates a few times—he was shit anyway. You know when you have to pretend to come because you just want it all to end? Yeah, it was *that* bad." Soraya nodded, as though she knew perfectly well. "Anyway, out of nowhere he ghosted me and when I finally managed to get hold of him he used the pathetic 'it's not you, it's me' excuse. I fucking know it's not me—you never made me come, you bastard!"

She shouted the last bit, which caused people to turn her way and laugh under their breath. Soraya's face colored.

"Well, he sounds like a knob," she said, looking at her phone for an escape. She saw someone had re-posted one of the illustrations she had posted online. It made her smile, momentarily.

While she would never call herself an artist, Soraya had always drawn, even as a young child. She mainly drew people, animals, and plants. The backgrounds to her illustrations tended to be pastel-colored, the outlines of her drawings black and thick.

She was self-taught, so her illustrations didn't always turn out as she planned. She hadn't mastered the art of drawing eyes, so always drew them as shaded-in semicircles, and coined that her "style."

In her art she attempted to reflect the world around her. She sometimes drew women in underwear, their stretch marks on show, their belly pouches hanging proudly. And yet, despite drawing women in this way, and knowing it was normal, she still had hang-ups about her own body.

"And then Magnus totally fucked over my friend Lucy," the blond girl hissed under her breath. "It's been like six months and she *still* isn't over him. He's a total fuck boy."

Soraya's ears pricked up. She locked her phone and looked at the girl in front of her properly for the first time. "Wait . . . what did you say?"

"Yeah, you know Magnus? He's behind you but don't turn around," she said. Soraya squinted her eyes as though trying to recall who he was. "Lucy dated him for four months before she found out he was sleeping with other girls. She actually thinks she loved him—though I'm not sure if it was just because he looks the way he does and the sex was really good. I'm not surprised though; if you've slept with that many people you *have* to be good. Otherwise, what are you even doing?"

The girl's words fitted the impression Soraya had gotten from others about Magnus during their three years at university. If someone had said this yesterday she would have brushed it off, not cared at all. Now though, she felt a weird desire to leave the conversation; she didn't want to hear more. She found herself justifying his actions, and she didn't like it.

"Oh, shit," Soraya said, lifting her phone up as though she'd received a message. "Sorry, I need to find my friend. He's looking for me. Talk later, yeah?" She got up without waiting for a reply and left the room, not taking a second glance at Magnus. But she could have sworn she felt his eyes on her.

The rest of the night was a blur of dancing, and conversations lamenting the end of an era. The queues for the toilets were ever-growing. Someone had mentioned that one of the basement bedrooms had an en suite. Soraya went to check.

There was no one down there, which struck her as odd, but she did find a toilet. She spent a long time looking in the mirror trying to fix her makeup, but her hands were shaky and her vision blurred. She steadied herself against the sink and took deep breaths. She hated this part of being drunk—the point at which it was too late to do anything but ride the wave of the spinning world.

As she came out of the en suite she saw Magnus sitting on the bed. His back was to her and she wasn't sure whether to walk out of the room without saying anything, or to acknowledge his presence.

"Hi," she said, despite herself.

He turned and gave her a smile. Her palms were clammy, her heart beating too fast. Part of her longed for someone to walk in, but a small part also hoped no one would.

He patted a spot on the bed next to him. "Sit," he said.

She hesitated.

"Or don't." He shrugged.

She went over and sat down next to him.

"I've not seen you at a party before," he said.

"Yeah, it's not really my . . ." She was going to say "scene," but thought again. It wasn't that it wasn't her scene; she had just never been invited to one like this before. Even now, she hadn't been directly asked; Oliver's boyfriend, Charlie, had invited them along. "I prefer more low-key gatherings."

Magnus looked at her for a long while. Being this close to him meant she could smell him for the first time. His aftershave was musky, earthy almost. With him this close, she noticed his eyes were red.

"You're very drunk, aren't you?"

"No," he lied. "I mean, aren't you too? You look it."

She had sobered up a little since sitting down next to him, but the room was still spinning. Focusing her gaze on him kept her grounded, so she did that.

He put his hand on her thigh as though to steady himself, and she felt herself go very rigid. This always happened when boys tried to touch her. She closed her eyes for a few seconds.

"So, Soraya," he said. "Let me guess what you do with your nights instead. You're 'alternative,' so you go to Corsica or Bussey Building and listen to techno music while you're high on MD? Or you prefer to have intellectual conversations drinking artisan coffee with your friends?" He had a smile on his face.

Her mouth was open in astonishment. In reality she liked pop music, secretly still enjoyed *Twilight*, and drank instant coffee. But she thought it best to omit those details.

"And you've never done those things yourself? What are you, antidrugs? How very un-Goldsmiths of you."

"If you need to take something to have a good night, then you're not having a good night, is all I'm saying."

As he spoke she noticed he had a small gap between his two front teeth, like she did. She felt a strange warmth towards him then.

"So you've never taken anything before?"

"I'm not saying that," he said quickly. "It's just a slippery slope, that's all."

He was the first person she had spoken to in her three years at university who wasn't blasé about drugs. She remembered the exchange she had overheard between him and his dad at graduation and wondered if that was the reason for Magnus's stance against drug taking.

He shifted, and Soraya became acutely aware that his hand was still resting on her thigh. She was struck by how attractive his hands were—she had never had such a thought before. Hands, she had always felt, were just hands—and yet looking at his did something to her. She could describe them in no way other than manly. She realized she had never been this close to a man before, in this way at least, to have made such an observation. When she looked at him, he didn't seem to notice what he was doing.

"So, you're going to tell me my description of you isn't right?" he challenged.

"You're such a dick." She playfully pushed his shoulder—which was as hard as it looked. His hand covered hers as though to stop her and their eyes locked. His other hand was still resting on her thigh.

"I didn't say it was a bad thing," he said.

"Well, it's my turn now," she said. "You're a rugby player, so you like sports, drink lots of beer, eat a shit ton of protein, and sleep with lots of girls. Oh, and brag about it too, am I right?"

"I'm not like that," he said softly. "I guess we're both wrong about each other."

Her throat was dry.

Magnus leant in closer, so close that she could feel his breath on her face. She recoiled, stood up quickly.

Words from her childhood about zina being the ultimate sin, and having to explain yourself to God once you died, rang in her head. She was a bad Muslim in every way, it seemed.

"I need to find Oliver."

For a split second Magnus had a wounded expression on his

face. Just for an instant. Then he relaxed and flashed her a big grin.

"OK, see you later, Soraya."

It was only once she was outside the room that she felt like she could breathe again. She climbed the stairs to the hallway, which was now heaving with bodies and laughter. She disliked herself for not leaning in with Magnus. Why couldn't she just kiss someone, even someone she didn't particularly like, and get it over with? Why couldn't she be normal?

She climbed the second set of stairs and tried three rooms until she found Oliver. He was straddling the windowsill, joint in hand.

"Help," she said, clambering down next to him. Outside the window was the flat roof of the ground floor, and people were sitting on it. Soraya knew without asking that Oliver had refused to sit on the roof, not because it was unsafe, but because it was dirty. He often wore extravagant outfits—not gaudy, but well thought out with attention to detail. Despite it being late summer, and warm out, he had chosen to wear navy wool trousers with a red Kenzo jumper tucked in. Underneath the jumper she could see a cream roll neck. He enjoyed layering.

"And why do you need help?" Oliver took an elegant swig from the bottle of red wine he'd stashed outside the window, his pinkie sticking out.

"Magnus," Soraya breathed, but then she pulled herself together. It was in this moment she remembered she was drunk. Or perhaps dizzy from the interaction she'd just had. She straightened up, gave herself a light slap on the face. Oliver didn't bat an eyelid. "I think he was going to kiss me, you know, just now."

"Magnus? Why? Tell him to leave you alone."

"Well, no . . . I think I wanted him to." With drunkenness came candidness.

"You want to kiss Magnus Evans?" Priya said, poking her head in from outside the window. "As in, rugby lad Magnus Evans?"

"OK, can we not shout?" Soraya said.

Priya nudged Oliver to move away from the window ledge so

she could climb in. He hopped off and stood inside the room. Soraya was suddenly self-conscious and looked around. Was she being loud? Upon inspection, it seemed no one was focused on her. But then, why would they be? She shook her head again.

They moved to sit in a corner of the room.

"It's not that I want to kiss *him* in particular," Soraya began. "I just think, you know, it might be nice to get it over with, and he seemed like he was going to kiss me."

Priya nodded, while Oliver had a gleam in his eye.

Priya hadn't known Soraya was a virgin for the first two years of their friendship, had just assumed she wasn't because she wore short skirts and dark lipstick, and for some reason apparently that meant she was more liberal in her views on sex. It was only when they were high one time in third year that Soraya finally divulged her secret. Priya was surprisingly reasonable about it, but that didn't mean she truly got it.

Like Oliver and Soraya, Priya came from a restrictive background. Her Pakistani family didn't allow her to behave like the English people around her, but instead of rebelling at university like Soraya, she had done it in secret throughout her teens.

"Yes!" Priya said. "Use them like they always use us."

"I mean, you could do much worse for a first kiss," Oliver said. "At least he's fit."

"Your Brummie accent was proper strong then," Soraya replied, laughing.

"OK, also would not go that far, Oliver. He's not fit at all." Priya shuddered. "But he'd be good practice. Technique-wise."

"I mean physically fit. You'd obviously not have deep emotional chats with him, but . . . oh, come *on*." Oliver got his phone out, began typing, and fairly quickly brandished a picture online of Magnus Evans, stark naked with a cushion just about covering his genitals. The caption was the monkey covering its eyes emoji. "You can't say he isn't hot. Just look at those abs and thighs."

Priya wrinkled her nose. "He's not *my* type." She preferred skinny indie boys who dressed in vintage clothing, and whose Tinder pictures were either of them on their skateboards or else of them drinking coffee. Soraya thought her taste in men mirrored Priya's, though she refused to go on Tinder. She didn't like the idea of judging people solely on their looks—online anyway. "But you should do it, Soraya. It'll only last a few seconds, and it'll be funny."

"I don't want it to be funny," she began. "But the guys I like never seem to like me back and, at this point, I just want to get it over with. Oh, God, I don't even know *how* to kiss!"

Oliver took a last puff of the joint he was smoking and dropped the butt into a glass. It still had someone's drink in it. He had an uncanny ability to look perfectly sober, and act it, even when stoned.

"Most thirteen-year-olds don't either. They just do it," he said.

"But what if—"

"OK, let's just cut straight to the chase. Soraya, do you want to have this hanging over you forever? It's all you talk about lately, that you've never been kissed," Priya chimed in.

"Guys, could you be less loud?" Soraya breathed in deeply.

She'd done so much at university and yet when it came to men she'd done nothing. Who knew when an opportunity like this would come again?

She resolved to take action. To do what she wanted for a change, rather than let her life be dictated by her parents and their views.

If she was truly being honest, she didn't know what her thoughts were about sex before marriage. She'd grown up assuming she would wait, and at one point in her life she'd liked that idea. Liked that there would be only one person for her. That their relationship would be halal. That it wouldn't have to be kept a secret from her family. It was only at university, however, that she realized the likelihood of finding someone who would wait until marriage was low.

And she didn't know if she wanted to wait anymore.

But quite frankly the thought of having sex with someone terrified her, so it was pushed to the back of her mind every time it arose.

While she still wasn't quite sure how she felt about sex before marriage, she now knew that she wanted to kiss someone before marriage. Wanted to know what it felt like. Even if it was embarrassing, at least she would never have to see him again. Any experience at this point was good experience. She just had to push past her guilt, and the fact that objectively he was the last person she'd choose to have her first kiss with.

"Oh, God, I'm going to do it," she said, before mock-heaving, at which Priya cackled loudly. "I'm going to ask Magnus Evans out."

Chapter 6

SORAYA

London, 2014

Hey, do you fancy going for a drink sometime?

Immediately after sending Magnus the Facebook message, she locked her phone and turned it facedown on her bed.

Two days had passed since the party, and despite Priya's and Oliver's goading her to ask him out immediately, she'd put it off until she had had the time to think about it logically.

She had written a list of pros and cons in her diary, which she kept hidden under her pillow, but while there were many cons, the one pro outweighed the rest: she'd finally get it over with and be able to move on with her life.

It wasn't as though she was intentionally a twenty-one-year-old who hadn't been kissed. When she was a teenager it was virtually impossible for it to happen, but she hadn't abstained from kissing at university for any particular reason. She had wanted to do it, but, setting aside the guilt she felt at thinking such thoughts, the guys she liked never showed interest in her anyway. And could she ever feel that irresistible pull towards a man who was not her husband when she was weighed down with Muslim guilt? When the thought of attempting to kiss someone made her feel sick with worry?

She needed to accept that life wasn't like fiction; her first kiss would be logical rather than magical.

While Magnus had spoken to her and paid her some attention, she was under no illusions: he paid every girl attention. She was not singled out. She'd seen the way he flitted around the party, talking to an array of women, lapping up their attention. So perhaps he was the perfect subject. One date. One kiss. Then it would be done. And they'd likely never talk again.

That was her thought process when she pressed send.

As soon as the message was sent, however, a whole manner of cringeworthy scenarios clouded her mind.

She was almost tempted to contact him again and say the message wasn't meant for him, but she reminded herself that she wasn't a teenager anymore. She needed to be confident in her actions.

Her phone pinged a few minutes later. She grabbed it, almost dropping it in her haste.

MAGNUS: *Hey. Why not? When you thinking?*

She stared at the words for a long time. *Why not?* What did that even mean?

SORAYA: *Next Friday? I'm going back home this weekend.*
MAGNUS: *Sounds good. Where's home?*
SORAYA: *Brighton—you ever been?*
MAGNUS: *I have not. But I've not had the right tour guide before.*

Soraya snorted and was about to reply when he double-texted.

MAGNUS: *P.S. I knew you were posh;).*
SORAYA: *WELL. Just because I'm Southern doesn't mean I'm posh . . . and anyway I kind of have Northern roots. My brother and sisters were born in Liverpool actually.*

It was refreshing to say "sisters" rather than "sister" and know he wouldn't think anything of it.

MAGNUS: *That's a real stretch at saying you're Northern, but I appreciate you trying.*

Her hands were clammy from their conversation, and she felt light-headed. She hated this reaction to what should have been a normal, easy interaction.

Unexpectedly, they continued talking for the next few days.

Through their messaging, she discovered he was into a lot more highbrow literature than she'd expected. His favorite texts from their course were *Tender Buttons* (a book Soraya gave up attempting to read two pages in) and *Antigone*. Whereas she much preferred studying writers such as Joan Didion—whose writing style Soraya appreciated as much as her fashion sense. These conversations left her wanting to keep up with him, almost wishing she enjoyed more classic literature.

Through their messaging she was reminded of her seminars at Goldsmiths, in which her personal reading tastes weren't considered highbrow. She'd responded to this by writing her dissertation on a variety of contemporary romance novels, arguing that they were in fact empowering for women.

She and Magnus talked a lot about university, but nothing personal.

He did reveal that in their first year he had made it a point to memorize key details from essays about the texts they were studying for the seminars. He said he wanted to seem clever. Such admissions made her think he didn't speak to everyone in this way. She, in turn, told him she often felt like the dumbest person in their class when she struggled to keep up with the reading and seminar discussions. He replied saying that she came across quietly confident, in his opinion. This comment made her smile, and she wanted to believe it, liked the way he imagined her.

She still hadn't told Oliver or Priya about the conversation she'd overheard between Magnus and his dad at graduation. She decided she wouldn't, ever. It wasn't something they would understand anyway.

FROM: Hannah Gordon (hannah.gordon@agencyrus.co.uk)
To: Soraya Nazari (SorayaNazari@aomail.com)

Hi Soraya,

I hope you're well and had a great weekend!

```
    I have just heard from the client
at Purple B and unfortunately you
have been unsuccessful. They did
offer some feedback which you may
find useful:

She is a very smart girl and
presented herself well. We were just
concerned that she may be a bit
timid for our role, which involves
meeting with very tough clients. I
would also advise her to elaborate
on her answers more when in
interviews as she came across quite
quiet and nervous.

    I'm sorry I couldn't bring better
news but I'm sure if you work on
your confidence for next time you
will do well! Interviews are always
great practice. Even if you are
unsuccessful, just make sure you use
the feedback.
    I'm sure we will be able to find
something else for you soon.

Thanks,
Hannah
```

Soraya glanced at the email, skimming over sentences until certain words jumped out at her, words such as "unsuccessful" and "timid." She barely gave herself pause to take in the news, but instead rang Parvin.

"Would you say I'm timid?"

"Um . . ." Parvin paused, clearly taken aback by the question. "A bit, yeah, why?"

Why had she chosen to phone her sister? Soraya hated her honesty. She wished Parvin would bother to lie, to make her feel better. She could hardly end the call so abruptly though. Instead she forced herself to continue with it.

"In what way am I timid?"

"I don't know . . . you aren't very assertive, are you?"

Soraya bit her lip, held her phone tight, and looked out of her bedroom window. She could see the railway tracks from New Cross Gate station, a train slowly moving past. It was all rather gray. She studied the scene closely, her nose almost to the glass. The people on the train were smaller than ants, going about their lives.

"I just got rejected from a job," she said finally.

"Oh—they said you were timid?"

"Well, yeah." Her breath steamed up the window, so Soraya sat back and drew a love heart with her index finger in the condensation.

"Well, you can always work on that."

Soraya didn't want to work on it; she didn't want to have to change herself, and quite frankly she didn't even want the job that bad. She wanted a job in which she could be timid and that would be fine—but what job was that?

There was a pause.

Soraya lay down on her bed, put her feet up against her slanted wall, not sure how to word what she would say next. "Do you ever get Muslim guilt?"

Despite it being a made-up phrase, Parvin knew what she meant. "Sometimes, but then I remember we aren't hurting anyone, so why does it matter?"

While Parvin's words were not quite what the Quran decreed, they gave reassurance all the same.

"Why? Are you seeing a boy or something?" she pressed.

"Not really," Soraya muttered.

"Care to elaborate?"

"Nope."

"Oh, quit worrying and start living, Soraya," Parvin continued. "Maybe that's why you're so timid, you're always stuck in your own head."

That comment made Soraya want to say some not very timid things in reply. She settled for "Well, that was rude."

"But remember to be careful," Parvin added, a strange edge to her voice.

"Careful?"

"Like . . . you know." And then she whispered, "Remember to always use protection."

Soraya's cheeks colored, the urge to hang up becoming even greater. "OK, stop. I'm not stupid."

"No need to get snappy. Aren't you going to ask what's new here?"

"Fine. What's new?"

"Well, for starters, Amir has a new girlfriend. She's very quiet. Almost too quiet."

"Huh?"

"She came round for dinner, *again*! She's only twenty, which I thought was a bit weird. They talk about getting engaged a lot, but I'm not sure she's that into it."

Soraya could feel her irritation turning to outrage. It was one thing for her brother to have "secret" girlfriends, of whom he had many, but another to flaunt them while simultaneously preaching about Islam to his sisters. And her mum and dad's lack of care about the whole situation brought her anger all the way home. Soraya breathed in deeply, telling herself, *It's nothing new.*

"That's quite a big age gap . . . interesting. Wait, why do you think she isn't into it?"

"She just giggled whenever it was brought up. She was quite timid, actually."

"Like me, you mean?"

"Well, no, you're a bit more timid than her."

Soraya's jaw tightened. She got up from her bed. Perhaps she could work on her timidness, starting with her sister.

"OK, I've gotta go, bye!"

She hung up before Parvin could say anything else. Instead of dwelling on the email from the agency, as she inevitably would if it stayed in her in-box, Soraya decided to delete it.

She spent the rest of the day drawing a new illustration. She drew what she imagined her sister Laleh to look like now, and she was smiling. But despite her attempts to draw a woman in her thirties, she couldn't help but give her teenage qualities, from that one photograph she had of her. Her cheeks were chubby, her eyes youthful and carefree. That was all she knew of her sister.

She wondered why Laleh had ruined her life, leaving her entire family, for a man. How it seemed, judging from the women in her family, that men always seemed to ruin women's lives.

She texted Parvin then: *Do you ever think about Laleh?*

Parvin replied: *Always.*

Soraya let out a long breath. Contemplated replying, but didn't quite know what to say. What was there to say, when she didn't know Laleh at all, knew nothing about her?

Her mind began to wander to Magnus. And not for the first time she asked herself what she was doing. A bubble of panic rose in her stomach. She pushed the thought down, vowing to interrogate it at a later date if necessary, hopefully never.

She refreshed her mailbox again and had no new emails. Looming over her was the fact that without any income, and with her quickly dwindling student loan savings, she'd soon have to move back home.

Chapter 7

NEDA

Neda was acutely aware of the middle-aged men who walked past her in the streets, the way their gazes lingered on certain parts of her body: her breasts, thighs, bottom, even her wrists. Everywhere but her face. It seemed women weren't allowed to walk down the street without being looked at, whistled at. As though walking down the street was akin to being a painting in a gallery or—depending on how you looked at it—a freshly drained lamb in the markets.

She wore a knee-length skirt and a fitted blouse, attire she thought suitably conservative while she worked part-time in the admin department at the hospital. She wore similar outfits to university.

Skipping breakfast, she ran to the bus stop, her feet slamming against the hot ground. She swore she could feel the heat through her sandals. Beads of sweat ran down her forehead; her underarms were already damp with perspiration.

The houses down her street blurred before her eyes, their mismatched grand gates and cream brickwork merging into one. Children played with footballs in the road, their laughter ringing in her ears.

It was only when she slowed down, due to a stitch in her side, that she noticed her neighbors standing outside their houses chatting together. They turned to look at her with amused, inquisitive expressions. She gave them a wave, conscious that it was considered rude not to give them a proper greeting. This was made more embarrassing when she rounded the corner and saw her bus driving away.

She stopped again and rested her hands on her hips while she caught her breath. Grudgingly, she raised her arm limply and hailed a taxi. A red car stopped in the middle of the road and the man inside gestured for her to hurry. Dashing over, she jumped into the back seat.

"The general hospital. Quickly, please, I'm late," she said, before leaning away from the driver. Her now damp back was sticky against the leather seat.

"Sure," he said, looking at her through his mirror.

She exhaled, still catching her breath, making a mental note to get fitter. Looking out of the window, she saw great green trees, colorful cars with large rounded tires, and women wearing miniskirts, which seemed to be getting shorter by the day. Murals of the Shah were painted on the buildings they passed, his angular face and dark eyebrows commanding, but despite their grandeur such murals were so commonplace seeing one was like seeing her own face in the mirror.

The taxi driver took a right when he should have taken a left, and began to make his way down an underpass, in the opposite direction from the hospital.

"Where are you going? The hospital is the other way," she said sharply, before letting out a tut. "How do you not know where it is?"

He said nothing, and the silence dragged on. Her hands were suddenly slick with sweat, her whole body damp in the heat.

"Excuse me, sir? Where are we going?"

"To my house," he replied gently, his gaze on the traffic ahead.

Her whole body felt cold then.

"What?" she yelled, looking at the meter. He was driving at 120 kilometers per hour, like all the other cars on the motorway. She looked at the door. It was not locked. "Why?"

His grip tightened around the steering wheel. "I need to get something from my house first."

"What?" Her thoughts were jumbled—what did he need to get

and why had he let her get in the car when he had errands to do?—and each new question jostled its way to the front of her mind. And then one jumped out, stuck in her throat, and lodged itself there.

Was she even in a taxi?

It wasn't always clear-cut, regular cars and taxis weren't easily distinguishable. Arguably, anyone could be a taxi driver. She'd heard before of girls being abducted by men pretending to be taxi drivers, but it never happened to people she knew, not people like her.

"Let me out now!" she yelled.

"Darling, that's not possible, we're on a motorway," he drawled.

She peered at him. He was old enough to be her father, even had the same thick black mustache and receding hairline Baba had.

For once Neda was speechless.

"You have beautiful legs," he said, again quietly.

"What?" she spat. She wanted to smack him, beat him, and that's exactly what she planned to do when the car stopped.

"I saw you running. Lovely, lovely legs."

"Take me back, now!"

"Why did you get in the car, then? Dressed in a skirt like that." He let out a low whistle.

The car slowed as he drove down an exit ramp, and then there were shops again, people walking the street, billboards of glamorous American movie stars, cinemas, and French restaurants. It was bizarre that those around her shopping, hand in hand, were unaware that she was being abducted.

He continued driving more slowly now, needing to seem inconspicuous among the pedestrians nearby. Neda's hand was firmly on the door handle. It slipped against her clammy palm.

She pulled on the handle while the car was moving.

He noticed and attempted to speed up. She closed her eyes and pushed the door open, jumping and rolling into the open gutter. She landed roughly on her side in a stream of dirty water, one of the many that ran along the streets in Tehran. Immediately she felt a surge of pain and wondered if she'd broken her shoulder or arm.

She could almost feel the dirty brown water seeping into her grazed legs and arms.

The car sped off with its passenger door still open. She wanted to make a note of the registration plate, but all she could do was lie dazed in the water, her heart beating painfully loud and fast in her chest, her whole body numb. Passersby ran over.

"What happened?"

"Are you OK?"

"What's going on?"

Concern was etched on their faces. But all Neda could think was that she'd had enough. Had enough of men leering at her, of her friends being groped in the street. Abductions such as these were commonplace and yet nothing was being done about it.

She wanted control.

A week later she joined the Islamic Society at university. It was something she had always meant to do, but had put off as a not quite pressing task. To begin with, she tentatively sounded out the idea of wearing a hijab to her friends.

"It's much better—you have more freedom, in fact!" she said to her best friend.

"Oh, come on, it's so old-fashioned," the friend replied. "I bet you won't last a week."

"No, it's Islamic. As Muslim women we should wear it—"

"Neda, just because you were stupid enough to get in a car with a donkey doesn't mean you should preach to us, understand?"

And when Maman saw Neda attempting to leave the house one day wearing a hijab, she stopped her in her tracks.

"What are you doing?"

"I have my reasons, Maman," Neda began. "If you don't like it, talk to Allah, not me."

Maman's mouth was wide open. But because there was nothing she could say, all she did was scowl. It was at that point Maman and Neda finally stopped even trying to understand each other.

Maman couldn't ask her daughter to take her hijab off. Her family classed themselves as Muslim despite Neda being the only one to wear a hijab and pray five times a day. They prayed even if they were not stringent about when and how many times a day, whereas prayer time had always kept Neda sane and calm. It gave her something to work towards. And in times of hardship, it gave her something to hold on to.

Her family liked Western ideas, the ones the Shah had introduced to Iran, though admittedly not the way these had escalated. It was the cause of many heated discussions during family parties. There were those who appreciated how the Shah had transformed Iran into a modern country, and those who focused on the spreading slums, the widening gap between the rich and poor. What they all wanted was democracy and modernity, while upholding Persian culture—an impossible combination, it seemed.

Neda was unsure where she fitted into all this. Her reason for wearing a hijab was twofold: she would become closer to Allah, and she would protect herself from those around her. She tried to explain this to her friends: that it wasn't going against the Shah's regime; it wasn't a political statement as such, but a personal one. But conversations with others were much the same as those with her maman and best friend; they didn't understand her way of liberating herself. Instead they turned defensive because they saw Neda's hijab as a reminder that as Muslim women they too should be covering themselves, and they didn't want to.

And so, Neda became one of only four girls at her university to wear a hijab.

Chapter 8

SORAYA

Brighton, 2014

Soraya was guilt-tripped into going back to Brighton every other weekend. All her mum had to say was either "We miss you" or "Family is important" and she would make arrangements to travel down. Soraya's already nervous disposition meant her mum's hidden messages dug deep inside of her. They translated to: appreciate your time with us because one day we'll be gone. Rich when her mum herself had left Iran over thirty years ago and rarely went back to visit her own mother.

The four-story Nazari house was embarrassingly cluttered and everything inside was mismatched. It might have been a nice place to be had they known how to decorate it. The basement, which would be a separate flat in London, was where Parvin stayed, when she wasn't living and working in Bahrain. Amir occupied the farthest room on the ground floor, with his own back entrance, all the better for sneaking girls in. On the second floor were their mum's and dad's separate rooms. They were well beyond the two-beds-in-one-room stage, and in the past year had chosen to keep to separate spaces. However, this was not a welcome transition. Her dad had moved into the room none of the family had gone into for over a decade, and claimed it as his own.

Soraya resided in the attic, which had an abundance of natural light, something she missed in her London flat. Being in this bedroom in the daytime, with the sun shining on her face, was enough to lift her mood. It was curious how similar to houseplants humans were. How sunlight could lift you up when you were perilously close to drooping.

Soraya sat on her bed, the sheets cold against her legs. Her laptop was open and she was working on an illustration.

When her anxiety was heightened, drawing helped calm her; it gave her hands and mind something to focus on. Friends sometimes asked her to draw for their zines, or she posted photos on her Instagram, developing a portfolio for herself, though she'd never tell anyone that was what she was doing. If she said it aloud and enough people knew about it, that meant if she failed everyone would know. Then her shortcomings would become abundantly clear to all.

She heard the staircase creak under the soft footsteps that were making their way up to her room.

"Soraya!" Parvin called, in a voice an octave too high.

"Yeah?" Soraya was always aware of how low and moany her own voice sounded in comparison to her sister's.

"What you doing?" Parvin plopped her small body down onto Soraya's bed. She was wearing leggings and a baggy jumper, yet somehow still looked chic. Soraya looked at her own outfit: black jeans and a tucked-in white T-shirt. She could see a small roll of belly fat. When she straightened up it flattened.

Quickly, she closed her laptop. "Nothing—"

Soraya wasn't given the opportunity to finish as Parvin spoke over her. "Oh, God, I have to tell you something!"

"OK . . ."

"Amir snuck a girl in last night."

Soraya was irritated but not surprised. One rule for men and another for women was the running theme in their family.

"Really? The girl you were talking about on the phone?"

"No, someone different. This one is loud, a bit classless too. Terrible hair." Her sister shook her head.

"His type then," Soraya muttered. Parvin nodded. "If he snuck her in, how did you see her?"

"I heard them laughing outside the back of the house, and saw them out of my window. He doesn't even try to be inconspicuous, but hey, that's Amir." She paused. "Wait, are you going to *cry?*" Parvin asked.

Soraya hadn't realized her irritation at these double standards was so plain to see. If she was about to cry, though, she doubted Parvin laughing in her face would help.

"No, I'm just tired." During the silence that followed, Soraya picked at the skin around her nails. The dry, hard pieces were best, and when she found one she yanked hard. The act stung ever so slightly. "You know what though," she said, her voice rising. "Imagine, just imagine, if we ever brought a boy home."

Parvin laughed, a high-pitched, girlie sound. "They would kill us, not invite the boys round for baghali polo."

Soraya's phone pinged. They both glanced at it.

"Magnus, ey?" Parvin said, snatching Soraya's phone from the bed.

Soraya smiled. "You don't have my pass code." Her smile turned into a frown when she saw Parvin sniggering. "What?" Soraya climbed off the bed and dashed to her sister's side. "Oh my God, how did you get in?"

"Your pass code is your date of birth." Soraya snatched back the phone from her sister. "So . . ." Parvin plopped herself onto the mattress. "He can't wait until Friday, apparently." Soraya's cheeks colored. "What's happening Friday?"

Soraya put a finger to her lips and tiptoed a short distance down the stairs. Seeing that the coast was clear, she went back up and shut the door. "Could you be less loud?"

"Mum went to Lidl, Amir's in town, and Dad's two floors down watching TV. Not that he even listens to us when we're in the same room as him. I'm not stupid."

Soraya couldn't help but be paranoid despite Parvin's words; imprinted in her mind was a memory of her dad telling her when she was a teenager that he would kill her if she talked to a boy.

"It's nothing."

"Oh, come on, spill."

"It's honestly nothing."

Parvin gave her a piercing stare. "If you say so."

Soraya opened her mouth, almost said a word, so that a strange groan came out, but then quickly shut it.

"Huh?"

"Nothing."

Parvin raised a perfectly threaded brow. "OK . . . whatever it is, I think you should go for it. You're only young once."

Her sister had had numerous long-term boyfriends that she had hidden from the family, even sometimes from Soraya. It would be only when she was going through a breakup that Soraya would learn that Parvin had actually been dating someone for years. Her sister had mastered the art of leading a double life.

Parvin went to look at herself in the full-length mirror. She leant close to it, focused on her face and then her hair. "Enjoy your youth and not having gray hair," she sighed as she pulled on a few.

The staircase groaned again, but this time under heavy, slow footsteps. Soraya resisted the urge to roll her eyes at the prospect of what was to come.

"Hello, girls," their dad said as he entered the room.

Parvin, still assessing herself in the mirror, said, "Hi, Dad."

Soraya grudgingly said, "Hi."

His face was red and his clothes hung baggily on him. She wondered if he had always been so thin. It was rare that Soraya properly looked at him these days. His presence often filled her with anger, so much so that she refused to settle her gaze on him most of the time. Refused to really look at her dad.

She hadn't always felt this way about him; once she'd even liked him. However, years of hearing her mum's complaints about him had built a growing resentment towards her dad, and Soraya had told her mum this. But despite knowing exactly where her youngest daughter's unhealthy hatred of her dad came from, her mum continued to express her frustration with him to Soraya. And Soraya loved her mum too much to turn her away when she needed to vent; she felt her mother's anger viscerally when she complained about her husband. Amir and Parvin dismissed their mum's complaints, so she had no one else to talk to. She would never tell her friends, not even her best friend, Mena; her pride was too great.

But looking at her father now, Soraya felt pity. His gray T-shirt had a ketchup stain on it, and small holes in the hem. Where did the holes even come from? And when was the last time he had changed his clothes? Her mum had once said he was a handsome man, that all her friends were secretly jealous she had married a onetime professional footballer.

"Do we have any food in the house?" their dad asked, giving a toothless grin. He had forgotten to put his false teeth back in.

And then any sympathy she'd briefly felt for him completely disappeared. Soraya hadn't expected much. But as usual, her low expectations were met with an even lower outcome. This was the first time he'd seen her since she'd come home. He'd given her no "Congratulations," made no mention at all of her graduating. No apologies about him not attending her graduation ceremony, no explanation. Nothing.

Instead, he asked if there was any food in the house, a hint for someone to make him something.

"I don't know, why don't you look?" Soraya said. She was bolder because it was clear he was in good spirits today.

Soraya knew just how to approach him in his various moods. Now his eyes were wild, his movements shaky, erratic, his voice loud and excited. In this mood he would happily take sarcastic comments and frowns, might even throw money at his children in an attempt to get them on his side.

Sensing the situation, Parvin said, "Dad, we have some oven pizzas in the fridge. I could put one in for you?" Despite living in this house for decades, he still didn't know how to work the oven. Or didn't want to know. Didn't think he needed to.

"You're my good girl, you know that?" He rubbed the top of Parvin's head, and then looked at Soraya. "You are too, don't feel left out!" He came over to her and she held her breath. He ruffled her hair too, a bit too roughly, but probably not intentionally so. He pulled it too, in the act.

"Ow!"

"You're such a moody girl," he said. "What are you girls doing today then?" He stood in the middle of her room, like a boulder she wished she could remove. But for once he was in a chatty mood.

As in all situations, Parvin knew exactly what to say and do.

"We're going to town, and I'm going to buy Soraya lunch to celebrate her graduating."

"Oh, yeah! My youngest daughter the graduate." Soraya felt a faint hope expanding in her like a balloon. "What are your plans now then? Are you applying for jobs?" And then they were popped with a needle, confusing her. In some ways it was worse than disappointment, this feeling. She didn't have time to fully form a hope before it was snatched away from her.

"Don't you want to congratulate me?" This was what Amir and their dad often called Soraya's "back chat."

"Congratulations," he said, going over to her again to pat, or rather whack, her on the back. "You know what, girls? Lunch is on me, wherever you want to go."

"Maybe Jamie Oliver's then," Parvin chimed in, excited by her father's offer.

He rummaged inside his trackie bottom pockets and produced two twenty-pound notes, which he gave to Parvin. He didn't have much money, so would regret that later. "There you go, take your little sister on a girls' day out and enjoy yourselves."

Another popped balloon.

While Soraya would rather go for lunch with Parvin than with her dad, she wondered if it was asking too much for him to want to spend time with her. That was why she and Oliver had bonded so closely when they first met: they both had dysfunctional families. Families who pressured them into acting a certain way, and then were vocally disappointed when their creatures didn't turn out as they were expected to.

"Thanks, Dad!" Parvin jumped over to give him a half hug, not wanting to risk inhaling the stench. And this was how she and Soraya were different. Parvin's takeaway from this would be that their dad paid for them to go out for lunch, a nice thing to do. But all Soraya could think was that he was too lazy to spend time with them, to attend her graduation, or even to make up for that by going out to lunch with them. Instead he preferred to pay them off. With money he didn't have. And perhaps Parvin was fine with that, but Soraya knew she never could be.

When Soraya had finished binge-watching *The O.C.* in the early hours of the morning, she made her way down the two flights of stairs to the kitchen for a snack. As she reached the ground floor she saw that her dad was in the living room watching TV. She took the door straight into the kitchen, instead of walking through the other room in front of him.

She could hear the TV narrator talking about a murder that had occurred. His voice was classically American, ominous, unremarkable.

Opening the fridge to get out a bottle of milk, she realized her dad hadn't called out from the living room. She put the milk bottle on the counter and walked to the door connecting the two rooms, a box of cereal in her hand. Her dad was lying on the sofa with his back to her. His headphones were plugged into his laptop. Soraya forced herself to stand there for a moment, trying to understand what she was seeing playing on the screen. At first all she saw was flesh. Breasts. Normally when Soraya caught him watching porn, she would quickly look away. Shake her head. Mutter something under her breath along the lines of "disgusting." But today she willed herself to understand what he was watching. On his screen was a girl going down on another girl.

His clothes were all on, his hands still by his sides. This made the whole sight stranger. He was a passive onlooker, observing. It seemed he took no pleasure in it. But then, perhaps he wasn't an expressive person. Soraya didn't really know him that well.

She also wondered, as she always did, why? Why in the living room? Why in their public space, when he had taken a bedroom that wasn't his anyway and made it his own? Couldn't he watch porn there?

"Ridiculous," she said under her breath, following her own ritual unthinkingly.

And he continued watching, completely unaware.

So Soraya returned to the kitchen, poured the milk and cereal into a bowl. Returned the items to their respective places and headed back to her room, turning off each light as she went.

It wasn't anything new.

She left the bowl of uneaten cereal on her bedside table and took a shower. She turned the dial so the water was hot, almost scorching. She got in, held her breath as the water stung against her bare skin. She breathed through gritted teeth, focusing on nothing but the water.

When she shut the water off, she wrapped herself in a scratchy towel and went back to her bedroom, not sure why she had done that. But it helped her feel a little cleaner.

By now the cereal was soggy and unappealing.

Chapter 9

SORAYA

London, 2014

Soraya met Magnus in one of the nicer bars in Brockley, one she had never been in before. She wore a black turtleneck jumper tucked into a midi-length baby pink skirt, and silver cut-off Doc Martens. Over this she wore a black duster jacket and a silver mini backpack. It was an outfit she'd deliberated over for an hour, until she forced herself out the door because, despite living only fifteen minutes away, she was already late.

Magnus was there when she arrived, sitting in one of the booths looking at his phone. Something about seeing him there—dressed all in black, which suited him a lot more than the green top he'd worn at the party—sent her anxiety into overdrive. There was a reason why she always liked a certain type, and why Magnus was not included in it. He made her nervous, and not in a good way. He reminded her of the boys at school who had made fun of her.

What was she doing? And why had she let herself be egged on by her friends? She was beginning to think this was a very bad idea. It didn't help that she'd been out the night before, her comedown well and truly sparking the negative feelings she had about herself and how this date would go.

As she edged closer he looked up and said, "Hey," before standing up and leaning in to hug her. She hugged him back, raising herself onto her tiptoes. He smelt very good, like cinnamon and citrus fruit combined. When she let go, they slowly disentangled themselves. Wanting to create some immediate distance, she quickly sat opposite him in the booth.

The red and black walls gave the bar a boudoir feel. The waiters wore waistcoats and bow ties, and the host had a fancy mustache. Slow contemporary music played in the background, jarring with the retro décor.

It was a hipster bar through and through.

Ordinarily, Soraya would have felt right at home, though she'd probably deny that to him, but something about the kind of people around them made her feel out of place. Made her feel immensely stupid for being the one to suggest coming here. She hadn't known it would be like this.

She grabbed a menu; it was an old hardback novel with a menu insert stuck inside. Her book was *To Kill a Mockingbird*. Magnus's was *The Catcher in the Rye*. The whole concept was completely unnecessary.

"So," he began. "What you having?"

She looked over at the bar, finding the thought of alcohol nauseating at that moment.

Oliver had broken up with Charlie a couple of days before because he had caught him messaging other guys on Grindr. In order to be a supportive friend Soraya had feigned enthusiasm for his suggestion of a night out in Elephant and Castle the night before. They'd ended up in a club until 4:00 A.M. She hadn't taken a great deal of MD, but enough that her first meal of the day had been at 5:00 P.M. Her insides still felt hollow. "I kind of had a big night out last night," she said slowly. She didn't want to mention casual drug taking because his stance on it was clear from their first conversation. "I think maybe just a Diet Coke."

Magnus laughed and scratched his head. "To be honest, I have a big game tomorrow morning so wasn't planning on drinking either."

"Why did we go for a drink then?" she said, laughing.

"I don't know, you're the one who suggested it." He let out a quick laugh. "No problem, two soft drinks it is."

He left to go to the bar, which gave her the opportunity to wipe her now sweaty palms against her skirt. In fact, she felt as though her entire body was perspiring profusely.

When he returned with the drinks she asked him about his

week. It wasn't as though they could go straight into kissing. Or could they? She imagined leaning in, grabbing his face, and mashing her mouth to his. But then what would she do? The thought made her inwardly cringe. She sat on her hands.

"Are you OK?" he asked.

Or maybe she was outwardly cringing.

"Yep, yep. Fine. Sorry, what were you saying?"

He'd been at work—he tutored children in English in Lewisham—and then showed her his bandaged hand. His pinkie and ring finger were bound together.

"I spent some time in A & E too," he said. "I had a rugby match on Tuesday."

"Oh, shit," she said. "Did you win at least?"

He looked down at her, a smug and competitive glint to his eyes. "Yeah, obviously." He winked.

She remembered what he'd told her when they were messaging, about how he was a writer, had even written a draft of a novel. Though he wouldn't tell her what it was about.

It was difficult to correlate the different versions of Magnus: the one she had known in their classes, the boy who was often quiet but clearly smart and studious, the person she had been texting and who now sat in front of her, and the boy she saw online. He posted so many pictures, mainly selfies pouting in the mirror with his pecs out. This person ticked the stereotype of a university rugby player, a *lad*. This was who she had assumed he was for the past three years. And yet, through their texting he'd presented a very different version of himself, and she couldn't work out which one was the façade. Though she wasn't sure why she cared. She had one task for this evening and didn't need to make it more complicated for herself.

Still, she couldn't help but ask, "How's the writing going, then?"

He was leaning his elbows on the table. His arms strained against the fabric of his shirt.

He frowned. "OK, I guess." He took a long sip of his drink. His hands were large and calloused. She watched as he lifted his glass, trying to imagine that hand cupping her face as he kissed her, but every time it came, she would nervously block the image from her mind. "Do you write?"

Soraya chuckled nervously. "No, I can't write."

"Have you ever tried?" His eyes were wide, encouraging, and she had to remind herself that this was the way he spoke to everyone with a vagina, not just her specifically.

"Beyond writing in my diary, not really. Me and my friends have been talking about creating our own literary journal though." It was an idea Priya, Oliver, and Soraya had been floating around for a while, but so far they'd failed to put it into action.

"That'd be really cool." He paused, as though deliberating what to say next. "You know, I saw your drawings on Instagram. You're really good."

Her face colored with the knowledge that it wasn't just she who had been social media stalking.

"I think people would pay good money for your illustrations," he said. His confidence was contagious. No one had ever told her that; rather they had agreed with her that drawing was a hobby, nothing more. "I know I would," he said, smiling.

"Thanks. I'm trying to develop my style more, especially now we've graduated. I'd love to be able to do more detailed drawings. Like Studio Ghibli style, colorful with lots of landscape detail."

"Studio Ghibli?"

"You've never watched any Ghibli films?"

"No . . ."

"You need to."

"I'll hold you to that then," he said. "Is this what you want to do now we've graduated then? Work on your art?"

Art. Again, she'd never been given permission to think of what she did as "art." It wasn't that her mum didn't support her drawing—she liked to look at the pieces—but she was firmly set on drawing being a hobby. She sometimes made Soraya feel embarrassed even to think about it as something more than that. So Soraya didn't.

"I don't really know. Part of me wishes I had chosen to study graphic design instead of English. I'd love to have a visual job. I keep applying for marketing jobs but I don't even know what they would involve." It was easier being frank with him. Perhaps because she knew their time together would be short-lived.

"I wouldn't worry too much if you don't know what your plans are yet."

"Says the boy who knows exactly what his plans are," she joked. He had told her he planned to do a master's degree next year, provided he got enough funding.

"I'm older than you, though."

"You are?" This was news to her.

"I'm assuming you're . . . what . . . twenty-one, twenty-two?"

"Twenty-one."

"I'm twenty-four. I did a different course for a year before I started this one, and took a few years after that to figure out what I really wanted to study. So, I've had more time to think about it."

Magnus explained that he'd studied law at Leeds but dropped out. "It just wasn't me." He shrugged. "It was hard telling my parents I was dropping out—especially because I'm the first in my family to go to university—but I knew I couldn't spend another two years studying it. I probably would have failed, to be honest."

Soraya couldn't imagine dropping out of university. In her family, once you committed to something you stuck to it, even if it turned out to be a huge mistake.

"I thought it would be awkward being a bit older starting uni again, but I joined the rugby team and quite a few of them are older too, so it turned out all right."

"What does being part of the team entail, exactly?" she asked.

He looked up at her and smirked. "Um, I don't know, you play rugby?"

"I get the feeling it's like a brotherhood."

He snorted. "A brotherhood?"

"Yeah. You always hang out in packs."

"Packs," he repeated slowly, a small smile on his face.

She worried that she'd said something stupid and began picking at the skin around her nails. Magnus put his hands over hers quite suddenly.

"You shouldn't do that," he said quietly.

He played with her fingers as though it was the most normal thing in the world. Just his touch on her hand sent a flutter through her.

She began to worry if the hair on her fingers was visible. If it was, he didn't seem to care. He began stroking her palm, drawing patterns on it with his forefinger.

If this was what he did to other girls, Soraya suddenly didn't care because it was working. She had thought being so close to him would be repulsive, that him touching her wouldn't be enjoyable, but she'd been wrong.

"You say exactly what you're thinking, don't you?" he said, the ghost of a smile on his lips.

"And that's a bad thing?"

"No," he said. "I like it. It just catches me off guard. You're not how I expected you to be."

"How do you mean?"

He removed his hand from hers and ran it through his hair. It looked like he was trying to find a way to say the words without offending her. "You've got this exotic look about you. With your big dark hair and dark makeup. In lectures it would always be you and Oliver sat next to each other by the side, looking quite bitchy—no offense. You never talked in seminars, either. I figured, don't take this the wrong way, that you'd be a bit stuck-up. But you're all right."

She ignored his "exotic" comment. It was interesting how she could ignore problematic language when it came from someone she now found attractive.

" 'All right'? Gee, thanks."

"You know what I mean."

And she did.

"What about me, then? Did you ever think about me?" He gave her a look which made her laugh.

"You just seemed like a typical lad."

"Great. Care to elaborate on that?"

"Like, I'll always remember you wearing running shorts in lectures in winter. You liked the attention it brought."

He was smiling. "Well, that's an astute observation. It clearly caught your attention, though, no?"

"Is that what you wanted? To catch my attention?"

He looked down for a moment before speaking, which made her notice her quickening heart. "Maybe."

After two more rounds of soft drinks, Magnus offered to walk her home, an offer she might have found sweet if her mind wasn't already reeling at the prospect of what was to come. It was abundantly clear why he wanted to walk her home.

When they were outside her door she wished time would just move forward so she wouldn't have to deal with the present. But she did. There she was, outside her flat, with Magnus.

He was exactly a head taller than her. She had to lift her chin to look at him. She now felt tipsy in his presence, felt the warmth that usually came with alcohol, the way you saw people through different eyes when you'd been drinking. He wasn't how she had imagined he would be. Whether he was pretending to be someone else didn't actually matter in that moment.

"So," he said.

"So," she replied.

His brown eyes bored into hers. Throughout the night she had avoided his gaze, but she returned it now, and allowed herself to be pulled in by him. Countless times she tried to explain to herself what happened next, but all she knew was that she slowly leant in. Deep inside her, she suddenly, desperately, wanted to feel his lips against hers. Wanted his arms to encircle her.

Magnus leant in too, and their lips touched. He put his hand on the back of her neck, sending shivers through her, drawing her closer to him.

And just like that Soraya Nazari had her first kiss.

She got the impression that Magnus didn't notice how awkward the kiss was, for her at least. As his lips touched hers, it was too late to decide between fight or flight. She had already selected fight when she leant in first.

Rather than enjoy the moment, she remembered everything she had Googled about kissing. She puckered her lips and touched his hair, gripping his curls gently between her fingers. She opened her mouth slightly and was not surprised when his tongue entered it. She didn't quite know what to do once it was in there. But she thought confidence was key.

When she practiced biting his bottom lip, lightly, he groaned in response, and pulled her closer. He had no idea, it seemed, that this was her first kiss. And she would never tell him.

She liked the way his arms felt when they were around her, and the way he cupped her face in his hands.

When they separated from each other, she said, "Sorry, I haven't kissed in a while." She couldn't help it; she felt as though she had to give a disclaimer, just in case he was smiling to stop himself from laughing, though a part of her doubted that.

"Don't be silly," he said. His eyes were fixed on her mouth and he ran his tongue over his bottom lip before he bent down and kissed her again. This time she let herself close her eyes, and follow his lead, finding that she was enjoying the experience.

"Shall we go inside?" he said, his voice husky, as he nodded towards her flat.

Caught up in the moment, she almost said yes. She had to remind herself that he wouldn't be satisfied with kissing all night, and that was all she would do with him.

"I want to take things slow," she said. "I feel like no one does that anymore."

She saw something in his eyes, surprise and then something like a challenge being accepted.

"Sure," he said, before kissing her again. This time the kiss was deeper, one hand cupping her face, the other tightly holding her waist. And just when she began to melt into him, just when she fully let herself go, he abruptly pulled away, a smile on his face.

"See you later then, Soraya."

It was only when she was back in her flat that she allowed the situation to fully sink in. Inexplicably, she wanted to see him again. Wanted to kiss him again. And perhaps, for the first time, she considered the very real possibility of going further.

Chapter 10

NEDA

Tehran, 1977

The atmosphere was heavy and humid. Disruption was stirring.

Some people wanted change, though others, the minority, were happy with the way things were. There were many, many demonstrations demanding change for different reasons. Often the students at the University of Tehran would mask their demonstrations against the Shah with complaints about the high university fees. Iranians were generally inquisitive by nature, and each protest often became much larger than anticipated. It wasn't just Neda who liked gossip.

Despite this, when all around is slow-building chaos, the disorder becomes normalized, and so her mind was elsewhere, on more immediate concerns, like the fact that it was her final semester of university.

The air-conditioning in the coffeehouse Neda sat in with her girlfriends made the atmosphere stale, but it was appreciated nonetheless. Her hijab hung loose, exposing the top of her head. Underneath the enclosing fabric she wore a long-sleeved striped T-shirt, with flared jeans and clogs.

"I heard she was flirting with Tariq even though she's engaged to Hamid . . ." one of her friends said.

"Tariq! But she said she didn't like him." Neda leant forward, as though being closer to her friend would give her further insight.

"You know Pouran, she loves the attention!"

"Oh, stop looking so worried, Neda dear. It's not a crime to flirt," Shanauz said.

Neda opened her mouth to say, *Actually it is according to Islam,* but thought better of it. She didn't want to be the preacher of the group. Instead she drank her café glacé. The sweetness of vanilla ice cream mixed with strong, nutty coffee was a delight, and she had to force herself to slow down.

A man made his way over to them and the group of women stopped talking. He had long shaggy hair and a well-groomed beard. "Ladies," he said. "Do you mind if we join you?" Behind him a group of young men sat drinking their beverages. One of them smiled at the women, but the other two kept their gazes down-turned as they took exceptionally long sips of their chai.

Her girlfriends wagged their eyebrows, excitement stirring. Neda frowned, her small lips turned downwards. She was disappointed. She wanted to continue gossiping.

"Oh, why not!" one of the women said, without consulting the group. Chairs were moved around and the four men joined them at their table. One man opened a pastry box to expose a dozen shirini, varying from nan-e nokhodchi to ghotab.

One of the shyer men distributed the sweets to each person. It took him a while to get to Neda because each of the women said she didn't want the shirini when they were first offered, to which the man insisted, and back and forth. Taarofing was something Neda could not stand, despite it being ingrained in Iranian culture. She wished instead people would do, and say, what they wanted without wasting time.

Once the man was closer to Neda she recognized him from university.

He had caught her eye on several occasions, smiling at her in the corridors. It was only when Shanauz had said "He's always smiling at you" that she began to take proper notice though. Neda seldom smiled back. It was wrong, she thought, and what was he smiling *at* exactly? She didn't want to encourage him; she wasn't that kind of girl.

One of his bouncy brown curls fell in front of his face and he laughed, powerless to brush it back with his hands full. He blew it away, and in so doing pulled a face that made Neda laugh too. She covered her mouth with her hand.

He was in front of her now, smiling broadly. His teeth were small and white, crowded together but straight. They were like a child's, the sight endearing. Neda picked up a kolompeh, a date-filled cookie, without fuss. He raised his eyebrows in surprise.

"Merci," she said, her eyes not meeting his. She had gained a tan on her face, causing the freckles across her nose to appear more prominent.

"It's my pleasure. What's your name? I seem to see you everywhere."

Neda's friend sitting next to her peered at the box of treats, desperate for a snack to go with her chai.

"I'm Neda." She felt her cheeks coloring under the attention.

"I'm Hossein, nice to meet you." And then he continued the rounds.

"See," the woman next to her hissed. "We told you he likes you. He played football professionally, you know." Eyebrows were raised.

"No! Not professionally?" They gave her knowing looks. Iranians liked to exaggerate, but all the same . . . a *footballer*. Neda wondered if her dad would approve, wondered what Hossein's family were like . . . She forced herself to snap out of it. There were more important things in life than worrying about men, besides the small fact that he hadn't even shown any real interest, let alone serious interest.

And would he—or any man for that matter—support her wish to continue studying? For her to work and not be made to look after the house? She knew even the more modern men these days were not quite comfortable with their wives working, and she could never give up her studies.

When they went back to the university lab, where Neda studied biomedicine, she knocked over a vial and it smashed on the floor.

"Something or *someone* on your mind?" one of the girls asked. The others cackled.

Neda rolled her eyes. As she cleaned up the glass with a dustpan and brush, she wondered what Hossein studied. She had never seen him or any of his friends working in the lab. And when her friend said he "played" football professionally, did that mean he no longer did? Did he give it up to go to university?

"Shanauz," Neda said, when she found her friend on her own in a corner. "What do you know about Hossein?"

Shanauz smiled, put down the glass in her hand, and drummed her fingers on the countertop. "Oh, now you care."

"Come on, I'm just curious, you know me . . ."

"Yes. That you actually love a gossip."

Neda smiled. "He seems to be everywhere lately."

Shanauz pushed her fringe out of her face. Her hair was thick, with choppy layers; eyes smoky, lined with kohl. Neda wished she knew how to do her makeup like that, without being laughed at by Maman.

"He studies sports something or other and I think he got here on a scholarship. Though, if you ask me, his parents must be rich. Have you seen the clothes he wears? Always brands. Adidas, Puma, Levi's . . ."

"I don't care about money, is he *good*?" Neda's eyes were worried, her lips tight with concern, and she wasn't quite sure why.

"He went around and distributed shirini to us when he really didn't have to," her friend said. "I've never seen my baba do anything like that for my maman. Hossein seems like a modern man."

Neda remembered his smile, the floppy hair covering his face. She smiled at the memory, before pulling herself out of it and getting back to work.

Weeks passed with other similar encounters, and each time he asked her more about herself. In their new routine, Hossein and his friends would join her friends during their breaks. The men always provided the group with shirini to go with their hot drinks, a fact Neda had noticed beginning to show on her waistline.

"What do you want to do after university?" he once asked her.

"I'd like to work for a while, complete a master's, get a PhD maybe." She wanted to see his reaction, expecting him to back away, realizing talking to her had been a mistake. Instead he nodded, impressed.

"Being a doctor would suit you," he said, reassuring her of something she realized she had been doubting. "I bet you have many suitors." This comment surprised her.

"Not particularly."

"That's a yes then?" he said, peeking up at her as he sipped his coffee. She noticed he had strong hands, the veins pronounced, and the hair on his arms was dark. It was the first time she had observed a member of the opposite sex in such a way, and she imagined what it would feel like for him to hold her hand, found herself longing for him to do so.

She pinched her leg under the table.

Despite sitting in the coffeehouse with their friends, they had angled their bodies away from them and towards each other, so Neda could imagine they were having coffee alone. However, she still wanted their meetings to be somewhat halal with chaperones present, and having her friends close by was a comfort to her.

"I've had two offers," she said slowly. "But neither was quite right."

"I'm not surprised. You're very beautiful and intelligent," he said. "You're blushing! Don't worry, we can change the subject." He gave a soft laugh, which made her blush even more. When he laughed he had a perfect dimple in each cheek.

Of the two men she'd received offers from, one vehemently did not believe in Allah and the other was twenty years her senior. They both approached her baba directly, and he made his disapproval of them very much known, which was a relief to Neda. The proposals went nowhere quickly.

Eventually, she began asking Hossein questions.

"How many siblings do you have?"

"Three sisters, no brothers. I always wanted a brother, it would have made it easier when my baba, you know . . ." He looked uncomfortable when he spoke about his father. He had died in a car accident two years ago.

"He's with Allah now, be assured of that," Neda said.

Hossein muttered a prayer before taking some tokhmeh from a bowl.

She learnt that he had played football professionally, but during a collision with another player had sustained a double compound fracture of his left shin. Following the incident he was unable to play again.

"Thank Allah, I'm able to walk, and even play friendly matches with my friends," he had said when he first told her. "I'm very lucky."

He walked with a slight limp, and it was more pronounced when he walked quickly.

She also discovered he studied sports science, which explained why she hadn't seen him in the labs.

Despite their increasing closeness, she said nothing of Hossein to her parents. They were already busy with their nine other children; she didn't want to concern them with no-news.

While peeling potatoes in the kitchen one evening, one of Neda's younger sisters, Rabeh, whispered in her ear, "I've heard about you and that footballer."

"What?" Neda hissed, looking around.

Her brothers were all in the living room, smoking and playing card games with their dad. Her eldest four siblings, two brothers and two sisters, were already married and moved out. Neda was next.

She was conflicted about what she wanted. She felt an increasing obligation to relieve the family of their financial worries. But she also wanted more time, was frightened of change while also longing for it. Her opinion on the matter changed every day.

"People talk," Rabeh said. "Are you not going to tell Maman and Baba?"

"Nothing has happened, we've not really spoken seriously." Neda was on edge. "Go put the samovar on."

Rabeh complied and began preparing the chai.

"Listen," Neda said. "It's important you don't say anything to Maman or Baba until it's official, *if* it's ever official."

"Why do you want to lie to our parents?" When Rabeh spoke Neda noticed a bit of tokhmeh stuck in her teeth, which added to her annoyance. "I thought you were meant to be the pious one."

Neda made a noise deep in her throat and quickly told her sister, "Oh, shut up and peel the potatoes, then."

After dinner, when everyone was asleep on the floor in the living room, Rabeh came over to Neda and attempted to rest her head against her chest. But Neda pushed her away.

"What?" Rabeh said.

"I was serious before," Neda said.

She could hear her sister exhale sharply. "You're always serious, sister."

Neda turned away from her, closing her eyes.

The only light in the room came from the streetlights filtering through the crack in the curtains. That evening a sense of dread crept its way into her belly, and she struggled to shake it off.

She felt she should cherish these moments, falling asleep among her family. They struggled, but they stuck together and everything worked out OK. Allah was watching them. It was a comforting feeling, like eating a large bowl of steaming rice after a long day. Despite their house being shabby, only one toilet to be shared between eight of them, and the cockroaches that regularly emerged from the cracks in the floors, it was home. She often daydreamed about being a child again, and envied her youngest sibling, Zahra, for having more years to enjoy being young and free.

So as she lay awake that night Neda tried to appreciate the things she ordinarily wouldn't have. The familiar hum of the fridge, her dad's loud snores, her younger siblings creeping over to her in the night for a cuddle, the laughs they had before lights out, all of them chatting, playing games, making fun of each other. Soon all of this would be over; her childhood would be over.

And then she felt crazy; she was twenty-one years old, her childhood already technically long gone. It was over when she had her first period, eight years ago. And perhaps, she thought, the next step in life would be even better, exciting even. That was if Rabeh kept her mouth shut.

Her dad's snores were louder, echoing around the room.

"Eh!" someone yelled in exasperation. Neda and Rabeh sniggered under their covers.

A small kick. The snoring stopped.

"Wha—" her dad said, confusion thick in his voice. Everyone was silent, pretending to be asleep. He shook his head, scratched it, and then turned over. Everyone had a smile on their face, happy for the momentary quiet.

She felt a tap on her shoulder. Rabeh. Neda could see only the outline of her face, but thought her sister was smiling at her. She held her pinkie finger out to Neda. "Your secret is safe with me, OK?"

Through sleepy eyes Neda wrapped her pinkie around her sister's a tad too tight. "Promise?"

"Promise."

Chapter 11

SORAYA

Brighton, 2014

"These English people kiss anyone," Soraya's mum said, raising her hands in exasperation.

The familiar drumming chorus of the *EastEnders* theme tune came on.

"Who wants a cup of tea then?" Her mum got up to fill the kettle as the *Coronation Street* music began. "Hey, pause it," she yelled. Her dad complied.

With the TV paused, the hum of the kettle brewing was loud in the background. Their living room and kitchen had an archway between, but it was essentially one large room with two doorways accessing it from the hallway.

The family were not fans of the minimalist look; they threw nothing away. The living room was cluttered with books, papers, broken printers, and numerous Iranian vases. And a plethora of Persian carpets. The rugs overlapped each other on the floor, and three hung proudly on the walls. When Soraya was ten years old she had seen them installed there after school one day. Horrified, she had asked her mum, "Why?"

"I saw someone do it on TV, and theirs aren't even *real* Persian carpets," her mum had replied.

"What's your plan now, then, Soraya?" Amir asked. He was sitting on the floor, his back against the sofa their dad lay on.

"Um, get a job?"

"Have you been applying?" their dad asked. As he spoke a piece of pistachio he had been chewing flew out of his mouth.

She hadn't told the rest of her family about her failed interview.

"I only just graduated," Soraya said.

"You've had all summer to apply for jobs," Amir chimed in, and then he smugly added, "I got my first job two weeks after my last exam."

"A job you hate," she replied.

"A job that means I've saved enough for a deposit on a house," he retorted. Amir worked as an accountant, not because he was particularly talented in mathematics but because it was what their parents wanted.

"Soraya did a creative subject though, it's different," Parvin said.

"We told her to study medicine, or even law, but she didn't listen," her dad said.

Soraya clenched her fist, letting her fingernails dig into her palm. She pressed harder until it hurt. They thought she was like them: intelligent. Like her mum, who taught biomedicine at the University of Sussex. Like Amir, who got a First in accounting. Like Parvin, who despite working only part-time for a travel company, earned 70,000 pounds a year, tax-free, in Bahrain, which allowed her to alternate her time between there and England. Soraya struggled with education, always had, and wanted so bad to find a subject she was naturally talented in.

Failure hung over her. She had applied to eighteen jobs in total, received twelve rejection emails, and the others hadn't responded to her yet.

"Do you need help?" Soraya asked her mum, walking into the kitchen.

Her mother was pouring hot water into a teapot; the sweet aroma of spices, predominantly cardamom, filled the air. Not allowing it to brew properly, her mum poured the tea into mismatched mugs.

Soraya had been to Tehran a handful of times with the family when she was younger. Her memories of Iran were hazy, but prominent among them was how perfectly her khale Rabeh made tea. It was always brewed at just the right temperature. She remembered her khale criticizing her mum for her rushed tea making, and her mum playfully swatting her sister with a dishcloth.

Now her parents went to Iran every year without their children. It was easier to explain the absence in the family if none of the children were there. Soraya never felt comfortable in Tehran anyway. She was always regarded as a foreigner, despite looking like the people there. In England she had the reverse problem. In England she was Iranian, and in Iran she was English. Always a foreigner, never belonging.

"Thank you, darling." Her mum handed Soraya two cups. "This one is your dad's"—she pointed to the faded mug holding tea which was black with no sugar—"and this one is Amir's," the milky tea with a lot of sugar.

Soraya carried them through to the living room and put them down in front of her dad and brother; they were received without thanks. She went back to her mum to retrieve hers and held the steaming mug close to her.

"Ignore them," her mum said, without looking up. She poured the remaining tea, and then looked for some biscuits to put on a plate. "They don't know how hard you've been trying."

This understanding made Soraya teary-eyed but also produced impostor-like feelings. Had she been trying hard? She had applied for so many jobs, read up on how to write the best cover letters, and taken her time filling out the applications. But was her heart in it? Did she even know what she wanted to do?

"I always tell students it takes time, so don't be disheartened. It's difficult to get your first job, but you'll get there." Her mum patted Soraya on her forearm.

"Your dad made such a mess of the house today," she continued in hushed tones.

Soraya didn't reply.

"I work all day and come back to biscuit crumbs on the floor and jam smeared on the remote control."

"Tell him to clean it up then." Soraya sighed, repeating the same conversation they always had.

"Like he would listen."

They returned to the living room with the chocolate biscuits, which were devoured within two minutes.

Then her dad pressed play and *Coronation Street* began with one character almost being caught having an affair.

"Again!" her mum cried, shaking her head. "Her partner is so kind as well."

"They all drink too much and this is what happens," her dad said, as though he was an expert in such matters.

"Wait, I thought that other guy was her husband?" Soraya said.

"No, they divorced and now she's going out with his friend," her mum explained, dunking her biscuit into her tea.

"When did that happen?"

"Months ago."

"So why is she with him again?"

"They got drunk at a party and kissed," her dad said.

"They always go to the pub and drink. English people must spend so much money on alcohol," her mum mused.

"You do know this isn't representative of English people's lives?" Soraya said to her parents.

They often had this conversation too.

"No, this is what they're like. This is why we don't drink alcohol, it makes people do bad things."

"It's exaggerated for TV, though, they've got to make it interesting."

"Mum and Dad think our English neighbors all meet in the pub every day and cheat on each other," Amir said, laughing.

"Oh, shhh," her mum said, turning the volume up.

Watching the soaps was an important pastime for her mum; she seldom watched TV with the exception of the soaps. They were the only moments in which she had time to herself, and the only real time she bonded with her husband over a shared interest.

The Nazari family were fans of late dinners, which meant eating at 9:00 P.M. Soraya and Parvin were only just setting the table. While Soraya dished up the pasta, Parvin added side salads to the plates and their mum took the garlic bread out of the oven. The men were watching football in the other room and occasionally Soraya could hear yelps, though she wasn't quite sure whether they were cries of joy or of anger.

"Food is ready!" Parvin called.

Their dad went straight to the fridge. He took out a large bottle of Diet Coke that no one else was allowed to drink and poured himself a glass. He filled the glass only halfway; by this point his obsession with having Diet Coke was not out of pleasure but compulsion. He had to have Diet Coke with every single meal. Soraya often wondered whether he even liked the taste anymore, or whether he gave himself as little as possible because he didn't actually want it. His habit at this point was so regimented, and his willpower so weak.

He refused to eat at the dinner table, preferring to watch television rather than talk to his family.

So once more only four of them ate together.

"This tastes lovely," her mum said.

"You cook well," Amir said between bites. "It's a good skill for a woman to have. Especially when she marries."

Soraya rolled her eyes.

"You should learn how to cook too," her mum said to him, smiling devilishly. It was strange, but also delightful, how the only fully practicing Muslim in the family was also the most feminist in some ways. "So that when you and your wife come home from work, you can take turns cooking for each other. Unlike me and your dad . . ." Soraya thought she heard her mutter then, "Who doesn't even work."

"Mum's right, stop being such a misogynist." Only Parvin could say this to Amir without him flipping. "It should be equal."

"Sorry, *Paris*." He gave her a look.

Parvin pressed her lips together and pretended she hadn't heard him.

Amir had heard her friend call her Paris once, and had played it against her ever since.

"Like Paris Hilton, isn't she famous because of a sex tape, like that Kardashian?" Amir continued.

Soraya wanted to interject that actually Kim Kardashian was an intelligent businesswoman, but Parvin spoke before she could.

"English people don't know how to pronounce my name, it's easier to call myself Paris," she said. "You don't have to mention it *all the time.*"

"You should be proud to be Iranian. Why do you want to be named after a European city? A racist European city at that."

"It just makes my life easier, it's really not that deep," Parvin said. Soraya noticed she had stopped eating her food and was now using her fork to push it around her plate.

Despite the obscene amount her job paid, it was clear she didn't enjoy her time spent abroad, having to behave and be a certain way around her friends there. Appearance was crucial, and she often lamented not having meaningful conversations with anyone or making any deep friendships.

"We shouldn't be changing ourselves to make *their* lives easier," Amir said. "And on the topic of transgressions, you two need to dress more modestly, I was embarrassed at Soraya's graduation."

A collective internal eye roll from both Parvin and Soraya.

"It's no wonder that boy cheered for you in the crowd, Soraya, you proper had your legs out. Even if you say he was gay, I bet Mum was embarrassed." Why couldn't he just say *he* was embarrassed? To which Parvin and Soraya could, in some alternate universe, say they were embarrassed by *him* when he voiced his sexist views.

Soraya was about to defend herself when her dad shouted, "What boy?" from the other room.

Soraya put her fork down.

"No boy, Amir was joking!" her mum replied quickly. Soraya wasn't sure if it actually happened but she could have sworn her mum kicked Amir under the table. His body jolted slightly. "Just eat your food." She gave Soraya a look then that said: *You'd better be careful and not be talking to any boys.*

Soraya felt a flicker of guilt. Normally their speculations were groundless. But not anymore.

Chapter 12

SORAYA

London, 2014

They met at the V&A Museum. It was Magnus's idea. At first when Soraya asked him what his plans were for the weekend he said he was going there alone, and invited her along seemingly as an afterthought, but she got the distinct impression that this was his way of asking her on a date, without actually asking her on a date.

Walking through each room, Soraya struggled to concentrate. She wasn't quite sure what she was doing or why she was seeing him again.

"Do you go to galleries a lot then?" she asked.

He smiled to himself and looked down, as if what she'd said was funny.

"Sometimes." He paused before grinning at her and admitting, "Not really. I thought this was something you liked, that's why I suggested it."

She didn't know what to say to that; all she knew was that this comment would be something she would dissect later, no doubt turning his sentence over in her mind repeatedly until it meant nothing, but also everything.

"Is this something you like doing?" he asked.

Soraya shrugged. "I don't make a point of coming but I probably should do more of it."

They stopped in front of a painting. The colors were dark, a moody mess of gray and black paint. They stood there for quite some time, quietly observing.

"Do you believe in God?" Magnus asked.

The question took her by surprise, and she laughed although she didn't find it funny.

"Random much? Yes," she said. "Do you?"

"I'm not sure, probably not."

He continued to look at the painting.

"Why did you ask?"

"I was just thinking about this painting. The artist said it's meant to represent death, the nothingness of it."

"So you seriously don't believe there's a reason we're here?"

"It feels too convenient to believe in a God." He shrugged.

Soraya began walking, moving away from the painting and towards another exhibit, one that she hoped was less morbid. Of all the people to be seeing, she thought, she had to pick an atheist.

She felt his warm hand close around hers then, which made her stop.

"Are you annoyed at me?" He looked like he was repressing laughter. Even their hands touching was enough to make her hyperaware of her body in a way she had never been before. It was dizzying and embarrassing.

"No," she said quickly.

He moved his hand to lift her chin, tilting her face upwards so he could see her more clearly. She imagined how they must look to outsiders. His muscles strained beneath his Fred Perry jacket, whereas she wore an oversize vintage wool coat and dark lipstick. They didn't match; she was podgy in places he was taut. He was white, fully British, whereas she was Middle Eastern and English, and most of the time confused about what that meant. And yet with him this close, she wanted to kiss him, no matter what it looked like from the outside.

He leant in closer, his breath warm on her face.

"Promise?"

All she had to do was move an inch and they could quite easily be kissing.

"Promise."

He looked like he was about to close his eyes, so sure they would of course kiss that she moved away.

"I'm dying for a coffee, shall we go?" she called over her shoulder, leading the way.

Chapter 13

NEDA

Tehran, 1977

Another day, another round of chai. Except in Neda's case she needed something a lot stronger. She had an exam at the end of the month and had been in the lab since 6:00 A.M. The bags under her eyes were pulling her to the ground. After her melancholy moment, she concluded her dad's snoring all night was simply annoying. And after waking up so early, she needed an endless supply of strong coffee.

While her friends popped sugar cubes in their mouths before taking leisurely sips of chai, Neda swallowed bitter espresso.

Hossein sat by her side but seemed to be avoiding looking at her. He wasn't as chatty as usual. Instead he was tearing bits off a newspaper and rolling them up. It was like he wasn't aware of what he was doing and the mess he was making.

Neda sat very straight on the wooden chair, half in conversation with her friends and half willing Hossein to say something, *anything*.

It was an excruciating couple of minutes before finally he presented her with a folded piece of paper. She looked up at him and there was a very small smile on his mouth. His large brown eyes, however, were sad, perhaps even scared.

"Hossein, where are the shirini?" his friend asked.

"Oh!" he said, theatrically hitting his forehead with his hand. "I forgot to collect them." He turned to Neda. "I'll be back." They were sitting upstairs and he walked down to the café counter on the ground floor. He wore his long-sleeved Adidas T-shirt, sleeves pulled down to cover his hands, something Neda herself did when she felt self-conscious.

Her friends were chatting cluelessly, giggling at the jokes the men made, some of them arguing with each other. One friend believed women were better than men and often liked to demonstrate this in conversation.

"Men are stronger, you cannot deny that, azizam," one young man was saying.

"Oh, really?" her friend began, drawing breath. "Why is it then that we are working in a laboratory, will go on to make medical discoveries, while you are . . . what? Playing with a ball outside? Studying people kicking a football?" There was a ripple of laughter, and Neda had to bite the inside of her cheek to stop herself from smiling.

"If a woman was running the country, you'd see, we would be modern *and* care about those less fortunate than ourselves. Men can't multitask. Look at the Shah . . ."

This caused a debate between the group over the government, no longer dividing according to their sex but following the opinions of their respective classes and adherence to religion.

Neda suddenly remembered the folded piece of paper in her hand. She opened it up, and written in red pen were the words:

Dear Neda, will you marry me?

Shanauz noticed her sitting very still, staring at the paper with all the weight it carried.

"What is it?" she asked, taking it from her friend's hand. When she read the words she yelled in surprise. People turned to look at them. "Sorry, sorry, it's nothing." She scooted closer to Neda and whispered, "What did you say back?"

"He went to get shirini from downstairs, I haven't been able to say anything!"

Shanauz clapped her hands together. "I knew it—I just knew it! I always get these things right." In that moment she looked like the Cheshire Cat, her joy greater than her friend's.

Though Neda was pleased, her heart seemed to beat too quickly, and she thought there must be a mistake. He was so beautiful that she couldn't believe he felt the same way about her. Remembering how nervous Hossein had been, though, made her feel powerful and important. Her response mattered to him. *She* mattered to him.

She knew she must marry eventually, and she wanted it to be to Hossein, whom she found unbelievably attractive and intriguing. She didn't think he'd ever not surprise and amaze her.

When he came back to the table with a box in his hand, his friends surrounded him, keen to get a sugary pastry to go with their tea. He peeked up at Neda across the table and she smiled at him, nodding slightly. He smiled back, understanding what this meant.

Later, when he had the chance to sit next to her, they discussed how he had to ask her dad first, before anything could be done. She knew her maman would jump at the idea of her marrying Hossein; it didn't matter who the suitor was as long as it meant one less child to feed at home. Not for the first time Neda wished her own mother cared more about her, wondered what that would feel like.

"Of course I will ask him. I just can't believe you said yes," Hossein told her, the color returning to his face. He gripped his curly hair in both hands, adrenaline running high.

"Why do you think so poorly of yourself?"

"I see men looking at you, Neda, I'm not stupid . . . I am a very lucky man though."

Men did look at her, but Neda thought it was because she wore a hijab. That said, she knew she was attractive, she wouldn't deny it. She always thought it strange when women pretended they weren't aware of their own beauty.

"Why, Hossein, I am lucky too," she told him.

Chapter 14

SORAYA

London, 2014

For dark hair, leave on for up to ten minutes.

Soraya had left the bleaching cream on her arms for fifteen and her skin was beginning to tingle. She pushed past it. *They're thinking of white people hair.*

"You're going all out, aren't you?" Oliver said.

She applied the light pink hair removal cream above her lip, her tweezers ready in one hand. She was leaning into the bathroom mirror. "It'll all probably grow back in like an hour," Soraya said with a sigh.

She stretched over the sink towards the mirror and plucked from her chin the stubborn black hairs that seemed to return daily.

She could see Oliver looking at her reflection. "Our friendship really has reached new lows if I'm now OK with you watching me pluck my chin hair," Soraya said.

He sat on the closed toilet seat and crossed his legs. He had on his graduation suit styled down with a turtleneck underneath, and despite the backdrop not being overly glamorous, she still resisted an urge to take a photograph of him. He looked like he belonged in a Kooples advert with the caption "Oliver has been with himself for the last twenty-one years, and is loving it."

Their bathroom was minimally decorated, the blue walls matching the navy tiles on the floor. The toilet was also blue. It was not quite the vibe Soraya and Oliver were going for. But overall their flat was decent, despite some of its more quirky features.

"I'm just strengthening our friendship, you know, we need to see each other at our best and our worst." He had his phone in his hand, and a small catlike smile on his face.

"What?"

On his phone was a picture of three men posing nude with their hands covering their genitals. In the background was a wall full of pictures of women in lingerie and swimwear, presumably taken out of the kind of magazine Soraya hated. She didn't understand why Oliver was showing her such a crass photo until her gaze fell on one of the men's faces. Magnus Evans looked back at her. The image had been posted last night.

Soraya's jaw dropped, and in the process a small clump of Veet cream fell into her mouth. She spat it out and quickly rinsed her mouth.

"Symbolic," she said through gritted teeth.

Oliver didn't seem to notice what had happened. He continued swiping through his phone.

"You know, he reminds me a bit of Terry."

"Terry? As in the guy who once sent me an unsolicited dick pic? *That* Terry?"

Among the boys Soraya had almost kissed was Terry. He was the "mature" twenty-three-year-old student that she'd had an unsuccessful back-and-forth with online in third year. He was too forward, and attempted to kiss her randomly in the library, so she eventually blocked his number and avoided him on campus.

"Yeah, he has similar qualities," Oliver mused. "Maybe you're developing a taste for lads? Maybe lads *are* your type?"

"Magnus isn't my type," she said slowly. "Anyway, I'd rather not talk about Terry, I still feel scarred by that picture."

"It was so red," Oliver said.

Soraya shuddered. "Moving on . . ."

"So what are your plans for tonight, just hair removal?" he asked.

"Pretty much. I might put on a face mask too."

"Well, the offer to come to Bjork's house with me still stands," he said, not meaning it. She got the feeling Oliver didn't want her to meet his other friends, didn't want to mix them together. She could never understand why, but in light of seeing pictures of their escapades (weekends away in Coventry on coke) she didn't care enough to press the matter. This other friendship group consisted of rich "creatives" who were funded by their parents to go to coffee shops with their MacBooks and focus on their art, which mostly meant scrolling though Tumblr.

"You know my horoscope says change is going to come this week," he said. Oliver had downloaded Astrology Zone to his phone and was persistent in trying to get Soraya into it too.

"Hmm. Have you spoken to Charlie at all?"

Beyond his infidelity, Charlie was undeserving of Oliver anyway, white in both skin color and personality, but it was hard to say that to Oliver without sounding like a biased best friend.

"No," he said, firmly moving on. "Your horoscope says tonight you will understand a lover a bit better." He had an amused expression on his face.

She tried to pay little attention to what he was saying because she was lying to him. She never lied to Oliver. She didn't even know why she had lied. She'd had every intention of telling him Magnus was coming over, but when he said he wasn't going to be in had reconsidered.

She didn't want to have to explain why she was seeing Magnus again. Oliver still thought it was a one-off date. She didn't want to be teased for trying to have "kissing practice" with the biggest player at their university, or be told that going on more than one date was dangerous.

She already felt guilty for possibly being the worst Muslim ever, and didn't need Oliver adding to her perpetual worries. It wasn't as if she saw a future with Magnus, or even wanted one with him, even if he wasn't a fuck boy; they were too different. How could she ever bring him home to her family? An atheist rugby player who posted almost-naked photos of himself online. The thought was as unimaginable as it was ridiculous. She knew she would never marry a man like him, so her intentions from the start in the eyes of God were not good. If she saw a future with Magnus, saw something beyond a few meetings, at least she could justify what she was doing to herself, if not to God.

And yet when Magnus messaged her she couldn't help but invite him over.

She stared at herself in the mirror, looking ridiculous and barely resisting the intense urge to scratch her arms.

Using the mini plastic spatula, she scraped the bleach off her arms, skin tingling in relief with each swipe. It was ceremonial, really, the shedding of her roots to conform to Western standards.

"So, this is your room," Magnus said, walking into her bedroom.

They planned to watch her favorite Ghibli movies, *My Neighbor Totoro* and *The Cat Returns*. Soraya trailed behind him. When she'd first opened the door to let him in she found herself momentarily speechless, which made her want to slap herself. She reminded herself repeatedly that he was a lad. Tried to remember the awful pictures of him in her brain. And yet now, as she walked behind him, her gaze fell to his bottom, the sight of which rendered her speechless. His shorts were tight across his bum, and through the material she could make out the definition of his thighs. He wore a navy Goldsmiths hoodie; on the top left-hand side of the chest it bore his name, and the university crest—an open book atop a leopard.

Seeing the room through his eyes, she was sure he'd think it was childish. Her bedspread was floral and pink, her lamp pink gingham, and a Hello Kitty cushion was propped up against her pillows. Why did everything look so pink all of a sudden?

Her sketchbook was on her desk. She saw his gaze linger on it.

"Can I?" he asked, lifting it up before she had the chance to answer.

"Sure," she said pointlessly. She hadn't thought he'd want to look through her belongings. When she noticed her diary left on the bedside table, her heart suddenly quickened.

"Are you sure I won't find any drawings of me in here?" he said, smirking.

"God, you have such a big head," she said, her voice flat, concern focused elsewhere. She walked backwards, retrieved the diary unobserved, and slipped it under her pillow. All while he was facing her desk, hand on the sketchbook cover.

"I'm merely asking," he said. He flicked through the book while she stood there, one arm now wrapped around her stomach. She wished he would say something, anything.

"You're crazy talented. You know that, right?"

She squeezed herself tighter, grimacing, before taking the sketchbook from him and throwing it onto her bed. "Do you want a drink?"

He pulled her towards him and bent his head to meet hers, drawing her into a kiss. The whole movement was so natural and swift that she didn't have time to think about what was happening. As his lips touched hers she became breathless.

This was all so normal to him, and completely alien to her. The urge to move her body closer to his was strong, but so too was the desire to move away.

And for the first time in her life she wanted to know what a man looked like with no clothes on. She wanted to know what *Magnus* looked like with no clothes on. And if she wanted to, she could probably see him undressed tonight.

All her life she had been taught to resist men; it went against her entire upbringing to enjoy his company. Men had the ability to ruin lives. But when he pressed his body to hers all such thoughts died away. Her body responded by pressing back against his. His hand found her behind, which made her laugh. Soraya was sure this was not the reaction she was meant to have, but Magnus smiled against her lips.

"I'll get the wine," she said, keen for an escape.

She wasn't sure if this was a terrible idea. Maybe they should have just watched the films in the living room. What stopped her from doing that was the thought that Oliver might sense Magnus had been here.

In the kitchen, Soraya inspected the wine Magnus had brought, not that she knew much about wine. It was red. She poured them each a glass although there was only one wineglass, which Oliver had accidentally stolen from the pub around the corner. They had been drinking in the smoking area when he had seen someone he'd had a short fling with. Not wanting to have an awkward interaction, he and Soraya had walked quickly back to their flat, and it was only when they were home that he realized he had taken his glass with him.

She returned to her room to find Magnus sprawled across her bed, perfectly at home. She handed him the wineglass and she drank from a mug.

"Classy," Magnus commented as he took a large gulp.

She brought her laptop over to the bed.

"I saw the photo you posted," she said, sensing a need to fill the silence.

He pressed his lips together to stop himself from smiling. "Did you like it?" he said, a glint in his eye.

"What were you guys even doing?"

"It was a laugh," he said, leaning forward. "What, you don't take naked photos?"

"I would literally be killed if I did that. Not that I'd want to."

"By who?"

"My parents . . ."

"Oh, they're strict?"

"Muslim. Same thing."

There was a short silence before he said, "Where are you from again?"

Soraya gave him a look. It was curious, she thought, how much debate there constantly was online about asking people where they were from, whereas immigrants happily asked each other. It wasn't rude or suggestive to them, simply a question. She got the feeling Magnus was asking in this vein, despite being a white man.

"I mean, where are your family from?" he amended.

"Where do you think?"

"Well, you look a bit like Cleopatra with your eyeliner, fringe, and cheekbones. It's one of the reasons I noticed you in lectures actually."

Soraya grimaced, inwardly begging him to stop.

"Egyptian?" he guessed.

She snorted. "No, Iranian."

Whenever Soraya had revealed her background growing up she received mixed (but equally ignorant) responses:

1. "Don't they all live in huts there?"—from those who thought Iran was just a desert
2. "Do you mean Iraq?"—from those who thought Iran and Iraq were the same country
3. "Isn't that where all the terrorists go before an attack?"—from those who thought all Middle Eastern countries were filled with terrorists

Magnus's response surprised her. "That's really cool."

"I wouldn't say it's *cool*," she said, quietly.

"You wouldn't?"

"I mean, like growing up it didn't feel cool. There were only a few ethnic minorities at school. I just felt different, and kids are little shits, so they made it known we were different and that was a bad thing."

She hadn't meant to say this. In fact, it was exactly the kind of thing she did not divulge to people she didn't know very well, but she couldn't help herself. There was something about him that made her feel as though she could tell him this. It was strange and she was not sure how much she liked it.

"I'm sorry," he said. He stroked the back of her hand. "I bet they're all fucking losers now, and look at you."

She snorted.

"Don't get me wrong, I like being Iranian. I just guess I still have hang-ups from going to basically an all-white school. That's why I like London so much—it's so different to where I grew up."

"I like that about London too. It feels like you can be anyone here and that's fine, no one cares."

She wondered what he meant. Who did Magnus want to be, and was that the person he truly was? She had seen his different sides now, each one contradicting the other. She almost wanted to ask him, "Who do you want to be?" but she pressed her lips together instead.

They didn't get past the opening credits of *My Neighbor Totoro* before they became distracted. There was a small smile on Magnus's face, his brown eyes gentle and appealing. Soraya leant in to kiss him, intending for it to be just a small kiss, but they ended up kissing for half an hour.

She was nervous to begin with, but he had an uncanny ability to put her at ease. Kissing him was unlike anything she'd ever experienced before. He touched her cheek at first, and as it escalated his hands bunched her hair. He lifted her up so she was sitting on top of him.

But then guilt engulfed her. It told her that she shouldn't be doing this, that she was a bad person. She shut her eyes tight, trying to stop the images of her family watching her like this, of God watching her, from creeping in. It was infuriating; she wasn't even entirely sure why she should feel guilty.

She dug a fingernail into her palm, Magnus was none the wiser. With the sharp pain she gained clarity, and pushed past the guilt, and began kissing his neck.

Eventually he looked up at her, his eyes wide, his lips swollen and a deep pink. Somehow his top had come off, exposing his broad shoulders and hairless chest. In the moment she enjoyed the feel of his muscles against her and allowed her hands to explore his chest and back, to feel how ripped and taut they were. He looked even better than in the photos.

His hand trailed its way lower, past her breasts and to the waistband of her underwear. In the heat of the moment she had let him take her clothes off, with the exception of her bra and pants. She was glad she'd worn semi-sexy lace underwear.

Sensing her stiffen, he stopped. "Are you OK?"

"I just . . ." She didn't know what to say. Here was a man many women wanted naked in their beds, a man who wanted to pleasure her, and she couldn't allow it. She didn't know how to explain why she couldn't. "I'd like to take things slow, like I said before."

"Of course, I'm sorry. I thought you wanted . . ." He trailed off, an edge to his voice.

She shut her eyes. It wasn't his fault.

"I know, I wanted it. It's just . . ."

"It's OK."

"It is?"

"Of course. We'll only do what you want to do. That's important to me." She could imagine many men saying this and not meaning it, but when Magnus said it she knew he did. She'd expected to feel shame or embarrassment when this conversation came up—which didn't explain why she had allowed herself to be in this situation in the first place—but she didn't feel like that at all. "It might be nice to take things slow," Magnus said. They lay in silence for a while, her head leaning against his shoulder. She liked the way he smelt of man, sweat, and musky cologne.

She looked up at him, about to say something when she noticed a dark mark on his neck. "What's that?" Soraya said, gasping when she realized exactly what it was.

Magnus got up and looked at himself in the full-length mirror. He laughed. "Well, you were kissing my neck for quite a while." He shrugged, coming back to the bed to sit next to her. He looked incongruous in her room, almost too big for it. She supposed that was because she had never had a man in her room before, Oliver being the exception. But despite being tall her friend had the catlike ability to make himself appear smaller.

Suddenly Magnus had a smile on his face. "I think you're trying to mark your territory."

She let out a short laugh. "Absolutely not."

He lay back on the bed, arms crossed behind his head, the picture of ease. "Trying to ward off other girls," he said. "I don't blame you, to be honest."

She swatted him with her Hello Kitty cushion, horrified at what he was saying. Despite this, the sight of him lying on her bed bare-chested was startlingly attractive. The biceps she'd once thought too much were now immensely appealing to her. She imagined him lifting her up and pinning her to the bed. The weedy indie boys couldn't do that.

"You have such a big fucking head," she said.

"Yeah, but you love it."

Chapter 15

SORAYA

London, 2014

"Let me get this straight. You're seeing him *again?*"

There was only so long Soraya could keep something secret from Oliver. She did live with him, after all.

"I just feel being with him will be good practice for when I meet someone else," Soraya answered, cringing as she said the words aloud. They'd sounded much more reasonable in her head; saying them out loud she sounded like a monster.

Truth be told, she didn't know what she was doing. She knew from what happened to Laleh that being with a man was dangerous—let alone being with someone like Magnus who she couldn't quite work out. And yet, here she was.

"Just to clarify, this isn't *Angus, Thongs and Perfect Snogging.*" Oliver lifted a vintage velvet dress from a rail and held it against Soraya's body. "This would suit you, by the way."

She took the dress from him, checked the price tag. It wasn't actually expensive but she wasn't sure she could justify any unnecessary purchase with no student loan or job prospects.

Oliver began rummaging through another rail. He had an impeccable eye for finding gems within a hoard of moth-eaten garments.

She put the dress back. "I thought you and Priya liked my plan."

"Yes," he said slowly. "But I know you better than she does. You aren't the type to just use a guy for sex—"

Soraya opened her mouth to protest but he waved his hand in front of her.

"OK, not sex. 'Kissing practice,' as you so eloquently put it. But what happens when he wants to do more? What's your plan then, exactly? Because I'm sure if you asked Priya, she'd say 'Just do it!' "

"I've already thought of that, actually."

"Oh, really. Pray do tell." He turned around, giving her his full attention.

She hadn't thought of that.

"You know what," she said, picking the dress up again, "it doesn't even matter. I'm trying this on."

Before she turned away she caught Oliver smirking and rolling his eyes.

It was the first time she had been to Magnus's house.

She was wearing the newly purchased velvet dress; it was tight on her waist, and flared out in the skirt. She dressed it down with Doc Martens so he didn't think she was making any special effort for him.

She knocked once, lightly, but no one came to the door. Shifting on her feet, she was debating whether to knock again when she saw a figure approaching behind the stained-glass door panel.

"Hey, you," Magnus said, once he'd opened the door. "You look amazing."

"Thanks," she said, avoiding his gaze.

This time she hadn't asked to see him, he'd messaged her to ask if she wanted to come over for dinner. It struck her as an odd, couple-like thing to do, and she almost said no, wondering if she had taken this experiment too far. But another part of her was intrigued; no man had ever made her dinner before.

As he led her into the house, she noticed how messy it was. Two bikes cluttered the hallway, making it a tight squeeze to get into the living room and kitchen. The floorboards had holes in them, and the walls were painted a strange shade of off-white. The house had a masculine smell to it that she wasn't fond of.

She heard voices coming from the living room and her stomach clenched. She had hoped the house would be empty.

As they entered the living room, three athletic-looking boys stood there with their jackets on.

"This is Soraya," Magnus said. "Soraya, this is Henry, Luke, and Callum."

She wasn't sure who was who, but waved awkwardly in their direction.

"So this is her," one of them said. He was blond with patchy facial hair. "Don't worry, we're off to the pub so you have the place to yourselves."

The others looked like they were repressing laughter. She grimaced, and when Magnus put his hand on the small of her back, resisted the urge to move away from it.

"All right, all right," he said. "We're going to make dinner anyway." With his hand still on her back, Magnus gently propelled her in the direction of the kitchen.

It was rectangular and tidy but not necessarily clean.

She heard the front door slam shut.

"Why were they laughing at me?" she said, her eyes narrowed.

Magnus was busy pouring pasta into a pan, so the silence was broken by the hard shells hitting the aluminum. On the table was a packet of Quorn mince. She'd half thought he was joking when he'd said he was considering becoming a vegetarian like her the last time they'd spoken.

"They weren't. What are you talking about?"

She said she needed to use the toilet.

It was upstairs. Safely inside, she told herself to stop acting crazy.

She looked around, not wanting to touch anything. There was facial hair in the basin, and an empty bottle of soap. By the toilet was a pile of magazines with naked women on the covers. Her jaw dropped when she saw this. She knew young men were the target market for such magazines, but didn't think people she'd studied with actually still bought them. Questions arose about why these magazines were by the toilet, and the possibilities made her mutter "Ew" under her breath.

When she made her way back to the kitchen, Magnus was chopping vegetables and putting them into a frying pan.

"Why do you have those magazines in your bathroom?" she asked.

He jumped slightly, not realizing she was back.

He opened his mouth to say something, but shrugged. "I don't know, really."

"Do you think those magazines are good? That objectifying women is good?"

She was reminded suddenly of Lucy—the girl he had been seeing for a few months and then dropped like she meant nothing.

He put the knife down and leant against the counter. "Some would argue it's empowering." He looked like he was resisting the urge to laugh.

Soraya bit her lip, wishing Priya was here to deliver the perfect comeback. But then she wondered if Priya would agree with him.

"Well, I don't like it."

"OK," he said, and began walking out of the kitchen. She stayed there, not quite knowing what to do. He returned moments later with the magazines in his hand, raised them in front of her, and then put them in the recycling bin. "There."

"Just like that?"

"Just like that."

"Won't your friends be annoyed?"

"They'll get over it." His eyes locked onto hers. Her breath caught. He grabbed her by the waist and drew her closer to him. When their lips were inches away, he said, "I like you."

She gulped, her throat suddenly tight.

Not knowing what to say back—because he wasn't meant to say that—she leant in and kissed him. He was tentative with the kiss, gentle almost, but she put her hands on his face in an attempt to escalate it. She'd rather that than feel the guilt she was feeling now.

Her brother and dad claimed men universally said whatever was necessary to get a woman into bed. "You don't know what my friends say behind girls' backs," her brother would tell her, shaking his head.

Wasn't this exactly what was happening right now? But wasn't Soraya a more than willing participant? In fact, worse than that, wasn't *she* the one using him?

Magnus lifted her up easily, bringing her out of her head, so that she was sitting on the countertop, his hands around her waist. He bent down and his lips met hers again. When their tongues touched Soraya didn't think about it, but let herself enjoy the sensations that followed. She closed her eyes and turned her mind off. His tongue stroked hers, and it sent butterflies to her stomach. Her body became supersensitive to his touch, and she wanted more. So much more.

Magnus broke the kiss. Soraya opened her mouth to protest, but his lips found her neck and the delicate skin under her ear. He kissed her ever so softly there, something he had not done before. A moan escaped her lips. This took her by surprise, and as he continued kissing her she felt warm. Her eyes fluttered shut and her legs found their way around his waist, locking him to the spot. She could feel his hardness against her. His hand traveled underneath her dress and found her breasts.

He touched them, and she was surprised by how good it felt. And then his other hand trailed up her thigh.

He momentarily broke the kiss, and all she could do was stare at him; she didn't know how this went, or what would come next. All she knew was that she suddenly wanted it very much. She nodded her head ever so slightly. He pressed his lips to hers again and they kissed more fervently than before, his lips hungry for hers, his tongue caressing hers.

And then his fingers found her. She'd never been touched there before and just the way he brushed her made her feel as if she might explode. With him she felt arousal, whereas before him she had always been searching for it. He took it a step further, and that's when she felt it.

Pain.

Thoughts such as "broken seal" screamed at her, sudden and venomous. She almost recoiled from them. She knew it was sexist and perhaps if the act was pleasurable she might have pushed past it, but it hurt. And he had no idea because she hadn't told him she hadn't even touched herself there, had never put anything up there—not even a tampon—because she had always been told not to.

Then it began to feel good and her body moved of its own accord. But even then, she couldn't let go, couldn't enjoy it. Her mind was in a whirlwind about what it would mean simply to enjoy this man being so intimate with her, when she was unmarried, when she saw no future with him, when she was using him. Her jaw was tight, and she shut her eyes in an attempt to block out the tirade of thoughts.

It was all too much, and despite the feelings that were very much coursing through her, she remembered the last part of her mum's sermons.

God is watching.

That thought was like a shower of ice-cold water.

"The food," Soraya said softly. Her legs slackened their hold. Magnus didn't pay attention to her words. "Stop," she said again.

He removed his hand and stepped back. "Huh?"

"I can hear the food burning." She pointed to the frying pan. At least she was telling the truth. The vegetables he had been frying were now blackened. That said, she didn't dare look him in the eye, as though her eyes would reveal everything. The real reason why she was seeing him. That she had no intention of seriously dating him. That she was a virgin. A fraud.

He laughed. "Oh, fuck, shall we just order pizza?"

"Yeah, let's," she said, getting off the counter and pulling her dress down.

Only a couple of minutes ago she was a normal twenty-one-year-old woman. But now her in-between state—of thinking of herself as a Muslim but not acting like one—was asserting itself again.

It was inescapable.

Chapter 16

SORAYA

London, 2014

All Soraya knew about her sister Laleh was that she had left the family fifteen years ago to be with her boyfriend. Laleh had been just seventeen years old then. She was subsequently disowned by the family. Though Soraya was never quite sure whether this was because Laleh had disowned them first.

Soraya had been too young to actually remember Laleh when she lived at home. This was both a blessing and a curse. She couldn't miss her sister because she didn't know her—but wasn't it weird not to miss a sister you hadn't seen for fifteen years?

It was only recently that Soraya thought about Laleh more frequently. Perhaps she finally understood her eldest sister a bit more. Understood what it was like to want to see a boy behind their parents' back. But resounding in her mind were so many unanswered questions. Why couldn't Laleh just have waited until she was eighteen, and off to university, before having a boyfriend? Was any boy really worth leaving your family behind?

Soraya's image of Laleh was always blurred, never fully formed. She had seen pictures in the photo albums that were kept hidden away. Laleh at sixteen, in her school uniform, smiling at the camera. She was so naturally beautiful, her eyebrows thin and shaped and her lips a perfect Cupid's bow. Her hair had been cut into a long bob, slightly frizzy in the way teenage hair always is.

Soraya reached under her pillow to retrieve her diary. She wrote in it when she couldn't make sense of her emotions. Lately the majority of her entries had been about Magnus. She opened the last page and the photograph she was looking for fell out.

Her sister's face stared back at her. She had a mole between her eyebrows that always struck Soraya as unique. She tried to imagine her sister in her thirties. Would her hair be thinner, sleeker? Would she be bigger in maturity?

Laleh wasn't on social media. At least not under Laleh Nazari. No one in the family talked about her, and it wasn't until Soraya was much older that she realized how strange that was. When she tried to bring up the subject of her sister the atmosphere always changed and she was abruptly shut down. After a while she learnt not to try.

Every few months Soraya would attempt to find Laleh online. She would Google-search her, check every social media platform for her sister. But there was no trace of her. It was clear she didn't want to be found.

In some of her daydreams Soraya pictured Laleh living in Paris, or somewhere equally glamorous, in a café somewhere, drinking espresso, not thinking about the family she'd left behind. Her image of her sister was always as a teenager, like the girl in the photograph. She could not imagine what Laleh looked like now.

In Soraya's nightmares Laleh was living in a tiny flat, struggling to make ends meet. Or worse: on the streets. Homeless because her parents had abandoned her when she was seventeen—would rather lose their daughter than accept she had a boyfriend. Surely, the whole point of families was to be there for each other? Not disown a young person for falling in love.

That was the problem with the forbidden love that Soraya relished reading about: it was easy to idealize only if you ignored the wreckage it caused.

Soraya doubted Laleh was still with that boyfriend. The statistical odds were against them. They had been a teenage couple who idealized love. She imagined that when Laleh had left home cracks had begun to form. How could they not? It was a sad thought.

She put the photograph away and tucked her diary back under her pillow.

Either Laleh was doing well and wanted nothing to do with them. Or she was doing bad and needed them, but couldn't reach out.

The two thoughts haunted Soraya.

Staring up at her ceiling, feeling the ever-present emptiness inside her, she couldn't help but wonder if she was one step closer to being like Laleh.

To being tarnished.

Or perhaps free.

Chapter 17

NEDA

Neda hid Baba's bottles of wine in the cupboard, placed heavy blankets over them, and cleaned the house thoroughly. The good dishes were out, and the freshest, largest fruit had been bought. Watermelon was cut into thick slabs and placed in a clear bowl. Cherries, apples, cucumbers, plums, and peaches were artfully assembled in dishes. Maman had ruled that all the women should wear hijabs for dinner.

Say what you want about Maman, she knew how to adapt to her children's various suitors during a khastegari.

The sofreh, a large floral sheet, was on the floor; not the one the family sat on to eat every day, this one was special, for guests only. Displayed on it were dishes of ash, adas polow, salad olivieh, and jujeh kabab. Neda's family, minus Neda's already married siblings, sat on one side of the sofreh, and Hossein, his mother, and three sisters sat on the opposite side. His sisters, surprisingly, did not wear head scarves. Neda had assumed they would and could tell her own sisters were resentful that they had been made to wear them.

"You have a cute house," Hossein's mother commented.

Neda and Rabeh cringed. The woman's words were laced with double meaning. It made Neda conscious of her surroundings, seeing them through an outsider's eyes. She noticed for the first time the water stains on one wall, that the cracks in the plaster weren't normal, everything that indicated they were in some way inferior for living in a place like this. She wished she could stop this seeing, and go back to being clueless about their shabby home.

"Cute," Maman repeated slowly. "Thank you."

The familiar hum of the air-conditioning filled the silence.

"What is it you study, Neda dear?"

Neda puffed out her chest with pride. "Biomedicine."

"But you finish this year, correct?" It became clear Hossein's mother didn't actually care what the subject was.

"Yes."

"That's good then, so you can look after the house following marriage."

Neda looked over at Baba. He was leaning against the wall, legs crossed. He pursed his lips but said nothing.

"Yes, of course, Neda is a lovely cook and very clean," Maman said, slightly too quickly. You could almost smell the desperation in the air, seasoned with reluctance from Baba, in addition to the strong stench of the kebab.

"Very good." Her soon-to-be mother-in-law looked at Neda approvingly. "Well done. You would be surprised . . . girls these days are forgetting all their home skills in favor of academia. This is apparently the modern normal." She wrinkled her nose dismissively.

Hossein had a smile plastered on his face; he was equally uncomfortable with his mother's comments. Neda was soon distracted by thoughts of how straight and white his teeth were, and how he was soon to be hers.

He had already made it clear he would support her studying and working, so his mother's words did not faze her, but Baba's reactions to them did.

She was reminded of one of their conversations after Hossein gave her the life-changing note.

"You're the only man who asked me first and not Baba," Neda had said.

"I wanted this to be your decision." Hossein looked down at his hands as he spoke. "I didn't know if your dad was strict, and the last thing I would want is for this to be an engagement you didn't want." He stared deep into her eyes then, earnest as ever. Looking at him in that moment, Neda wondered how someone so beautiful, with eyelashes so long and eyes so welcoming, could also be perfect within.

She was brought back to the present.

"He's my only son, you know how it is," Hossein's mum continued, taking a tentative bite of her kebab. "When his father died it was very hard on us . . . and having three girls and only one boy! Ay, it has been difficult, but this boy has been a real man of the house. He's very special to us; I just want to make sure he has a good wife, you know. A good girl like Neda, I mean. I can tell she is a good girl." She said the last part quickly, realizing all of Neda's family were looking at her, their smiles turning into grimaces. "The food is lovely, by the way."

"What about Hossein?" Baba said, breaking his almost steely silence.

"What about him?" she said.

"He's at the same university as our Neda," her father said. "But what exactly is it that he's studying?"

His mum didn't answer immediately and looked down as she spoke. "Science as well."

Neda frowned unconsciously and her dad picked up on it.

"Really?" he said. "I thought it was something different."

"It's sports science, sir," Hossein said, his voice steady. "I played football too, professionally, but I had an injury."

"He's very good, he could even be professional again one day," his mum added. "Inshallah his leg will heal fully."

Ignoring this, Baba continued speaking. "And how are you going to provide for Neda?"

"I've been working at my uncle's factory part-time," Hossein said. "I've got savings and inheritance money. And once I graduate, I will find a full-time job, hopefully relating to my degree. I'd love to coach football at the very least."

Maman smiled.

The topic of conversation moved on to Neda's virginity.

"She's a good Muslim girl," Maman said. "Obviously." And yet her hands were clasped together tight. It was like seeing a policeman in the street. Even though you're doing nothing wrong, there's still that small ball of anxiety in your stomach, as though somehow you might be. That's how Neda imagined Maman felt during this conversation—it was how Neda was feeling, anyway.

"Yes, I don't doubt that. I would obviously like to see the sheet afterwards, though."

Maman almost flinched before saying, "Of course!"

Neda caught Hossein's eye. He looked like he wanted to laugh while she wanted to cry. He winked at her and she felt the tension in her shoulders release. She almost smiled back, but quickly brought her gaze down. Better not attract attention. But she peeked at him one more time, and though he was now looking at his mother, he still had the glimmer of a smirk on his face.

At the end of the evening it took at least forty-five minutes for Neda's family to say goodbye to Hossein's. There were after all thirteen of them, and Iranians are very particular about their goodbyes. A proper leave-taking consisted of three kisses on each person's cheeks, an invitation to a future dinner, thank-yous, a compliment, another goodbye, another offer to meet up over dinner, additional thank-yous, and then a formal goodbye before Neda's family walked Hossein's to their car.

While their families were preoccupied, Hossein managed to stand next to Neda. They smiled at each other, giddy that it seemed to have gone smoothly and their wedding was actually going to happen. Neda's heart beat fast every time she looked at Hossein. He both terrified and excited her. Even standing next to each other, they kept at least a ten-centimeter gap between them; there would be no real touching until their wedding night. And yet despite this, Hossein's hand found Neda's—for a few seconds—and brushed against it. It was everything she had imagined it would be; his hand was warm and strong. It sent a funny feeling through her body. She looked at him sharply, denying how her body felt, focusing on what she *should* feel.

He laughed, running his hand through his hair. He seemed totally at ease, making Neda feel like a fool for being so uptight. He accidentally touched her and she was making a show of herself.

Neda opened her mouth to speak but was interrupted by Baba. He leant in to say goodbye to Hossein, shook his hand before kissing his cheeks.

"Get home safe," he said.

Baba was a small man with a kind face. She wished she could have taken a photograph of Baba and Hossein together—her old life with her new life. Instead, she imprinted the image of them in her mind permanently.

As Hossein climbed into the car, he gave Neda a small bow.

"Goodbye, future wife."

Chapter 18

SORAYA

London, 2014

There was something intrinsically special about standing in a well-stocked bookshop. Excitement and longing, for all the books there was not enough time to read, hung in the air.

Magnus and Soraya had begun their date by walking along the South Bank, and it was there that they stumbled upon Foyles Bookshop. It had been a month since graduation, since they first spoke, which felt like so long ago now.

They were looking at the new releases section when Soraya blurted out, "When are you going to tell me what your book is about?"

He looked taken aback.

"It's about families, I guess," he said, walking over to the paperbacks on one of the center tables. She thought he would continue speaking but he did not.

"Care to elaborate?" she asked, following him.

He laughed and grabbed her face between both hands, locking her in place.

Her eyes widened at this, and he responded with a smirk and the slight raise of one eyebrow.

He moved closer to her, so that his nose was almost touching hers. Her breath caught suddenly; she'd come to realize he had that effect on her. She didn't like it.

"You're nosy, you know that?" he breathed.

Just when she almost leant in, she became conscious of the

people around them and moved backwards. He must have had the same thought because he let her go at the same time.

"I guess it's inspired by my relationship with my dad," he said finally.

The resignation in his voice, and Soraya's memory of his dad at graduation, made her feel bad for asking.

To prod further was to enter uncertain territory; this whole thing was only meant to be about one kiss. Poking into sticky family situations would only complicate things further.

"Oh, yeah?" she replied, throwing the ball firmly back into his court.

"Yeah. I mean, I don't think it'll go anywhere. I just write for fun."

She noticed the way his whole demeanor changed when he spoke about writing. He was usually so confident, knew exactly what he was doing, but here, in the realm of writing, he did not.

They moved to another section of the bookshop. Soraya noticed a shelf marked "Feminism and Feminist Theory." She power walked towards it, knowing he would follow her like she had followed him.

"What are your thoughts on feminism?" she asked, her heart beating oddly quickly. She knew exactly what she was doing though; she was hoping he would say the wrong thing, that her initial assumptions about him would be confirmed as correct all along: that he was just a typical lad. Confirmation of this would make not seeing him again a lot easier.

She was conscious of the fact that she was no longer using him, that the lines were blurring, and what they were doing had now become something real. They would never work as a couple, though, she knew this, for a number of reasons, including

1. He was renowned for dating girls on rotation.
2. He had previously said he didn't believe in monogamy.
3. He didn't believe in God.

When she wasn't with him, Soraya questioned what they were doing, and why she had let it go on for so long. And yet . . . she liked being with him now. Somewhere deep inside, she knew she looked forward to their meetings. So, she needed him to say something wrong now—to cause an argument, to give her a reason to call it off.

But a small part of her was rooting for Magnus. She pushed down on that part.

She didn't look at him but picked up the nearest book and pretended to read the blurb, though her eyes were skimming over words her brain did not take in.

She could feel his presence behind her. "It's good?" he said.

She put the book down, turned around to face him, a challenging look in her eyes. "Good?"

"I mean," he said, "what do you want me to say? It's bad?" He was smiling.

"So you have no opinions on the matter, then?" she asked quickly. "It sounds like you could take it or leave it, like it's not something you've considered before."

He frowned. "I obviously care about equality between men and women. I'm not a complete dickhead. I just don't really get why you're asking me, to be honest. It's like you want me to say I don't agree with it or something?"

She was clearly not being as subtle as she thought.

"Of course I support women's rights, *obviously*," he continued. "Why the hell wouldn't I?"

Soraya sat on one of the wooden benches nearby, and Magnus sat down next to her. She looked at her hands as she spoke, something close to shame creeping in. "You hang around with boys from uni who are known for treating girls badly," she said, in as steady a voice as she could manage, though the fire in her belly had died down now. What she didn't say was: the way *you're* known to treat girls is pretty bad too.

"I'm not them, though."

"But you're friends with them."

"Not all of them. My actual friends are pretty sound." He paused. "I don't like that you still see me that way."

Her heart began to beat quickly again.

"We've hung out quite a few times now," he continued. "Surely you see that I'm not like that by now?"

She swallowed her own saliva with difficulty; her throat felt too tight. She felt thoroughly put on the spot. It wasn't like she didn't deserve it though.

"It's just you hear so many things . . ."

"But you know me," he interjected. "Right? From what you've seen of me, do you really think I'm like that?"

His eyes were imploring her, and she felt another wave of shame. She hadn't really thought about what she was saying, about how it might make him feel. She hadn't thought about his feelings at all since she had known him, come to think of it.

"No, I don't," she said, surprising herself by how true the words felt when they came out of her mouth.

He visibly relaxed, like her opinion of him really mattered.

And all Soraya could think in that moment was *Oh, shit.*

After twenty more minutes spent browsing—and then purchasing—books, they continued their walk along the river, passing teenagers at the skate park, the various chain restaurants and amusements.

Their conversation had moved in a much lighter, much safer, direction; Soraya had learnt her lesson.

"How are you finding post-uni life now?" Magnus asked.

They stopped to lean against one of the railings overlooking the usually murky Thames. But today the clear blue sky was reflected in the water and brightened it, giving the illusion of a perfectly blue river.

"It's weird," Soraya confessed. "It's not what I thought it would be."

"How so?" Magnus was looking out into the distance as they spoke, which allowed her to gaze openly at his face. She decided she appreciated his broken nose. It was the only thing about him that wasn't conventionally attractive, and that made it more special. He had mentioned in passing how he'd broken it on two separate occasions, during rugby games, and had given up on having surgery to correct it. He'd laughed it off at the time, but she could tell it was actually something he was bothered about, beneath it all.

"I was really looking forward to 'beginning life,' but I don't think I realized how everything would change—and not for the better. I thought everyone would stay in London, that starting a career would be simple. That everyone would still see each other, as normal, but apart from Priya and Oliver, I haven't seen anyone since graduation. I guess I just didn't think it through, not that I really had a choice in the matter."

"Yeah, it's definitely not easy. Most of my friends have gone off somewhere else as well."

"Let me guess, Australia or Thailand, or both?"

He gave her a wide smile. "Yes! And can I just ask *how* is everyone flying off to Australia and Thailand? Where did they even get the money? I swear the ones who left were the ones who were always going on about being skint. If that's their version of skint . . ."

"It comes from the bank of Mummy and Daddy," Soraya finished.

She wasn't unaware of the privilege in her own life, that her family now lived comfortably, but her parents were not well off enough to pay her rent or give her money for flights to the other side of the world. It was interesting, she thought, how no matter how well you were doing in life, there was always something you didn't have and longed for—and yet someone elsewhere would be wishing for exactly what you had.

"God, there were so many posh people at our uni. Like worse than just posh people—posh people pretending not to be posh—like they think it's actually cooler to be poor," Magnus said, shaking his head. They began walking again. He gave her a look then that made her both laugh out loud and also feel deeply offended.

"I'm not posh!"

"Yeah, yeah, 'I'm not posh,'" he said, mimicking her Southern accent badly.

Her mouth hung wide open for a few seconds before she playfully shoved his shoulder. How was it possible for anyone's shoulder to be rock solid? She knew her bingo wings were not quite the norm at twenty-one years old, but Magnus seemed to take things in the complete opposite direction.

He put his hand over hers before she could remove it, and then somehow they were holding hands, like it was the most normal thing in the world. What was worse was that she quite liked the feeling of his hand enclosing hers, liked the protectiveness of the gesture. This information would of course never be shared with Priya or Oliver.

"I'm not," she protested again. "Like, I'm genuinely not. It's just my accent."

He narrowed his eyes, but there was a teasing edge to his otherwise detective-like expression.

"How many holidays do your family go on a year?"

The question was so specific it surprised her. "Um, I don't know, we don't always go on family holidays. Probably like once every five years and they're always a bit of a fail."

"What kind of school did you go to?"

"State school." This question, however, she understood. She'd been so surprised entering student halls in first year to find most of the people there had been to a private school. Though she also felt a sense of pride that she had achieved the same grades without her parents having paid for a private education.

"How many bathrooms does your family home have?"

She laughed. "These questions . . ." She thought for a moment. "Three."

He raised their clasped hands in the air as though celebrating a triumph. "See, I told you."

She stopped walking and gave him a half-joking scowl. "You're so annoying," she said. "We're genuinely not like loaded or anything. We have a nice house because my parents lucked out and bought one in Brighton years ago when it was cheaper, but they came to England with literally one suitcase each and a Persian carpet." She'd heard the story many times, but saying it out loud sounded a bit too exact. Why did they need to bring a rug with them? Who did that?

She felt herself getting a bit too defensive. Why did she even care what he thought? Except, she knew she cared very much.

"To clarify," she continued, "I'm not saying we're in a bad position or anything, like I'm very lucky, I'm just saying that we're not posh."

He smiled down at her then. "You're cute when you're annoyed, you know," he murmured.

She understood, then, why the girls at the house party lapped up Magnus's words, because right now she was doing the same thing. One minute she was annoyed at him and the next she was putty in his hands—and it needed to stop. But not right now.

There was an uneasiness in the pit of her stomach. It took her a moment to locate the cause: she had come to really like Magnus. She liked his brain and the version of herself that she was around him. "You're being mean," she breathed. "And presumptuous."

He came closer so their lips were almost touching. "I'm joking," he said, before kissing her. The kiss was slow, romantic. "I quite like arguing with you," he said after a moment.

She disentangled herself and narrowed her eyes.

"You know you said I see you in a way you don't like? Well, you see me in a way I don't like."

In fact, perhaps part of the reason Soraya never quite integrated at university, she thought, was that she couldn't connect with the other students there. Lack of sexual experience aside, every year friends of friends at university would return with stories about their summers abroad, and she could never understand how they lived as they did, always thought she was the one who was doing something wrong, like she had to keep up with them or be left behind.

"How would you like me to see you then?"

It was such a simple question, but one she struggled to answer. She shrugged her shoulders.

A niggling part of her wished she had brought up the subject of his dad. She imagined that his probing linked back to his family somehow. But the problem was, if she mentioned his dad, he might ask about hers, and that would lead them into territory she couldn't face. It would only lead to more lies, or even worse: the truth.

Chapter 19

SORAYA

It had become a given that Soraya and Magnus would see each other at least twice a week. As time passed they went for dinners in central London, crazy golf in Shoreditch, and long walks on Hampstead Heath.

They reached an invisible milestone when Magnus sent her his novel in progress. It was when they had been steadily dating for two months that she was finally given the opportunity to read it.

Despite repeatedly asking him to send it, when she got the email with the attachment and nothing in the body of the email, she began to fear opening it. What if it wasn't good? Would she have to lie?

It was a worry she needn't have had. She read his book in just one day; it exceeded her expectations. The prose was dreamlike and whimsical, while also managing to be very precise. It was full of contradictions in a pleasant way. It was a lot darker than she'd thought it would be, featuring a working-class, dysfunctional family on the verge of collapse. Magnus was always so positive when they met that the novel was an insight into a different side to him. One she could very much relate to.

He asked her to go with him to buy a new winter coat, something she relished doing because despite now finding him attractive, she still hated his clothes. As she picked out the perfect coat, part of her wondered if she was helping the next girl he would be with, one who would be dating a far more fashionable Magnus. She tried to dismiss such thoughts.

When he invited her to watch him play an important rugby game, she lied and said she already had plans. She was wary of integrating herself into his life because this was only meant to be temporary. It had already gone on for too long. She didn't envisage them having a future together, and if they attempted to have one it would end badly, that much she knew. While on some levels they were alike, fundamentally their attitudes towards many aspects of life were completely different. They would never marry, ultimately, and that meant one day they'd break up. She didn't want to put herself in a situation in which she could get hurt, didn't want to be one of the many women who were discarded by Magnus.

That he'd invited her into a public space was also worrying in another way: it hinted that he wasn't seeing anyone else.

And yet, despite all of this, they continued seeing each other. After each date they'd go back to her flat or his house and put on a film, although they never got past the opening credits before they began kissing. Their clothes would come off, hastily. Each time it escalated more and more, but they still hadn't had sex. On this point, Soraya was adamant. She got the sense he saw this waiting as a tactic, that by playing the long game he'd eventually win. But little did he know, in some way this was a game for her too. She'd stay with him until the issue of them not having had sex finally became too much, and then she knew they'd break up.

She wasn't ready to have sex, didn't know how to come to terms with everything she had been taught about the importance of preserving one's virginity. Nor with how what she had been taught differed from what she believed, that virginity was a social construct.

It was when they went for a walk in Nunhead Cemetery that Soraya decided she needed to end things with Magnus. But not for the reasons she had originally believed would cause her to break up with him; rather because she realized she was developing very real feelings for him. She didn't want to fall for him. Didn't want the messiness that came with being emotionally involved with someone like him. She decided she would do it in the evening, via text message because she was a self-professed coward.

Autumn leaves crunched under their feet as they studied the Gothic tombstones.

"You should pursue writing and getting published, if that's really what you want," Soraya said.

Magnus scratched his head, looking away. He always looked away when they talked about his writing. She reached up to his face, pulling it towards her so he'd be forced to look at her.

"I mean it," she said, more softly this time.

"I appreciate the sentiment," he said slowly. "But it's not something someone like me can seriously consider."

She expected him to expand. But he didn't.

"Someone like you?"

She resisted the urge to point out that for him as a white man, a career in writing was very much within his grasp.

"You know, my dad's a plumber and my mum works in Matalan. It's just not what we do where I'm from." He let out a long breath. "There's no job security in writing. God, I don't even know if I'm any good."

"You are," she reassured him.

"Even if I was, I wouldn't know where to begin. It feels wrong even to dream about it . . . God, I sound sappy, don't I?"

She smiled. "No, you don't."

"And anyway, why don't you take your drawing seriously?" he shot back at her.

"That's different—"

"How? You're talented, Soraya, but you're scared. And you don't need to be."

"Like you?"

He sighed in frustration.

"I just feel like a bit of a loser lately," she confessed.

He looked at her and frowned. "You're not a loser."

"I keep getting rejected from jobs," she said. "Office jobs, retail jobs, everything." She still had some savings left, buying herself extra time, but this could go on for only so long.

"They aren't meant to be then. Things happen for a reason, you know. Something good will happen for you soon, I know it."

They stopped walking to observe the architecture of one particularly stunning mausoleum. It was large and looked Victorian, reminding her of something otherworldly.

"Why did you want to come here?" she asked.

"I think there's something really beautiful about old cemeteries. I sometimes come here to think. Or get inspiration. I thought you might like it." He looked down self-consciously.

She did. Though she found it odd to enjoy being in a cemetery, the reminder of the fragility of life surrounding them. How short it was, really, in the grand scheme of things. And how we'd all end up in the same place, no matter who we were. No matter where we were from, what religion we were.

His hand found hers and he began stroking her palm slowly, absentmindedly. He was making this so hard for her.

"Have you brought other girls here?" she asked, unable to stop the words coming out of her mouth. She wished she could swallow them back, not wanting to hear the answer.

"No," he said quickly.

"Why not?"

"It never felt right. I come here for quiet, for stillness. I don't think I could bring just anyone here."

He didn't say more on the matter, and she didn't press him, despite desperately wanting clarity on what that even meant.

She thought back to the party, when she was told Magnus had been dating a girl for four months before dumping her. She couldn't imagine him doing that, but then the girl probably couldn't either.

"You know what," he said. "How about we make a deal? I'll try and take my writing seriously if you take your art seriously too."

She rolled her eyes. He put a hand in the air to stop her from speaking. "Come on, just say yes. It could be fun." He flashed her a smile and her heart fluttered. How had she ever not found him attractive? Now all he had to do was smile at her and she melted, became putty in his hands.

"Fine, OK."

He gave her hand a squeeze and they continued walking up the path. And she knew when they left the cemetery that she wouldn't break up with him, that she had never truly planned to do so.

She was in too deep, and it would only end in disaster.

Chapter 20

NEDA

Tehran, 1977

"What's your favorite color?" Neda asked, her voice pitched too high, her hands firmly clasped together. They walked side by side through Park-e Shahr, stopping occasionally to observe the fanciful sculpted shrubbery, leafy trees, and pink roses.

Hossein laughed, running his fingers through his hair as he pondered the question.

The smell of roasted nuts lingered in the air from the vendor they walked past. Neda's eyes closed briefly as she inhaled the scent, reminding herself that the nuts often smelt better than they tasted.

It was the first time they had been alone, albeit not quite on their own in such a public space. There were other families, friends, and couples all around them.

"I don't have one," he finally said.

"Really? You must!" She started to feel silly, childlike almost, for asking him. But she'd had no practice in talking to the opposite sex—apart from family members—and wasn't quite sure what to say or how to act. So she feigned confidence.

The leaves crunched softly under their feet as they walked. Despite finding the noise satisfying, Neda longed to hold on to the last of summer, willing it to continue just a little while longer. She had gotten good grades and would begin working soon, perhaps continuing her studies the year after if she was granted a scholarship.

It was curious how quickly life changed. Numerous friends had become engaged to men from university. It was quite unlike the American movies they watched; in Iran it took only a few meetings to become engaged, and then married.

And Neda finally felt ready. The more she got to know Hossein, the more enchanted she became by him. She knew she would do anything to make him smile, to make him happy.

Children ran past them, playing tag, almost bumping into Hossein in the process.

"OK, well, I guess if I had to choose a color, I'd pick red."

"Ah," Neda said.

Hossein smiled. His arms swung as he walked, narrowly missing her. Part of her wanted to lean into him, and she had to scold herself for such thoughts. "Why just 'ah'?"

"Well, you could pick any color in the whole world. Turquoise, silver, peach, magnolia—even plain old purple. But instead you picked red."

"It's a classic color." Hossein folded his arms in mock offense. "Well, what's yours?"

"Oh, there're too many colors to choose from. I don't really have a favorite." Her lips were held in a small smile as she repressed laughter.

"Oh, you . . ." Hossein touched her hand and brought it to his chest. "You're infuriating, but somehow I love it."

Love.

Neda was breathless. Just the touch of his hand on hers was enough to make her whole body shiver in a way it never had before. Their eyes connected for only a second before he let go and they continued walking past a large lake. Despite being artificial it was still beautiful, the sight of the water calming.

"I've always wanted to ask you—why do you wear a hijab when so many of your friends don't? Have you always worn it?"

She gave him her reasons, getting herself into knots when she tried to explain that while she was doing it to follow Islam as instructed in the Quran, she was also doing it for herself. When she said this he nodded, as though he understood perfectly.

"You're so brave," he said. "Unlike anyone I've ever known."

At this Neda scoffed. "I know what people think—that I'm old-fashioned."

Hossein stopped, so Neda did too. A couple behind weaved their way past, mildly irritated by the obstacle in their way, swinging their clasped hands as they walked.

"Well, I don't think that. You're taking action, standing up for what you believe in . . . it's admirable. I wish I were like you. In fact, I have something I need to—"

A man selling single red roses cut him off. "Buy one for the beautiful khanum?"

Neda opened her mouth to refuse, though secretly she hoped he'd buy her one. Hossein gave the man money, his back to her. When he turned around, in his hands were a dozen or so roses.

She grinned; it was the most genuine smile she'd given in a very long time. As he handed them to her he swore under his breath. "The thorns," he explained. She looked down and saw he hadn't got the roses wrapped, so his palm was encircling the sharp barbs. She laughed, and then they were both laughing at the ridiculousness of the situation.

Racing around Neda's mind in that moment was the word "love" and how easily, she realized, she could fall in love with this man.

Chapter 21

NEDA

Tehran, 1977

"Are you sure about this, Neda?" Baba's voice startled her, causing her to spill water from the can she was holding onto the cracked tiles in their garden. She moved it back towards the flower beds she had been watering, paying particular attention to the red roses that were in bloom.

"Sure about what?"

The silence that followed made her pause in what she was doing. Her father had a worried look on his face and his hands were folded together, which she knew was a sign that they were itching to fidget. She had seen him peel the skin from his fingers when he didn't know she was looking. As she grew older she had realized the man she thought was the fountain of knowledge and wisdom had cracks underneath just like everyone else.

"Baba?"

"I have a bad feeling about Hossein," he said slowly. "But you seem so certain, so sure. I didn't want to say anything before, but now I feel I have to. He doesn't seem good enough for you, Neda."

"What? You didn't say anything at the khastegari—"

"You looked happy. I thought maybe I was being overprotective . . ."

"So, what's changed since then?" She shifted on her feet, feeling almost dizzy, as though the one thing she wanted more than anything was close to being snatched away. She hadn't realized she felt as much as that for Hossein until this moment. "Maman loves him, why can't you?"

Baba's face hardened and he tutted sharply. "Watch your tone."

Neda muttered an apology that she didn't mean.

He stepped closer to her, but instead of looking at her he watched the roses she had just watered, brushing his fingers over their petals.

"Of all my children you're the most intelligent, you know that, don't you?"

She said nothing in response.

"I know your mother gives you bother because of your ambition. It's because she doesn't understand. You're destined for things much greater than this." He pointed at the small garden they shared with the other residents of their building. "When you first said you wanted to wear a hijab, I couldn't understand it. You'd be making your life so much harder. But you were so determined, just like you are with your studies, like you are with everything you do. I want to make sure you're happy. As your father it's my duty to advise you."

"But, Baba, I will be happy with Hossein. You don't understand, he's had such a hard life. After his dad died he had to be a father to his sisters, to look after his whole family. He's a good man. I know I'll be happy with him."

She knew what she was doing, knew if she mentioned Hossein's hard life it would soften her baba.

Or so she thought.

He snorted in response. Neda smiled automatically until she realized he was laughing at her.

"You're young, azizam, marriage is hard, you don't know the other person until you're living with them and then it's too late. There's something not quite right about him—he seems very melancholy, no?"

"What do you mean, 'melancholy'?"

"He has a sadness in his eyes. When no one is looking he seems *sad*. Do you want to live with someone like that?"

Neda was momentarily speechless. Her baba viewed Hossein in a very different way; he saw emotions as a weakness, a flaw, when it was precisely Hossein's softness that attracted Neda to him.

"You don't know him like I do. And you didn't give any of my siblings this hassle when they got married!" She blurted out the words and once she began she couldn't stop. "You agreed to this, and now you're trying to make me doubt myself, and him, and it isn't fair. He's just shy, and he's had a hard life." Her eyes were filling; she hoped the tears wouldn't discredit what she was trying to say.

"He's a loser!" her dad bellowed. "Why not marry someone with a job, stability, a good family? Why sell yourself so short?"

She could feel what she most wanted slipping rapidly through her fingers and it made her all the more determined, all the more certain that she wanted the thing she was trying to hold on to. Neda was the type of person who wanted something all the more when it was taken away from her, or even if its being taken was merely suggested.

In all the romances she secretly read, the characters had to face obstacles, but she didn't want that for her and Hossein. This wasn't *Romeo and Juliet;* it should be simple. Two people who like each other enough to marry. To be with each other forever.

Baba looked at her face then rested a heavy hand on her shoulder. "Neda, don't get upset."

"If you think I'm smart, believe me when I say I want to marry Hossein and only Hossein."

He sighed, disappointed but resigned.

"He's good, Baba, believe me."

The glimmer of a smile traced his lips, and she relaxed.

"You always get what you want in the end, don't you, azizam?"

Chapter 22

SORAYA

London, 2014

Magnus let go of the lead and the black Labrador bolted off into the distance, sniffing various leaves and sticks as she went.

Soraya was overwhelmed by the novelty of being with a dog; she was more of a cat person. A fact Magnus was keen to change.

"I don't mind cats," he had said. "But dogs are better, fact."

"Dogs are needy, but with cats you have to win them over; it makes their love so much more special."

Magnus rolled his eyes. "You haven't met the right one yet." He winked. She laughed at that.

"Are you calling yourself a dog?"

He pushed her jokingly, making her laugh even more.

She had never been to Clapham Common before. Magnus's friend had asked him to look after his pets while he was on holiday, and consequently Magnus was house-sitting for the week.

The dog came bounding back to them, jumping up against Soraya's thighs, almost knocking her over in the process. She pretended to laugh, patted the animal's head, hoping she would back off.

"Holly, sit," Magnus said. The dog complied. With her legs back on the ground she did look cute. Soraya tentatively patted Holly's head, finding the fur not quite as soft as it looked.

Magnus waved a plastic toy in the shape of a bone, pretending to throw it multiple times before he launched it off into the distance.

"How does your friend afford to live round here, and with pets? Who even has their own pets at our age?" she asked.

Before they went for the walk Soraya had been given a tour of the house and met the quiet resident tabby and white cat, named Tyson, who was rightfully suspicious of her. She was taken aback by how polished the house was; the walls and carpet cream and pristine, except in the kitchen, where the floor was gray marble. They even had a Nespresso machine. A symbol, Soraya thought, that you had made it in life.

"His dad bought it," Magnus said, in a tone she knew very well. They had had many conversations criticizing those whose parents handed everything to them, especially in London. They knew, however, it was because this was something they would never have; if they could, they were sure their opinion on the matter would be different.

"I always wanted a dog when I was younger," Magnus said, bringing Soraya back to the present.

"Did your family not want one?"

"Well, they had one when I was little, but I don't remember it. When she died I think my dad was quite cut up about it, so they never wanted to get another."

"That's sad," Soraya said, trying to envisage Magnus as a child. "What were you like growing up? I can't imagine it."

Holly ran towards them with the toy in her mouth. Soraya pulled it out and mimicked Magnus, pretending to throw it multiple times before hurling it as far as she could. It wasn't a long way. She wiped her now wet hand on her coat.

"I was a bit of a geek really." He looked sheepish. "I didn't fit in at school."

"Seriously? That's not the vibe I get from you at all. I'd have guessed you'd have been popular."

He shook his head. "Not really. I mean, I guess I hung out with the more popular lads, but I never felt like I belonged when I was with them. Stuff at home was always intense, and I never told anyone about it. I definitely didn't tell them I wrote stories." He let out a short laugh. "*That* would be a surefire way to get the piss taken out of me." She noticed the tops of his ears were pink.

Magnus wrinkled his nose. "I sound pretty lame, don't I?" he added quickly.

"No," she said. "Not at all. You keep surprising me."

He gave her a sideways grin. They reached the bandstand and walked up the steps to stand under its canopy. She gazed out across the common, at the pond in the distance, the people walking around it through orange leaves scattered on the ground.

She knew then that Magnus, like her, put a mask on to cope with his dysfunctional family. While his response was to become more extroverted, she, by contrast, became more introverted. She wished, so much, she had it in her to tell him about her dad. She wondered what he would say, whether he'd feel comforted by it, whether they'd both feel less alone.

"What were you like growing up?" he asked.

She thought for a moment. "I wasn't unpopular, I wouldn't say, but I wasn't popular either. I'd say my time at school was quite unremarkable. I wasn't really allowed to do anything fun— sleepovers or parties or anything like that. So, I don't know, I found growing up a bit boring at times." She was careful to omit the occasions on which it was far from boring, but distressing, when her dad would get angry, or when Laleh was mentioned.

"I get parties, but why weren't you allowed to go to sleepovers?"

She took a sip of the coffee they'd bought before they began their walk, thinking about how she'd word this.

"When I was a teenager my parents were suspicious that instead of going to sleepovers I'd really be with boys. Or"—she let out a small laugh—"when I was younger, my mum always thought someone's dad would be a pedophile so they were doing it to protect me."

"Wait . . . what? A specific person you knew—their dad?"

"No, just other people's dads in general. It doesn't make much sense but she must have read about something like that happening in the news. They're superprotective. I guess living in a foreign country, you have to be on your guard. It was only when I was older that they switched their suspicions towards boys. It was really shit at the time. I just wanted to be normal. I guess I'll never know what a girlie sleepover is like."

"Were they strict with your brother too?"

Soraya snorted. "No, different rules apply to boys, in my family at least. It pisses me and Parvin off so much."

Magnus simply nodded. Probably because there was nothing else he could really say. After a short pause, he said, "You have another sister, right?"

At this, Soraya began to cough on her own saliva from the shock. "What? Why would you ask that?"

"When we first started talking you mentioned having more than one? Or did I get that completely wrong?"

Soraya was left with a decision: tell the truth or lie.

"As far as I'm aware, I only have one sister," she said, pretending to laugh.

Her phone pinged with a WhatsApp message. She knew she shouldn't check it immediately, but her mind ran wild when she received texts from her family. They were the only ones she spoke to on WhatsApp.

It was from Parvin: *Found out Dad has been taking zopiclone. Explains why he's sleeping even more lately . . .*

Soraya's heart sank.

She quickly Googled zopiclone. A highly addictive sleeping pill.

"Hello?" Magnus waved a hand in front of her face, giving her a start.

Holly was sniffing another dog in the distance.

She put her phone in her pocket and wrapped her arms tight around her body.

"Sorry, I was miles away." She said the words but could feel the hollowness around them. Knew she couldn't pretend to be calm anymore. She often felt this bubbling in her chest, like if she didn't vent to someone she would explode. Her hands were itching to get her phone back out of her pocket, to reply to Parvin, to text Oliver, to throw this hot potato of information until it was no longer just her burden, until the pain was spread around.

"Hey, you OK?" She could tell even though Magnus was trying to help her, he was also distracted by the sight of Holly leaping about in the distance. "Hold on one minute," he said, before running over to break up a dog fight, dragging Holly back with him. "Probably time to take her home anyway."

They walked in silence. Soraya was aware she should say something, but her brain couldn't figure out what exactly, what a normal thing to say would be. All she could think was that this news was hopeless for her dad, who wasn't even stabilizing; he just made himself worse and worse.

After Holly had been fed, they sat together on the sofa, next to the cat, which was curled in a ball. Soraya absentmindedly stroked him as he purred contentedly.

"What's up?" Magnus said, putting his forefinger beneath her chin, lifting her face so he could see her better.

She let out a shaky breath that surprised her.

"Family stuff," she said. "My dad isn't really well . . . it's quite difficult to explain." She knew from past experience that when she said this people tended not to push further, accepting an ambiguous explanation of her dad's medical condition.

Magnus didn't surprise her.

"Ah," he said. "I'm sorry. Do you want to talk about it?"

She shook her head.

"What can we do to cheer you up?" He gave her a tentative smile, which made her heart jump.

"I don't know. Whenever me or Oliver are upset about something we put on a playlist we made on Spotify, with songs that either cheer us up or relate to how we're feeling."

"You're really close with him, aren't you?"

"Yeah, he's my best friend. Probably the only friend I've ever had that I've been able to be truly myself with."

"Why couldn't you be yourself with friends before?"

"My Brighton friends didn't really ever understand why I grew up the way I did. Oliver instantly got it. His parents don't really understand him either. They still don't accept him being gay, you know, they think they can fix it somehow. It's pretty fucked up."

"Really fucked up." There was a short silence before Magnus said suddenly, "Let's see this playlist then."

She took out her phone and handed it to him.

"Robyn." He nodded in approval. "Pitbull? Flo Rida?" He laughed. "What are these guys doing here?"

She folded her arms defensively. "They've produced some of the best feel-good songs of our generation."

He barked out a laugh, pulling her into a hug. "Whatever you say, Ms. Nazari." He kissed her head. Still hugging her, he put on "Fireball" by Pitbull. She began to laugh. "I don't ever want you to be sad," he said into her ear. She drew back then, looking into his earnest eyes, which contrasted so markedly with the upbeat music.

She felt something else bubbling within her and knew she had fallen for him. It was too late now to fight it. She leant in to kiss him, expecting a quick peck in return, but it was surprisingly tender, loving even. He put both his hands to her face as she wrapped her arms around his neck. When they stopped kissing, he rested his forehead against hers for a moment. This felt more intimate than anything they had done before.

"You're really special to me, you know that?" he said.

"I . . ." She stopped herself from continuing. "You're pretty special yourself."

Chapter 23

SORAYA

London, 2014

They were meant to meet at the cinema thirty minutes ago. Magnus still hadn't arrived. Soraya stood in a cinema lobby that was now almost empty. She had two tickets for *Gone Girl* in her hand.

How many times can you ring someone before it's just embarrassing? She had already rung three times and sent numerous text messages.

To begin with, she thought he may have just been late, but now she had a sinking suspicion that she had been stood up. Either that, or he had forgotten, a thought equally terrible in that moment. Like whatever they had was forgettable. Her jaw was tight, and her mood rotated in a loop among irritation, anger, slight optimism, and then humiliation. Ultimately, though, she decided she was stupid to think she mattered to him, that he wouldn't drop her suddenly, like he had all the other girls he had been with before.

So instead of ringing him again she texted Oliver and Priya to explain that she'd been stood up.

PRIYA: *The question is . . . WHY ARE YOU STILL SEEING HIM? I thought this was a temporary thing?!*

SORAYA: *It is, but that's not really the point.*

OLIVER: *How . . . odd. You may as well come back home. We ordered Domino's.*

SORAYA: *What if something's happened to him??*

PRIYA: *I hope something has happened to him. Respect yourself and leave. NOW.*

Despite her harsh words at times, Soraya knew Priya didn't mean to offend. Oliver had coined the statement "That's just Priya" to excuse her bad behavior. Over the years Soraya had learnt how to handle her when she became too much, her opinions grating.

She locked her phone. Magnus was now forty minutes late.

On the bus home she kept expecting him to message or ring. But nothing.

Once in her flat she could hear Priya and Oliver chatting in the living room. She prepared herself. A strong smell of cheese and oil hit her and she instantly needed a slice of pizza, slipping back into her old ways of comfort eating. She hadn't even realized she'd stopped doing it since she'd begun seeing Magnus.

Priya looked like she wanted to say something, but Oliver spoke before she could.

"Are you OK?"

"I'm fine," Soraya lied. "I mean, maybe his phone ran out of battery or something."

"Why did neither of you tell me you were still seeing him?" Priya asked in an accusatory tone, clearly not reading the room.

Oliver picked up a large slice of pizza and took his time chewing it.

"I mean, I'm still using him," Soraya said, aware Oliver knew she was blatantly lying, her voice wavering. "Can we just not talk about it?" She sat on the sofa with them.

They watched *Will & Grace* reruns in silence.

"Oh, God, is this what ghosting is?" Soraya suddenly asked. "I've heard about it but never thought I'd actually experience it . . ."

Oliver passed her the last slice of pizza, which she took silently. It was lukewarm and doughy in her hands. She took a bite, chewing loudly but tasting nothing.

"That's a yes then," she continued. "How fucking embarrassing. You know, I was meant to be the one to end it. Not him."

"I never get why it's called 'ghosting.' Isn't the whole point that ghosts don't go away?" Priya said thoughtfully. Oliver and Soraya looked at her in silence. "I'm just saying."

Perhaps it was karma for attempting to play with a player.

Chapter 24

NEDA

Tehran, 1977

As was tradition, a tray of herbs and spices, a silver-plated mirror, hard-shell nuts, painted eggs, a large Quran, coins, sweets, and a needle and thread had all been laid on an expensive silk sofreh. They symbolized the joining of two forces and were considered a token of good luck, from the family and from Allah.

Neda had fought hard for this, for Hossein, for the right to be his wife, and now that their wedding was about to happen she was surprised by her physical reaction to the commitment she was making. Her stomach churned; her entire body felt jittery, adrenaline pumping. In many ways she knew such feelings were perfectly normal; what bride didn't feel nervous before her wedding? Who didn't have doubts in the back of their mind? Anyone who said they didn't, Neda knew, was lying. Saving face because they assumed such thoughts were unusual. It was an endless cycle of deception. Marriage was putting yourself into someone else's hands and accepting one future out of many different options. But it was also a great thing. It was the joining of two people, and meant gaining a companion for life. This would be the start of Neda's adult life, really. So it was no wonder she was nervous about making such a change. That was what she told herself, repeatedly.

Facing her, in the room where she and her family slept, the room she grew up in, were Hossein, his mum, Maman, Baba, and their two respective Imams. Neda and Hossein sat on wooden chairs next to each other while everyone else stood, looming over them, not helping her anxiety.

The conditions of the marriage were reiterated. Both parties had agreed to the settlement, after much back-and-forth between the families. It was odd to Neda how little both she and Hossein cared about the specifics of the contract, all they wanted was to be married, but their families treated the whole affair as a business matter.

"Do you consent to marry Hossein Nazari, on the terms listed?" her Imam asked.

Tradition dictated that she say nothing, to keep the groom on his toes, until the Imam asked the same question for the third time. Then she said, "Yes, I do."

Hossein's Imam then asked him, "Do you accept Neda Haghighi as your wife?"

Hossein replied, "I do."

And with that, Neda Haghighi became Neda Nazari.

Once the ceremony was over, she was surprised by the lightness she felt. The way one feels when one no longer has a choice or power over something. When the decision is made and there can be no more wondering whether what one is doing is right, no more worrying about the implications of such a decision forty years later. There was no going back now, and Neda was glad.

The second party, the actual wedding, weeks later at Hossein's family home, was much larger and a more nerve-racking experience, which made little sense because the deed had already been done: she was now his.

Neda had gone to the beautician's in the morning with her friends to get ready. The hair on her entire body was removed, a rigmarole of hair-removal powders and creams. She had never felt so smooth, so polished. Her eyes were outlined with kohl, her eyebrows arched like the wings of a bird. She felt overdone, yes, but the thrill of seeing someone else in front of the mirror, Neda *Nazari*, sent flashes of excitement through her.

She wore a white lace wedding dress. A veil covered her face, partly obstructing her vision. She preferred it that way, not being entirely open to the eyes of other people as well as not being able to see the expressions of those around her.

It was late October now and Tehran was cooler, but despite this, while preparations were being made—both to herself and to the house—she kept a fan by her side. The soothing whir that often lulled her to sleep was her comfort now. It calmed the flutters in her stomach, drowned out the voices calling to her from her childhood. She was both excited and terrified, longing for and repelled by this change.

And when Neda tentatively voiced her fears with friends and relatives, some married, others engaged, a handful single, she discovered they held—or had held—similar sentiments. Marrying meant gaining a new family in your virtually unknown husband.

"Shahd's husband is a monster," her aunties would gossip.

"Like mine then!" another woman would declare with a laugh, her sad eyes not matching her shrill, only half-joking response.

"All men are monsters," another would shout.

"Not mine," a woman newly married into the family would say, to which everyone would think: *Lucky khar* or *Just you wait.*

"It's normal, Neda. You've always been indecisive, and this is a huge decision. But it's the right one. I see the way he makes you smile," Shanauz had said. "And he is *beautiful,* so if you don't want him, I'll have him . . ." Neda had laughed then and hit her friend playfully on the arm. No one knew her as well as Shanauz did; Neda hoped she was right.

The more Neda spoke to Hossein, the more convinced she became that he was different from other men. Her dad was kind but didn't understand her decision to be a practicing Muslim. Didn't quite get why she disapproved of his drinking. He was too Western, she thought. In contrast, her brothers were old-fashioned in many of their views, mainly regarding the aspects of Islam that had nothing to do with them. They believed women should be at home cooking, cleaning, or breeding—definitely not working once married.

Neda had had conversations with Hossein about her working and he simply said, "Do whatever you want, azizam." He was accommodating; wanted her to be happy, and would readily assist her to achieve such aims. "I'm just so thankful to Allah that you said yes," he often said, the tops of his cheeks pink. He made her feel beautiful, special even.

So, yes, Neda was frightened of marriage, but she also realized that Hossein was different. That with him she could live the life she wanted; that her life didn't need to change drastically, not if she didn't want it to.

The men celebrated upstairs and the women downstairs—this was Hossein's mother's idea, common among highly religious families, and not at all what Neda's siblings' weddings had been like. There was also a communal room where the sexes could mix—something Maman had encouraged. The music was loud, and while supposedly no alcohol was consumed, there was an air of drunkenness. People were high off each other's excitement. Neda sat talking to old friends while her relatives danced in the middle of the room.

And then she was urged to dance too, hands were pulling her up, and her body was suddenly moving. She had rehearsed the moves many times before. The term "two left feet" very much applied to Neda, but from their cheers no one seemed to notice—or at least they didn't let it show—how terribly she was dancing. But then, given Iranians' love of whispering behind each other's backs, they probably noted how she swung her arms a tad too wildly, curved in an unflattering way, her hair tucked behind her rather prominent ears.

When she sat back down, she looked at her surroundings properly. From within a large picture frame Hossein's father was frowning into the camera. He wore an army uniform, his jawline strong and pronounced. Looking at it, she wondered what he would think about his only son marrying her. She shook her head, forcing herself to be present in the moment.

She couldn't help but admire the gold and other valuables displayed in cabinets around the living room. It was clear women dominated this house; everything was in its place. And yet there was a sterility to the cleanliness.

Even louder roaring erupted from the women. One of Hossein's sisters patted her knee.

"Hossein!" someone said, breathless with excitement, or perhaps from the dancing. Those who wore hijabs quickly put them on.

Hossein walked towards them in his wedding suit. Just looking at him Neda felt herself blushing. She hoped those around her believed it was from embarrassment and not desire. His hair was long at the front. As he made his way towards her a strand fell in front of his eyes. It reminded her of the first time they spoke, and she resisted the urge to move it from his face.

He sat next to her, accepting the congratulations of those around him. Photos were taken. By the end she felt her cheeks straining from smiling.

"How are you feeling?" he asked.

"OK . . . how about you?"

"I'm exhausted," he said, before letting out a boyish laugh.

Neda breathed out in relief. "I'm glad you said that, I'm so tired. I just didn't want to say it."

He leant in closer. "I can't wait to leave."

"Me neither." Neda giggled. She didn't think she had ever done so before. Was this what married life was about? If so, it wasn't something her aunties had mentioned. In their tirades about men they omitted the weightless feeling of happiness, the way one's cheeks hurt from smiling so much.

"By the way"—Hossein tilted his head so his lips almost touched her ear—"you look beautiful."

And she felt it. She was aware that some of the women were looking at them critically, particularly those on his side of the family, but so be it—they were married now and this was only a small public display of affection.

"I'm just going outside for some air," Neda said.

It took her even longer than expected to leave the room since relatives had a plethora of things to share with her: complaints about the food, compliments on her dress, and anecdotes about how only yesterday she was a baby and now she was a married woman.

When she eventually made it to the courtyard she let out a deep sigh, feeling the constraints of her dress against her stomach as she did so. She leant against the wall. Music could be heard coming from upstairs as well as downstairs, the competing tunes both lulling and overwhelming her.

There were lemon trees in full bloom surrounding a small rectangular pool. Because of the number of guests in the house, they had all removed their shoes in the courtyard, rather than inside by the door, and it looked like there were hundreds of pairs cluttering the ground. Behind her she heard movement. Inwardly she groaned. All she wanted was a moment of quiet to herself.

As she turned, a big, fake smile plastered on her face, she was surprised to find Hossein standing there.

She relaxed.

"It's so hot inside," he said, breathing in fresh air and sighing it out.

"You look so handsome," she heard herself say.

"Thank you," he said. He smiled, moved his head down and then back up, like he didn't know what to do with himself. He checked that no one was nearby before cupping her face. His hands were warm and soft.

"I'm going to kiss you," he said slowly, looking into her eyes for a beat. "I've wanted to do this ever since I first saw you, Neda."

"Do it then," she muttered.

He leant in, brushed his lips across hers, and put one hand behind her head, keeping her there. The kiss deepened, and while Neda's hands were still firmly by her sides, her lips moved with his. She wasn't sure what she was doing, but went along with Hossein, following his lead as though it were the most natural thing in the world. After all, he was just as inexperienced as she was, and that gave her a sense of comfort. They were having their first kiss together, and it was so special.

They were interrupted by a sound of disgust. Neda recoiled from her husband to find her portly, red-faced amu Ahmad before them. He jabbed his finger in Hossein's face.

"You aren't good enough for her!" Neda's uncle yelled, pushing Hossein, who stumbled backwards, tripping over the pile of shoes and falling to the ground. Neda's eyes widened in horror.

"Amu, what are you doing?" she shouted, pulling him away from Hossein.

Up close she could see his bloodshot eyes, and the smell that radiated from him made her recoil. "Alcohol? You're drinking at my wedding?"

"I told your baba, this man isn't good!"

"Get off him!" Neda helped her husband up. His expression was unreadable, apart from the tightness of his jaw.

"You're drunk. Sober up, old man," Hossein said, his voice steady.

"Why did you marry him, Neda? Why did your baba allow it?" Her uncle picked up a shoe from the ground and threw it against the wall just as Baba entered the courtyard, a look of rage on his face.

He walked over in what felt like double time until he was face-to-face with Hossein, shoving Neda out of the way.

"You won't see your little girlfriend anymore, no more! You hear me? You want to laugh at *my* family? Disrespect *my* family?" He spat on Hossein's feet. "No! Do you hear me?" His shouts echoed around the courtyard's walls, and it was only then that Neda noticed the music had been turned down. In true Iranian fashion everyone was eavesdropping.

Her entire body was in knots. She couldn't quite process what was being said, so she missed some words.

"You're mistaken, *Baba*," Hossein said. Neda could detect the sarcasm in his voice. She clutched her chest and shut her eyes for a couple of seconds. And when she opened them, all she saw was Baba's raised arm, which swung towards Hossein's face. Luckily for him, Hossein ducked just in time. Unfortunately for Baba, that meant he stumbled and Hossein caught him.

"Get off me!" Baba exclaimed, pushing away from him.

Baba looked at Neda as though remembering for the first time that she was in fact there, watching everything fall apart. "I'm sorry." He shook his head and ran his fingers through his hair before proceeding to yank on it.

"Baba!" Neda said. "What's going on?" She looked over to Hossein, whose gaze was cast down, and then to her uncle, who had somehow sobered up and simply stared at his brother. All roads led to her father. "Baba?"

There was a long silence.

"You coward," he muttered to Hossein. "We found out your husband has had a girlfriend for the past few years, and it overlapped with the khastegari," he explained to his daughter.

"That's not true—" Hossein began. Neda raised her hand and gave him a deathly stare.

"Let Baba finish."

"A girl came to me just now to tell me she 'loves' Hossein, that he promised to marry her and then left her."

All Neda could think in that moment was how much she wished she hadn't heard those words. How she wished she could go on being ignorant, feeling special, feeling like she'd made the right choice. It was all ruined. *Everything.*

"I was once with someone, it's true. But we had a sigheh, Neda." Hossein's voice was pleading as he watched her back away from him. *Sigheh.* A temporary marriage. "We realized we weren't suited, and that's when we separated. And then I met you, Neda. I swear on Allah, Neda, please believe me."

She looked over to her dad, registered his expression of defeat. It was too late.

They all knew there was little to be done now.

Chapter 25

SORAYA

Brighton, 2014

"Wakey, wakey!"

Days after being ghosted by Magnus, Soraya woke from a deep sleep to find her bedroom door open and her mum's silhouette in the doorway. Somehow it felt better to be in Brighton, rather than London, when she felt so burnt. In Brighton she could pretend she hadn't been ruthlessly rejected, because no one knew she had been seeing anyone to begin with.

"It's twelve o'clock. Why are you still asleep?" her mum said, walking into the room. She pulled the blinds open, one by one, bringing too much light into the darkness. Soraya pulled the covers over her head. "Ey, why is your laptop on your bed while you sleep? I always tell you about the radiation!"

Soraya had fallen asleep working on an illustration of Nunhead Cemetery; it was the first time she'd attempted a landscape drawing. It looked more macabre than she had originally intended, but she appreciated the effect so far.

"I'll get up in a minute," she groaned, and then on reflection groaned a second time. She was twenty-one years old, recently graduated, an adult, but in many ways it was as though nothing had changed since she was fifteen. Hadn't she slept until noon then, and hadn't her mum always said "Wakey, wakey" then too?

How much longer would she be in this no-man's-land of unemployment? Every entry-level job advert she saw—even unpaid work experience—listed a requirement for the candidate to have

prior experience. You needed work experience for work experience.
An outlandish cycle Soraya wasn't sure how to bypass.

And she still hadn't heard from Magnus. It had been three
days. She checked when he was last online on Facebook Messenger,
and the time stamp confirmed it:he was ghosting her.

"Parvin and I are going to Marks and Spencer today, get ready,
we're leaving in half an hour." Her mum had a smile in her voice;
she loved M&S.

On the way there they passed Waterstones, and Neda saw the
latest Jojo Moyes in the window. She ushered them inside to purchase it immediately.

"Can I borrow that after you?" Soraya asked.

"Of course, darling."

"Mum, don't you want to read something a bit different?"
Parvin said, picking up a book entitled *The Happiness of Pursuit*.
Soraya rolled her eyes.

"Ah, my books bring me happiness, but thank you anyway,
azizam."

Soraya bought *Gone Girl* by Gillian Flynn. The film was tainted
for her now since she'd been stood up by Magnus, but she supposed
she could at least enjoy the novel instead, when she was feeling a
little less burnt, that is.

On the way to M&S Parvin explained how in *The Happiness of
Pursuit* there was a link between quests, challenging yourself, and
happiness. "It's about taking control of your life," Parvin continued. "Something we should all be aware of." Despite her initial re-
sistance, Soraya began to be intrigued by the sound of the book.
But it also made her nervous; did she feel unhappy because no intellectual challenge lay ahead for her now? What quest did she
have to follow?

After browsing M&S for forty minutes, her mum had a huge
pile of clothes in her arms. They were mainly gifts she was stockpil-
ing for her family. Soraya was never sure if it was a universal cus-
tom, or if it was just her family, but every time her parents went
back to Iran they had to bring gifts for each family member. Every
single one. So whenever there was a sale they jumped on it.

"They're going to be very happy," her mum said. "Everyone knows Marks and Spencer is good quality. And look, this top is only three pounds!"

Parvin found some underwear on sale, and Soraya refrained from purchasing anything. They didn't exactly stock items in her style, and even if she did find something, she couldn't indulge. She was using Jobseeker's Allowance now to get by, and had spent her overdraft to pay the rent this month.

She was, however, looking forward to their customary afternoon tea in the café. Parvin and Soraya were aware that with its plastic chairs and harsh lighting the place was hardly classy, but afternoon tea as a threesome had become a tradition for them. There was also the fact that their mum always insisted on paying for it.

Over two platters of mini vegetarian sandwiches, scones, and cakes, her mum began her usual tirade.

"Parvin, darling, you need to think about getting married soon," she said in between bites of scone that had a bit too much cream on it for her high cholesterol.

Parvin was quiet for a moment. "It's not that easy, you know, Mum."

"We've shown you many men and you're not interested in any of them." Her mum's voice had a worrisome edge to it, which often annoyed Soraya. It was as though being single at twenty-eight years old was quite literally the end of the world.

"You showed me a takeaway worker I have *nothing* in common with. And then Raoul, that weird fifty-year-old."

Soraya stifled a laugh.

"It's difficult. We don't know many people here." Her mum's back was slightly hunched as she reached for a cheese and onion sandwich. "In Iran two men proposed to me before your dad." Parvin rolled her eyes at Soraya. They'd heard the story so many times.

"Well, how do you expect me to find someone if you don't want me to date anyone? Men don't just fall out of the sky and propose."

"Muslim men do." Her mum smiled and nudged Soraya with

her elbow. Soraya wasn't quite sure why she did this but smiled anyway.

"Yes, but would a proper Muslim want me?" Parvin said.

"And why wouldn't he?"

"Well, there's the obvious: I don't wear a hijab. And I don't want to wear one." Parvin didn't look her mum in the eye. Instead she ate the icing from one of the cupcakes.

"Some men have open minds. You're a good girl."

"Yes, but *where* are they?"

Her mum paused, realizing she didn't actually know where they were. Or how to find them. It had been different for her generation. It seemed she had not considered how her children would meet their future partners in England without dating beforehand.

"Have you tried looking online?" she asked Parvin.

Soraya stifled a laugh, almost spitting out her tea.

"Online dating?" Parvin asked, no doubt imagining Tinder.

"There must be some kind of Muslim dating site, or that one that is always advertised—e something . . . "

"eHarmony?" Soraya said.

"Yes, that one!"

"I'm OK, Mum, I think I'll pass," Parvin said.

"You're not getting any younger, darling. You will regret not getting married soon. You want to have children, a family. You can't do that anytime, you know."

Seeing her sister being backed into a corner, Soraya couldn't resist intervening. "Lots of people don't get married until they're at least in their thirties. Times are different now. You forget, England is not like Iran, that isn't how people get married here."

"But what about having children? Biologically women become less fertile in their thirties," her mum said, turning to Soraya. "And I was going to ask you—you're not talking to any boys, are you? You're acting different lately." Her eyes were fixed on Soraya's.

Soraya couldn't even look away because that would make it seem like she was avoiding scrutiny, *which she was*. She knew she shouldn't have piped up. Her mum had a sixth sense about these things; she could always tell when her children were hiding something. Even if the thing they were hiding was now in the past.

"No," Soraya said, forcing a puzzled expression onto her face that felt beyond farcical.

"Are you sure?"

Soraya broke eye contact, turning to Parvin while also reaching for a sandwich. "Mum, you're being so dramatic. Obviously not."

"What's going on with Amir's girlfriend anyway?" Parvin asked, saving Soraya from the conversation from hell.

"Oh, he says he likes her and that she's a nice girl. Don't ask him about her, though, he gets embarrassed."

"Why is he allowed a girlfriend?" Soraya said, before mentally scolding herself for her outburst. "I swear he's cheating on her anyway."

Her mum sighed. "It's different for boys."

"You don't really believe that, do you?"

"Boys can't get pregnant. If one of you got pregnant before marriage . . ." She shook her head, her words sharp, a contrast from before. "It would ruin your life. That's how it's different."

Soraya said nothing. The silence felt heavy.

She had long since given up arguing with her family about the hypocrisy in their logic. If Amir got a girl pregnant, what would happen then? Why was it any different for him? She knew if such a thing happened her family would accept the situation, and this knowledge infuriated her. Laleh had left the family to be with her boyfriend, and yet her brother was allowed to bring girls to the house. Such thoughts often left her red-faced and teary-eyed if she attempted to challenge her family. So she'd learnt to let the whole subject go.

Parvin moved the conversation along by asking more questions about the girl. Soraya eventually joined in. Better to indulge in the injustice than have the injustice turned back on her.

In the evening, back at the house, Parvin ran over to Soraya in the living room and whispered, "Can you hear that?"

They were both silent for a few seconds, but it was long enough to hear quiet moaning. At first Soraya thought it was coming from her dad's laptop, but he was usually so careful and wore headphones. Besides, he was upstairs.

Parvin's eyes widened. "Ewwww."

Soraya wanted to block her ears. The moaning became louder.

Her mum came into the living room from the kitchen, blissfully unaware. Both girls looked at her, grimaces on their faces.

"What?" she asked.

Then she heard it.

"Amir? Astaghfirullah."

She grabbed the TV remote and turned the volume up as high as was needed to drown out the sounds.

The showiness of her brother, having exceptionally loud sex in the same house his sisters and mother occupied. Soraya couldn't even imagine doing that—she'd be disowned, like Laleh. Or worse. Much worse.

A potent feeling bubbled up within her. She felt shame on hearing them, finding the act of sex disgusting. This wasn't the first time she'd regarded it this way, and she wondered how her family had managed to imprint their views on her so deeply that the most natural human act could repulse her. Perhaps it was years of being told sex was wrong and dirty by people like her brother who freely engaged in the activity themselves.

It was different when she was with Magnus. He was the first person to somehow break through this wall and make her see things in a different way. It stung that now she still had no idea what had happened to make him stand her up and then ghost her. None of it made any sense.

"This house is mad!" Parvin exclaimed.

Soraya continued grimacing until her phone pinged with a message.

It was from Magnus.

Chapter 26

SORAYA

Soraya had just gotten to the twist in the book she was reading, *Gone Girl*, which made her sit up in bed, book firmly in hand.

"As if," she muttered, turning the pages quickly, her eyes skimming over the words. She wasn't ordinarily a fan of thrillers, but romances held little appeal for her now. They reminded her of how embarrassed she should be. A story about a psychotic wife attempting to ruin her cheating husband's life suited her much better. Her phone rang. Another missed call from Magnus. It had been a week since he had texted her and he was becoming more persistent.

Her hand twitched, but there was no point. No point in talking to him. She'd always known their time together had an expiry date. It was a game, and it finished with Soraya getting burnt.

His excuse was exceptionally flimsy: he broke his phone. Apparently, he had not seen her messages. Even if she believed this, which she didn't, the two of them were too different ever to be a real thing. She knew they could never be long-term, so really it had ended at the right time. Before anyone got too attached.

And yet despite her logical rationale about why this was a blessing in disguise, burning within her was rage. She wanted to answer his calls and tell him quite frankly to fuck off and leave her alone, but she also wanted to question him about why he thought it was OK to simply ditch her, and not get back to her for days. They weren't in the Stone Age, if his phone was broken he could have Facebook-messaged her—or even emailed her. And even if he somehow had no way to contact her, that didn't explain why he didn't meet her as planned. There was really no excuse. Priya's words were imprinted in her mind. *Respect yourself*. And that she intended to do.

Instead of replying to Magnus, she wrote a long, scathing diary entry about how disgusting he was. She didn't even necessarily believe her own words, which annoyed her, but it felt good to get it out, to make him seem as small as he made her feel.

After another five hours in bed, during which time she had finished reading the book in between refreshing Indeed for jobs, she got up, put on a pair of old gym shorts and a baggy T-shirt. She wasn't quite sure who she was kidding dressing to go for a run but decided she needed to try. To clear her mind and move her body.

She ran down the stairs of her flat, hoping to give herself some much-needed adrenaline. When she opened the main door to leave the building, she jumped in surprise.

"What—"

"You weren't answering my calls," Magnus said, his hand still in the air as though about to press the buzzer.

She wanted to say, "So get the hint," but the retort stuck in her throat. She couldn't be that cutting in person, not with him standing in front of her, looking at her the way he was.

She shut the door behind her and continued walking, pretending she hadn't seen him. This whole situation had become too sticky. She hoped putting a little distance between them would prevent her from becoming stuck in it.

"Soraya," he called from behind her, grabbing her hand. She shut her eyes, wishing she was more normal. If she was they would have gone back to her flat to talk about this, rather than arguing in the street.

She shrugged herself free and turned to look over her shoulder at him. "I don't know why you keep calling me."

He sighed and put both hands in his hoodie pocket, pushing them down.

"Why are you ignoring me?"

"That's rich."

In typical London fashion passersby remained unbothered by

their public argument. She continued walking towards Telegraph Hill.

"Would you just stop?" he said, matching her pace.

"I have somewhere to be. So I can't really talk."

He looked her up and down, and she remembered her tragic ensemble and makeup-free face, and realized this was the first time he'd seen her like this.

"The gym?" he asked.

She let out a frustrated sigh. "What do you want?"

"I don't get why you're so mad at me. My phone broke, otherwise I would have texted you back. It was only a few days—"

"Oh, come on, you stood me up at Peckham Plex! That's not OK—"

Realization dawned on his face. "Oh, shit! I totally forgot we were meant to meet . . ."

Soraya began walking at an even brisker pace. He followed along effortlessly while she was struggling to breathe properly.

"It doesn't even matter."

"So you forgive me?"

They walked up the steep street, the park where Soraya had planned to go for a run within sight.

"I'm not annoyed with you. I mean, your whole 'my phone broke' excuse is complete bullshit but it's fine. You don't owe me anything."

"Soraya—"

"We don't need to have this conversation." She was smiling, despite feeling anything but happy. "I'm not a fan of being stood up. But it's not like we were going out or anything. So, really, it's not a big deal."

He bit his bottom lip, studied her for a moment, his eyes pensive. "If I tell you the truth, will you listen to me?"

She shrugged and together they walked through the gates to Telegraph Hill. Ahead was a picturesque view of the city, the Docklands buildings bright and shiny against the gray sky.

They sat down on the cold grass.

"I went back home," he explained. "To Leeds."

"Right . . ."

"I went because my dad was missing." He spoke so quietly she wasn't sure she'd heard correctly. "My mum was worried so I got the train up and we went looking for him together."

"Did you find him? Is he OK?"

"Yeah, he's fine. He went on a binge with one of his friends and didn't want us to know. Left his phone in a pub, that's why we couldn't get hold of him."

"Does he normally go on binges?" Soraya wasn't sure if she would have asked this question if she hadn't heard what she had at graduation. What would she have said if she didn't already know?

She could tell Magnus was avoiding her eyes, staring out at the view.

"Yeah, he drinks a lot. But he'd been sober for a few weeks, not that that ever lasts. That's kind of why I don't like going home. I only ever go at Christmas."

"I'm sorry," she said, the words sounding feeble.

His shoulders slumped, making her realize how tense he was.

"I didn't mean to, you know, upset you. It's just once family stuff takes over, it *really* takes over. It probably sounds like another crap excuse . . ."

"No, it doesn't," she said, putting her hand over his. His vulnerability was touching. She had never met anyone else whose parent had an addiction; it was often isolating, like she was alone in her pain and suffering. "I get it."

"You do?"

She was given the opportunity to relate, unburden herself.

Yes, because my dad is a methadone addict.

Her dad had been addicted to drugs for the last twenty-eight years. It was the reason why he was barely aware of anything. Soraya had only ever known her father while he wore this mask; she had never met the man he was before. He occasionally attempted to quit, but managed to last only a week at most. She would be surprised to see him with healthy color in his cheeks, rather than permanently red-faced. He seemed sadder at these times, but at least it was a human emotion, it reminded her that her dad was just that: a human being.

She didn't know a great deal about how he became an addict. Her mum had once told her he began smoking opium with friends in the late eighties, when they lived in Liverpool, and then he couldn't stop. Doctors had put him on small doses of methadone, and they had tried to wean him off by gradually lowering the dosage, until he was supposed to stop completely. His dependency meant that he could go only a few days without drugs before he had to start the process again, and so it continued that way.

Generally, he was content with being on a low dose for the rest of his life. Sometimes he slept all day, taking a cocktail of sleeping pills, sacrificing a fix in order to have a blowout the next day with two days' worth. Sometimes, he still bought drugs illegally, as well as taking his prescribed medication. He thought no one noticed his particularly high days, but they did.

When she opened her mouth, she felt sick. She could never say it aloud.

She willed herself to, but just couldn't. Her mum had always told her to tell no one; since she was a small child she'd been given that solemn instruction. It was different from having an alcoholic parent, more shameful somehow, more scandalous. She couldn't imagine saying the words, didn't want to have to act like it was OK when it wasn't, didn't want to see the way Magnus would look at her differently once he knew.

He turned his head to face her, as if sensing her thoughts.

She gave him a small smile instead. "Yeah. Family is messy sometimes, but they're family. You'll do anything for them. I get it."

His eyes were warm as he smiled back. She noticed, too, the same look he'd had in his eyes at graduation. The vulnerability, the disappointment. They really weren't so different, not really.

"I really am sorry," he said.

"I know," she said. "It's OK."

She wasn't quite sure if they were in fact OK, but the look of hope on his face made her heart beat out of time, and suddenly she wanted so desperately for it all to blow over, so she said it anyway.

"So, we're friends again?"

She nodded. "Sure."

His eyes narrowed slightly. "You really sure? You can have a go at me some more if you like? I deserve it."

She shook her head. "If anything like that happens again, just give me a heads-up, that's all I wanted." The words felt foreign in her mouth, like she was asking a great deal of this man, even though she knew she wasn't. She wasn't sure if she should still be trying to play it cool, almost worried that she was coming across too invested in whatever it was they were, but she didn't have time to overthink it because he smiled softly at her, and caught her hand in both of his.

"I promise."

That evening they engaged in an activity that proved them to be more than friends.

His hand was around her waist. He drew it lower to the bottom of her stomach. Her pouch. Her smile faltered and she put her hands over his and lifted it higher to her waist.

"I don't like my stomach," Soraya told him.

"Well, I do," he said, and pushed the duvet away, crawled down the bed, and kissed her lower stomach. She squirmed.

His hand was on her inner thigh, which stopped her short. She suddenly felt very, very warm. A chuckle escaped her lips; she was light and giddy. A stark contrast from the way she'd felt in the morning. "Every time you say you don't like something about yourself, I'm going to kiss it, to make you accept that you're perfect."

Soraya let out a snort.

"What if it's my personality? You can't kiss a personality," she said, between gasps as his fingers seemed to trail higher.

"Yeah, you can." His lips pressed down on hers, gently opening them, and when their tongues met she knew what he meant.

She somehow ended up on top of him, his hardness pressing against her. In moments like these she felt confident, conscious of the way her long, curly hair tumbled down her back. He kissed her sides.

"Do you feel how hard I am for you?" he whispered, in a low voice.

His words sent shivers through her. She said nothing. His hand cupped her chin, making her look at him.

Being forced to really look at him, she was reminded of how different he was from all the other men in her life. He was both strong and soft. His pale skin, his lightly haired body, his freckles . . . it was all alien to her. In some ways she was made uncomfortable by how attracted she was to him. She knew there were countless articles written about dating white guys, and white savior complexes, but she didn't care in that moment. She couldn't deny the way her body reacted to his despite him being so completely opposite to her.

It made her realize how much she'd missed him when she thought they were over, and that was dangerous. More so, how easily she could forgive him after he ignored her for days, and how her mind was desperately trying to push that fact away.

"You're always hard," she joked.

"That's because you're so fucking sexy." He grabbed her bum, and she blushed.

"Says you. You're the hot one," she replied quietly.

"What was that?" he said, relishing this conversation.

"I said, you're hot, Magnus." She rolled her eyes.

"Please tell me more . . ."

Soraya got off him and lay down beside him. Mimicking him, she began kissing his body.

She kissed his bicep, then his six-pack, trailing kisses lower and lower until she felt embarrassed. And completely clueless.

He saved the situation by swooping her up so she was straddling him again. He gripped her underwear with both hands and pulled at the lace of her pants with his fingers.

"I get the feeling you're only after me for my looks."

"Obviously." She was smiling when suddenly Magnus grew serious. He looked at her, really looked at her.

"I'm glad we're OK again," he said, before kissing her long and hard. Then he was on top of her, making his descent down the bed, pressing his palms to either side of her upper thighs. His fingers tightened against her underwear as he pulled, ripping them apart. She barely had time to be annoyed because what he did next made her very, very happy.

Chapter 27

SORAYA

Brighton, 2014

Soraya remembered a conversation she'd heard her mum having with her khale. She wasn't even meant to be listening, and didn't suppose her mum thought anything of it at the time. She certainly doubted her mum would ever imagine that Soraya had thought about it ever since on a weekly, sometimes daily, basis, even though it had occurred just before she left for university, three years ago now.

"Poor girl," her mum said in Farsi into the phone receiver. "Yes, but it will be better than her husband leaving her because she didn't bleed."

Then her mum laughed softly, though it wasn't real, Soraya knew that. It was a trait she had inherited, a nervous tic when silence would be too telling. Another thing women needed to stop doing, but did anyway.

"I never said she won't bleed, Rabeh. You need to relax. I'm the uptight one, not you."

Her mum glanced up then to find Soraya watching her. She looked away quickly but continued sitting at the kitchen table, hearing nothing but her mum's conversation and the low hum of the fridge-freezer.

Tyzer, their orange cat, jumped up onto the wooden table and Soraya stroked his rough fur. She leant in to his body, inhaled his weirdly warm smell before giving him a peck on his small head.

When her mum finished her conversation she shooed Tyzer off

the table. "All this hair everywhere," she muttered. That was the reason they were never allowed a dog; dog hair was considered unclean and would make praying difficult. Soraya often wondered why cats were considered different from dogs in this respect. One of many questions she never asked.

"What were you saying to Khale Rabeh?"

"Fatima's wedding is in two weeks and she was worrying about all the preparations."

Her mum sat down next to Soraya and began opening the letters on the table, shaking her head at the bills. "Stupid TV license." She couldn't understand why they had to pay for Sky, the television itself, the electricity it used, *and* the monthly TV license.

"Did you say something about blood?" Soraya's Farsi skills were poor, but her understanding was much better than her ability to speak it.

"Yes, her fiancé's family are very old-fashioned and want to make sure she's a virgin, so they're asking for the bedsheets from the wedding night."

Soraya's jaw dropped. She snapped it shut then opened it again to speak. "That's still a thing?" She remembered in "The Bloody Chamber" Bluebeard joking about wanting to wave the bloody sheet around. She thought it was something that happened only in ancient times or fairy tales.

"So they hand the sheet to his mum? Isn't that really gross?"

Neda shrugged. "It's just the way it is. She's getting a test done by a doctor beforehand, just in case she doesn't bleed, and then she'll have a certificate confirming she's a virgin. That's what Rabeh was worrying about—your cousin is scared about the pain of the test."

There was a silence until her mum said, "*This* is why it's important to be a good girl."

Soraya wasn't sure why this was a valid reason—to have a painful test to prove you're a "good girl."

"You don't say that to Amir. Does the boy have to have a test to see if he's a good boy?"

Her mum laughed then and shook her head. "No" was all she

said. It was as though she knew how ridiculous the double standard was but didn't care. How could she not care?

And yet here Soraya was, having just done things that definitely did not make her a good girl with Magnus, a white atheist she would most definitely never marry. A man whose body count, if you will, topped most people's at the university.

Could she imagine herself ever having sex with him? The thought terrified her. She imagined a splattering of blood, an inescapable sense of regret immediately afterwards. Once it was done there was no going back. That was the awful thing about losing your virginity; when it was gone, it was gone. But what even was virginity? How could something you weren't fully conscious of be so important?

Soraya would be the first person to say virginity was a construct, that women weren't objects to be kept shiny and new, and yet when it came to herself, she sometimes wondered whether she did indeed want that. Granted, her liaison with Magnus had left her feeling somewhat used—they had, after all, engaged in some sexual activity, even if they had not gone all the way. And then she realized how fucked up her own analogy was and pushed the thought from her mind, resolving not to think about it again until she really needed to.

It was only when they were together, when his hand trailed up her thigh and his breath was on her neck, that she wanted it to all be over. She wanted to give in and no longer think about whether she would go to hell, or whether she would one day be engaged to a Muslim man who would make her take a test, and whether she would feel shame after. But unfortunately, she could never quite let herself go to that extent.

Chapter 28

NEDA

It was impossible to forget what had happened on her wedding night, but in time Neda learnt to forgive, or at least told herself that was what she was doing. Hossein proclaimed his innocence, vehemently and unwaveringly. But the fact he had had a girlfriend before her and kept it secret displeased her. *What went wrong?* she had asked. *We were too different,* he replied. *She was kind of crazy,* he said another time. *She didn't have good morals,* he commented later. *She wasn't you.*

Neda presumed, and rightly so, that if she had had a boyfriend in the past, Hossein wouldn't have wanted to marry her. However, it was unsurprising really that his expectations of men's and women's morals were vastly different. He was, after all, a man, no matter how different she'd once thought he was.

But he was still Hossein. The same man who unwaveringly rooted for her, no matter if she was trying out a new recipe or applying for scholarships to do a master's degree. He always voiced his faith in her, made her feel boosted by his belief in her.

She couldn't leave him; it would be humiliating. Not just for her, but for her family. And she couldn't divorce him for no reason; only men had that power. Anyway, she wasn't sure she wanted to lose him, despite everything.

In time she began to wonder whether it was right to judge someone based on their past. Whether she was no better for begrudging him something he did before he had even met her, if that was in fact the truth, which deep down she believed it was. Surely word would have spread sooner if Hossein had been with the girl while they were engaged? Their social circle was small and Neda knew all the gossip.

As they settled into their new life together, she began working as a medical laboratory assistant, and Hossein continued working at his uncle's factory and coaching under-sixteens football.

It was once they were living together that Neda really noticed his slight limp. The way, every morning when he woke up, he carefully stretched his leg. He had never explained his injury to her in detail. It was only when she saw his prescription for painkillers that she understood the extent of his injury.

"My leg almost had to be amputated at one point," he said, casually buttering himself a piece of bread one morning when she asked about it.

"*What?*" Her mouth was agape.

"My injury was more serious than my mother likes to admit. But I'm OK now, thank Allah." He looked up, as though he could see him above.

Neda muttered, "Alhamdulillah." Then, "But your mother said you might be able to play again?"

Hossein smiled, shaking his head, his eyes sad. "She *wants* me to be able to play again. The doctor has already said it's over. I made my peace with it, but she . . . she had her hopes set on it. She knew how proud it would have made my dad."

Neda looked at her husband across the sofreh. She saw him in an unaccustomed light, saw him as he was when she accepted his proposal, when she was so excited at the prospect of a new life with this man. He was the same man, the same good, kind man; he had just made a mistake. And that was when she finally forgave him, deciding he had suffered enough already.

The longer they lived together, the better acquainted they became with each other's habits. At first it was awkward for them both; they had never lived with so few people in a house before, everything they did magnified, no longer masked by hordes of family members. They took it in turns to wake each other up for fajr prayer. And when they went back to bed, they snuggled into each other until they fell asleep.

Whereas Hossein liked to press snooze on his alarm for as long as possible, Neda woke up immediately to get ready for the day ahead. She always made them breakfast. In return, on the nights he wasn't coaching, he would collect dinner from their favorite pizza shop on the way home from work.

And of course they engaged in the activity only married people could in a halal way. It was something she enjoyed, to an extent. But wasn't sex always for the man, anyway? His body reacted in different ways from a woman's, it was more obvious with its clear ending, the predictable release.

She thought back to their first time, a haze now. They did not have sex on their wedding night. That had been filled with awkwardness tinged with bitterness. Hossein slept in the living room without any argument.

It was weeks later, once the ice had thawed, that he had made her smile again with his boyish charm. All she remembered was the sudden haste, both his and hers. She had made the first move, and that was important. It had been drilled into her what would be expected of her, what she would finally be allowed to do with Allah's blessing. There was fumbling and pain. A lot of pain.

"It's like sticking a sausage into a needle hole!" her cousin had once joked, and her relatives had cackled. At the time Neda had been fairly young and hadn't quite understood what was meant. But upon losing her virginity, the reference became clear to her. Hossein wasn't quite patient. He was gentle, yes, but not patient. All Neda remembered of that night was being uncomfortable and shedding a tiny amount of blood. She had imagined a bucketload, a dramatic signifier of what they had just done; her passage into womanhood. But instead it was anticlimactic, a few watery drops.

The lack of blood made her panic.

"It's so strange, I expected more," she ventured to say to him the next morning.

"Everyone's different, it's normal." He shrugged. The implication of his statement scorched her. She was reminded of his girl-friend, and a barrier was raised between them again.

"Really?"

"Azizam, I know you were a virgin, don't worry."

Despite his words Neda felt her heartbeat quickening. *She* knew she was. "What about your mother?"

"There's blood, isn't there? If you weren't a virgin, you wouldn't have been that uncomfortable. Don't worry, it'll be better next time." He brushed his hand across her bare stomach, causing shivers to run through her. And then suddenly his lips were upon hers, and there was never the chance for Neda to ask, both bitterly and boldly, *how* he had such wisdom.

Chapter 29

NEDA

It was on their first anniversary that Neda realized she was in love with Hossein. It was a peculiar feeling; a sort of bubbling, like a volcano, deep in the pit of her stomach. They were cuddling in bed, his strong arms gripping her midriff as he nuzzled his face into her hair. She relished this intimacy. They would hold each other for hours, with Neda rattling off any piece of information she could about her day while he would listen, commenting, asking for more. They would laugh about nothing for hours, until their neighbor hit a broomstick against the wall. This was what companionship truly was. She had tried to keep the words in, not say them, but human nature wouldn't allow her that.

"I love you," she said, in a small voice, partly hoping he wouldn't hear, but she had to say it.

He curled his bad leg around hers and pulled her to him, impossibly close. "I've always loved you," he said, bashfully.

"You often say these things," she said doubtfully. "But why? How is that possible?"

"Azizam, you're the smartest person I know, so caring, so *good*. Just being with you, I can feel your goodness. You forgave me when you didn't need to." He kissed the top of her head. "The worst thing you do is gossip, and I can tell you feel so guilty even about that. It's cute. You're cute."

"I wish you and Baba got along."

He sighed. "He doesn't want to talk to me. He thinks he already knows me."

His chest hair scratched against Neda's neck and she moved away. "Maybe he just needs more time," she mused.

"It's a hard thing giving your daughter away . . . I could try again, I suppose?"

Hossein had rung Baba numerous times and shown up at her family home, but he was always met with the same icy silence, or if Baba had to talk it was monosyllabic, causing Maman to overcompensate.

The arrival of a letter in the post soon shook up their routine. Shook up their entire lives.

"What do you think?" Neda tentatively asked Hossein. They sat cross-legged on the sofreh. He had a piece of bread lathered in honey almost to his mouth, and he held it there contemplating her words. A drip of honey fell from the bread and left a trail on the sofreh.

"What do *you* think?" he asked, surprising her.

"I don't know . . . it's a great opportunity, but I only applied on a whim, I didn't think anything of it. I was hoping I'd get a place at a university in Tehran. And also we have this." She gestured to their tiny one-bedroom apartment. Her family had provided them with key pieces of furniture, and she knew they'd struggled to do that despite the place being so small. But tradition dictated that the man's family pay for the wedding and the woman's the furniture. "And, of course, you have your job, and you might not want to move," she added quickly. While Hossein gave her free rein to speak her thoughts, she sometimes wondered if he was almost too good to be true. She didn't want to overstep any unseen boundaries.

"I can find another job." He broke into a grin. "It could be an adventure."

"And so many of our friends are moving abroad."

"If we can get away before things become even worse here . . ."

Was it treacherous, she wondered, to abandon one's own country when times had gotten difficult? Neda and Hossein went together to small demonstrations in the streets, with hundreds of others, shouting for democracy, for a new leader, but it was dangerous, and despite always displaying outer strength, she didn't want to have to fight anymore. There was talk of friends of friends being taken to prison, tortured for speaking against the Shah.

Neda wanted out. But would she be able to leave her family behind?

Perhaps it would be easier if she left. Her baba's profound dislike of Hossein sometimes got to her, though she tried to remain impartial. Every time she saw her family she was reminded of what Hossein did, and their opinions of him rubbed off on her. Try as she might, she would come home feeling colder towards her husband. She was easily thawed, but she hated the feeling, hated that it had to be like this.

And it wasn't just that. Her own country's universities didn't give her a scholarship, but the one application she'd sent abroad, on a whim, to England did. Perhaps it was a sign? Allah telling her it was time to move on.

"Let's go," Hossein said. "Let's see what freedom and democracy can really be like."

"Do you think?" Excitement and fear stirred in the pit of her stomach.

"Neda, this is an amazing opportunity for you. A university in England—*England!*—wants to pay you to study in their program. I'm so proud of you, and you need to take this—you'll regret it if you don't. It's only a year after all, and it could be the best year of our lives. Not many people get this opportunity; we need to take it."

Neda's heart fluttered. He saw something could make her happy and he wanted her to do it.

"Are we mad?" she asked, laughing.

"Aren't we all a bit mad?" He leant across the sofreh and held her face between his hands. "We're going to England."

Chapter 30

SORAYA

London, 2014

Soraya moved from behind the counter, a position she'd been in for fifteen minutes.

She had begun working full-time at a high-end clothes shop. It had all happened quickly; she was invited to interview at twenty-four hours' notice, and then told she got the job on the spot. She began work the following day. While it wasn't her first choice of occupation, she knew anything was better than unemployment.

She struggled with her thin heels as she plucked them from the lush carpet and picked her way over towards the customer. Heels were compulsory for all staff. The French-inspired décor attempted to be glamorous; the furniture was light pink and the spiral staircase leading upstairs to the personal shopping area rose-gold. On each clothes rail were no more than five items, all equally spaced and arranged in size order.

The customer, a sour-faced woman dressed all in white, ignored her greeting. Only to be expected.

Despite this, Soraya drew in closer, her manager Guy's eyes on her from the other end of the shop, keen to find something to criticize her for. To blame her for a missed sale if she didn't say the exact words she'd rehearsed from the company manual.

The woman was looking at the rail of clothes, grabbing items and fingering them before discarding them.

"Good afternoon. How are you today?" Soraya said, a smile plastered on her face; she could feel her cheeks twitching ever so slightly and dug her nails into her palms.

"Fine, I don't need help," the woman said, bypassing a conversation she didn't want to have. What she didn't seem to notice was that it wasn't a conversation Soraya wanted to have either. It was in these moments that Soraya felt despair. She thought about Oliver, who had managed to get a paid yearlong publishing internship while she was still stuck working in retail, still being rejected by graduate employers—and customers—daily. She tried not to feel jealous.

"OK, well, give me a shout if you do!" Soraya turned on her heel and moved back to the counter.

Guy edged towards her, his brow furrowed. His turtleneck jumper and plaid suit combo gave him an annoying air before he even opened his mouth. The high neck looked like it was choking him, but his pink nose gave him a misleading appearance of child-like innocence.

"Well, *she* didn't want to talk," he said in his Essex accent, holding back a smile. His hands were thrust deep into his trouser pockets and he rocked on his heels.

"I know," Soraya said, holding back a laugh.

"She's looking at that coat. Why don't you ask her if she wants to try it on?"

Guy often put Soraya in uncomfortable situations where she had to bear the brunt of a customer's aggression. She was about to make another wobbly descent when a colleague came down the stairs to take over.

"Oh! It's three already . . ." Soraya said.

"Ah, right, I suppose you can go home now."

At this she bolted to the staff room, promptly removed her heels, and rubbed the soles of her feet, which were pink and sore. She slipped on trainer socks and pulled on her cut-off Doc Martens.

When she left she noticed Magnus waiting outside to meet her. For a minute he didn't see her. She used this opportunity to look at him freely for once. He was leaning against the concrete wall by the shop, one leg propped casually against the wall, the other stretched out in front of him. He had a book in his hand, his head bent in concentration.

As she stood staring at him, passersby muttered when they had to walk around her, obscuring him from her view. It was only when she was pushed, accidentally or otherwise—this was London—that she went over to him.

"Whatcha reading?" she said, close to his ear.

He started, ever so slightly, and then grinned, lifting up the cover so she could see. *1984.*

"Interesting," Soraya said, pursing her lips.

"I'm sorry it's not one of the excellent works of literature you read," he joked, before she swatted him. He shoved the paperback in his coat pocket. "How was work?"

"Same old, same old . . ."

"It's not forever." He began stroking her palm, caressing the sensitive area. All of London, the hustle and bustle of it, faded away when she was with him. Or rather, she became part of the crowd, excited to be there, for a change. Until recently she had felt tired of the city.

Something fluttered deep within her and she forced it back down. She was making things harder for herself. There was an expiry date on whatever their relationship was, and it was fast approaching. She could feel it.

"I know." She yanked his hand slightly so they could begin walking.

"I have some news . . ."

"Really, what?" They were heading towards Oxford Circus, Magnus leading the way, when he turned right onto a side street.

"An agent got back to me today."

Soraya stopped but Magnus continued walking, pulling her hand.

"Hold up! I didn't even know you'd sent your book out yet. This is huge!" Soraya said. "Why are you not jumping up and down?"

He suppressed a grin. "I don't want to jinx things."

"You're not jinxing *anything.*" She planted a kiss on his lips, swatted his arm. Soraya still didn't feel comfortable kissing in public from an irrational fear that someone who knew her family would catch her. She played this off as not liking PDA. "You deserve this," she insisted.

Despite being happy for him, she felt a tinge of jealousy too.

They'd made a promise to each other, and while he was soaring, she was here, being bossed around in heels for minimum wage.

She had added some illustrations to her Instagram account and finished off the drawing of Nunhead Cemetery, but she wasn't exactly pursuing her dream. She wasn't sure that was her dream. Or even if she *had* a dream. How could she pursue a dream if she didn't know what it was?

In many ways she felt ashamed to be this directionless, like she was the only person from her university to have no idea what she wanted to do now that she had graduated. In her dark moments, she wondered if there was something wrong with her. "Anyway, the agent asked to meet up next week to discuss representing me."

"This is amazing! I hope I feature in your acknowledgments."

"Of course." He nudged her playfully with his elbow. "It does clash with rugby practice but I didn't want to seem difficult from the get-go . . ."

Soraya resisted the urge to say, "It's only *rugby* practice," because she knew that wouldn't go down well. He took rugby seriously in a way she couldn't understand. She'd assumed he'd stop playing once they graduated.

"This is such good news," she said instead, beaming at him, feeling the strain of the smile pulling against her cheeks. "This calls for a toast."

They made their way to a nearby pub, and Magnus ordered a bottle of red wine. She wished she'd told him sooner that she didn't have a particular fondness for wine. But by this point, it had been too long and she wasn't sure how to broach the subject.

"To your book," Soraya said, raising her glass to clink his.

Magnus's cheeks were flushed. She realized he didn't like too much attention when it came to his writing; he became bashful and embarrassed. It was a side of him she rarely saw.

"It's not a sure thing," he said.

"Even getting this far is very impressive. You do know that, don't you? And why would she want to meet about representing you, if she wasn't serious about it? Have faith in yourself."

He took a long sip from his glass. She attempted to mimic this but was struck by the earthy tanginess of the wine, and inwardly shuddered.

"I just don't want to get too excited. I don't feel like I'm the type of person who could be an author. Even calling myself that makes me cringe. It feels way beyond my reach."

She put her hands over his.

"Don't ever think that. You can be anything you want to be. You're talented at writing, Magnus. I'm not just saying that because you're my . . . whatever, I'm saying it because it's true."

He was about to counter her point when she added, "Anyway, there are lots of mediocre white male authors, so I wouldn't worry. What's one more?"

He pushed her arm, laughing.

"You're such a dick," he said.

"A dick you like very much," she said quickly. They looked at each other and burst out laughing again. "Sorry, that was really bad."

They spent the rest of the night talking about their plans for the future, what Magnus would say to the agent, what his next steps would be if he were signed. When the conversation turned to her future she felt paralyzed. How could she still not know what she wanted to do? She clung to this idea of working in marketing, having an office job, because that was what everyone else was doing, that was what her idea of success was. Work in an office for a big company and you will have made it. But was that even true?

Magnus was always encouraging, no matter what she said. Some days she would say she wanted to be a professional illustrator, others work for a marketing company, sometimes even that she'd like to do a master's in graphic design. Every time he would nod along, showing no judgment whatsoever about her chaotic, confused mind.

"I wanted to ask you something," he said. She noticed the tops of his ears were pink and his face was flushed, from his alcohol consumption, she assumed.

"Yeah?"

"Well," he said, tripping over his next words. "More that I want to tell you something, actually. Just that . . . I'm not seeing anyone else."

His words hung in the air. His initial nervousness made sense now. She resisted the urge to smile. She felt powerful in that moment, knowing that what she said next was important to him. It was a strange, but wonderful, feeling.

"Neither am I," she said, resisting the urge to say "obviously." Because to Magnus this fact wasn't obvious, she realized.

He smiled then, a big, goofy smile that was contagious. "Let's keep it that way, yeah?" He winked and she let out a laugh.

"I'll try." She paused for a moment. "I have to ask you something, though. Once in one of our seminars you said you didn't believe in relationships, that you think they're wrong. Has that changed?"

Initially, he looked surprised, but then he leant back, a pensive expression on his face.

"I know the time you're talking about," he said. "The book we were studying reminded me of my parents. How they're stuck together—or at least feel like they are. I never want someone to feel stuck with me, or vice versa. It's probably one of my worst fears, in fact. But . . ." He trailed off, tracing the top of his glass with his forefinger as he thought through what he would say next. "I guess with you I'm trying to just let go of that fear. We aren't our parents. And I like you a lot. I kind of actually want to be yours."

"I want to be yours too."

Before Magnus, she would have thought this to be excessive, but she meant it. She liked the idea of them belonging to each other. She knew then that she was falling in love with him.

When they got back to his house, she avoided his housemates by going straight to his bedroom while he shouted hello to them before following her up the stairs. As soon as his door was closed, he leant forward, his lips finding hers.

He stopped for a moment, moved an inch, and they looked each other in the eye. His deep brown gaze was warm and mysterious. That said, she knew exactly what he was thinking. She was thinking it too.

They may try and do things with you. Don't let them do that.

Ten minutes later came the moment she had to stop him from taking it too far, as she always did.

"I don't know . . ." she said, not sure how to finish her sentence.

Frustration was clear on Magnus's face. "Don't take this the wrong way, but when do you think we can stop waiting?"

She wished she knew the answer to that question.

"I don't know," she sighed. "What's the rush?"

"There isn't one . . . I'm just dying a little over here." He laughed humorlessly. "I want you so bad."

"I want you too, it's just . . . like I said, I want to take it slow. I don't know what else to say."

She couldn't even be sure at this point whether she was lying or telling the truth.

He looked as though he wanted to say something else, but instead he bit it back, kissed her on top of her head, and pulled her towards him. "It's OK." He encircled her in his arms and legs, and it was this act that felt the most intimate. Their naked bodies pressed against each other. And soon she heard his breathing slow as he fell asleep.

This position both panicked and softened her. His hands around her middle, almost trapping her. But that this person wanted to sleep next to her, felt comfortable enough to do so, and that he was hers to snuggle against, was almost too much for her. She wondered how people handled this level of intimacy as teenagers.

The guilt remained, heavy and hard within her. She could almost see herself from a bird's-eye view and shut her eyes as though to erase the image. But she couldn't. She saw her own naked body and this large white man pressed up against her. Imagined her dad and brother walking in and seeing them like this. Began wondering, again, how she could call herself a Muslim when she was in bed with a man who didn't even believe in God and whom she would never marry. And yet she liked him, more than she wanted to admit.

She wondered, as usual, why everything in her life had to be so complicated.

She pulled his arms up, so they were around her waist rather than her lower stomach, so she could move around more freely. Then she got out her phone, and opened Instagram, seeing that he had posted a picture he had taken of her in the pub. She was holding a glass of wine and smiling, and from an outsider's perspective they seemed like a perfectly normal couple. The picture had only three likes, whereas the photos of him alone tended to have significantly more.

She'd asked him in the past not to post pictures of her online because of the risk of her parents seeing them, but he must have forgotten. She wasn't sure what was worse, that she was clearly alone with Magnus in the picture, or that she had alcohol in her hand. If Magnus wasn't asleep she would have asked him to delete it, but a small part of her liked that he had posted it. It showed that he was proud to be with her, that he wanted people to know they were together. This fact made her heart swell in both a pleasant and an anxiety-inducing way.

Perhaps she was being overly cautious. Her parents didn't even have Instagram. This level of paranoia was what her parents had reduced her to. Would she ever not worry about every single thing in her life?

She resolved to not say anything to Magnus about the picture; they could have this one small thing at least.

"Relax," he said, sleepily.

"Huh?"

His hand curled around her tighter, his leg molding itself to hers. He snuggled into her. "You keep moving."

"Whoops, sorry!" She gave her signature humorless laugh, and put her phone underneath her pillow.

But he was asleep again and didn't notice what she had said.

"I really hate wine," she whispered into the quiet darkness.

Chapter 31

SORAYA

Brighton, 2014

Soraya stared at a pile of clothes she had been meaning to donate to charity for years now and wondered whether she was incapable of letting go, of her childhood, of past teachings. She had always assumed that once she moved out she'd live the life she craved, would gain freedom. So why was she holding herself back? Why did she have no life goals? What did she truly believe in?

"Jendeh!"

Whore.

There were loud footsteps. Quick and heavy. She closed her laptop and got out of bed.

Her dad slammed into the room, his face a deeper shade of red than normal.

"You jendeh!" he spat, crossing the room towards her.

She backed away from him until her head hit the sloping ceiling. She swore under her breath and applied pressure to her scalp. Her heart felt like it was attempting to escape her chest; it pounded hard and erratically.

Her mum came running up the stairs. "Hossein, stop, please!"

Tyzer jumped off her bed, tail low, and ran down the stairs.

As her father approached Soraya, she noticed his eyes were dark and wild. His raised hand slapped her hard across the face. Her cheek stung. The act caused her to hit her head again against the attic ceiling. The collision caused a bang. It sounded worse than it felt, but Soraya knew this wasn't the end.

She ducked down to run around him. "What are you talking about?" she yelled. She'd had enough nightmares about this happening. She usually woke up with a start around now.

But this was real.

"Zainab saw pictures of you on a boy's Instagram, drinking alcohol. You fucking slag!" He stepped forward again and her heart sank.

Zainab had found it because Magnus tagged her in the picture, and his account wasn't private, and Soraya had been stupid enough to forget how nosy her relatives in Iran were. She felt as though she was drowning with weights tied around her ankles. She couldn't move, couldn't think properly. Her dad had this effect on her; only he could make her feel like she was drowning.

She wished she could be invisible, like she often felt, and run away from this crazy man, this crazy family that constantly attempted to control her.

A memory from her childhood came back to her. Her dad had caught her in a big group of classmates, talking to a boy. He'd dragged her to the car then, told her if she ever did anything like that again he'd kill her.

She remembered her sister telling her that when Laleh left, their dad dragged Parvin away from Amir in the living room and simply told her, "If you ever disobey me, I will lock you in your room and never let you out."

"It was like a switch flicked on in him when Laleh left," Parvin had said. "And it hasn't turned off since."

Soraya now looked towards the stairs, where her mum stood, unintentionally in the way. She was cornered like a wild animal, with an even wilder predator shouting profanities at her.

"I don't know what you're talking about—"

"You fucking liar!" Her dad scrambled on her dresser for an object, any object, and threw a photo frame in her direction. It hit her. The unexpected impact with her face was enough to make her to fall to the ground. Her head stung with a sharp, throbbing pain. Her entire body went to jelly. She wanted to stand, but when she put her hand to the floor to try to lever herself up, she found she didn't have the strength.

At the same time, rage bubbled inside her. Why was she at twenty-one years old still ruled by this useless man? She hated that he reduced her to this—a pathetic mess on the floor, while her mum cried. Her mum was always unhappy, always crying. Where was the justice?

She wished he would disappear instead. Wished he'd stop controlling them, burdening them.

She heard another crash and looked over to see he'd thrown down her TV. He picked up the watercolor set she'd been given for her birthday and smashed it against the wall. He had the ability to ruin everything; he destroyed and destroyed until everything was broken.

"Hossein, stop!" her mum shouted.

"This is your fault." He turned on her then. She had a hand on his shoulder and he pushed her off him. She fell full force and the look on his face was one of surprise. As though he wasn't aware of his own strength. Soraya and her mum both lay crumpled on the floor. Seeing him touch her mum in that way changed something in Soraya.

"Neda," he said softly, bending over her, hand outstretched, as though he hadn't meant to hurt her.

Neda ignored his hand, instead keeping her gaze on him, her jaw clenched. She managed to stand up unaided, on shaky legs.

"Don't you ever touch her, don't even—" Soraya began.

Anger returned to his face then, bringing him back to the reason he had pushed his wife, despite the brief moment of remorse he had shown.

"What? What did you say?"

"Leave Mum alone—"

He gave a short, harsh laugh. "You think your mum is innocent? She let you go to London, let you live with that *gay* boy, let you wear short skirts, and this happens. Like fucking *Laleh*." He spat in Soraya's face. Saliva ran down her cheek and into her hair. She tried to wipe it off but it was gluey and elastic. It stuck to her skin. She wiped her hand repeatedly against her pajama bottoms. "You're lucky Amir isn't home. He'd kill you, he'd fucking kill you!" her father ranted.

"For what? I've not done anything!" she shouted. "You're a bully, all you ever do is bully all of us, and I'm so sick of it!"

His eyes were wild, hungry for confrontation, and she'd stupidly fed him. He reached out and grabbed her by the hair, pulling her towards him. She was about to groan with the pain of it when he smacked her across the face again.

He hit her harder this time and her face felt like it had been branded by a hot iron. Her vision blurred. A contact lens had come out. She cried, couldn't help it, tears gushing down her face, and sobbed loudly. As if she had been reduced to an animal, her cries were feral, unrestrained.

"I told you before. Everything we do is for you," her father shouted. "We came to England for *you,* your mum works like a donkey for *you*." His voice rose after each word, until he was bellowing.

Soraya looked over at her mum. Her head was bent low in resignation. Her lips were turned down and in that moment she noticed how much her mum had aged. Her wrinkles looked deeper, her body smaller. In particular, her hands looked tiny, childlike. *How had she ended up with such a monster?* And why wouldn't she leave him?

"I'm ashamed of you," he spat.

Soraya shut her eyes for a moment, willing this to be a nightmare. Wanting to wake up and have a normal dad. A calm, boring family. Not this.

She hated him so much then. It was a familiar feeling but it was in this moment that she felt it charge her veins until she had to resist the urge to scream.

"What's going on . . . ?" Parvin stood at the top of the stairs, looking in at the chaos.

There were shards of glass on the floor, the television upside down, paint on the walls. Her mum held her face in her hands and Soraya stood facing their dad, her cheeks wet with tears, blood dribbling from her nose. The silence in the room was almost audible.

Parvin's presence seemed to calm her dad's fury. He backed away from Soraya and turned towards her sister, forcing a shaky smile onto his face. "Nothing, darling."

Soraya didn't know what she wanted him to say, but it wasn't that.

"Nothing?" she let out. "You call *attacking us* nothing?" Her voice echoed around the room.

"Don't exaggerate." He scratched his bald head. "You're always talking back, always going against what I tell you, having a fucking *boyfriend,* drinking alcohol. And now you're saying I *hit* you . . ."

Parvin looked again at the spectacle in front of her.

"Why do you never bother her?" Soraya said, pointing to her sister, not sure where her boldness was coming from. Was it Parvin's presence? Or had she simply had enough?

Her dad ignored her, turning to make his way down the stairs.

"I asked you a question!" Soraya called after him. She wiped her face with the back of her hand, tears mixed with blood.

He turned, his eyes dark again. "Do you want to know why? Because she listens to me, she doesn't back chat like you, like *Laleh.*" He said the name as if it was a dirty word. "I see *her* in you. You act just like her. And I don't want to be embarrassed again. Do you fucking hear? No more of this. If I hear you're still with this boy, *any boy,* you can fuck off out of this family. No more shame. Do you hear? No more!"

He went down the stairs, pushing Parvin out of the way. And he was right about one thing: Parvin was more obedient. She let herself be shoved aside without protest, something Soraya would never allow. Something in her always wanted to have the last word with her dad, wanted somehow to bring justice home. But instead more chaos ensued, and her mum was caught in the crossfire.

"I hate him," Soraya whispered. Her voice was strangled. She barely recognized it as her own.

"What happened?" Parvin asked, rushing to her mum's side.

"Zainab saw a picture of Soraya on a boy's Instagram. There was alcohol too." Her mum turned to Soraya. "What is all of this?"

"It's not what you think—"

"It doesn't matter. Whatever it is, just stop it. Your cousins in Iran are nosy and they gossip. Don't give them anything to gossip about. You don't want to end up like your sister." Her mum rarely said Laleh's name. It shocked Soraya that her dad had named her.

"Why won't you just leave him?" Soraya wailed.

"And where would he go? He's a *druggie*, Soraya. He could never survive on his own. And at the end of the day, he's your dad." Her mum shook her head and breathed in deeply. "You know you shouldn't be hanging around with boys, you're Muslim."

As well as her mum's, Soraya could also feel Parvin's eyes on her. It was as though her sister was judging her, not for what she did, but for how careless she had been.

She had been too reckless, pretending to be a normal girl with a normal boyfriend. That wasn't her, so why had she tried to live like that? Why had she let Magnus post a picture of her online? Why didn't she just tell him to delete it when she saw it?

"Soraya, listen to me. No more messing around with this boy, do you hear me? I know you live in London now, but remember Allah. Remember you're a good Muslim. No more of this, please."

Looking into her mum's tearstained face, Soraya nodded once. Her actions had consequences. They inadvertently harmed those she loved. No good would come from being with Magnus.

They weren't like English families, who could go months without talking to each other; the Nazari family were close-knit, just like most Iranian families. It was part of their culture. To cut her dad out of her life would mean cutting her mum out too. And that was unthinkable. Her dad was wrong about one thing, though. Soraya wasn't exactly like Laleh; that wasn't something she could do. Perhaps she was too weak, but she loved her family, and she would never leave them.

Soraya's heart ached with the knowledge that they were stuck with this drain of a man until death intervened—theirs or his. And she was so tired of it.

So, so tired.

Part
TWO

Part
TWO

Chapter 32

NEDA

Liverpool, 1978

In the time Neda had been married to Hossein she'd noted three things about him:

1. He was always worried about something. Since moving to England his once perfectly manicured nails had been reduced to stubs. It looked painful, and yet when they watched television she noticed him biting them, again and again.

2. He would go weeks without calling his mother or sisters, whereas Neda called her family every other day. It made her wonder about his character, especially when his mother would then ring Neda's mother to find out how they were.

3. He was not a practicing Muslim. He slowly stopped praying while they were in Liverpool and when questioned would say, "My relationship with Allah is between me and Allah."

She knew his dad had been religious, and slowly began to realize Hossein chose her, one of four hijabis at the university, because doing so would have made his father happy. That wasn't the only reason, but she was sure it was one.

Still, she had questions. But she couldn't broach them, because to do so would incite conflict, and Neda knew it was best to avoid such situations. Especially now they were in a foreign country away from family.

Neda enjoyed the breeze, the way the cool air brushed against her face. It was the beginning of autumn, the days still fairly warm, the leaves beginning to fall. All around was excitement at the changing season.

They had arrived with one suitcase each, a rolled Persian carpet, and an abundance of pistachios. They had rented out their flat in Tehran to a newly married couple.

Hossein had used a substantial amount of his savings and inheritance to pay for their plane tickets and a deposit on a flat in England.

"It's an investment in our future," he had said simply, as though nothing worried him. She wondered if this was truly his personality or a front he put on for her benefit. Either way, it put her at ease. In this way they were well matched; she was anxious enough for both of them, always planning ahead, whereas he shrugged off any hiccup in their new life.

The city was not quite what they had both expected. Of course, they had seen England in the movies, but Liverpool looked different, more industrial and in some areas run-down and dangerous. Neither of them said this to the other, fearful that voicing such opinions would shatter the shininess of this new chapter in their lives. Besides, Hossein's excitement that John Lennon had once resided in Liverpool, and had drunk at the infamous Ye Cracke pub, managed to overshadow their doubts.

Neda had been so nervous about her first day in class: that she wouldn't understand anyone, that she would be picked on by lecturers, that people would stare at her.

Her fears were unfounded for the most part. Despite her English being basic, the handouts helped and no one chose her to answer questions. The teaching techniques in England, it seemed, were kinder.

She was right, however, about the staring. But it wasn't just at her. She was among a handful of foreign students who had gotten in on scholarships, and they too were stared at. She wondered what made her stand out: was it her hijab, her skin color, or both? And were they curious or resentful stares?

At the end of her last lecture of the day, she expelled a deep, low sigh. While her energy was almost depleted, she still went to the library to go over what she had been taught. There was a reason she had won a scholarship; Neda had to be top of her class, even if that class was in a foreign language.

While in the lecture halls surrounded by foreign people she felt out of place, in the library Neda felt at home. She belonged. The musty, familiar smell of old books, the hushed tones, and the studious quiet, this was what Neda loved. She found an empty table and spread the contents of her bag onto the surface, marking her territory, before going off in search of textbooks. Really, she needed to buy them, but they were too expensive. The bursary she was given by the university would be best used towards rent, until Hossein found a job. The only copies the library had left were for reference only.

She had been there for an hour when she felt a tap on her shoulder. Neda assumed she had done something wrong and prepared to apologize. But when she turned she saw a petite woman with a crooked nose and glistening white teeth, smiling brightly at her.

"Sister," the woman said, "I just wanted to say hello."

One look at her and Neda's posture softened; she smiled back. "Salam," she said.

The woman sat down next to Neda, her large hazel eyes bright with interest. "It's so rare to see a hijabi, I had to say hello." Despite having an Iranian accent, she spoke perfect English, each word crisp and deliberate.

"Have you been here long?" Neda asked in Farsi. "Sorry. My name is Neda."

"I moved here a month ago," the woman said, her smile fading momentarily. "I miss home, but I can't complain." She shrugged. "I'm Mena."

"Did you come here with your husband?"

Mena laughed, covering her mouth just as she was given dark looks by people trying to study a few tables away. "Hell, no! I left Iran to get away from men," she stage-whispered, reminding Neda of her friend Shanauz.

Neda chuckled softly. "Men are everywhere, you can't escape them."

"Unfortunately . . ." She looked down at Neda's ring finger. "So, you have one then?"

"I came here with my husband, yes." She clasped her hands together.

"And he studies?"

Neda hesitated. "No."

"Oh, he got a job here?" Up close Neda noticed the white spots on Mena's teeth. It made her like the other woman more, with this evidence that she wasn't quite perfect.

"Yes . . . he's working in a restaurant at the minute. But he hopes to find something else. It's hard here, you know, but I'm sure once we're settled he'll find something that suits him better."

"Inshallah," Mena said.

"Yes, inshallah," Neda repeated.

And so began a blossoming friendship. They met in the library, often by chance.

Mena would bring various pieces of fruit with her, and Neda would bring a flask of coffee and two cups. She learnt that Mena's family had wanted her to marry, but she applied for scholarships abroad in secret and narrowly missed marrying a man twenty years her senior. Her family couldn't stop their daughter from going; the bragging rights of having a child studying in England were too great.

"The man I was meant to marry looked awful! His belly was like this!" She indicated with her hand a large rounded stomach. "And he had huge teeth." She bared her own teeth and pulled faces.

Despite her loudness, which at times made Neda feel uncomfortable, Mena reminded her of home, and for that she was grateful. The dramatics of every conversation, every situation being high stakes, was typical of the way her family and friends spoke back home. English people, Neda thought, seemed calmer, less interested in storytelling and complaining, or observing the minute details of life. They did things and moved on, instead of talking about things long past.

The pair went to English evening classes the university put on for foreign students. They took trips to the cinema and found themselves watching romantic comedies, horror movies, whatever was playing, to master the all-important language.

They recommended their favorite romance novels to each other, beginning an informal book club where they would discuss what they had read each week. It began a couple of months into their friendship when Mena gingerly slid a book across the library desk to Neda, cover facedown. Mena had a look of glee on her face.

"What is it?" Neda said, turning it over. "Eh!"

The cover showed a woman and man in an embrace, her head thrown back in some kind of ecstasy, the cut of her dress exposing her décolletage. The cover alluded to scandal and drama, key ingredients of Neda's favorite romances.

"It's really good, Neda. I would recommend! Unlike anything I've read before . . . It made me realize how tame the books I had been reading were."

"How could I bring this home to Hossein? He'd laugh at me!" Despite her words, Neda put the book in her bag quickly.

"When can I meet this mysterious husband of yours anyway?"

Neda hesitated. She hadn't introduced them for a reason. Hossein was growing more and more irritated by the lack of decent job prospects for him. He had approached football clubs to help with coaching, but no one wanted him—not even for small children—and he'd offered to teach for free. In their coming to England his dreams had been shattered, rather than what he'd believed would happen, that he would be introduced to a world of new possibilities.

"He works long hours," Neda lied seamlessly. "I barely see him myself." This part, at least, was true.

Six months into her new life in Liverpool and Neda was deep into her master's, the intensity of her work schedule catching up with her. During this time, Hossein gave up trying to find a job related to his field. Instead he worked in a restaurant during the week and at a taxi firm on the weekends. It was "cash in hand," and though Neda didn't quite know what that meant, he seemed to bring home wads of money.

One Sunday morning, while he was asleep after doing a late shift, she cleaned up after him. He had told her the money was good during night shifts, as English people coming home late didn't question the high fares due to their intoxicated state. They also often tipped generously. His job as a taxi driver meant Neda was alone most evenings on the weekends, a fact she grew to accept. Mena would often go to discos and clubs, something Neda disapproved of.

Alcohol caused people to make mistakes, ruined lives. She couldn't understand why, despite this, people continued drinking. She knew firsthand from her dad's bad moods the morning after that it affected not only the drinker but also those around them.

Hossein had left his trousers on the floor, as though he had literally stepped out of them and gotten into bed. His socks were abandoned near the door, and on the kitchen table was a greasy takeaway box. When she went to pick up his trousers, seeing that there were mud stains on the legs, she decided to put them to soak in the bath. His clothes always smelt heavy with aftershave, something he hadn't really worn in Tehran. She removed the belt from the loopholes and fingered inside the pockets to remove loose change. She checked his back pockets and felt something square and soft. She pulled it out.

A condom packet.

She sat on the wooden chair in the section of the studio flat they liked to call the "kitchen." Her mind whirled, wondering what excuses, explanations there could be.

The room was deafeningly quiet. Her mind shook, her breathing almost stilled. She put the packet back in his pocket and returned the belt to the loops. She pocketed the change for herself, put the trousers in their original place on the floor, and left the flat.

She used the money to buy herself a coffee and a vegetarian

fry-up from their local café. The smell of nonhalal sausages taunted her. The waitress was chatty, but Neda was in no mood for conversation. She stayed there for an hour, staring into space in between bites of food she couldn't taste. She felt tired, drained of any joy she had had.

When she returned home Hossein was awake. His smile still, annoyingly, dazzled her. He was so beautiful, and perhaps that was the problem. Perhaps she should have married an ugly man, and then he might not have cheated on her.

"Where did you go? I missed you." He gave her a suggestive look, and pulled her into a hug. His breath was minty fresh, and his hand lingered on her bottom.

She wiggled out of his grasp, unpinned her hijab, and folded it neatly into a square.

"How was work?" she asked.

"Good! Tiring, but you know I'd do anything for you." Again, a suggestive look. Ordinarily, she would have been lulled by both a sense of obligation and an appreciation for this man who worked hard so she could follow her dreams. But something was off. Something had always been off. Hadn't she always known?

She said nothing. Neda believed in obtaining proper evidence before drawing conclusions. This was no different from the experiments she conducted in the lab. She would never conclude something without solid evidence, without doing the proper tests and assessing all the variables. So, she decided to do just that.

She experimented on her husband.

Chapter 33

SORAYA

London, 2014

Some people are radiators, and others are drains. Hossein Nazari was a drain. He sucked the life out of people. When he lashed out, those around him became shells of themselves. And Soraya was now empty. She hadn't spoken to her dad. Or Parvin. But her mum sent daily WhatsApp messages asking how she was, followed by a plethora of emojis ranging from pink flowers to the kiss face. It pained Soraya to be pitied by her mum. But her mum was also stuck with her dad, had endured a lifetime of him.

She thought back to when she was a child and her mum described the first time her own husband had hit her.

It was a hard smack across the face during an argument; before that he had only broken things when emotions ran high. Her mum was so shocked she was rendered speechless, she'd told Soraya. He bought her flowers the next day, and her favorite chocolates, blaming his addiction for his actions.

Soraya had researched the link between drug addiction and violence, and didn't know whether it was a good enough excuse. Hadn't he used it often enough by now?

Why won't she leave him? Soraya asked herself, gripping her hair hard and pulling. It was the dead of night. Oliver was out in Soho, and she had avoided Magnus by saying she was back in Brighton. She hadn't told him what had happened there.

In the solitude of her bedroom she allowed herself one small scream. Again, she felt like a caged animal, unable to escape. Even

Parvin was on their dad's side. She told Soraya that she needed to be more careful, that she was stupid for being so reckless. There was no sympathy in her texts, and talking to her sister made Soraya feel even more alone. She left Parvin's most recent message unread; she didn't have the energy to reply.

Despite the winter chill creeping into her bedroom with its single-glazed windows, she was warm in her bed, the back of her neck sticky. She wrapped her heavy hair in a bun, even considered chopping it off with the kitchen scissors. But wouldn't that be cliché?

She walked over to her full-length mirror. She had lost weight, her cheekbones jutting out more, and no longer considered this a glamorous attribute. She looked unwell. The bruises on her face had faded into a slight yellow-green. MAC concealer and thick foundation covered them from the outside world. The only person who had seen her injuries was Oliver; they held no secrets from each other.

Sick of her own reflection, she turned off the lights and stared at her dark silhouette. On the bed, her phone vibrated. She grabbed it and answered the call without thinking. Then wished she had considered what she was doing.

"Hi," Magnus said softly.

"Hi," Soraya replied.

"How come you're up?"

"How come *you're* up?" Soraya was aware her voice was flat.

"What's going on with you?" His harsh tone made her shut her eyes; they stung from tiredness. Silence lingered. Soraya's throat tightened.

"Are you even in Brighton?" he asked.

Her eyes opened and she flicked the light switch on. "Why would you ask that?"

Magnus sighed. She had never heard him so down, so frustrated. *And it's because of me.* Not for the first time, she wished she didn't have the complications that came with her upbringing—or perhaps, rather, that he had the capacity to understand her situation.

"I'm just . . ."

"Just what?" Magnus asked, holding on to her words.

"I'm not feeling well."

"Oh, come on. Is it us? Are you not into me anymore?"

"I need to go, I'm sorry."

Soraya hung up and instantly regretted it. She hoped he'd ring back.

He didn't.

The connection between Magnus and Soraya was different after her dad hit her. She knew he felt it too. Their texts to each other were less frequent. As well as Muslim guilt there was the danger of being caught again, of being disowned, of her dad's power over them. It wasn't just her safety she feared for; it was her mum's. And even Magnus's. What if her dad told Amir she was seeing a boy? What if they somehow came head-to-head with Magnus? What if they visited her flat unannounced, only to find him in her bed? The men in her family were unrestrained in both their emotions and their pride. She'd been stupid to think she could have a normal relationship.

Her family catching her with Magnus had become a recurring nightmare. In her dreams Magnus would be in her family house in Brighton. Soraya would try to sneak him out, down the two flights of stairs, without waking anyone. She never succeeded and often woke with a start as her dad's hand came pounding down on her head.

Such thoughts continued for hours, her mind tormenting her with possibilities.

Her relationship with Magnus had gone from an experiment to real, and she'd never truly considered the potential fallout with her family before.

She attempted to write in her diary, but her words were jumbled, not full sentences, illegible in places. She looked at her pros and cons list about Magnus. It felt so long ago now since she had made it, she envied her past self for being so clueless as to what was to come. She tucked it under her pillow.

The shrill buzz of her doorbell startled her. It was 2:30 A.M. She tiptoed into the hallway. Despite not actually having been asleep, Soraya felt a twitch of irritation at Oliver.

She picked up the intercom receiver. "Hello?"

"Soraya?" It was Magnus.

If it hadn't been the middle of the night, she would have hung up. She looked down at herself. She had stains on her white T-shirt, and despite the cold she wore shorts. Dark, thick hair covered her legs, stubborn and strong. He had never seen her like this.

Her finger hovered over the buzzer.

"Come on," he said softly. She shut her eyes and pressed the door release.

The phone was still in her hand as she heard him climb the stairs. His heavy footsteps brought her out of her reverie. She opened the door to him.

The light from the corridor was bright, a contrast to the darkness of the flat. Her eyes had adjusted to the gloom, but it surprised Magnus and he had to squint to see inside. He lingered by the door.

His face was so soft, his lips perfectly plump and pink. She'd forgotten how beautiful he was. How attuned she was to his emotions, how she could feel concern radiating from him. But despite all this, seeing him again in her flat, she felt viscerally that he did not belong here. With her, in her world. His life was open, uncomplicated. Hers was not.

"What are you doing here?" Soraya asked, not meeting his eyes and focusing her gaze on his shoulder. He wore a navy ski jacket with a fur-trimmed hood. The one they had picked out together on their shopping date.

"Are you not going to let me in?" His lips curled slightly, about to smile, but upon seeing Soraya's stony expression he stopped himself. She noticed him breathe in deeply.

She moved out of the way and signaled with her hand for him to come in. As he stepped farther into the flat, his scent invaded her senses. Musky and sweet, with a rush of the outside cold. She breathed it in at first then stopped herself. It would only make things harder.

He didn't turn on the lights, and neither did she. Her focus was now on his beat-up trainers.

From the corner of her eye, she saw his hands move and then

they were cupping her face, tilting it up, forcing her to look him in the eye. His hands were ice-cold.

"What's going on?" he asked, barely above a whisper. His fingertips brushed the bruise around her right eye. She winced. He turned the light on then. "What happened to you?" he asked, his voice tight.

Tears began to well up and Soraya dug her nails into the palms of her hands in an attempt to distract herself.

"Please talk to me."

"I can't," she said.

He bent forward and wrapped his arms around her. She let herself relax into him. One tear rolled down her cheek. She was thankful for his hood, which absorbed it before he could see.

"Do you want to sleep?" he asked. The question surprised her, but this was Magnus, and somehow he always understood. She knew that, she just didn't want to admit it sometimes.

She nodded.

They went into her bedroom and she nestled herself back into bed, under the cool duvet. He removed his coat, trainers, jeans, and belt, so he was wearing only a T-shirt and boxers, and got into bed next to her. He spooned her, kissing her head gently. He put a protective arm around her waist.

She turned in his arms, so she was facing him, and raised herself higher so her lips could touch his. He kissed her back hesitantly, not deepening the kiss.

"I want you," she whispered.

With those words he grew hard, but he continued with the chaste kisses.

She broke the kiss and felt bold enough to look him in his eyes. "Don't you want me?"

He sighed deeply. "It's not that, Soraya. I really want you. Just not like this, not when you're upset." He stroked her cheek gently with his rough fingertips.

"No, you don't." She turned away from him, uncomfortably aware of what she was doing, but doing it anyway.

His hand was on her shoulder, turning her over so she faced him. "Soraya, you don't know how much I want to . . ." He trailed off, shook his head. "I need you to talk to me, tell me what's going on. What happened to you?"

"And I need you inside me."

The words surprised even her. She wasn't sure she meant them but in that moment she needed the distraction, needed something, anything.

He groaned ever so slightly. "I want that too." He cleared his throat. "But it wouldn't be right. I want you to really want it. Do you understand?"

"You're always trying to have sex with me, why is now different?"

Magnus flinched at her words. "I'm not . . . do you think that's what I'm doing?"

"You always seem disappointed when we don't end up having sex, and now I'm telling you I'm ready."

He closed his eyes and held them shut for what felt like hours.

"I'm sorry if it's come across like that." He moved his body slightly away from her. "I didn't mean—I never wanted you to think . . . I'm sorry."

"I don't want you to apologize, I just want you to . . ." She paused, unable to say the words again. "You know."

"Can't we just cuddle for now?" He moved closer, kissed her head again.

"Don't you find me attractive?"

Another groan. "Obviously I do, Soraya. Do you know how many times I've gotten a hard-on in public just from you giving me a peck on the lips?" He let out a small laugh.

Unsure what possessed her, Soraya sat up straighter and positioned herself so she was straddling him. She could feel *him* and it both frightened and thrilled her.

He placed his hands on her lower back, holding her there.

She leant down to kiss him, and the kiss was surprisingly deep, his tongue stroking hers as she ground against him.

She worked her way to removing his top, exposing his chiseled torso. But then she stopped kissing him suddenly and just sat staring at his chest.

"What's going on?" he asked.

"I don't get why you're with me."

Magnus let out a frustrated sigh. "What do you mean? Why are you saying this now?"

"You're . . . you. I mean, you're hot, smart, and well, no offense, but *normal*. And I'm a mess . . ."

He caught her chin with his hand and brought her face down close to his.

"You're gorgeous, intelligent, interesting, funny, sexy," he said. "Maybe I should be asking you why you're with *me*?"

The combination of him pressed against her and his words made her nipples harden. Magnus noticed this and looked her directly in the eye. His hand held the bottom of her T-shirt and she nodded, allowing him to lift it off. He pulled her down and drew his mouth to her nipple. She groaned in response.

"The sounds you make . . . I could literally come just from hearing you moan."

She breathed deeply.

After a few minutes he spoke. "Are you going to tell me why you have a black eye?"

It was like he had thrown a bucket of ice-cold water over her. "Magnus, now isn't the time."

He rolled her over so he was on top of her. His legs straddled her. Her bare chest exposed at this angle made her self-conscious, so she crossed her arms.

"I can't . . . I can't do this with you whilst this is all spinning in my head, Soraya."

"But surely this is more fun than talking?"

"It's very, *very* fun." His eyes darkened a tad. "But I need to know what's going on—why did you lie about being in Brighton? What happened to you?" He touched her bruised face.

"It's too long to explain."

"We have all night."

"I don't feel comfortable talking about it."

"Soraya, I'm supposed to be your . . ." It sounded like he was going to say "boyfriend" but stopped himself. "You know. But you don't tell me anything. Don't you trust me?"

She sighed and didn't know where to look. "My dad," she said, and then stopped talking, and breathed deeply. Magnus's gaze was hard, pensive. She didn't know if she could say it. Her mouth was dry, her body impossibly warm and clammy. "They saw the picture you posted of me at that pub."

There was a short silence.

"What do you mean?"

"I told you they were strict. I'm not allowed to be with boys or drink alcohol. Both of which were in the picture."

His face crumpled. "So your dad did this?" He couldn't hide the anger he felt quick enough. "Because we're together? That's crazy."

She didn't say anything.

"I don't get it," he said.

"I don't know what to say."

And *this* was why they could never be a thing. Why their relationship would never work. He didn't—couldn't—understand her culture. How had she been so blind to this before?

"Is it because I'm white?" he asked.

She sighed deeply. It was a sigh of frustration, of tiredness.

"Not really. It's because you're a man."

He lifted himself off her and sat on the bed next to her. He fixed his gaze on his hands. The distance and silence between them stretched.

Soraya's mind whirled from thought to thought. She hated silences; they allowed her mind to run wild, fleeting ideas and troubling memories all vying for her attention. It was even worse when she was with someone, like now, because she was also wondering what they were thinking.

"Say something," she finally said.

"What happened after he hit you?"

"He threw things around, including my mum." She spoke so quietly she wasn't sure Magnus could hear her. "He hit me when I tried to defend myself, and then denied it all to Parvin." Her breathing was unsteady and she had to stop talking.

"Didn't anyone try and help you? Your brother or sister?"

"Amir wasn't in. My dad's convinced Amir would have been on

his side. I doubt it, he's not a monster, but he doesn't know any-thing happened, which is probably for the best. Parvin is too much of a goody-goody to defend us. I'm not talking to her at the mo-ment." Soraya looked away, wiping a stray tear. "It's fine, it doesn't matter."

"It's *fine?* Soraya, how is any of this fine? This is just . . . it's mad." Magnus grabbed her face between his hands and forced her to look at him. "None of this is fine."

Tears began to roll down her cheeks. She shook him off.

"Talking about it won't make it better."

Magnus made a frustrated sound, hands balled into fists. "I know he's your dad but I just want to . . ." The veins in his arms protruded.

He surprised her by pulling her into a tight hug. "Don't go back there," he whispered into her hair. "You don't deserve to be treated like this."

"It's not that simple. They're all I have."

"They're abusive, Soraya, you can't go back there. Has he hit you before?" He looked at her carefully.

"No . . . well, not like that. He's always had a temper. The only similar time was when I was fifteen, and there was this park near my school that we all went to. I was there with friends and briefly spoke to a boy, and my parents found out—one of their friends drove by and saw me—so they dragged me home. My dad spat on me and hit my leg, said he'd kill me if I did anything like that again, and I just remember being so shocked." Soraya choked on the last word, and covered her mouth with her hand.

"This is so fucked up," Magnus whispered.

His words were only semi-comforting. He was missing the point, focusing on her dad's rage as though it was a singular prob-lem, not an issue a lot of British Muslim girls faced to some degree. It wasn't Hossein Nazari that was crazy, it was the attitude of many men in her culture, the way they saw their daughters as pets to be controlled.

"I don't know what to do," Soraya said, her mouth pressed against his chest. He didn't loosen his hold, and she was glad. "I like being with you, but it's so complicated. My brain is just . . . I feel guilty all the time when we're with each other. I feel like I'm already going to hell. And then there's this pressure from my family, and I'm so scared I'm going to get caught again." While she spoke Magnus continued to hold her, stroking her back gently.

"Why hell?" he asked, quietly. She imagined the frown forming on his face, uncomprehending yet again. "You're a good person, Soraya."

She rolled her eyes.

"Having a boyfriend before marriage is reason enough to go to hell. I don't even pray or wear a hijab. I mean, look at me. I'm semi-naked with my white boyfriend, and five minutes ago I invited you to *you know,* and *you're* the one who stopped us!" She paused to breathe deeply.

It was obvious he didn't know what to say. "I can't pretend to know how to be a good Muslim, but what we're doing doesn't feel wrong to me. We're not hurting anyone, and the way I feel about you, Soraya, I've never felt like this about anyone. It can't be wrong to feel this way about another person."

She squeezed her eyes shut, aware this conversation was a prime case of the blind leading the blind. She knew next to nothing about Islam and didn't practice her religion at all. She believed in God, but apart from that what did she know that Magnus didn't? What did she know about religion, heaven and hell, that he didn't?

"I'm falling in love with you, Soraya."

Speechless, she kept her eyes shut. Unintentionally, he had made things so much harder for her.

He needed to stop talking. Stop saying the words he was never meant to say. It wasn't meant to be like this. And yet part of her was glad it was.

"You don't have to say anything," he said quickly. "I just want you to know. To know that I'll always be there for you."

"Magnus . . ."

"My dad used to hit my mum when his drinking got really bad," Magnus said. "She'd have black eyes, and I'd hear her telling her friends she got them from slipping in the shower or some other crap excuse. But I heard them shouting, her screaming, so I always knew." There was a brief silence. "I just want you to tell me things. I *want* to help. You need help, Soraya, you know that, right?" He said the last bit quietly.

"How can anyone help?"

"You can't go back to them after all this and pretend nothing's happened. You need to talk about these things. Bottling it up won't help."

"My mum always told me not to tell people about us."

"It's important to, though. Especially me."

"I can't. I want to. So many times, I've wanted to."

"What's stopped you?"

"Well, I don't know . . . maybe that then you'd realize how fucked up my family is. I didn't want to add to the stereotype of coming from a dysfunctional Muslim family. Plus, I was scared it'd put you off."

"Soraya, it's me. I'm not going anywhere. There's nothing you can say that will change that."

"I was told to break things off with you, to be a good Muslim."

He loosened his arms so that he could look at her face. "What did you say to that?"

"I said I wasn't going to see you anymore."

He nodded. "And do you want that?" Magnus's voice was controlled, in a way that surprised and irked her. But it was a good question.

She opened her mouth, once, twice, three times, but didn't know what to say. No words would come. Her usually busy mind was suddenly blank.

"That wasn't why . . . I don't know what I want."

He grabbed her hand, began stroking the back of it.

"There's something I never told you." She felt the familiar buildup, of wanting to tell him something, and usually she'd push it back down. Except, this time, she let it rise, let the words come out. "My dad's an addict like yours."

The room was silent bar the hum from the pipes, which groaned momentarily. Soraya almost wanted to comment on it, create a joke out of it, distract them both from what she had just said. But she didn't.

"Really?"

"Yeah."

"Why didn't you tell me this before?"

They heard a key turn in the door and then the sound of it closing. Oliver's lazy stumble to the kitchen, the lights being switched on. Soraya listened to his movements for a while, imploring her senses to distract her from this situation.

"Soraya?" Magnus pressed her. His expression was concerned, eyebrows furrowed. She settled her gaze on the small mole at the center of his neck.

"My mum always told me to keep it secret. I have school friends I've known nearly all my life and they still don't know. Oliver is my only friend who does. My dad became addicted to opium originally, I think. And now his doctor prescribes him methadone, which he takes every day. My parents always told me to hide it, hide his secret. As though his shame is ours too. And I guess, in a way, it is."

Magnus looked intently at her. Now all she could focus on were his brown eyes, and the flecks of gold in them. "You've done nothing wrong," he breathed. "I'm so sorry." He rested his forehead against hers, holding her like she was precious.

She had never been held this way before.

Chapter 34

SORAYA

London, 2014

On one of the rare weekends that Soraya wasn't working a Saturday shift, she spent the day with Oliver. It was the first time they had hung out during the day in months; their schedules constantly clashed now. They could go days without seeing each other despite living in the same house. Oliver worked nine to five Monday to Friday and her shifts varied each week. Sometimes she would work late and by the time she returned home he would be getting ready for bed.

She had missed him, missed his energy and the way that she felt completely comfortable around him. Unlike any romantic interest, their friendship would never end, and unlike family, he had no unrealistic expectations about her and how she should act—he accepted her for who she was.

They had begun the day at Deptford Market, a short walk away from their flat. The market sold an array of bric-a-brac, furniture, brand-new, secondhand, and vintage clothing. As usual, it was the vintage jeans section that Oliver immediately headed over to. On the huge folding table were piles and piles of denim, all five pounds—Lee, Levi's, and Wrangler were the brands they both particularly kept an eye out for. Then once they had collected a variety of jeans, they assessed whether they would actually fit them, whether they were high-waisted enough, and whether alterations could be made.

The air was sharp and cold, making the rummaging not quite

pleasant, but it was their tradition and for that reason Soraya was content to be rifling through the stiff fabric for a potential treasure.

"How are you finding your job anyway? We've literally not had a chance to speak about it in person until now," she asked.

Since their first year at university Oliver had known he wanted to work in book publishing, and every summer he would do unpaid work experiences at the big publishing houses, returning at the end of each two-week stint with a pile of books and a huge smile on his face, motivated to make his dream a reality. It was inspiring seeing someone know exactly what they wanted and run after it. Inspiring but still not enough to push her into action.

"It's good," Oliver said, but his voice was pitched a little too high on the last word, discrediting him entirely. "I don't really want to talk about it."

"You sure?" she asked, undecided how hard to push.

"Yeah, it's fine." He sighed. "My love life on the other hand . . ." He let out a low whistle. "That is wretched. Every so often Charlie texts me—always on a weekend at like three A.M. mind—and I just wish he would fuck off. Can you find me a Magnus, please?" He smiled but she knew he didn't really find it funny.

"Do you reply to Charlie?"

"Sometimes, but I always feel dirty afterwards, like I'm doing myself a disservice."

Oliver's honesty was refreshing; he didn't sugarcoat things and often said what everyone else was thinking.

"It's whatever," he said quickly.

She knew not to prod too hard with him. Unlike her, Oliver didn't word-vomit his feelings but processed them internally in a possibly more healthy way.

He fished out a dark-wash denim that almost looked like a winner, until he realized it was dangerously low-rise. He sighed, throwing it on the top of the pile before asking, "How are you feeling about everything with Magnus now?"

She had of course told Oliver about her dad immediately after it happened, but hadn't really explained how she was feeling about Magnus and their relationship following the incident.

"In some ways I feel relieved that he knows everything. Well, not everything . . ." But did he ever need to know about her intentions when she first messaged him? People began relationships for stranger reasons every day, but now that things were irrevocably different between them, now that she really knew who he was, she couldn't help but feel guilty. "It's a bit weird between us now— I can't tell if I'm being paranoid but it feels like he's acting a bit colder towards me."

Oliver folded a pair of jeans over his arm and looked at her for a moment. "How so?"

They shuffled a little to the side, so other shoppers could access the table.

"I could be totally imagining it, but I don't know . . . he looks at me a little different, seems to think a lot more before he speaks. I guess that's inevitable after everything he's learnt about my family, but I'd hoped it wouldn't be the case. It kind of feels like he thinks I'm made of glass now, like I'm supersensitive."

"I don't want to tell you not to trust your instincts, but you *are* very paranoid a lot of the time." Oliver smiled before adding, "You're right though—if anything, it would be weirder if he acted like everything was perfectly fine. Like it was before. It shows he's trying, at least. You'll find your groove, trust me."

She gave him a faint smile back, not sure she believed his words, but not wanting to continue this conversation. This was her worst fear coming true: when she told people about her dad, about her often dysfunctional family, they would see her differently.

It was clear Oliver could feel her need to change the subject because he said, "If it makes you feel any better, I've resorted to putting on a posh accent in the office."

"Erm, what?"

He moved over to the stallholder, cash in hand. "Everyone is so bloody posh in publishing, it had to be done!"

She began to laugh and grabbed his arm. "Wait, Oliver, you can't be serious?"

"Honest to God—or should I say Allah?—I am. You would laugh in my face if you heard it. It's the only way, firstly for people to understand me, and secondly for me to be taken a bit more seriously. This is what graduate life is, Soraya, hiding your Brummie accent from posh white people in the workplace."

"Right, I need to hear it!"

"Yeah, I'm afraid that's happening never."

Chapter 35

SORAYA

London, 2014

It was a misconception, Soraya mused, that the baring of one's soul brought relief. In her case, sharing unraveled further issues, further destructive thoughts.

Despite knowing it was futile, she couldn't help but compare her relationship with Magnus to those of other couples on social media. On Instagram couples proclaimed their love for each other, with shots of their picturesque dates and selfies that showed them to be aesthetically pleasing couples.

Since the incident with her dad, Soraya and Magnus had not been on any outdoor dates, unless you counted popping to the supermarket. She could see this was getting to Magnus—the extrovert who loved nothing more than going to the pub—that and the fact that they still had not had sex fully. She didn't want him to grow to resent her; didn't want even to be thinking such thoughts herself.

Magnus's living room was cut in half by a wooden divider; on the other side of this was a bedroom. Tonight all his housemates were out, which was why Soraya had no qualms about sitting in their communal space. She always found conversations with them painfully awkward.

The room was furnished with items most likely found in the street, along with a large television. The sofa was covered in faded blue velvet and it sagged. But despite this, in some respects the room was cozier than her and Oliver's living room. It was more lived-in, with stacks of DVDs, and photos on the walls—of them on nights out, during rugby practice, and a picture of Magnus's bare bottom, with a middle finger obstructing the full view.

She got up to look at the pictures in more detail. Her eyes gravitated towards a picture of a few of them, indoors somewhere but clearly drunk, and her eyes scanned the group to find Magnus. And when she did her heart stopped momentarily. His gaze followed hers.

"Anyway, I didn't tell you about the editor I met, did I?" he said, trying to distract Soraya.

"Is that her?" she found herself saying, not aware the words were even coming out of her mouth. She wished she could put them back in, swallow them, digest them, and bring them out at a later date, or maybe never.

In the picture, Magnus held a blond girl close, his arm around her waist as she kissed his cheek. All that could really be gauged about the girl was that she was everything Soraya wasn't. Except she wasn't slim, she had large breasts, which seemed ridiculously perky, and her golden hair was styled into curls.

"Who?" he asked.

"It doesn't matter."

Silence.

Soraya sat back down on the sofa, picked up a slice of the pizza they had ordered from an independent restaurant nearby. Magnus had originally suggested they go out for dinner but she'd felt too uneasy, her palms perspiring at just the thought of it. Images of her dad finding out she was still seeing Magnus, him taking it out on her mum, flashed before her eyes. She'd already told Magnus how she felt about them going out, but either he forgot or he didn't understand the severity of her anxieties.

On the TV was a documentary about killer whales. Magnus looked like he was concentrating on it now. She wished she could be like him sometimes, worry less, see the world through different eyes.

She scrolled through Instagram, taking nothing in. Moments later, he sighed heavily and switched the television off.

"What are you annoyed about?"

"Nothing, it doesn't matter. What were you saying about the editor anyway?"

Another deep sigh from Magnus. She felt like sighing back. Surely she had more to sigh about?

"I totally forgot about that picture. I'll take it down." His voice was cold. He walked over to the wall, ripped the photograph of him and the blond girl away, crumpled it into a ball, and threw it on the floor.

"You didn't need to do that." Her hand tightened around her phone. She wondered why he wouldn't answer her original question. Why he wouldn't just say who the girl was. Was it because the girl in the picture wasn't Lucy? Was it someone else? How many had there been? They were just so different, Soraya couldn't help but compare herself to every other girl he had been with. She bet their parents didn't hit them when they found out they were dating him, she bet they didn't have issues with not wanting to be seen outside with him. She knew these comparisons were futile, but she couldn't stop herself.

Magnus returned to sit next to her, his expression glum. She ruined everything.

"Tell me about the editor then!" she said in an attempt at enthusiasm.

"I don't want to now."

Soraya leant into him, really looked at him. His face, usually so manly, looked childlike suddenly. And up this close she noticed the faint freckles scattered across his nose.

"I'm sorry," she said.

He leant back then grabbed her wrists with both his hands, before linking their hands together. "You've nothing to apologize about."

"You're in a bad mood because of me."

"I just want things to be like before," he said. "I guess that's a stupid thing to say." He said the last part quietly, almost to himself.

Something about these words stung. She couldn't quite place what it was. She knew he saw it on her face, the hurt.

"I want you to realize you've done nothing wrong. None of what happened was your fault. You're a good person."

She could feel her eyes watering then. He was saying this because he understood, because he had been in her position, and had blamed himself. She knew this, objectively. But she did not feel as if she was a good person. She was always letting people down, and now she was dragging Magnus down too. She had messed everything up.

"I don't know what to say," she mumbled.

He sighed, rubbing her held hand with his thumb. "I just want you to be happy."

She wanted that too, but it felt like a selfish wish. Shouldn't she want to make him happy? Wouldn't that mean giving him things she wasn't sure she could give him? Was there a middle ground?

"Let's just have a nice night," she said.

He looked like there was more he wanted to say, his mouth half open, but he snapped it shut, sat back in the sofa.

He nodded and nothing more was said on the matter.

Chapter 36

NEDA

Liverpool, 1978

The next weekend Neda stayed up until Hossein came back at 4:00 A.M. She had become a deep sleeper. The way he struggled with the key must not have registered with her before. When he finally entered the studio flat he lurched around for a moment or two and then, upon seeing Neda sitting on the bed with the lamp on, stopped short.

"Why are you up?" Hossein said. His voice was slurred, and that was when she knew.

She shut her eyes tight, wishing she hadn't done this, wishing she hadn't put herself in this situation.

"I couldn't sleep."

He began walking slowly towards her, his steps more deliberate and controlled since he knew he was being observed. Despite this, she could smell sweat and alcohol on him. The bad smell seemed to roll in waves towards her, mocking, taunting.

"I need to piss," he said, going into the bathroom. She could hear him urinating, and it went on for a long time. And then the shower. The hum of the old boiler and water trickling.

She bit her lip hard, not knowing how to dispel her anger.

When he finally came out, in just his boxers, his hair wet, he didn't meet her gaze.

"Why can't you sleep?" he asked, grabbing himself a mug of water.

"Why are you walking like that?" she said.

"Like what?" He took a long sip, wiping his mouth with the back of one hand as some of the water trickled down his chin.

There was a long silence.

"Like you're drunk," she finally said.

She had expected him to say many things, but he surprised her. He laughed a full-bodied, wholehearted laugh.

"Oh, so what?" he said.

Her heartbeat quickened. She had rehearsed this moment, and had a range of arguments memorized, but they all involved Hossein's denial of his wrongdoings.

"So?" she repeated, buying herself some much-needed time.

"I work hard, Neda." He sighed, no trace of a smile left on his face. He walked closer to her. "I had a drink, it's not the end of the world."

"Not the end of the world? You're meant to be a Muslim?"

"And is your baba not a Muslim? What about your uncle?"

She felt her body tighten. She focused her gaze on the mug he had drunk from. It had a small chip on the rim, which irritated her. She was sure he had done that, though he'd never have said anything.

"That's different."

"Why? Please explain why it's different."

"They're the older generation." She waved her hand dismissively. "I thought you were like me, that you believed in Allah, that you wanted to follow the rules—"

"It was one drink!" he exclaimed. The expression on his face was deceptive, it might have been one of mild exasperation. And if she hadn't looked in his trouser pockets, if she hadn't already had her suspicions, she would have let the argument go then. Added fondness for an occasional drink to his character traits.

"Why do you carry condoms with you?"

He was silent for a moment. "What are you talking about?"

"Just answer me!"

He walked over to his trousers and emptied the contents onto the kitchen table. He removed his wallet, loose change, and keys. "No condoms, see," he said. "Are you OK?" He looked at her like she was mentally unstable.

She slammed her fist against the table, surprising even herself.

"Not today, no. Maybe you've used the one I saw in there." She shook her head in disgust, recoiling from him. "But I saw one last week when I was washing your clothes."

He closed the distance between them, looked into her eyes, searching for something. "You're joking, right?" When she didn't reply, he made a noise deep in his throat. "Oh, come on! I love you, Neda, I love you so much. Of course I haven't been with anyone else. Fine, I had a couple of drinks, OK? With some men I know. And, no, I'm not gay, so don't accuse me of that." His attempt at humor failed miserably.

"You're lying."

Again, he took a step towards her, picked up her hand, grasped it in both of his like it was the most valuable object on earth.

"I swear on Allah, on my mother's life, Neda, I have never cheated on you."

"You still haven't explained the condoms. Why do you need them with you?"

The tops of his cheeks were pink. "Fine, I was speaking to friends and they said a particular brand was good . . . better for women . . . and I wanted us to try them. Samples were being given out." He walked over to their bedside table, pulled open the drawer, returning with a packet in his hand. "This was what you saw. But obviously, with our different schedules, we haven't actually had the opportunity to . . . you know." Despite being overly confident in most aspects of his life, he was suddenly shy, embarrassed even.

Now Neda was embarrassed. And speechless too.

She went to bed and he joined her.

"Why aren't you saying anything?" he asked.

"Let's just sleep," she said, turning away from him, pulling the covers tight around her body.

"You never want to talk. Sometimes you have to, even if it doesn't feel good," he said quietly.

She pretended she didn't hear him, and eventually heard his soft breathing lull into sleep.

The next day, when he had gone to work, last night's events not mentioned, Neda washed herself more slowly than normal, basking in the act. The water was a touch too cold, but she enjoyed the clearheaded feeling it gave her. She laid her prayer mat on the floor, put on her chador, and began praying. With each prostration she felt relief, as though she was exhaling all her worries. She prayed for Hossein. For all his family and her own. She thanked Allah for everything he had given her. She asked that Hossein be given the strength to do better, be better.

Prayer times were her favorite parts of the day; they were when she felt most connected to the world. And when she'd finished, she could continue her day with clarity, all her worries and fears gone.

For now, at least.

Weeks later, on the anniversary of Hossein's father's death, they went for a picnic in Sefton Park.

Laid on a blanket were sandwiches, crisps, and fruit. While Neda had anxiously set everything out, Hossein was quiet, not himself. The only reason Neda knew the significance of the date was that his mum had told hers, who then told Neda.

They'd found a spot under a tree, in the shade, slightly apart from the other groups of people, some smoking weed, some dressed in a way similar to the Beatles, all shaggy hair and round sunglasses. While Neda disapproved of drugs, she couldn't deny how everyone who took them seemed more relaxed, less hostile.

Hossein had let his mustache grow. He blended in well with the others; it was only Neda with her hijab who stood out.

A few days previously a group of teenagers had shouted "Go back home, you fucking Paki!" at her. If she had not been with Hossein she might have burst into tears, but his strength, and the fact that he outright told them where to go, prevented her. She had been so concerned about stopping a potential fight that she forgot about the insult.

Neda handed him a cheese sandwich and began biting into her own.

After a period of silence he said, "It's been three years since my baba died."

"I know. I'm so sorry, Hossein."

Another long silence.

Hossein gazed into the distance, she assumed reminiscing about the past. Was he thinking about the last time he spoke to his father? The last words they shared? Or was he picturing the good times they'd had together—or, alternatively, the bad ones, and realizing how on reflection he would rather have had them than this?

"At least Allah's looking after him now," Neda said, and then uttered a small prayer. Hossein repeated the same words under his breath. She noticed prayer beads in his hand, which he rolled between his fingers. When he saw her looking at them he stopped praying momentarily.

"These are my baba's," he explained. "Were my baba's. He would sit in the living room, sliding the beads around and around for hours."

Neda gave him a small smile. "What was he like?"

"Strong, quiet." Hossein shrugged. "This will be the first year I haven't visited his grave."

Neda felt guilty then, despite it not being her fault. She put her hand over Hossein's, caressed his palm. He gave a faint smile.

"I wish he could have met you," he said.

"I wish we could have met too. I wonder if he would have liked me."

"He would have loved you, Neda. I know that for sure. He was always the religious one in our house, always encouraged me to find a good Muslim wife." Hossein smiled at the memory. "And I found one. I found a woman who is decent and good . . ." He touched her face lightly with his fingertips. "A beautiful, sexy woman."

Neda was speechless. He had that effect on her.

"I'm sorry if I'm sometimes distant. I'm trying to get used to this new place. It's amazing, but so different . . . I hope you understand."

"I do, Hossein."

They continued eating for a while, the silence comfortable. Until he suddenly said, "Do you ever think about death?"

Her chewing slowed. "Of course," she said. "Why?"

"It scares me. When I think about it too much, I start not being able to breathe. I'm physically incapable, and then I think I'm having a heart attack." He shook his head as though just remembering would inflict the same pain on him. "That's why I sometimes drink." The tops of his ears were pink as he confessed. "Since moving here, I think about it more and more, and I want to forget. Being away from home makes you aware of how insignificant you are, in the grand scheme of things."

Neda clasped her hands together. She looked up at the leafy branches and the way the sunlight filtered through them, the sky beyond so blue.

"As long as you believe in Allah, it's OK, there's nothing to fear. Have faith and you will have no worries, azizam."

He opened his mouth as if to argue, then snapped it shut. "Of course, but it's the great unknown, isn't it?"

"It's not the unknown, not if you believe in Islam." She tried to make her words gentle, instead of a lecture. She wanted him to agree with her, reassure her that he did believe in Islam and Allah.

Hossein lay back on the grass, his hands behind his head.

"Yes, of course," he said.

Chapter 37

NEDA

Liverpool, 1982

"I'm not happy here," Hossein said one evening, sitting on the end of the bed, twisting his hands together.

Neda had been putting night cream on her face.

"What?"

"I'm not happy."

"In this flat?" she asked. She knew what he meant but was hoping her pretense of ignorance would make what he'd said go away.

He sighed deeply before responding.

"It was only meant to be for a year. A brief adventure, not our whole life."

She walked around the bed and stood in front of him. "We agreed that after my PhD—"

"Oh, come on, Neda, let's be real. You don't want to go back."

So much had happened since they'd left Iran.

How does one country endure such change in five years? The Shah had been overthrown suddenly three years before. When they heard the news, Hossein and Neda held a party, just the two of them, in their flat. They bought a variety of nuts and the largest, freshest fruit, excited for the future.

They imagined an Iran in which the gap between rich and poor was no longer so stark, in which Neda's family would struggle a little less. An Iran in which the possibilities were endless, rather than restricted to a select few. It was an unknown future, but one that promised to be better. Iranian people were finally being listened to; their demonstrations had made an impact.

However, the day after their celebration, questions were raised. Who would rule the country now? With the Shah exiled from Iran, what happened next? News from their country wasn't documented in great detail on British television; Neda, Hossein, and Mena were perpetually on edge, though their English life continued in the same way as before. It was an odd feeling, being away from home when everything there was changing. They heard that Ayatollah Khomeini had been invited back into the country and how eventually he became its leader, declaring Iran to be an Islamic republic. How there were now hijab police; that every morning the people of Iran stood outside and chanted "Allahu Akbar, Khomeini Rahbar" in harmony; that some of those who supported the Shah were taken away while others fled the country.

It physically hurt to be away from their families at such a time. That said, the place they once called home remained unchanged in their minds; so despite seeing it on the news and hearing from family all that was going on there, they couldn't fully envisage the new Iran that was being talked about. But that didn't mean Neda didn't want to return there.

"Why would you say that?" she asked.

"You have something here—prospects. All I'll ever be is a taxi driver or a shop worker. In England I'm nothing. I'm a loser."

She sat next to him, took both his hands in hers. "Hossein, you're not a loser."

He pulled away, stood up, and crossed the room to put distance between them.

"I don't want to limit you—you know that. But life here isn't good for me. What am I meant to do?"

"Wait. Wait for me to finish my PhD. There's only a year and a half left."

"Neda, I know. *I know.*"

Her heart skittered momentarily. He couldn't, she thought. But the way he looked at her, he seemed certain.

"Know what?"

"You're pregnant, aren't you?"

She said nothing, looked down at her wedding ring. Spun the gold band around her finger while she thought of something to say.

"Fucking answer me," her husband said through gritted teeth.

"I think so, yes."

He walked towards her, his face rigid. "Why didn't you tell me? Did you not think I needed to know? And you say we'll go back home. How? Now we've got a baby on the way and you want to finish your PhD. You're setting down roots here. It doesn't matter to you if I'm included in your plan, though, does it?"

Her head snapped up. "Hossein, don't be like this." She struggled to find the right words . "I didn't tell you because I didn't know how to. We didn't plan this. It's come at the worst time . . ."

"So, now you don't even want my baby."

"No! Hossein, no. Don't say that." She breathed unsteadily. "How did you find out?"

"For someone so clever, sometimes you can be dumb. You left the pregnancy test in the bin."

He didn't clean the flat, so she'd assumed he'd never look in the bins.

"You don't have to be unkind," she said.

"You know what, Neda jaan, I will be however I want to be." He punched the wall, making her jump. "We're fucking stuck here now. Even if we wanted to go back to Iran, everything there has changed too. Nothing's the same."

"So why are you angry at me?"

"I'm angry at everything."

This was the first red flag from Hossein that Neda ignored. Three years afterwards his habitual discontent would develop into something much worse, something that would change their lives completely.

Chapter 38

SORAYA

London, 2014

Soraya didn't want to be at this party. She and Magnus had to be low-key after all that had happened, and not be seen out together. But she knew she needed to try to get things back to normal. That and the fact that Magnus had insisted she come.

They held hands on the way there, an act that made Soraya exceptionally paranoid that someone would see them, so she kept her head down as they walked. But when they got to the front door of the house where the party was being held and he'd pressed the bell, Magnus put both his hands in his jacket pockets.

They were standing outside a slightly run-down semi, a family house until landlords realized how much young people would pay to live so close to the university. Some of its former smartness had worn off—the low brick wall that separated it from the street crumbling, the brown paintwork chipped in places.

A redheaded man opened the door. He wore a crested rugby hoodie like Magnus's.

"Mate," he said loudly, grasping Magnus's shoulder, before looking at Soraya, with an amused expression on his face. "This is her, then?"

She tried to smile but instead her mouth turned downwards.

"This is Tommy," Magnus said.

"I've heard all about you, Sarah," he said, peering at Soraya.

She looked behind her, already aware there was no one else there. "Sarah?"

Magnus shifted on his feet. "It's Soraya," he said to his friend. "He's drunk, ignore him," he whispered in her ear.

Tommy opened the door wider to let them in. As they entered Soraya began to lick her lips, hoping to remove the dark lipstick she wore. She suddenly felt the need to assimilate rather than stand out.

She could taste the testosterone in the house. Magnus's presence next to her felt different.

The party seemed to be made up of

1. Men who engaged in sporting activity.
2. Girls who were excited by men who engaged in sporting activity.

But what stood out the most to her was

3. Everyone was white.

With the passing of time Soraya had slowly become somewhat white-passing. This was partly because her skin had naturally lightened, and she made a conscious effort to remove her perceived excess body hair. Beyond that, though, now that white people were trying to make themselves look ethnic, by tanning, dying their hair darker, and drawing their eyebrows thicker, people saw Soraya, who naturally had these features, as similar to those white people. At school, however, this was not the case. Her every difference was noted then—something to be made fun of. She was often called a "hairy Paki." Now she experienced the same feeling of being on edge around her peers that she had then, and knew she didn't belong here.

A group of people crowded around Magnus, guys handing him beer and girls sidling up close to him. Soraya was left to one side, behind everyone, unsure what to do.

She started writing a long message to Oliver about the entire situation, partly to have something to do with her hands. After a few minutes of this, Magnus must have realized she wasn't standing next to him but was by the door on her phone.

"Soraya, what are you doing?" he said, laughing. The group had parted to let him through and they were all staring at her.

"Sorry, I was just replying to a message."

He placed one hand on the small of her back and began introducing her to the group as simply "Soraya."

The guys he introduced her to were loud, large, and confident. They looked her straight in the face for a long while, as though they couldn't understand what he was doing with her. And in that moment, she didn't understand either.

The evening mostly consisted of Magnus being swept away by some friend or other, and Soraya sitting alone watching men play beer pong, or else observing the technique of slim yet busty girls who flirted with the boys before slinking away with them somewhere.

She could always hear Magnus—his booming laugh echoed off the walls as he encouraged his friends to down drinks and made crass jokes.

When one girl said she wouldn't down a drink that contained a mixture of beer, vodka, and white wine, he said, "Go to the kitchen where you belong then!" The girl laughed, hit his shoulder, and downed it while maintaining eye contact with him.

Soraya had to leave the room at that point.

In the living room an entire wall was filled with magazine cutouts of naked women. Their round, large breasts caught her eye frequently, tauntingly. She remembered the Facebook picture of Magnus semi-naked in this house, against the lewd wall, and wondered yet again why he thought it was OK, or why anyone here thought a wall of glamour models was appropriate for a living room. The thought of the men actually cutting these pictures out of magazines and then collaging them on the wall was weird and sad.

She tried engaging in conversations with people, but while they were drunk or high on cocaine, she was sober and small talk often fizzled out. She wasn't in the mood to drink or take drugs.

So she sat alone on a sinking sofa, picking at her split ends.

The sofa suddenly sank considerably lower, which made her fall sideways into the person who had sat down. It was Tommy.

"Sarah," he said loudly, putting a hand on her shoulder. "What are you doing here alone?"

She wriggled out of his grasp. "It's Soraya."

He bit his lip theatrically. "Whoops," he said. "You having a good time?"

"Yeah, it's fine."

He put his hand on her shoulder again and whispered in her ear. "Come on, tell me, did it really happen?" When he spoke a speck of spit hit her cheek.

"What are you talking about?" she asked, ignoring his saliva on her face. She moved her head back.

"Have you guys, *you know*, shagged?" He shook his head, laughing. "I feel like I was cheated out of fifty quid. So, come on, is it true?"

Her mouth was wide open.

"What are you on about?"

"The lads put a bet on whether Magnus could, um . . ." He trailed off, belatedly realizing this news would not be welcome.

"Could what?"

He slapped her shoulder in what he clearly thought was a friendly gesture. She noticed his red eyes. He reminded her of Mr. Blobby in that moment. An absolute mess.

"It was a little challenge. Nothing derogatory, honestly. You must know Magnus is a top shagger and all that? Everyone knows. We just thought it was funny that he was struggling to do it with you." In trying to reassure her, he continued metaphorically jabbing her in the stomach.

Her jaw was tight from suppressing the urge to reply to this, and her forefinger busy working at a flake of skin on her thumb while her mind was reeling.

A girl approached them. Holding a can of beer, she crouched before them, a smile on her face.

"Tommy, are you scaring Soraya off?"

"No!" he said, at the same time as she said, "Yeah, he is."

"I'm Rosie, by the way." She had mermaid-like hair and her jeans were low-rise, exposing her navel. "I've heard all about you."

Soraya felt she was on display, like a monkey at a zoo.

"Right," she said. "Do you know about the bet too?"

Rosie's face colored and she looked confused. Tommy was silent.

"Magnus bet the 'lads' that he could sleep with me, it seems. So you didn't hear anything about that?" Soraya said to her.

Rosie looked from Soraya to Tommy, her pink lips set in a frozen smile.

"No. I mean, Magnus told me you're . . . *you know* . . . but I don't think he was involved in a bet."

She gave Soraya a sympathetic smile that irritated her. She disliked it when girls like Rosie acted as if they were looking out for other females; it always rang fake.

A thin blond girl ran into the room then, naked apart from pink boy shorts, and began running around, giggling drunkenly. Following her was a completely naked man, who was cupping his genitals with his hands. Everyone began cheering, Rosie included. Everyone but Soraya, it seemed.

"Go on, Lucy!" they called. *Magnus's Lucy?* The girl who was in love with him?

"What the fuck is going on?" Soraya muttered to herself.

When they left to streak in another room, it looked like Rosie was about to get up, so Soraya asked, "What did Magnus tell you then?"

"Well, that you're a *virgin*." She said the last word quietly, like she had just said Soraya was part of ISIS. If Rosie really had been looking out for a fellow woman, she wouldn't have said that in front of Tommy.

He let out a howl of triumph. "I *knew* he was fucking lying! Imagine, Magnus Evans, who's slept with fifty girls, is now going out with a virgin." He laughed.

Fifty girls.

"I'm not a virgin," said Soraya. It sounded feeble after what she'd just heard. *Fifty* . . .

Rosie put a hand on Soraya's wrist. She wanted to yank it away. "It's OK, it's not a bad thing."

"Don't you ever just want to fuck though?" Tommy asked.

Rosie rolled her eyes, and they began discussing whether it was wrong that Soraya was a virgin. But she couldn't hear them properly anymore.

She scrambled to her feet, adrenaline going into overtime.

Magnus sat on a wooden chair in the kitchen, talking to two other boys. Her jacket and bag were slung over the chairback. Without saying anything, she yanked her jacket away, causing him to jump slightly.

He turned, and when he saw it was Soraya standing there he laughed, as though it was all a joke.

And maybe it had been all along.

He knew she was a virgin. And he had only been seeing her as part of a bet. She'd been right about him all along.

"I'm going," she said to him through gritted teeth.

She had to push past bodies to get to the front door. Leaving this party would be her salvation. She could process what she'd just heard once she was outside, away from the music, the people, the feeling of Magnus's eyes on her retreating back.

Except, it wasn't that simple. His hand was on her arm, pulling her to him in the packed hallway.

"What's going on? What's happened?" he asked, his voice harsh with drunkenness.

She shoved him away, ignoring curious looks from those around them.

"Just get away from me. I know. I know about everything. You make me sick!"

His mouth hung open, eyes squinting as he struggled to comprehend her words. She didn't give him time to think of an excuse, or attempt to explain himself; instead she pried the front door open and slammed it behind her.

Once outside she was determined to keep walking and not stop until she was a safe distance away from the house.

It was dark, the streetlights illuminating only isolated spots, leaving some areas in shadow. Soraya set off at a quick pace, hugging herself to keep warm. She often walked alone late at night in South London, and although she probably shouldn't she usually felt safe. It wasn't fear of the unknown that made her walk quickly.

Ahead she could see the main road, the red buses passing, people walking.

For now, she refused to think about what Tommy had said. She wanted to consider his words properly when she was home.

And yet the pieces were finally slotting together. Why else would Magnus have been so eager, so willing to wait? He had even said he was falling in love with her. But was it all a game for him? And had she been stupid enough to fall for it, fall for him? They hadn't even gone all the way, which made her wonder if part of the bet was the other stuff they had done. That thought made her feel physically sick.

When she reached the main road, it was busy with people, a world away from where she had been moments ago, and she let out her breath. Her hands were shaking.

"Do you have twenty pence?" someone asked her as she passed a corner shop. She couldn't look at them or utter a word in reply but stared blankly ahead. "Are you OK, love?" the person continued. But she kept on walking, fingers playing with the keys in her pocket. She let them dig into her palm and pressed the metal harder and harder, until she snapped out of whatever spell she was under.

At the bus stop, the board said her bus would arrive in twenty-three minutes. She didn't want to walk, although it would take the same amount of time to catch the bus as it would to return on foot. She didn't have enough money in her bank account to justify getting an Uber. So, she sat on the bench, watching the cars go by.

A group of girls in the shelter were talking animatedly.

After a few minutes she felt a familiar presence next to her. Her heart quickened, her stomach turning unexpectedly hollow.

"You need to leave me alone." Despite the coldness of her tone she was shaking. She clasped her hands tight together.

"Soraya?" Magnus touched her hand and she snatched it away. Her breathing was unsteady. She refused to meet his eye.

"Just go away."

She could feel him looking at her.

On the other side of the road was a homeless man, wrapped in a blanket, asleep. By his side were chicken-shop boxes.

"I don't know what you think you heard—"

She snapped her head around then.

"What I *think* I heard? Your friend straight out told me you were only with me for a bet." Her raised voice quivered on the last word. "That all of this was so you could win fifty quid after sleeping with me. That's what messing with another person is worth to you—just fifty quid. You knew I hadn't been with anyone before, you knew it all along." She shook her head, rage coloring her senses. "I don't even know why you're standing here. You don't have to pretend to like me anymore. You can go back to your stupid fucking friends."

"Oh, come on, kiss and make up!" one drunk girl said to them. The others cackled at her interruption. Upon seeing Soraya's answering glare they laughed even harder. Tears prickled her eyes.

Magnus stood in front of Soraya, blocking the girls from view.

"I know it sounds bad—"

"Was *all* of this a game for you? To sleep with a virgin? To prove you could do it, oh, so effortlessly?"

"Obviously not—"

"*Even* when I told you about my dad, you didn't think you should stop? Or was it too funny to stop? Is that why you invited me to the party, so you could all laugh at me?"

"Soraya, it isn't like that." He closed his eyes momentarily, but then something in him changed. His jaw clenched and the streetlights cast a shadow over his face. It made him look different. "Who are you to talk?" he asked her then.

"What?"

"I know you were using me too," Magnus said quietly. "I read your diary."

Chapter 39

SORAYA

London, 2014

In that moment she wanted to die.

"And?" she said in a pathetic attempt to call his bluff. "What's that got to do with anything?"

"The night you told me about your dad, you left your diary under your pillow. When you were showering, I read what you wrote in there. About me being gross, how you only asked me out to get 'kissing practice.' That you're a virgin."

"What do you want me to say?" she challenged. "Apologize for using you, when you were using me too? And you know what? I was right about one thing: you are gross." She wasn't sure how she managed to keep her voice so level.

Magnus ran his fingers through his hair, pulled at a strand.

"I wasn't using you! I wasn't even involved in the bet. I told them I didn't want to be a part of it. I admit, I did tell the guys we had sex just to get them off my back when I realized how much I liked you, that this could be something real. I wanted them to stop talking about the fucking bet, that's all. I know it all sounds worse than it was, it was just lads talking—"

"And yet that girl knew I was a virgin, so you had been telling people. Was she another one you were with whilst you were with me? One of the fifty. *Fifty*. Jesus Christ."

She saw his jaw tighten. "No, of course not. Rosie's one of my best friends. I just told her about what I read. I wasn't sure what to do. I didn't know if you really liked me or if all this was a game to you."

His excuses sounded as hollow as she now felt.

What was the point of defending herself when he too had lied to her—used her in a much worse way? Wasn't all this proof of how dysfunctional their relationship was? She always knew it would have to end, and perhaps on some level she had also known his affection for her was never real. Her family, it seemed, had been right all along. He had been after nothing but sex. All to win fifty pounds and bragging rights.

"Stop! I don't care. We don't need to hash any of this out."

He nodded in acknowledgment. "So this really was all about practice for you?" he said.

She tried to think of what she'd written in her diary. She hadn't mentioned her changing feelings for him, she didn't think. At least she would be saved that embarrassment.

His attitude towards sex was worlds away from hers. *Fifty*. The number was colossal. Unimaginable to her. How many other such bets had he made about other girls? Was Soraya merely one of many?

"Yes," she said. "It was."

"Fair enough," he said slowly. "I guess this is it then."

The words winded her. It didn't matter then that it was inevitable; those simple words of acceptance still had the power to wound her.

"I guess so." She began to walk away.

"This is what I mean," she heard him say.

Soraya whipped her head around. "What?"

"You can't face up to things. I don't believe you. I know you like me. I know this was more than just 'practice.' But you bottle up *everything*. I mean, you didn't tell me about your dad, that you were a virgin—plus there's all this stuff about someone called Laleh! Who even is she? We would never have been able to work because I don't know who the fuck you are."

"Oh, fuck you. You had a really good read of my diary then? Who even does that anyway? And maybe I didn't tell you everything because I knew you'd never understand!"

"What, because I'm white?"

She sighed with frustration. "Yes, because you're white! Because you're the kind of guy who sees an Asian girl you think looks *exotic*, and then decides, *You know what? I'm going to try and sleep with her.* For sport. For a laugh. How could you *ever* understand why I needed practice with guys, why I'm a virgin, why my sister was disowned, what it could possibly be like to grow up in my family!" She paused for breath and added, "*You* could never understand."

Magnus grabbed her arm.

"Soraya," he said.

She shook him off, shoved his chest so that he stumbled away from her. "No. Whatever this was, it's over. It's done."

The girls at the bus stop started making excited noises.

"Oh, shut the fuck up!" Soraya shouted at them, before leaving.

This time he didn't follow her.

Chapter 40

NEDA

Liverpool, 1986

"Baba kojas?"

Four-year-old Laleh pulled at her mum's thin cotton trousers while she asked where her dad was.

Neda looked down at her small daughter. Her own back was aching, the weight of the two babies growing inside her taking its toll. And yet when she looked into her child's large brown eyes, needy and loving, she couldn't help but lift her up and place her on her knee.

She combed Laleh's silky hair. "I don't know." Neda couldn't keep the worry out of her voice. She had no one to talk to. She could hardly trust her peers with her troubles, and didn't want to say anything to Mena lest her friend dislike Hossein even more. Despite her never voicing it, Mena's opinion of him was clear. Besides, Maman had always taught Neda to keep family matters private.

Mena had finished her PhD quicker than Neda, as she didn't have multiple pregnancies to contend with, and had moved to London the year before. It was only with her departure that Neda realized how lonely England could be.

Life with Hossein had its peaks and troughs, and right now they were in a trough.

She already had enough to worry about with the news from her family back home. Every day Neda feared a family member would be lost to the Iraq bombings. Sometimes she would ring and ring and receive no answer for days, and then would find out they were hiding in a basement, waiting out Saddam's attacks. Accounts of bombings over three thousand miles away shook her to the core. She wanted desperately to return but her family had encouraged her to wait it out, to take the opportunities given to her, not waste them. Wait until things had calmed down. But by now it had been eight years.

"You wouldn't like it here at the moment," her baba had said.

"Yes, she would! We're all wearing hijabs now, she'd *love* it!" she'd heard Rabeh say. Baba had shushed her.

"We're proud of you in England, azizam, just stick at it. So many people would kill to be in your position, remember that," he'd said.

One of her younger brothers, Ali, the most liberal of them all, had come to Liverpool to study two years ago. He told her everyone who could was leaving Iran. It was a comfort to have him in the same city, even though they weren't particularly close.

So, Neda held in her troubles and doubts. She often suspected her marriage had been a mistake but reminded herself frequently that Iranian marriages were different from English ones—and how quickly she was forgetting her roots! They weren't about true love or passion, but about companionship, having a partner in life. And didn't all relationships have issues to overcome?

What if your partner was cheating, though, as she now suspected Hossein was? That was recognized as grounds for divorce; if she had evidence, the courts in Iran would allow them to separate. But what would people say? That it was her fault for making them go to England, for not listening when he said he wasn't happy, for not being enough for him?

"Boys are stupid, Laleh azizam, remember that," she told her daughter.

"Why?" Laleh's inquisitive eyes grew larger.

"They cheat and lie," Neda muttered. Laleh looked at her strangely as if she understood this information. It brought Neda a wave of shame, that her four-year-old daughter understood the reality of marriage. But shouldn't she know early? And Neda was lonely, who else could she tell?

"You'll grow up to be strong, won't you?"

"I want to be like Popeye!"

Neda stroked her daughter's hair once more.

"Can we go to the park?" Laleh exclaimed, jumping off her mum's lap. Her little legs looked strong as a frog's as she hopped up and down, determined to get her way. Neda couldn't blame her for being bored in their shabby flat.

Once Neda got a teaching job at the university, which she did alongside her own studies, they'd moved to a larger place, but they still had an assortment of mismatched furniture. Hossein had saved for a year to buy a bigger television, which he was proud to own. The Persian rug they'd brought with them eight years ago was in the living room. It was important to Neda, something to remind her of her roots.

The walls were bare, with mold growing high up in one of the rooms. Neda frequently scrubbed it off, but it always came back. Often she heard the neighbors on one side, either arguing or having loud intercourse.

"Mummy's feeling tired," she said, with a deep sigh.

"Pleaaaaase?" Laleh gave her sad eyes. She was so expressive, so honest with her emotions; it was admirable.

Neda heaved herself off the sofa. "OK, but we can't stay out too late, my back hurts." She put a cardigan on and folded her silk scarf down the middle before wrapping it loosely around her head. Towards the end of her pregnancy she didn't mind letting some of her hair show; she lacked the energy required to keep fixing it.

She held Laleh's hand as they left the house. "Maybe your uncle will be in—" Neda barely had a chance to finish her sentence before Laleh struggled out of her mother's grasp and ran down the path, five doors away, to Ali's house.

Laleh banged on the door. Getting no response, she peered through the letter box. "Uncle Ali! I know you're in there!"

Neda struggled to catch up with her. "Laleh! Stop shouting!" she shouted, ironically. "If he isn't answering, he isn't in. Maybe he's at class. Come on, come on, let's go."

As they walked away, Neda looked back at her brother's flat and saw a curtain twitch. Perhaps her daughter wasn't speaking out of turn. But she knew how much her brother loved Laleh, and if he wasn't answering the door to her it was probably because he *couldn't* answer. Meaning he had a girl over. Neda shook her head. It seemed everyone came to England to transgress. All she had come for was a new learning opportunity.

The park they frequented was a short walk from their flat. As soon as they passed through the gate Laleh ran off and amused herself. Neda made sure to watch over her from a nearby bench. She knew it was safe here but had heard stories of strangers in parks. Despite this, she shut her eyes for a few seconds, to let the pain behind her lids settle.

"Neda?" a voice said. She opened her eyes and instantly focused them on Laleh. She was sitting cross-legged in a sandpit, determinedly creating a mound. Then Neda looked at the woman in front of her. Suddenly she felt too hot, and wished she was at home and could run herself a cool bath. The sun seemed to have settled directly above her head and was beating down on her navy blue hijab.

"Look at you! How many months along are you now?" Simran asked, perching on the bench next to her.

Neda knew the other woman from their local mosque, though she wasn't a friend Neda would have chosen for herself. Simran was a busybody who made Neda miss Mena even more.

"Eight, alhamdulillah. How are you? Your husband and children are well?"

Simran bent forward, staring into Neda's eyes. She often did this, as though rooting deep into Neda's soul and extracting incriminating evidence that she would eventually share. Her long black hair was tied up in a thick plait down her back. Even looking at it made Neda feel hot; she could imagine the clinging weight of it and scratched her own neck in response.

When Neda had reached seven months pregnant with the twins, in a fit of despair at the discomfort, she'd had her hair cut into a bob. Hossein had barely noticed.

"They're well, sister, thank you." Simran gave her another pointed look. "There is something I need to talk to you about."

Neda focused her gaze on Simran's hands and the henna pattern there. She remembered she'd once queued to have henna put on her hand by Simran at a henna party. She had shown Hossein afterwards and all he'd said, while laughing at her, was "Why do you have *shit* on your hand?"

She had ignored him for the rest of the evening while he insisted he was "only joking."

"Sister, are you listening to me?"

"What?"

Simran took a deep breath, grasped Neda's hands between her own. "Sister, people have seen Hossein hanging around with an Englishwoman. They saw him going into her house last night. Did he come home?"

It was like a sharp punch to Neda's stomach. She needed to leave.

Simran wore a look of grim satisfaction, as though now the heavy burden had been lifted off her shoulders and placed onto Neda's, she could rest easy.

"Sorry, sister, I feel a bit light-headed. I think it's the sun. I'm going home," Neda said.

Simran's expression dropped. What did she expect, Neda thought, that they would discuss her husband's indiscretions together? That wasn't how it was done. Not to Neda's way of thinking. Secrets should be kept within the family, always.

She got up with slight difficulty, gripping the back of the bench for support. Simran held her hand out to help, her face now pinched in something almost like sympathy. Neda was too embarrassed to take it. Embarrassed about everything. About her entire existence. Every imperfection became heightened; her mind had a way of pushing her even lower into the pits of despair. She was conscious of the way her stomach ballooned outwards, how swollen and fat her feet were, of the hairs she was too tired to shave from her fingers. Was it any wonder he strayed?

And now everyone knew about her husband's transgressions. He was supposed to be a Muslim man, her *good* man, and now everyone was talking about them, no doubt laughing at her stupidity for marrying a man with no morals. Every time she thought of them—the people in the mosque, his fellow takeaway workers, even her university peers—gossiping about her, she felt a pain in her chest. She tried not to think about it. She couldn't in front of Simran. She would not break down in front of anyone, fuel further gossip.

After many years, Neda finally understood why gossiping was haram.

"Neda?" Simran called after her.

"I'm fine, Simran," she called back. "Laleh!" Her child looked up, no doubt about to protest. "Now." The little girl trudged slowly towards her mother.

Neda grabbed her wrist and turned to wave goodbye to Simran. "Talk soon, sister."

"Neda, are you sure you're OK?" Perhaps she truly was trying to help. But better Simran had kept quiet than make Neda so painfully aware how badly she was failing in her marriage and in life.

"I'm fine, honestly. Say hello to your husband from me." Neda gave a forced smile and turned her head away before a tear ran down her face. She walked away as fast as she could. Laleh had to run to keep up, little legs struggling to match her mother's long strides.

"Mummyyyy, stoooop!" Laleh moaned.

Neda looked down at her daughter's pink, perspiring face, and slowed.

"Why are you crying?" Laleh said. This wasn't the first time she had seen her mum cry, and it wouldn't be the last.

"Your dad is a bastard." Although Neda said it quietly she knew she shouldn't have said it at all. Knew she was being a bad mother. That thought dipped her deeper into sadness. "Do you want some ice cream?"

Laleh looked up at her mum, pleased, but didn't reply.

"Is that a yes?" Neda pressed.

"Why is Daddy a bastard? What's a bastard?"

Neda's cheeks colored. "I didn't say that, azizam, come on." She tugged Laleh's hand to make her walk a bit faster. They stopped off at the corner shop on the way home and Neda allowed Laleh to buy any ice cream she wanted. When they were home she gave the child her coloring books and pens, which busied her nicely.

Then Neda went into the kitchen, opened the cutlery drawer, and emptied its contents into the sink. She filled this with bleach and hot, soapy water. After that she started on the plates. While they were soaking, she rested her back against the doorframe, breathing deeply. She wanted desperately to sweep the whole place and mop the floors. Instead Neda went to their bedroom, stripped the bedding, and put the sheets and pillowcases in the bathtub. She filled it with hot water and laundry detergent. Everything was left to soak, but a voice was still nagging at the back of her mind. There were other people in her household. The women Hossein had been with, *was with currently*, taunted her. They were in the sheets, in the cutlery her lips touched. She wanted to scream. If Laleh hadn't been there she *would* have screamed, without restraint.

She settled for walking to her bedroom, opening the chest of drawers, and removing a pastel pink cashmere jumper. It was her mother's; Neda had taken it as a souvenir of home. She inhaled the warm scent, bringing back memories of her busy, loving home. She buried her face in the soft fabric and let out a muffled scream.

She struggled to stop.

Then, in a moment of potential insanity, she and Laleh were in the car. It happened in a blink and Neda knew she was driving herself further into madness, but she couldn't stop.

Getting behind the steering wheel was difficult for her. The car was ridiculously cramped but she pushed the driver's seat back and proceeded in her pursuit. Her back was in pain; everything hurt. As she struggled she knew passersby were judging her. They openly stared, and when she met their eyes they didn't look away. She was a foreigner, and so she would be looked at. It wasn't anything new.

"Where are we going?" Laleh asked.

"To collect Baba."

"Where is he?"

"I don't know."

"So how will you find him?"

Neda stalled the car. They were still outside their flat. She tightened her grip on the steering wheel. It was too thin, too flimsy. She felt like a clown in a toy car.

"Stop asking questions," she hissed. She accelerated as she drove off, the tires screeching.

She drove, and drove, and drove. It was aimless, really. One port of call was the takeaway restaurant owned by Ziryan, a Kurdish friend of Hossein's. It was a place where her husband liked to loiter.

As Neda waddled into the shop, rubbing her back with one hand, Ziryan looked displeased to see her.

"Salam," he said.

"Salam. Have you seen Hossein?"

"No." He was cutting up a kebab behind the counter before putting the strips of meat inside pita bread. His bluntness didn't surprise her; he never gave her much time, presumably because as a married woman she was not deemed worthy of his notice. He preferred to deliberate over which of his blond cashiers he most wanted to fuck.

"When did you last see him?"

"He's *your* husband, why don't you know where he is?" asked Ziryan, still not looking up at her. He was too busy squeezing mayonnaise over the salad.

A sharp pain in Neda's abdomen jolted her. She gritted her teeth; she didn't have time for this.

She looked at his face, searching for answers. His dark goatee, something she hadn't really noticed before, now irritated her. The sight of the facial hair above his lip made her want to put all the equipment in the takeaway into the sink with bleach on it too. It shouldn't be allowed, she thought with disgust, having facial hair when you worked in a kitchen. She looked at his hands and saw him add lettuce to another wrap with his bare fingers. She wasn't sure if it was men in general who revolted her, but decided she couldn't look at him or his hands anymore.

Laleh was getting restless next to her, attempting to sit down on the floor despite Neda's strong grip on her arm. As the pain in her stomach came and went she tightened her hold, until Laleh moaned, wriggling away. "Sorry, azizam," Neda muttered, letting go.

Ziryan only then seemed to notice Laleh was with her. He flashed the child a grin. "Do you want a lollipop?" Laleh perked up. He grabbed a box from under the counter. "Which flavor do you want?"

"Strawberry!"

"Laleh, what else do you say?"

"Please. Thank you!" She snatched the lollipop from the box, as though a one-second delay would deprive her of it.

"Do you know where Hossein could be?" Neda asked. She breathed heavily, silently praying that whatever was going on in her body, be it wind, the babies moving, or even contractions, would soon pass.

He looked at her then. His eyes were cold. "No, sister. He's probably at home now, waiting for you and wondering where his dinner is."

Neda walked back to the car, aware the man was lying to her but also aware there was nothing she could do about it. She couldn't force him to tell her the truth. His loyalty lay with Hossein.

In this foreign country, who did she have on her side?

Chapter 41

NEDA

Liverpool, 1986

Neda's waters broke just as the *Coronation Street* theme tune came on. She had begun watching it to understand the colloquialisms of the English language better, but continued for the drama each episode promised. She felt the water soak through her trousers and into their sofa. She almost laughed. *Now,* she thought, *when my husband is missing and I've finally been given evidence that he's cheating on me. Now! When he's probably in bed with* her.

She called Ali, and he answered on the fourth ring.

Her second labor was both easier and harder than her first. Parvin seemed to pop out, quite suddenly, with one big push.

She came out so quickly that the midwife almost didn't catch her.

Amir was a struggle. Neda was so spent from giving birth to her second daughter that she didn't think it possible to pass another life through her body.

"Khar . . . come out," she said between gritted teeth. Her face was wet with tears. If Hossein had been there, she would have grabbed his hand. But he wasn't, so she balled her hands into fists instead.

"Come on, one big push," the midwife said from between her legs.

Neda thought about how much she'd like to push Hossein off the riverside and watch him drown, before giving that one last push.

Her palms were bloodied by the time Amir came out.

And then in turn Neda was given her babies to hold. She had somehow become a single mum of three children within the space of a day.

Later, her brother Ali arrived with Laleh in tow. Ali's skin was pale; under the hospital lighting it looked almost sickly. He was often mistaken for an Englishman. Anyone else from Neda's family would have been elated by that, but since he'd moved to England it only angered him. Despite enjoying aspects of the Western lifestyle, such as being free to have relations with numerous English girls, he prized his Iranian roots.

Laleh stood behind his leg, looking shyly at her mum in the hospital bed. After Ali saw the new babies, gave the appropriate coos, and all the pleasantries were out of the way, he looked at Neda. It was a long, hard look. He had bright blue eyes that bored into hers. Another feature that most Iranians coveted, but he resented.

"What?" Neda hissed.

"Where's Hossein?"

"I don't know."

"You don't know where your husband is?"

"I'm tired." Neda sighed deeply. She hurt all over. All she wanted was to go home to her own bed and sleep. Here the artificial light shining down on her was too bright, her bed too hard, and there was a draft coming from the air-conditioning that made her skin prickle.

Ali hissed. But he didn't raise his voice, didn't make a scene, too mindful of Laleh over in the visitor's seat with her Barbie. She was plaiting her doll's long blond hair and talking quietly to herself.

He bent low over his sister, hands on his narrow hips, willing Neda to snap out of her mood. "Sister, what's going on?"

"Ali, I'm *tired*. Do you understand? I just gave birth—"

"Yes," he talked over her. "And your husband should be here. He should have been here for you then. But you don't even know where he is. Is he OK?"

Neda laughed humorlessly and, in the process, wet herself a little. "He's fine, don't worry about *him*."

"Neda, what does that mean? You're not making sense."

"I don't want to talk about it."

"Eh?"

"Please take Laleh home. I need to rest."

"Sister . . ."

"*Brother,* he's with another woman and I don't know *where.* I don't know if he plans on coming back. I know *nothing.*" Her insides clenched; she felt ever more aware of her battered physical state. Her breathing was ragged and she felt light-headed. This must have become obvious even to Ali because he handed her the small carton of apple juice he'd brought with him. He knew it was her favorite; it reminded her of the fresh apple juice Maman used to make.

Her eyes burnt, memories of home threatening to resurface, and she couldn't reminisce about the past, not right now. Slowly, she sipped the drink through the narrow straw.

"OK. We need to find him," Ali said.

"Thanks for your input, Einstein. I just told you, I don't know where the bastard is."

"He's your *husband,* Neda."

"And? He's fucking other women."

"Sister, don't talk like that." He shook his head, as though he were virginal himself.

"He is! Everyone seems to know." Neda's voice hitched on the last word, a sob caught in her throat. She sipped the juice and concentrated her gaze on the foot of her bed.

"I need to have a word with him." Even without looking at him Neda could imagine what her brother was doing, clenching his fists. She almost wanted to laugh. Almost.

"I'm stuck."

Her insides felt empty, disconnected. Ali looked frightened, toes tapping anxiously against the floor.

"Mummy," Laleh said from the visitor's chair. "Doesn't Daddy want to see"—she paused—"Parvin"—another pause—"and . . . and . . ."

"Amir," Ali finished for her.

"Amir," Laleh said slowly, testing the name out loud.

Neda sighed. "No, I don't think he does."

Ali paled, mouth agape at his sister's truthfulness.

"Why?" Laleh asked.

Again, Ali looked from his niece to his sister, wondering if this was a normal exchange for them. Neda knew what he was thinking. He thought she was a bad mother. Even she thought she was a bad mother. How could she care for three children alone? She hadn't signed up for this. They were meant to be a family, a team. Not like this. She had thought the children would bond them, not push them further apart. She pinched her hand with her nails, to stop herself from sobbing.

"Your mum is being silly," Ali said, his gaze on Neda. "Of course your dad wants to see your brother and sister. He's just busy at work."

"When will he be back?"

Ali's mouth was forming a reply when Laleh interrupted him, crying: "Daddy!"

Neda's head whipped around to face the door. Hossein walked into the room with a grin on his face and a large bouquet of flowers in one hand. Laleh ran over to him and he lifted her up with the other arm, playfully throwing her over his shoulder and spinning her around. Her giggles filled the silence.

When he put her down, he messed up her hair and gave her the bouquet. "Go give these to Mummy," he stage-whispered in her ear.

Laleh complied and Neda gave her a tight-lipped smile as she took the flowers. She noticed the price had been left on.

All she wanted was to be left alone.

"Everything went OK?" Hossein asked, walking over to the bed. Tension filled the air, threatening to stifle everyone.

Ali and Hossein stood next to each other. Hossein seemed to tower over the younger man and in that moment Neda felt sorry for her brother. He looked weak in comparison to Hossein. But what he lacked in physique he made up for in youth. At nineteen years old he couldn't yet know enough about the world. Or perhaps he knew more than she gave him credit for—about the new Iran, dif-

ferent from the home she had left, and the way it had adapted to
suit men better than it suited women.

"Where were you?" Ali hissed at Hossein.

"At work," he replied, his face reddening.

"Don't lie, we know about you and the *whore*." All of their
conversations were in Farsi, meaning the hospital staff had no
idea what was being said. Had they known, perhaps they would
have asked the two men to leave, to give Neda the space she
needed.

"What did you say?" Hossein was in Ali's face now. Neda could
feel herself shaking. She looked over to Laleh and her heart broke
further.

"Stop it," Neda said quietly. But she was ignored. She wondered
why she was so quiet. Did she want what happened next? Perhaps
not consciously, but subconsciously it was entirely possible.

"You're embarrassing my family, laughing at us. She's my sister, have some respect. She just gave birth to two of your children.
She's too good for you. You're a loser, Hossein, a fucking loser!"

"Respect? You need to show *me* some respect." And then Hossein's fist connected with Ali's nose. Blood came pouring out, drip-
ping onto the floor and soaking Ali's T-shirt. He held his nose while
drawing back his other hand in a fist and punching the side of Hossein's face. He was so quick, he caught his brother-in-law by surprise. Then they seemed to jump onto each other, with no regard
for where they were or who would see. They were like wild cats
scrapping, the kind Neda had often seen in their garden in Tehran
while she was growing up, and she hated it. It was something she
didn't want to see: their hands held in front of them, flailing and
scrabbling to land a further pathetic blow.

"Stop! Stop! Stop!" she yelled, to no avail. She threw her empty
apple juice carton at them, but they took no notice.

She heard a tearing sound, saw Hossein had ripped Ali's
T-shirt, which caused her brother to knee him in the balls in retali-
ation. Hossein yelled out in pain, louder than Neda had when she
had given birth to not one but two babies.

Laleh watched from the corner of the room, her Barbie doll

clutched in one hand. Her expression was blank, though she backed away as far as she could from everyone.

A nurse came in, saw the scene in front of her, and called for help.

"Excuse me," she said sternly to Hossein and Ali. "Stop this right now."

Neda's midwife entered together with a male nurse. Hossein and Ali finally stopped fighting and stood up straight, as though they had done nothing. Their appearance betrayed them, their ripped, bloodied clothing an embarrassment.

Neda sank deeper into her bed at the sight.

The male nurse stood between them and called over to her, "Which one is the father?"

Something about the look on his face gave her the impression he thought they were fighting because they were both potential fathers, like this was a soap opera, not real life.

She pointed a shaky finger towards Hossein.

The nurse put his hand on Ali's shoulder. "OK, mate, I'm going to have to ask you to leave. Immediate family only."

"I'm her brother!"

"She needs her rest, love," the other nurse said.

Hossein smirked, let out a small laugh.

"You laugh at me?" Ali said, trying to step around the nurse.

"Ali, please," Neda said, quietly. He glanced at her then, a look of mingled hurt and understanding on his face.

"Fine, I will call you later."

He was escorted out.

The atmosphere inside the room was tense, with the remaining nurse and midwife talking between themselves and Hossein trying to catch Neda's eye.

"Are you OK?" the midwife asked her.

"Yes, thank you. I'd like to be alone, if possible, to get some rest." She gazed into the midwife's blue eyes, hoping she'd understand.

"Of course." She turned to Hossein. "Dad, Mum needs her rest, so unfortunately visiting time is over."

"Oh," Hossein said. "I barely got to see them—"

"I know, I'm sorry, but with it being a double birth, Mum is very tired."

Hossein grumbled something in response and began to move towards Laleh. Neda's heart broke for her daughter. She wished she could have covered her child's eyes, stopped her from seeing what a mess her family was.

"Laleh can stay," Neda said quickly. "I want her here with me."

Hossein surprised her by nodding before leaving the room, head bowed. She got the distinct impression this was all for show, for the nurse and midwife, so he didn't seem like the guilty party but Ali did. She knew Hossein well enough to understand he was an excellent actor when he wanted to be.

When her dad had left, Laleh went to her mum. Neda helped her up onto the bed and cuddled her.

"Are you sure you're OK?" the nurse asked. The midwife stood next to her with a look of concern etched across her face.

"Yes, thank you. They're not normally like that," Neda lied.

The nurse pursed her thin lips, looking at her for a moment before saying slowly, "There are services, you know, that can help women in your position."

Neda could feel her own expression harden. "I'm not in need of help."

The nurse nodded and both women left in silence.

"I'm scared," Laleh said, distracting Neda from her worries, her problems. She had a child—and now children—she needed to put before herself.

"It's OK," she whispered into Laleh's hair. "It's OK. It's OK." She repeated the words over and over, trying to convince herself, until they both fell asleep.

In Neda's dreams she was a little girl again, in her family's back garden in just her underwear, joyful as she played tag with her siblings. She heaved with laughter, from deep within her belly. Worry wasn't a word in her vocabulary; she hadn't yet experienced it.

She dreamt of a country long gone, and a time long past.

And she willed herself never to wake up.

Chapter 42

SORAYA

At twenty-one years old Soraya experienced heartbreak for the first time. All the music she had listened to forlornly while getting over a crush she had never even spoken to seemed crucially relevant now. There were many stages to her grief.

Denial came first. She went back to her flat, dry-eyed, found Oliver in the living room in his pajamas reading a fashion magazine. It was only midnight, but it felt so much later. She asked him about his day and made them both cups of tea.

"Magnus and I broke up, by the way," she said casually, between sips of overly milky Yorkshire Tea. Her hands had been curiously shaky when she poured it out. She made a mental note to buy a new kind of tea the next day, to remove any reminders of him.

Oliver had the cup raised to his lips. He held it there, squinting at her. "Huh?"

"Yeah, we broke up." Something about saying the words out loud brought their meaning home to her, but she shrugged this off.

Oliver put his cup down. "You seem very casual about it all."

His intent gaze, forcing her to meet it, produced tears. She'd always been a crier.

"He . . ." She didn't know what to say. Didn't know how to explain all that had happened.

Oliver got up without saying anything and returned moments later with a toilet paper roll, which he handed to her wordlessly. She blew her nose, wiped her eyes, and looked down at the tissue to find it covered in black stains. Her mascara had run, creating theatrical lines down the sides of her face.

"God, I look a mess. This is embarrassing," she said.

"I've seen worse. I don't really understand. I thought you were good now?"

She explained what had happened. Oliver gasped in all the right places, looking more offended than she was.

Coincidentally, "Independent Women" came over the speakers then, which caused Soraya to sob pathetically, "I don't want to be an independent woman," while not quite meaning it.

Oliver just looked at her for a moment. "You've always been independent, but I agree, perhaps now isn't the time for this." He pressed pause on his phone. They were left in silence. She wasn't sure which was worse.

"He's an absolute piece of shit," Oliver said, shaking his head. "It's a good job you were only using him. Imagine how you'd feel if it had all been real."

Oliver knew she had come to really like Magnus, and it was touching, really, how he was now pretending the joke had really been on Magnus. She just wished she could pretend too.

She mumbled something like "I guess."

"And you were the one to break up with him. You didn't give him power in the end."

She was too deflated to think of a good response to this. She nodded, said nothing. She didn't want to mention the other stuff. She was scared that if she told Oliver about Magnus's criticisms of her, he would agree with them. Or, worse, hearing them spoken aloud would make Oliver realize how annoying she really was, and then maybe he wouldn't want to be her friend anymore—because did she truly deserve a friend like him? She doubted it.

And at this point he was all she had left.

Soraya didn't eat ice cream or watch romantic comedies. She didn't rush out and get a new haircut. She was still, solitary. Her room became a fortress of misery that she couldn't quite leave. She called in sick and didn't return to work for a week, feigning norovirus.

During her week indoors, most of which was spent entirely alone, she remained in bed. Oliver's internship was made into a permanent position, and while she was pleased for him, this new development was in painful contrast to her own crumbling life.

Eating held no appeal whatsoever. It was shocking, really. She had spent most of her life attempting various diets, and now, despite having nothing to do but eat, food was abhorrent to her. It was as though by eating she'd be accepting the reality of the situation, resuming normal life, and she couldn't do that. And when she tried to eat, due to her stomach growling angrily, she chewed and tasted nothing. Her jaw hurt, swallowing was painful.

Towards the end of the week the reality of her situation hit home. She hadn't eaten in twenty-five hours. An accidental fast.

Every time she tried to read she would zone out, and her attempts to draw were shoddy. All the things she once loved were now tainted.

In bed, light streaming in from the sides of her curtains, the air outside her duvet ice-cold, she remembered the good times.

The way Magnus's stubble scratched her face when he kissed her. How he always held her face, like she was dear to him. How often he said she was perfect, so much so that she had begun to believe it.

It was funny, she thought, how he'd made her feel she was enough for him, when all along it had been a lie.

Chapter 43

SORAYA

London, 2014

Soraya zoned out. Only partly from the drugs.

It was at moments such as these that she began to understand her dad's addiction. Not that she was addicted, she knew that, but she recognized the great appeal of forgetting yourself—or rather accepting yourself. While intoxicated she became more open and people talked to her.

In the past few months, she'd rekindled friendships with people from university whose personalities revolved around their love of techno music and recreational drugs. They were not quite clean and very thin as a result of the comedowns that suppressed their appetites. But wanting to forget, and not be around people who were particularly happy, she tagged along with them on a night out. Oliver said, "I'd rather stick needles in my eyeballs than go," so he did not join them.

The smoking area was filled with hipsters of varying degrees, both old and young. Boys and girls were wearing vintage-looking jeans with sheer tops. Soraya half got the dress code and wore a mesh crop top and a tennis skirt with fishnet tights, but one of her thighs seemed the same circumference as both of her friend John's.

It was at times like these, when she felt most alone, that she wished she knew her lost sister. Perhaps Laleh would be on her side, would understand her in a way her other siblings never did. She resolved to get her mum alone and ask her about Laleh over Christmas, find out anything she could about where her eldest sister might be. She must at least try.

She had resigned herself to the fact that because they were a small family she would have to go home for Christmas. She imagined if she didn't show they'd probably drive up to London and bring her back.

So she drank to blot out the thought of

1. Bringing up the subject of Laleh with her mother.
2. Enduring her dad's presence.
3. Her entire relationship with Magnus being fake.

Despite everything, the last point was the one that hurt the most. She was familiar with family disappointment, but in matters of the heart this was a fresh, new kind of pain. She couldn't decipher what was real from what was fake in her relationship with Magnus and spent many nights mulling over their dates, playing detective. When in moments of despair she concluded it was all lies, she hated him even more.

She sipped her vodka cranberry laced with MD. She smacked her lips together, finding the taste bitter. For her, taking MD was no different from drinking alcohol; it served a purpose when partying, but she didn't need it to survive. That was how she and her dad differed. She resolutely told herself they were different. She was young with no dependents, and so her taking drugs occasionally would have no consequences for anyone else, but he had children, a wife—he should know better.

And when she thought back to Magnus, who was against drug taking, she wondered whether he saw drugs as being any different from alcohol. Yes, you often didn't know what was in the drugs and Soraya knew she was stupid for overlooking that fact—but everyone knew an alcoholic nowadays. The damage from alcohol was as bad as from drug addiction, but no one talked about it. Perhaps she took the MD to spite Magnus, and maybe that's why she had taken more than usual tonight.

Ungracefully, she got up from her seated position on the floor in the smoking area. "I've got to pee," she lied, needing a moment to herself.

She waded through sticky bodies to get to the toilets. The harsh lighting made her squint, and the sight of her reflection made her squint further. She smoothed her hair down and used a wet paper towel to wipe away her smudged lipstick. Her eyes were completely black, demon-like. She kind of liked it.

There were other girls in the toilet, in similar states of disarray, but they were with friends. She leant against the wall as she waited in the queue, took her phone out, and held it at a distance. Focusing her eyes, she opened the Facebook app. Searched Magnus Evans. Clicked on his profile and scrolled down. He had posted a picture three hours ago. It was of him and his housemates, beers in their hands in a pub. She scrolled down further. Twelve hours ago, a topless mirror selfie. Fifty likes, with comments such as "Your room is so messy Magnus," followed by an emoji, from the type of girl who would check him out at parties. The type of girl Soraya wasn't.

He usually laughed when she said they were checking him out, shaking his head, saying something like "No, that's just Beth, she's a friend." But Soraya knew the way a woman's mind works. They had been waiting for him to be single and now he was.

"Why did I go out with someone hot?" Soraya muttered. "Why couldn't he have been unattractive?"

She made a decision. She deleted his phone number. Deleted their WhatsApp messages. Unfollowed him on Instagram. She would have deleted him from Facebook but he would have known, and she didn't want him to think she was trying to get his attention. Instead she vowed to look at Facebook less. When she finished she breathed deeply.

A random girl asked her if she was OK.

"I'm A-OK!" she said, in that overenthusiastic way people do when they're pretending to be fine.

When she finally had the chance to pee, she remained sitting on the seat, staring at the back of the toilet door. This wasn't how she'd expected graduate life to be. She knew they said it was hard to get a professional job. But she hadn't thought it would take *this* long. Didn't think she'd be the only one of her friends without one. How many more application rejections, interview rejections, would it take until she caught one, just one? Her romantic life had been her only saving grace throughout the rejections, and now that had come crashing down. Her dad's aggression was nothing new, but Magnus had made her feel like, for the first time, she wasn't to blame, and that her dad's behavior wasn't excusable or something she should grin and bear.

She went back to the dance floor and feeling another wave, happily danced on her own to the techno music she usually deplored. She allowed herself to be swept up in the crowd of bodies, bobbing their heads, swaying to the beat. With her eyes shut she imagined herself surrounded by people who loved her, that she was weightless, everything fine.

When she opened them again she saw Laleh; her face was blurry but Soraya was certain it was her.

"It's you," Soraya said.

But Laleh ignored her. And when Soraya blinked she didn't see her there anymore, just the backs of people dancing.

She blinked again, and promptly forgot her hallucination. Her eyes were playing with her, leaving her confused. So she continued dancing. Later when her friends found her they swayed to the music together. She wasn't sure how long she danced, just continued until the waves ended.

They left the club at 6:00 A.M. and a group of them went back to John's house, to watch movies and smoke weed.

When Oliver texted to ask if she was OK, she replied:

I'm fine.

Chapter 44

NEDA

Liverpool, 1986

In the living room were two new additions: one brown and one cream cot. Inside the brown one was a blue fleece blanket, and in the other a baby pink throw. Hossein had kitted out each cot with soft toys—which Neda wasn't entirely sure was safe for newborns. As was his way, next to the cot were five packs of nappies—which would be too big for them—and two tubs of baby milk powder—which they couldn't yet drink. It was at least better than when he had attempted to give Laleh cow's milk straight from the bottle when she was a small baby. Neda's lips twitched with annoyance all the same.

They had moved to a larger two-bedroom flat when Neda was pregnant with Laleh. But as with all upgrades, it made another one seem inevitable. Neda wanted each of her children to have their own room, like English people often did.

As Neda struggled with carrying two babies and made her way farther into the room, she saw Hossein had placed a stack of baby clothes on the sofa, the labels still attached, the prices displayed.

This was his way of apologizing, by attempting to impress her. But instead it irritated her. The clothes were too expensive and the babies would grow out of them in a week. Had he forgotten that? Or was it because he was never truly a part of the process with Laleh, conveniently working every night as soon as she was born, and then sleeping during the day, leaving Neda alone with their first newborn? He was a part-time father then, but at least he was loyal, not embarrassing or degrading her.

She had called Ali from the hospital, as promised, and he collected her and dropped her off at home. He refused to come inside the house when he saw Hossein's car outside, but agreed to look after Laleh while Neda settled the newborns in. Perhaps stubbornness ran in the family, because Neda had insisted only Ali could collect her from the hospital, and not Hossein. She had said she would rather walk the two and a half miles home with two babies in her arms and Laleh by her side than get in a car with her husband. Her cheating husband.

Seeing his wife struggle, Hossein rushed from the kitchen and took one of the babies from the carrier.

"You're home!" He looked at the child in his arms. "Ah, little Amir," he cooed lovingly.

"That's Parvin," Neda said before putting the carrier on the floor.

He looked disappointed. "Of course, I got mixed up." Now he looked at Parvin as though she was an object to fear, holding her away from himself, his hands under her armpits. She began to cry.

Neda took her daughter from him, rocking her against her body. The crying soon stopped.

"They need their mother," he said.

"They need a father too."

Hossein's nostrils flared for a fraction of a second.

She held Parvin close. "Why are you making a fool out of me?" she said, cooing the words. She knew—or hoped—that he wouldn't do anything in front of the babies. While he had never hit her, he had broken things when he was angry. She wondered if one day he would snap—he wouldn't be the first man in her family to hit a woman. It was common back home for men to hit their wives, almost expected. That Hossein hadn't done it so far was surprising. But hadn't he done enough already?

"What do you mean?"

"Simran told me about that Englishwoman . . ." Her words trailed off. Something about her husband was different. He was agitated, his face an unusual shade of red. She noticed the way his hands shook. "Are you OK?"

Tiny beads of sweat rolled down his forehead.

"What's going on?" she said.

"Nothing is going on," he said, moving away jerkily, reorganizing the nappies, and taking teddies from carrier bags, placing them inside the cots. With each movement she became more and more aware of how unsteady he was. He wasn't drunk; this wasn't the movement of a drunken man.

She began to recall his behavior over the past few months. He had always been erratic, but this was different. This was the first time she'd truly looked at him in a very long time. She noticed how much weight he had lost, how he couldn't stand still.

She put Parvin in one cot and checked on Amir before going into the kitchen. She knew Hossein would follow.

He grabbed the ends of his hair and pulled, saying nothing.

"What is going on with you?" Neda asked, observing him. "Are you on the weed? Is that what this is? You've gone from drinking alcohol to smoking hashish?"

He gulped, stuttering, "No, obviously not." He turned away from her so he was in profile, fingering a crisp bag he had left on the countertop, folding it in half before attempting to rip it, but struggling.

He reminded her of Laleh then, how he wanted to be close to her with nothing to say, just needing her presence. But she wasn't his mother, she was his wife, and he had betrayed her. She didn't want to be a calming presence anymore, didn't want to give him comfort. Who gave her comfort?

"Something is going on with you, you're behaving oddly."

"I'm not, I've just not been feeling that well."

"You're telling me because you've had a cold that justifies cheating on me, hitting my brother? Have you lost your mind? Just because we're in England doesn't mean you can act this way."

"I didn't know what I was doing, you have to believe me, I'm not well," he said, grabbing her hands. His palms were damp and cold, and she resisted the urge to snatch her hands away. She couldn't look him in the eye.

"Your actions now aren't the actions of a sane man. I don't know who you are anymore. Not well? What's wrong with you? Eh?"

He said nothing.

"How would you feel if I slept with another man and then said I was unwell? That's not an excuse! What do you even mean, 'unwell'? Do you mean tired? You have the flu? Speak some sense."

"I'm in trouble," he said in a quiet voice.

"With whom?" She realized then she didn't know him at all. It seemed he lived in an entirely separate world from her, a world in which he had English lovers, got in trouble with people she had never met.

"I've made so many mistakes and I don't know how to take them back. I wish I could take it all back." His eyes were glassy. She had never seen him cry before.

"What's that meant to mean? Take what back?"

"I can't stop taking it . . . I can't. I've tried and I can't. Allah help me." He put his head in his hands and his whole body shook violently.

Her hand hovered over his back, but she couldn't touch him.

"What can't you stop taking? Alcohol? Have you become an alcoholic? What is it, Hossein?"

"I don't remember being with them, what they even look like . . . that's how bad it's got."

"What are you talking about, Hossein? That woman? *Women?*" she hissed. "You're making no sense. Have you gone crazy?"

He shook his head. "I didn't mean to, that's not what I mean." He paused. "I need to stop. I know I can stop. I do bad things because of it. I hurt you. It's not my fault, I don't mean to, honestly. I swear to you, Neda. I just need your help."

She slammed her hand down onto the table. "Help with *what?*"

"Opio." As he said the word he let out a sigh of relief, his shoulders slumping.

And the words he uttered made no sense to her. When she tried to repeat them they stuck to her mouth, gluey.

Yes, he had cheated on her. Multiple times. She knew that, even if he wouldn't outright admit it. Yes. But that was beside the point now, or rather the point had changed, he'd changed it.

In the silence, his face was pained, lips turned down to expose his small teeth—the teeth she had once thought were cute. Now she noticed how yellow they were. When had this man she thought she loved decayed? And how had she lived with him and not noticed?

"Opium," Neda whispered. "Oh, Hossein."

Chapter 45

SORAYA

London, 2014

Soraya left John's house at 7:00 P.M.

Her insides felt like they had been grated, her skin dry and fragile. She'd had a few hours' sleep on the sofa while *Friends* played in the background.

It was a brisk fifteen-minute walk back to her place. Her stomach growled angrily despite her not feeling hungry. On the way home she stopped off at the supermarket.

She was given odd looks by those around her. Perhaps it was because her hair was balled into a knot on top of her head, her fishnet tights now laddered, her eyeliner smudged. She knew she looked bad, but for the first time she didn't care. What did caring about her appearance ever achieve? It never made her happy.

She grabbed a Diet Coke and packet of crisps, and then ventured to the frozen food aisle for a pizza.

Her nerves were sensitive: the fluorescent lights too bright, her shoes too hard on her heels, her bag too heavy on her shoulder.

As she rounded the corner, the cold air of the freezers making her shiver, she saw a familiar back. She stood still like he was a snake and any sudden movement could be fatal. He hadn't seen her so she turned away slowly, deciding she didn't need the pizza after all.

Of course, at that exact moment, he turned and looked straight at her. His lips parted and then curled into a smile.

So, naturally, Soraya ran away.

She power walked out of the aisle and moved two aisles away to the cleaning products section. She paused there and began looking at the washing detergents, not quite sure what she was doing. Part of her was irritated that he was in the way of the pizza, and part with herself for cowering away from him. Allowing herself to be inconvenienced by him.

She felt a presence and could smell *him*. She let herself inhale the familiar aftershave before looking up. Magnus stood next to her.

"Why'd you run away?"

"I didn't run away."

"You did, you literally ran away from me."

He looked happier than usual, his cheeks flushed, his eyes animated. The breakup, it seemed, had done him good.

"Well, I guess I didn't want to see you."

He sighed, his expression altering.

"I don't like the way we left things, Soraya," he said, softly.

"Listen, it's all fine, whatever." She shrugged.

He put his hand on the shelf, leaning against it, a position that suggested he wanted a proper chat.

"If we're going to see each other around, can't we at least be friendly? Not that you will see much of me come January."

"What does that mean?" she asked.

He scratched his head, his face bent sheepishly low. "I'm moving." The words came out in a whisper.

"Where? Back home?"

"Not quite . . . Paris."

"Paris?" Her own voice sounded strangled, which embarrassed her.

"I've been doing a TEFL course and I found out yesterday I got a job teaching English at a school there. And . . . it hasn't been announced yet but I got a book deal! It's a cliché, I know, but there's something about being a writer in Paris . . ." The rest of his words were lost as the same word echoed in her brain.

Paris.

Paris.

Paris.

She knew she needed to curb her emotions before she began crying in front of him.

"Hello?" he said, with a nervous laugh.

"Sorry, yes, congrats! That's amazing!"

"How are things with you anyway?" She hated that question. She had nothing to offer forward.

"Fine, just fine!"

He narrowed his eyes.

Soraya stood up straighter and swayed slightly. She was really hungry now, her accidental twenty-nine-hour fast no longer novel but concerning. He put a hand to her shoulder to steady her. She flinched.

The hurt in his eyes was palpable.

"I just . . . are you OK? You don't look good."

She laughed shakily. "Gee, thanks."

"No, I mean . . . have you been out or something?" He looked at his phone. "It's half-seven?"

"I'm just on a comedown and really hungry." She laughed, not meaning to.

"You took drugs?" He looked worried, lines creasing his forehead.

She sighed. "I've always taken drugs, Magnus, it's not a big deal."

His hand was still on her arm. She wanted to shake him off but couldn't bring herself to do it. It would be the last time he touched her, and she hated herself for being so sentimental as to think that.

"You need to take care of yourself. Look at your dad . . ."

Her mouth opened involuntarily as rage bubbled inside her.

"What the fuck? You can't just throw that in my face." She pushed his hand away. "You're lecturing me for taking MD on a night out, like you don't drink alcohol? Imagine if I said something about your dad, chastised you for drinking because of his problems."

He shut his eyes and clenched his jaws.

"I didn't mean to . . ."

"Forget it. It doesn't matter."

She didn't even care about their argument, not really. She just didn't like that he was pretending to care for her and judging her as though she was struggling without him.

"There you are!" a voice said from behind her. Soraya turned to find a blond girl making her way towards them. She stood close to Magnus and they looked nice together, like they were a natural couple.

"I couldn't find you," the girl said, in a singsong voice.

Soraya stepped back, her breath hitching.

She was such an idiot.

Magnus looked totally at ease, which made the whole situation worse.

"Red or white wine?" the blonde said, showing both bottles to him. He was now facing her, but his eyes were still on Soraya.

"Erm, red," he said. "This is Soraya, by the way."

The girl turned, as though she hadn't realized Soraya and Magnus had been talking. She smiled brightly and Soraya might have thought she was nice if it wasn't for the painful reality that Magnus had already moved on with her.

"Hiya," the girl said.

"I'm late for a thing anyway, nice meeting you. Have fun in Paris, Magnus."

Soraya left, taking impossibly large steps, holding herself together until she was at the self-checkout.

Chapter 46

NEDA

Liverpool, 1986

They needed to leave Liverpool, that much Neda knew.

She held on to the idea that starting afresh elsewhere was all they needed. She worked hard to finish her PhD, her only moments of harmony and stillness in the very early hours of the morning, when it was still dark out and all her family were asleep. When she grew so tired that she couldn't justify continuing to work, she sat at the end of a bed and allowed herself to breathe. She gave herself only five minutes a day of peace and silence, and she savored them. She had pushed herself to her limits before, but this was different. She was tired. Mentally more than anything else.

She thought back to the day Hossein had told her about his addiction.

She was surprised but at the same time not. It explained his mood swings. Opium was common in Iran; many of Baba's friends were opium addicts. When she thought of them, she imagined them smoking it from a pipe in dark rooms and then lying on the floor, spaced-out for hours. Their wives would be expected to bring them chai on request, even light them up another puff if need be. Opium use was both common and life-destroying, creating zombies out of previously able men.

She hadn't imagined her healthy, fit husband would be among them.

And how had she not noticed? How had he successfully hidden something so large from her? It made sense, now, that his clothes always smelt so strongly of aftershave. He had been covering the scent of his sins.

"Why?" Neda had asked him.

He shrugged. "I have nothing here." She imagined he had rehearsed this story. His voice seemed cold, devoid of any true emotion.

She moved her head towards the living room, to the two newborn babies, to their little Laleh. "Nothing?"

"I mean job-wise," he said impatiently. "You're thriving here . . . I'm not. I'm a loser in this country."

"We can go back! I've always said we could go back. I *want* to go back. We agreed we would stay until things settle down back home, *if* things settle down back home, but we can go back anytime. What are these excuses?"

"Here is better for the kids, for you, for me, maybe . . . I don't know."

"So that's the real reason—you don't know? Who do you take those *drugs* with? Huh?"

"Ziryan—"

"I knew it!" Neda interrupted.

And through her forcing it out of him, she realized why he began smoking opium. To be accepted by people he deemed similar to himself; to experience momentary highs in which he felt happy and weightless. She understood the attraction of that, but opium? Didn't he think of his family?

"English people don't want to be my friends," he said. "And I don't want to be theirs! Fucking bastards."

But that wasn't all. It was clear to Neda that she had grown thicker skin than her husband over time. Years of being called a "Paki bastard," being told to "go back home," being told he looked "dirty" had gotten to Hossein. Isolated him. Pushed him towards anyone who would be his friend. *Peer pressure. Was Hossein a thirteen-year-old?* Neda thought bitterly. She wanted to have sympathy for him, because she knew that was what she was meant to feel, but instead resentment bubbled inside her.

The weight of responsibility, of having three children while working on her PhD and worrying about her family at home, threatened to break her sometimes. And here he was, getting high with his friends. With no support from him, she was being crushed.

"It was only meant to be a bit of fun, but you don't understand the feeling . . . the way I feel when I smoke it." He smiled then; it was the most genuine joy she'd seen in him in years. She felt sickened by the sight.

She gripped the countertop, her fingertips pale, and turned away from him, forcing herself to feel the correct emotions. To behave as was expected of her, to be the devoted wife.

But she couldn't.

"I can't look at you."

"Neda," he implored. "Please help me. You're my wife and I'm begging you: help me."

"How can I help you? Just stop taking it!"

"I've tried, Neda," he said. "I've tried to go without, but that's when I get angry and do things to you that make me hate myself. I'm not well—I'm ill." His expression was pleading with her to take this weight onto her shoulders; it was clear he expected her to fix his problems, relied on her to do so.

And she was unable to say no to him—she wanted her Hossein back. The man who made her laugh, gave her that weightless feeling.

"We'll take you to a doctor," she said after a moment. "They'll be able to fix this. But first, pray with me."

He looked uncertain.

"In times of hardship we turn to Allah," she said. "Your faith has been weak, we need to strengthen it."

Perhaps seeing that this was a way to appease his wife, no longer to be the object of her disdain, he nodded.

Night prayer, tahajjud prayer, was one of the most important prayers, so it was fitting that it was the one Neda and Hossein chose to perform together, to ask Allah to help him. Neda was confident that a connection to Allah would ground her husband when clearly his marriage to her had not done so.

After they settled the babies in their cots, they performed wudu.

It was important to center and quiet yourself, focusing solely on the act.

"Bismillah," they both said under their breaths before washing their hands, using their left to wash their right. This motion was performed three times before repeating the act, but this time the right hand washed the left three times. It was important to wash between each pair of fingers, and all the way up to your wrists.

As Neda performed the ritual, she looked at Hossein, noting the way he didn't quite clean carefully enough between his fingers. She repressed the urge to scold him and breathed deeply through her nose instead. He was learning.

Then, in turn, each cupped their right hand and drank from it, swishing the alkaline-tasting water in their mouths before spitting it out. Next they put more water into their cupped hands and inhaled it into their noses. Neda didn't like this part as much, but understood the need to clean every crevice of her body before talking to Allah. Following this came the washing of their faces, arms, elbows, heads, ears, and feet. Always in this order.

Ordinarily, people took it in turns to perform wudu, but Neda urged Hossein to do it with her. She didn't trust him to do it fully, and it was now imperative to her that he should.

They laid their prayer mats on the living room floor and Neda put on her chador. Hossein stood a little in front of her while they began their prayer.

From the corner of her eye she noticed Laleh sitting on the sofa watching them, doll in hand. It was good, she thought, that her daughter was seeing her parents praying together, witnessing the importance of a good relationship with Allah.

Neda didn't know where she would be without Allah; she imagined she would be lost, aimlessly wandering the earth. Islam gave her a reason for being, something to look forward to in the afterlife, the feeling that everything happened for a reason. Yes, everything. Even Hossein's opium addiction. Perhaps Allah was testing her. It was understandable, she thought, that her initial reaction was one of alarm, but now the shock had worn off she needed to remember what her religion had taught her. She could handle the bad; this was a test, after all, to see what she would do next.

The next day she booked a doctor's appointment, asked Ali to look after the children, and took Hossein to the surgery.

His doctor was a large woman who was sympathetic to his addiction. She breathed heavily, as though lifting her arm to sign his prescription was almost too much of an effort, would tip her over the edge.

"We'll put you on methadone," she said. "It's a safer alternative to opium. And we'll give you a dose every day. Gradually this dose will reduce until you no longer need to take anything. We'll do this slowly, how does that sound?"

Neda couldn't help but wonder how someone who seemed to have respiratory problems herself could help him. Help his entire family. She didn't want to take a slow approach; didn't want her husband to take another drug to survive. She wanted all of this nasty business behind them, and for things to be better again.

But of course she knew this way would be better. She shuddered to think of Hossein's temperament if he suddenly stopped taking his drugs. She knew from enough research on lab rats that it was medically kinder to wean a person off an intoxicating substance slowly. That didn't mean she liked it though.

If life with Hossein and their children was enough for her, why wasn't it enough for him? It was easy to blame his moral deterioration on his crumbling relationship with Allah, but she couldn't banish the thought that she was not enough for him.

She was reminded of a study of cocaine use she had read for her undergraduate degree in which some rats were given all the pleasures they wanted and some were given nothing. Those given nothing were more likely to become addicted to cocaine, while those already living in paradise refrained from taking it.

The evidence that perhaps she and her children were not enough for Hossein stung, because she knew she couldn't argue with science. She had built her career around it, taught postgraduates while writing her thesis. What would they think if she discredited science because it upset her?

Of course, she had further thoughts of divorce. But was it fair to leave her husband when he was so low, when he needed her the most?

Such thoughts are destructive, she told herself. *Support your husband.*

And that she did.

Chapter 47

NEDA

Brighton / Tehran, 1987–1990

It seemed Hossein couldn't—or perhaps wouldn't—stop taking methadone. He took the lowest possible dose of the bright green liquid for weeks, sometimes months, but when finally it was time for him to abstain from the drug altogether, he could manage without it for only a few days. In those brief interludes Neda saw something of the man she'd first married: her Hossein. The Hossein who valued her, who rarely raised his voice to her or the children, the man who was grateful for his family. And then he would come home red-faced once more, having gotten his fix from a dealer of some kind—or maybe even the friends who got him into taking opium in the first place—and it would all be ruined again.

He would ruin them again.

It was after his third failed attempt that Neda made the decision finally to move, to uproot her family and start afresh somewhere new. The summer after she handed in her thesis, the family moved to Brighton. It was easier to blame Liverpool, and the people Hossein spent time with there, for the destruction of their family. Brighton was their beacon of hope. By the sea—and hadn't Maman always told her water was calming? Could aid almost any ailment? Could the sea, then, save Hossein?

They left suddenly and without much thought for the logistics, but it turned out OK. It had to.

Neda became both housewife and breadwinner. They had lived

in England for ten years at this point and had been made British citizens.

Occasionally she indulged in fantasies of leaving Hossein, telling herself she had the power in their relationship, but she knew she would never do it. She couldn't leave him when he was so vulnerable, so dependent. What would he do without her? Where would he go? She knew he would end up homeless. Or, worse, dead. She had resigned herself to looking after him—perhaps this was Allah testing her.

Being an older sibling, Neda was aware that all her life she had been made to look after others. She was seeing the effect of this in her relationship with her husband. Objectively, she knew they were equals, that he shouldn't need her, much as she didn't need him. And yet she found herself mothering him, putting his needs above hers. It was in realizing this that she finally accepted the life before her. It was hard, but she knew what she had to do, knew what her role was to be, and how somewhere inside herself she even enjoyed it. Enjoyed carrying the load because without it what would she do? There would be emptiness, and what was more frightening than the unknown?

Their new life soon had a rhythm. Yes, Hossein was an absentee husband and father, but sometimes, *sometimes*, he showed he still cared. He watched television with the children and seemed absorbed in their interests; he even took them to school every morning on the way to the pharmacy to collect his medication. He occasionally bought Neda bouquets of flowers, saying, "But you're the most beautiful flower," which made her smile.

It was when his mother died suddenly in 1990 from a brain tumor that he entered the pit of depression. He did not cry when he found out. He simply went straight to bed and stayed there for twenty-four hours.

The entire family went to Iran for the first time in thirteen years.

Humid air greeted Neda as she stepped off the plane; it felt like home.

At the airport they were met by their family, holding red roses and signs that read "The Nazari Family." Her own maman and baba were there, at one in the morning. Her usually stony-eyed father had tears in his eyes instead as he hugged her and whispered in her ear, "Don't be gone for so long next time, eh?"

Both Amir and Parvin sat on her lap on the car journey home and seemed to marvel at the fact that in Iran it was acceptable to have more than five people in a car.

"Isn't this . . . illegal?" Laleh said. She was sitting on her father's lap.

"She looks so worried!" Baba said to Neda. "Tell her it's OK, everyone does this here." He chuckled.

Neda translated for her baba.

"She does know a bit of Farsi, she's just shy," she added quickly to her family.

Hossein said nothing, his gaze focused on the outside. He had been like this since he found out about his mother: silent. Neda herself hadn't yet experienced such a grief, so could only imagine what he was feeling. She wondered whether if he wasn't on drugs his reaction would be different, whether it would be something she could understand better.

Neither family was told about his addiction.

The country they once knew had become alien to Hossein and Neda. The shops and restaurants they remembered vividly had closed down, and the streets were full of women in black chadors. Gone were the days of the miniskirt. Neda remembered when wearing a small hijab was considered unusual, black chadors expensive and rare.

Tehran was run-down; its former brightness seemed to have dulled. The coffeehouse where Hossein had proposed to Neda was now boarded up, and Baba said it would be renovated into a takeaway soon.

The funeral was a blur of wailing, with Hossein's sisters pounding their hands on their mother's grave. Amir and Parvin hid behind Laleh's leg. Hossein remained dry-eyed.

During the will reading, he was given the entirety of his mother's savings and the family house as he was the only man. He distributed the money evenly among his sisters, keeping enough for his own family to buy a five-bedroom house in Brighton. Somewhere along the way he must have resigned himself to the fact that they would stay in England forever. Perhaps seeing the changed Iran made him realize his memories of a life he would return to were just that: memories. Life would never be the same for him, not now his mother had died, not since he had become an addict.

Chapter 48

SORAYA

Brighton, 2014

Christmas was always a confusing time for the Nazari family. Soraya had spent her childhood trying to get them into the Western spirit, to conform and for the sake of the presents. But each year was different. One year they would have a Christmas tree, another year they would get presents or else make a big feast, but it was never quite in sync, all the traditions observed together in harmony.

It was only when she was eighteen that Soraya gave up. This was also in part because at university she finally met people who didn't celebrate Christmas at all, and for once wasn't regarded with wonder because her Muslim Iranian family didn't fully celebrate the holiday.

So Christmas for the Nazaris was like any other day, except they did have one special meal that they ate together, including her dad. And they watched the *EastEnders* and *Coronation Street* Christmas specials.

When Soraya returned home there were subtle signs acknowledging something serious had happened: her mum was attentive, bordering on clingy. Parvin was formal; she said hello and goodbye to Soraya when Amir was nearby, but if they were alone together was stony in her silence. Soraya wasn't sure why her sister was annoyed with her—Parvin was the one who'd always told her to date. Then, when her dad hit Soraya, her sister just stood there, as though it was all Soraya's fault for getting caught. She should be the one to be ignoring Parvin, but she didn't have the energy to retaliate. Her sister's lack of empathy had become the topic of many rants delivered to Oliver. So she avoided Parvin around the house.

Her dad, however, didn't engage with Soraya on any level, pretending she was invisible. This she preferred. Amir was the only one who acted normally with her, because no one had told him what his father had done.

She messaged Oliver and Priya to organize a meetup to plan their literary journal idea once and for all. She needed something to look forward to. If Magnus was thriving, she needed to do something as well.

It was on Christmas Eve that she realized why her mum seemed to have moved on so quickly from the event that had shaken Soraya. She had a new reason to hate her husband.

It all began to unravel in the early evening, when Soraya heard a light tap on her door. She was binge-watching *Sex and the City* on her laptop, relating to Carrie during one of her frequent breakups with Mr. Big. Oliver had lent her the sixth-season box set as a holiday parting gift.

Her body tensed at the noise, and she felt like a caged animal once more. One that kept willingly returning to the same cage despite knowing the dangers. She clutched her blanket tight around her, as though it could protect her from whatever awaited her. It wasn't that she thought her dad would come in for round two, but behind that door could be any member of her family, each with the ability to derail her already delicate mental state. She was fragile, that much was obvious, or so she thought, and one further push could break her.

The door inched open and her mum appeared. She was wearing floral trousers and a baggy T-shirt. Her expression was of excitement tinged with sadness.

"Are you up?" she said, stepping into the room, closing the door softly behind her.

"No, I'm asleep." Soraya rolled her eyes and sat up straighter.

"You're a funny girl, ey?" her mum said before sitting down on the side of the bed. In her hand she held *One Day*, a book Soraya had lent her, which she put down on the bedside table. "The ending was so sad, I'm not sure I'd want to read it again."

Soraya made a small sound in response, despite the fact that *One Day* was one of her favorite books. She didn't want to discuss it now, or defend it against her mum, who wanted a happy ending in every book she read.

She noticed her mum peering at her, a forlorn look on her face. "What's up?"

"Why are you so moody?" her mum asked, placing a hand against Soraya's cheek.

Soraya moved away.

"Have you forgotten what happened when I was last here?"

"Of course I haven't. What can we do? Your dad is . . . you know how I feel about him. We're stuck with him." Her mum shrugged as though she had just said something mundane, and not heartbreaking. "You're a good girl, OK? Don't let him get you down."

Something about the sadness in her mum's eyes made Soraya soften beneath her touch.

Her mum smiled briefly before saying, "What do you know about this Match website?"

She'd expected her mum to say many things, but inquiring about a dating site was not one of them. "Why?" Soraya tried to keep her voice neutral, but a smile threatened her composure. Despite her mum's old-fashioned ways, she would ask about the most random things.

"I think *he's* on there!" she said.

"Oh," Soraya said. "I thought he was seeing that girl?" She didn't add that Amir was most likely seeing many different girls anyway.

"Not your brother," her mum said quickly. "Your dad!"

She explained that she had been suspicious of her husband's increase in Internet activity, the blue glow of his laptop screen always shining on his face in the middle of the night. So when he had gone into town she'd checked—a task that disgusted her. His laptop was always sticky, and there were crumbs between the letters on his keyboard. Usually her mum resolutely refused to touch it. On the odd occasion she had to move it from the sofa, she wore gloves.

"And open on his laptop was Match.com," she said, leaning closer to Soraya for dramatic effect. "Your dad is *talking* to women on Match.com!"

Soraya took a moment to process these words. She wasn't quite sure what she could say in response. "Right," she said, pausing again. Then, "Are you sure?"

Her mum tsked impatiently. "If I bring you his laptop, will you find his messages?" In some ways, her mother was the most intelligent person Soraya knew, having mastered subjects Soraya couldn't even begin to understand, but like many people of her generation, her mum was not particularly tech-savvy; she was completely naïve about how expansive the Internet was.

"I guess so."

Soraya had never seen her mum move so quickly. She returned minutes later with the laptop. She held it away from her body, careful not to let it touch her clothes. Under her armpit was a pack of Dettol wipes. She put it on the floor and gave the interior and exterior a wipe before placing the laptop on Soraya's bed.

Her dad didn't have a password on his computer. Perhaps he thought his lack of hygiene was a big enough deterrent to his wife and children, and until now it had worked. Soraya opened the website and it automatically logged in to his account. She clicked the mailbox button at the top, and her heart dropped at what she saw.

There were at least thirty messages from her dad to other women.

"Maybe it's not actually him," she muttered to herself. She clicked on his profile. What she saw made her do a triple take. "Oh, God," she said, smirking and grimacing at the same time. "He's using Amir's pictures! And has his name down as Hamid Nazari."

"That bastard," her mum said, standing up, hand on hip. They both knew it wasn't Amir on the site, the bio section screamed her dad. The bad grammar, the pictures chosen (family photos in which he cut out everyone but Amir), and the fact that it was his computer made that clear. But it left one question.

"Why, though?" Soraya said. "What's he hoping to achieve? It's not like he could actually meet them."

"He's a dirty, dirty man," her mum said, sitting back down on the bed. Her fingers laced together, she looked at the wall. "This isn't the first time he's done something like this, you know. I've always told you, men are bastards."

Soraya had been told about her dad's past exploits many times before. The same stories were repeated, changed slightly, exaggerated in different places each time.

She wished her mum told her friends about her problems, was less fearful of their judgment, instead of always off-loading onto her children.

It was this fear of telling other people about your problems, your flaws, that her mum had passed down to Soraya. Magnus had tried to shake Soraya out of that way of thinking, but the damage had already been done.

She couldn't imagine a world in which her parents liked each other consistently—or rather, a world in which her mum liked her dad. And yet, despite all this, the hurt on her mum's face was palpable.

"What are you going to do?" Soraya asked.

Her mum collected the laptop and left the room without saying a word. Soraya scrambled out of bed, put on her dressing gown, and tentatively followed her down the stairs.

But instead of going towards her dad's, or rather Laleh's, room, her mum walked down another flight of stairs, towards Amir's room. She tapped on the door twice sharply before entering. Amir was playing his Xbox. He was smiling until he saw the looks on their faces.

"What's going on?" He sat up straighter in bed. In one swift move, his mum turned off the TV, silencing the sound of gunfire. Amir made a noise of disapproval, but she shut the door and brandished the laptop in his face.

"Your father is pretending to be *you* on a dating site! Astaghfirullah." She muttered the last word.

She paused, and Soraya knew what she was thinking. That it was preposterous she had been reduced to this; Dr. Neda Nazari, a biomedicine lecturer who had written numerous notable research papers, a woman highly respected in her field, was sneaking around spying on her husband's laptop. Did she ever dream it would come to this? That this would be the life she led in England, surrounded by transgression, including that of her cheating husband?

In that moment, Soraya felt deeply sorry for her mother.

At first Amir was in denial. "You're being paranoid, Mum," he said, but then when he clicked through the website, like Soraya he realized the extent of his dad's disrespect. He, too, saw the messages. Messages they knew they couldn't show their mum.

And it made Amir even angrier to see the filth his dad was spouting to these unsuspecting women under his son's picture. Amir could actually have bumped into one of them in person, unaware that online his image was being used to ask them if they "wanted a bit of fun" . . . and both Soraya and he wanted to projectile-vomit when they read the explicit "fun" their dad was detailing. No one wanted to know about their parents having sex—or, even worse, their failed sexts to other people. And because their mum was so pure, one thing was clear to all: she deserved better.

These thoughts must have been swimming around Amir's mind as well until he couldn't take it anymore.

"Fuck this!" He scrambled out of bed, laptop in hand. Despite being in just his boxer shorts, a sight Soraya didn't want to see, he left his room without a care and stomped up the stairs. Her mum trailed behind him while Soraya lingered in the hallway. Resounding in her head was the question she often asked herself: *Why is my family such a circus show?* She had planned to talk to her mum about Laleh, but this news overshadowed everything.

Amir ripped open the door to their dad's room. He turned on the light, waking up their always-sleeping father, with their mum hot on his trail. Soraya now followed close behind, reasoning that the shouting would be worse if she couldn't see the action.

Their dad had been asleep on the single bed and was now

squinting at the crowd of people around him. The depths of sleep didn't soften his facial expression.

The bedroom still held hints of Laleh. There was the floral bedspread and teddies in the corner, even a stack of girls' magazines, featuring the *Friends* cast, and Justin and Britney. Why hadn't her parents thrown them out? Why had they kept these reminders of the child they'd disowned?

Laleh's basic cream wardrobe still had her clothes hanging inside. Every so often when Soraya was a teenager she would secretly go and try on these clothes that screamed of the nineties and imagine what her sister had been thinking when she left without them.

"What are you doing, idiot? I'm sleeping," her dad hissed, mostly to Amir.

His son's hairy chest rose and fell rapidly. "Why are you using *my* picture on a dating website?" He thrust the laptop in his dad's face, holding it by the screen, the movement awkward, mirroring his mum's earlier.

Soraya hid behind them both. She could feel her insides knotting. Amir was not exempt from a beating from their dad; if anything he would go harder on him, though it was rare. When Amir got expelled from school for a week for punching a bully who called him a "Paki," their dad had thrown the coffee table at him and kicked him out.

Their mum had smuggled him back into the house in the middle of the night.

"You're talking stupid, that wasn't me," their dad replied, turning away from the family to continue sleeping. His reaction wasn't surprising; it was confirmation that he knew he had done wrong. But, of course, he wouldn't admit that. He was burying his head in the sand, or rather in his duvet.

Amir put a hand on their dad's shoulder.

"Eh!" he said, slapping it away.

"Why are you trying to deny it?" he said.

"Don't talk back at me."

Amir sighed. "I'm not, Dad. I don't want to. It's just you've really upset Mum, and you've used *my* picture. Accept you've done something wrong—"

He was cut off when their dad pushed him. Despite the disadvantage of being in bed at the time, he gave his son a shove so hard it caused Amir to stumble against the wardrobe behind him.

The room was fairly small, all four of them in the space was a squeeze. Due to Amir's size, the impact of his back hitting the wardrobe made it shudder, a tremendous sound echoing round the house—or maybe Soraya imagined that. The impact her dad made on his victims always felt disproportionate to what actually happened.

"You shut up! Fuck off out of this house if you think you can talk to me like that."

Their mum stepped in then. She brought herself closer to her husband, a look of disgust on her face. Her index finger was raised, shakily, in front of her. It was a very Iranian movement, Soraya thought. She had only ever seen such passionate gestures from her parents or relatives. Her mother's bent finger, the power in it, the tension palpable. She wasn't just pointing at her husband, she was finally emancipating herself from him.

"You bastard!" she cried, her voice cracking.

Soraya's dad stood up then, discarding the duvet, seizing the opportunity to tower over his wife, as he had done for more than thirty years.

"What did you say?" he demanded in Farsi, his lip curled. Amir hung back cautiously. Soraya was torn between running in front of her mother and running away from them all.

"I said, you're a fucking cheating bastard!" her mum roared.

"I said, it wasn't me—" he continued.

"Oh, come on, Dad," Amir interjected. "Just stop. Tell the truth. It's bad enough you've done this, but to use my pictures? You've taken it too far. Have some respect—for Mum at least."

"She probably made the profile herself! She loves the drama!"

Soraya's mouth opened involuntarily, and despite forcing herself to pipe down, she still made a sound. It was enough to make her dad look at her. This was the first time he'd really looked at her since striking her weeks ago.

The sight of his puffy red face disgusted her. She looked down at her bare toes. Noticed the chipped baby pink nail varnish on her big toe. Pondered, despite the gravity of the situation, when she would have time to repaint it, and if she had any nail varnish remover in Brighton. It was uncanny that in dire situations, situations in which she was fearful, her brain still had the capacity to think mundane thoughts.

"What? *You* have something to say?" His voice was venomous. *"You?"*

Soraya resisted the urge to run away. There was protection in her being with so many people, and especially with Amir. Despite often behaving unfairly to her, he would always protect her against others. It was a fine balance; he would hurt anyone who did anything *he* deemed detrimental to her—for example, a boyfriend. Meaning she didn't always feel safe around him, because he could come to ruin the things she held dear, thinking he was saving her.

But in this case, she felt safe with him.

"Stop lying to us, we're not stupid." The words that came out of her mouth were spoken quietly, and yet it seemed the whole room was holding its breath, waiting for her to challenge their father.

"What did you say?" he yelled.

Sometimes he resembled a wild dog, she thought, desperate both to gain attention and to cause disturbance. It was innate, too ingrained in his being, to be considered a reaction. It was just him.

But what would happen if the people around him, for once, didn't back down?

Soraya imagined him exploding like a defeated villain in a game. But this, sadly, was no game. He was her father, and despite everything she couldn't ignore that. It made the pain worse.

"You heard me," she said, still speaking quietly. She could hear her heart beating wildly in her chest, was convinced everyone around her could hear it too. "We're always walking on eggshells around you, but enough is enough. You've been a shit dad, and a shit husband, and it's not OK. None of this is OK."

There was a momentary calm before the storm.

But then he surprised her. Instead of hitting someone—or her—as she had expected, he pushed past them and stormed down the stairs, his footsteps heavy against the floorboards.

Soraya wanted to scream, hit the wall, stomp her foot, break something, anything. He never reacted the way she wanted him to; he was incapable of normal human responses.

The look on Amir's face reduced her to tears. Pure disappointment. For her dad to disappoint Soraya was one thing, but it spoke something of the damage he had now caused if her brother, who idolized their dad, was disappointed in him too.

Then she looked at her mum. She'd expected her to be similarly affected, to be crying or angry. Instead, she was laughing.

Soraya's arms prickled with goose bumps. An urgent feeling of dread crept into the pit of her belly.

Her mum began cackling with loud and raucous laughter. "That bastard," she said, struggling to breathe. Both of her children looked at her, speechless.

She left the room then, laughing all the way down the stairs.

"What's going on?" Parvin asked, conveniently appearing once the action was over.

Soraya said nothing, walking past her sister and down the stairs, Amir close behind.

What followed was bizarre. Their mum continued laughing until she was face-to-face with her husband, the whole family gathered uneasily in the living room. Their dad had the television remote in his hand, but the TV was off.

"Has she gone crazy?" Parvin whispered to Amir.

He nodded his head, said, "I think so." He put his hand on their mum's shoulder and she shrugged him off, continuing to cackle, louder this time.

"Are you fucking mad? What's wrong with you? Leave me alone!" their dad said, his voice cracking.

Their mum blocked the door to the kitchen and the twins stood by the door leading to the hallway. It was unintentional, but Soraya appreciated the irony. For once, Hossein Nazari was the caged animal. He was cornered. And he didn't like it.

No one ever liked it.

There were grimaces all around. And silence. It ran around the room. Deafening. Soraya almost wanted to cover her ears, like this was a horror movie and she couldn't take the suspense. It was no wonder she was anxious all the time, she thought. How could a person be relaxed in a house whose occupants were always at war with each other, in which the husband and wife always involved their children in their arguments?

She had always felt jealous of school friends whose parents had divorced, because at least then their houses were finally quiet. Divorce sometimes affected children negatively, but so did a couple staying with each other when they were both unhappy.

Soraya hoped this was the last argument her parents would have. That this would be the final straw. If it was, she could endure the way her heart hurt now. But she doubted it.

She noticed her dad picking at his nails, how bitten they were, to the point where they looked painful.

"I know about Laleh," Parvin said suddenly. "I know everything."

Chapter 49

NEDA

She knew not to force the hijab onto her daughters. If she lived in Iran, it would be different, especially now it was compulsory for women to wear it. In England, she didn't want them to suffer the same abuse she and Hossein experienced. She wanted them to fit in.

She often wondered if this had been her first mistake with Laleh.

No. Her first mistake was letting the child witness her parents' dysfunctional relationship.

Laleh, now seventeen years old, was a brash young woman, with a level of confidence Neda could remember once having herself. She frequently talked back to her mother, and with Hossein often drugged up and asleep—his various medications made him sleepy—Neda had to attempt to tame her wild daughter alone. She had to do that while making sure Hossein didn't get wind of anything that was going on, *and* working full-time as a lecturer, *and* looking after her other three children.

In 1993 she had given birth to another daughter: Soraya. And it was Soraya she truly felt sorry for. Laleh, Parvin, and Amir grew up with a father who at least tried to be sober, in a family that tried to be normal and happy. By the time Soraya was born all the fight had gone from Hossein. His methadone addiction was no longer a secret in the family, his will to work dead and gone. He was a zombie who occasionally lost his temper, the man she loved a distant memory Neda still mourned.

Of all her children, Laleh was the one who most reminded Neda of herself as a child. Her intellect, her inquisitiveness, her nose always being stuck in a book, made Neda nostalgic for her own childhood. Despite all this, as soon as puberty hit and she entered high school, Laleh became moody, which was to be expected, then rejected reading, rejected anything of her former self.

It all began when Neda had found a love bite on her daughter's neck.

She had come home from work and Laleh was in the kitchen, still in her school uniform, eating a chocolate bar. "Baby One More Time" was playing on the radio. At first Neda noticed nothing, her brain distracted from her full day working at the university. Lesson plans and conversations with anxious students occupied her thoughts, but when she looked at Laleh she noticed how her daughter ducked her head low, and how her hair covered most of her face.

"What's going on?" Neda asked, slowly.

"What do you mean?"

"You're acting strange." Neda made her way over to Laleh until she was face-to-face with her. Then she saw it. Her daughter's neck. She made a noise of disgust. "*Laleh!* What is this?"

"I think it's a rash—"

"You think I'm stupid?"

Laleh sighed. "Mum, I don't know what you think it is?" She looked at Neda aghast. So much so that Neda began to wonder if she'd gotten it wrong. Was she projecting her own dirty thoughts onto her daughter?

The sound of Hossein's heavy footsteps on the stairs silenced them.

"What's for dinner?" he asked, coming into the kitchen while scratching his bottom. Laleh rolled her eyes and jumped up to stir a large pot simmering on the hob.

"I'm making spaghetti," she said.

He made a noise of disapproval. "I want rice," he said, walking into the living room.

Despite what had just gone on between them, Neda still felt a pang in her heart on seeing the way Laleh's face clouded over with disappointment at her father's dismissive words. And maybe also, in a strange, twisted way, at his failure to notice the love bite on her neck. Laleh was invisible to Hossein.

"I'm just saying, Laleh dear," Neda said to her later, when Hossein was busy watching television and the younger children were asleep, "be careful, be *decent*, and remember you're a Muslim. Allah is watching you."

Laleh rolled her eyes. "Sure, Mum."

Chapter 50

NEDA

Brighton, 1999

Weeks passed in a similar vein, except Laleh had no more love bites. She would occasionally stay out late, but overall she was quieter and more subdued, as though she had finally absorbed Neda's advice, recognized that her mother wasn't stupid, that she knew what teenagers got up to.

Neda decided she and Laleh needed some quality time together. So, they went shopping.

In the car Laleh was anxious. She bit her nails while her mother was talking.

"What's the matter?" Neda asked.

Laleh jolted upright and stared straight ahead at the car in front. Neda sighed.

"Is it about that boy?"

"What boy?" Laleh asked, her voice pitched too high.

They were in traffic now, and Neda put the car in neutral. She turned the radio down. It was a difficult position to be in. She didn't want to be too harsh and push Laleh away, but she didn't want to be too gentle and thereby allow her daughter to do haram acts. Where was the balance?

"The boy who gave you the mark on your neck."

"Can you drop it?" Laleh snapped.

Neda let out a breath and opened the window. The heat inside the car was stifling, combined with the moody energy Laleh was transmitting; some fresh air was more than necessary.

Despite Laleh's words, Neda got the sense that she wanted to say something. Wanted her mother to push her one last time. How she knew this, she could never describe. Perhaps it was a mother's intuition but she had a feeling the girl was saying one thing while meaning something else.

"Are you sure? You know you can tell me anything."

"Fine, I'm . . ." Laleh stopped talking. She made a choking sound, similar to the first time she realized she had a nut allergy.

"Are you OK? Tell me," Neda said, softly. The softness would soon turn. She clicked her indicator to the left. "You've been acting strange for a few weeks now, what's the matter?"

Still Laleh said nothing.

The radio broke the silence with the presenter cackling at a joke. Despite the gravity of this moment, the sun was shining brightly. The hottest day of the year, the presenter proclaimed.

"Did you fall out with one of your friends?" Neda asked.

"It's nothing."

"Don't lie to me, Laleh." They stopped at a red light, which gave Neda the opportunity to study her daughter more closely, as though doing that would give her the answer. And perhaps it would have if only she had understood what she should be looking for.

Then she would have noticed the way Laleh's palm was cupping her stomach lightly. Her new necklace, the pendant in the shape of a heart with a small diamanté in the middle.

"Laleh—"

"Mum, I'm pregnant."

Chapter 51

SORAYA

Brighton, 2014

All eyes were on Parvin now.

"What do you mean?" Soraya said.

Tears ran down her sister's face. She rubbed them away with the sleeve of her jumper.

"I can't hold it in anymore. I know."

"Know what?" Amir asked.

"Laleh left because she was pregnant. She has a daughter. *We* have a niece." She looked at her siblings.

In the silence that followed all Soraya could hear was her heart pounding in her ears as it thumped uncontrollably. Laleh had gotten pregnant. *We have a niece.* So that was why her family shunned her sister. But also, *that* was why her family shunned one of its own members? It made so much sense, and yet made no sense at all.

Secrets threatened to ruin the Nazari family, and this one, after fifteen years, was finally exposed.

Finally they knew the truth about Laleh.

A change had to come now.

Their mum was looking pale, backing away from them until she was against a wall. She leant on it, desperately needing its support. Soraya felt sorry for her, despite knowing now what she did.

"What did you say?" Amir asked his twin.

Parvin looked up quickly and then back down at her feet. Her fingers nervously removed the ring from her index finger before putting it back on. She did this three times until Amir grabbed her hand to stop her.

"I said, what did you say?" he repeated.

"I've been speaking to her, to Laleh. I found her online a few months ago. She got pregnant when she was seventeen, that's why she left. Her daughter's name is Zara, and she's fourteen now . . . she looks just like Laleh did."

"What? And no one thought to fucking tell us?" Amir said angrily. "You kept this from me for *months*? You're meant to be my twin." He moved away from Parvin, shaking his head. "Well, where is she?"

Their parents were speechless, as though they had never expected this day to come. Perhaps they thought after fifteen years they had gotten lucky and would never need to explain disowning a pregnant seventeen-year-old.

"Is no one going to answer me?" Amir looked around the room.

Soraya had expected her dad to say something, but he sat quietly on the sofa, his head slumped.

All she could do was watch the scene unfold; for the first time in her life she had nothing to say.

"They live in Edinburgh," Parvin said. "She's lived there since she left."

"I don't get it," Amir said. "None of this makes sense. Why did she run away? Mum and Dad made out she left to be with her boyfriend, but she would have needed us if she was pregnant. Why leave?"

Parvin and Soraya stared blankly at their brother, who clearly had no idea how hypocrisy and misogyny worked in most Muslim households. Surprising, because they imagined he would be the one to enforce such rules.

"It's always been different for you, Amir," Soraya explained. "How come you're allowed girlfriends but we aren't?"

"That's different—"

"It was my fault," their mum choked out. "I told her to leave."

"Why would you do that? What she did was wrong, yes, but family is family," Amir said.

Her mum was crying now. Her dad had his head in his hands.

"She told me," Parvin said slowly, looking at her dad, who was avoiding her gaze. "She told me Dad rang her when she had left because Mum told him what had happened, and he said he'd kill her and the baby if she tried to come back. He said she wasn't welcome and wasn't his child anymore." Parvin said all this quietly. If the atmosphere hadn't been as tense as it was, perhaps they wouldn't have heard. But they all heard those words loud and clear.

Soraya's head was spinning. She too had to lean against the wall for support. Her dad's hatred spanned two generations, touched so many people. He was the reason her sister had run as a teenager, afraid and pregnant. He was the reason they hadn't met their niece, had been estranged from their own sister. Soraya had to shut her eyes. Her hands were clenched into fists, and she wanted so bad to beat them against his chest and make him leave. Force him out of the house.

"Were you ever going to tell us?" Amir said. "Either of you?"

Her mum stood straighter. "I wanted to, so many times. I wanted to bring her home. But your dad said no. He said he'd do horrible things to her, to me, and I realized it was better for Laleh to stay away. She would have a better life away from us."

"Blame me! You always blame me. She was seventeen years old, having a *bastard* child." Despite his harsh words their dad said the last part of this quietly. "What was I supposed to do?"

"This family is so fucked up," Soraya let out.

"What? You want to end up like your sister? Is that why you have a boyfriend? You want a baby? To have your life ruined?" her dad said.

Soraya could feel Amir stiffen next to her.

"Boyfriend? What? Why are there so many secrets? What boyfriend?" he said.

"You don't need to have secrets because you're a boy!" Parvin snapped.

"I just want you all to be decent, OK?" he said. "Everything I say is so you don't end up . . ."

"Like Laleh?" Parvin laughed in his face. "Yeah, OK."

"I never stopped talking to her," their mum said quietly. "I always send her money, text her, call her." Tears still streamed down her face. Soraya was struggling to keep up. "I never stopped caring."

"What?" Their dad looked confused, but the anger had left his expression and what remained was betrayal. He had never suspected his wife to be capable of such deceit, even if it was necessary.

"You think I'd disown my own daughter? Never talk to her again? Never speak to my granddaughter? You're the idiot."

He put his hands to his almost bald head, as though forgetting he had no hair left to pull. "I was doing what I thought was right."

"Right for who?" their mum asked. "You're nothing like the man I married. He was understanding, loving. He would never have made me disown my precious child."

"You all think I'm so heartless. Like I don't think of Laleh, like I wanted this to happen—"

"You never let us talk about her!" their mum shouted. "She's become like that evil character in Harry Motter, Potter, whatever it is—"

"Harry Potter," Soraya interjected, and then quickly shut her mouth.

"I didn't want her behavior to influence our other children. For them to think sleeping around is OK, that it's OK to fuck up your life and act like English girls." He looked his wife in the eye, solemnly. "But don't you ever think I simply washed my hands of Laleh. She's always in my dreams. She never goes away. Even when I want her to leave me, she's always there." He shook his head.

"She's your daughter, of course she won't *go away*," their mother said. "How did you become so selfish, so self-centered?" She looked like she was about to spit on him, an expression of pure disgust on her face.

Their dad noticed this. Soraya saw the way his shoulders slumped, and it was as though something clicked in him. She noticed his eyes were suddenly very shiny, but couldn't believe what she was seeing.

"Yes, I know, I'm the worst. I'm bad, worthless. That's what you all think. You think I don't know this either? That I ruin every-thing?" He looked at Soraya then, and she diverted her gaze to the floor, hoping he would stop staring at her. His eyes on her made her feel uncomfortable, her heart beating even faster until she wished she could run. "You especially, you've always hated me, haven't you?"

Soraya shrugged her shoulders, unable to form words.

"Everything I've done has been for my family, even if it doesn't seem that way. Sometimes you're rude, you have no manners, so I get angry. But I didn't mean for things to get the way they did be-fore, you know that . . ."

"That's no justification for the things you do—the things you did!" Soraya snapped. Her body shook; tears were desperate to es-cape her eyes.

"I—I didn't mean to hurt you, any of you." He looked to his wife briefly. "I can't do this anymore. What's the point in any of it?" He said the last part quietly, almost to himself.

All eyes turned to him.

"Hossein, what are you talking about?" their mum said sharply.

"I do everything wrong. No one respects me. No one even likes me. What am I doing here?"

The question was vague; Soraya wondered if he meant in En-gland, or in existence altogether. It was something she often won-dered, but hearing it said aloud was chilling. Such talk belonged only in movies, felt totally unexpected coming from her emotion-less dad.

Despite such apparent candor, part of her didn't believe it, didn't believe her dad was truly in as much despair as he made out. It seemed to her that he was trying to distract them from all the secrets that had been revealed. From all the wrong he had done. Even though his tears were real, she believed his reasons for them were quite different from what he wanted them to believe.

"Dad, you've done so many bad things—you're hardly the in-nocent person in all this!" Soraya said.

"I can't believe we have a niece you didn't tell us about," Amir said quietly to his twin.

Her head was down. "I'm sorry."

"It's the drugs I take. They make me so angry—" their dad was saying.

"No, Hossein, don't blame everything on something else. What about the online dating, eh? Are you going to blame drugs for that too?"

Suddenly he slammed his hand against the coffee table, making them all jump, except for their mum, who perhaps expected this reaction.

"My life is shit. I sleep all day. You all work, have fun, enjoy life. I have nothing. I went online pretending to be a normal man and talked to women so I could *feel* something, anything!"

"But you never think how I feel. All you think about is yourself," their mum said.

"Does this even matter right now—we've found out why Laleh left, and the fact you both hid the reason from us!" Amir interjected.

"It does matter because he's my husband and your father," their mum hissed. The vehemence of her voice surprised her children. They had never seen their mum so angry, especially towards them. "He sleeps all the time, doesn't work . . . the least he could do was not cheat on me, on us. To think, once upon a time, I believed you were a good man, Hossein."

"It wasn't cheating, we didn't meet—"

"This isn't the first time—I'm not stupid!"

Their dad was picking at his nails, but there was nothing left to pick, they were virtually nonexistent.

"I'm sorry, OK! I'm sorry!" he shouted. "I'm a loser. My family thinks it . . . even my fucking doctor thinks it. I can't do anything right."

"Yes, you are, Hossein. You are a loser! So stop feeling sorry for yourself and do better," their mum said.

He seemed shocked by these words, a look of pure hurt on his face. His wife had never been so outspoken before, so brutal.

"Neda, how could you say that?"

"Because it's true. I've had enough." She crossed the room and went upstairs, leaving him sitting with his hands on his head. For the first time ever, Soraya saw her parents as they really were. They were vulnerable, and they had no idea what they were doing, winging a failing relationship. She could almost see them in their twenties, making bad decision after bad decision, never speaking to each other. Her dad bottling everything up, and her mum talking to her children but not her husband about their problems.

Amir went over, put his hand on his father's shoulder, patted it gently. "It's OK, Dad."

"It's not OK. Everything's a mess. I just want to sleep forever. If I could take a pill that would let me sleep forever, I would. What's the point?"

"Don't say that, Dad!" Parvin cried.

"I want to go back to Iran, back to my sisters, I need to get away from here," he said. "I've wanted to go back ever since we moved to England. I've never liked this country."

"But we're your family," Amir said.

"And all I do is make you upset." He looked straight into Soraya's eyes. "I don't even know who I am anymore."

Part
THREE

Chapter 52

SORAYA

London, 2015

The rest of Soraya's days in Brighton passed quietly. Neda avoided her husband until Amir dropped him off at Gatwick Airport a week later. Everyone was still taking in the shock of his departure.

The news about Laleh had changed everything. It wasn't as though the thought that her oldest sister may have gotten herself pregnant, and that's why she left, hadn't crossed Soraya's mind before. But she had always dismissed it, hoping her parents were not capable of keeping such a huge secret for so many years. It made sense, though. Soraya had never understood, really, why Laleh would leave her family for a boy so young. Now everything made sense.

They all agreed they wanted to see her. Progress. Her mum said they needed to be patient, though. While they were now ever more keen to reunite with Laleh and meet their niece, Laleh might not be willing to see them so quickly.

As people needed to be sold overpriced clothing, Soraya returned to London on New Year's Day.

A week later she arranged to see Oliver and Priya. It was the first time in too long that Soraya had been able to feel excited about something. It gave her hope.

"Where is she?" Oliver asked, just as a petite girl with a messy bob walked up the stairs, coffee cup in hand. "Priya, hello! Loving the new hair by the way."

"Hey! Thank you, and sorry I'm late, guys," she said, sitting down next to Soraya. "Hey, you."

"Hiya." Soraya smiled at her. She could smell Priya's perfume, sweet and floral, as she sat down. Priya wore bright red lipstick and a pair of glasses with thick black frames. However, the first thing Soraya noticed were her huge pineapple-shaped earrings. She had recently gotten a job at an art gallery. Soraya was not sure what exactly her friend did there but it seemed to suit her.

"I can't believe we're finally doing the journal. It's only taken us two bloody years." Priya laughed, pulling her laptop out of her bag. "Shall we dive straight in?"

"OK, so the theme could be . . ." Oliver said, letting the sentence hang as he tapped his pen against his nose.

"Growing up?" Priya said.

"Nah, too cliché," he said.

"Sex!" Priya exclaimed, a grin on her face as she typed away.

"Again, cliché." Oliver sighed. "I know it's not really a cliché, but don't we want it to be something new . . . fresh . . . something that means something to us?"

Priya looked furious for one millisecond. He didn't see. But Soraya did. She often saw things others didn't. In fact, she could almost feel the resentment rolling off Priya. Oliver's dismissal of her idea wasn't intentional, he was only trying to brainstorm random ideas. Whereas Soraya knew Priya believed in her ideas; they were thought out. To her, this was original stuff.

"Breaking free?" Soraya said, very quietly. It was more of a mumble really.

"What was that?" Oliver asked.

With both her friends now looking at her, Soraya struggled. Her ideas always felt stupid, unless someone told her they were good. Only with positive affirmation could she see her potential.

"Nothing, I was thinking aloud."

"Did you say 'breaking free'?" Priya said.

"Yes, I know it's totally lame. It's a *High School Musical* song, in fact!" Soraya gave a fake laugh.

"I think it works," Oliver said. "You could write about sex in breaking free, growing up, and . . ." He looked at Soraya in a peculiar way. But she knew what he was thinking. And he knew what she would say if he said it. She wasn't a writer. And she wouldn't write about her dad.

And besides, had she broken free? Or was she still chained to him? Her parents still spoke on the phone, but their relationship seemed different now. Her mum had more control. With her dad away, and everything out in the open, the air around them was clearer, there was less tension in the family.

Soraya hadn't broken free from Magnus, emotionally at least. She thought about him every day, still struggled to sleep while re-hashing how it all went wrong, how he was now in Paris, that it was really over.

She wondered about Laleh. Soraya had always assumed Laleh had left the family for freedom, but now she realized she had really been forced out. Her imaginings of her eldest sister, the type of person she might be, changed once more. She would finally get to meet her, soon she hoped, and while the thought made her nervous, it broke the cycle of wondering around her sister. She'd finally be able to see Laleh, rather than let her imaginings take hold.

"Hmm," Priya mused. "Breaking free. I like it."

In the weeks that followed Soraya led them towards their goal. They decided to create a biannual literary journal and it was the first time in a very long while that she felt like she had a purpose, like she was in charge of something important.

There was the question, first, of funding. Soraya had no savings; all the money from her hours at the shop went towards rent, and each month was a struggle for her. She wouldn't ask her mum. This was something she wanted to do independently, and to ask for help would forfeit the pleasure she felt in the process. So Priya and Oliver offered to band together to cover the cost of printing.

Next was finding people to write in the journal for free. That was easy. They used their pool of Goldsmiths friends, who had a lot to say. The journal would include poetry, articles, and short stories on the theme.

Soraya filled every spare moment with tasks for their journal. Every time she thought of Magnus, she looked up different design techniques. It provided her with a good distraction, but that didn't mean that every day she didn't remember him, didn't think back over every date and turn over every detail to assess whether he'd been pretending then.

It was a week after their meetup, and after work Soraya scrolled through her phone on the bus, her mind too distracted to read. Her mum had texted her to say that she had been speaking to Laleh, and told her that the family now all knew what really happened. Laleh was apprehensive to meet them with Zara. Soraya imagined if she were in Laleh's shoes she would feel the same way. That didn't mean her sister's reluctance didn't sadden her, though.

She went on Facebook and clicked on Magnus's profile. She wasn't sure why she was doing it, it was clearly emotionally cutting, but she couldn't help herself. It was almost involuntary.

What she saw made her pause, eyes focused on the image. He was tagged in a photo by a girl called Angélique. The picture showed him sitting outside a café with an espresso cup in his hand, smiling into the distance, tagged somewhere in Paris. The caption was "the boy." What did that mean? The boy. *Her* boy?

After a minute had passed, Soraya realized she was still staring at the picture blankly, her vision blurry. She put her phone in her coat pocket. Removed her headphones. In such a mood she couldn't concentrate on music; the sounds spiked her anxiety levels. She needed a clear head to focus on what she had just witnessed.

Her hands were suddenly cold, clammy. She hated the way her body reacted to things, the way her heart speeded up, but she also managed to feel outside of her body at the same time.

The bus was fairly quiet apart from the group of teenagers jokily arguing at the back.

"Don't be a pussy, man," one of them was saying. But the sound was muted, and all Soraya could focus on was "the boy."

She looked out the window, out at London. Watched as the bus went over the river. She looked at the London Eye, and then Elephant and Castle with its busy, ugly roundabout, bursting with people, until the bus went down Old Kent Road with its takeaways, launderettes, and hipsters walking by. Some of the people she saw looked as lost as her dad. As each image passed her by all she could think about was Magnus.

He'd moved on so quickly, she thought, so ruthlessly.

She didn't even know how anxious she was until she looked down and saw she had ripped the skin by her nails with her teeth, her eyes stinging with a mixture of tears and liquid eyeliner.

Familiar feelings she thought she'd managed to shut out invaded her thoughts. Did she miss Magnus, or did she miss being liked by him? Somewhere, deep inside, she wondered if maybe she had loved him, but didn't want to admit it to herself. He had even said he was falling in love with her. Was that true? Or was that part of the lie too? It was cruel, in a sense, that their relationship had ended before she could find out. Suddenly she could no longer talk to him. And that's what hurt the most. That someone she'd spoken to every day, she would never speak to again. If she contemplated talking to him, sending him a message, friends scolded her. They scolded her for trying to talk to someone who didn't want her anymore. Someone who had never truly wanted her. Soraya had acted just like these friends when other people were going through a breakup, she understood where they were coming from, but they weren't in her relationship, they didn't know how she felt about Magnus. Not really.

Another wave of anxiety. A minor detail Soraya kept choosing to ignore rose to the surface of her mind again. *It was all a bet*, she reminded herself. *I was one of many.*

Chapter 53

SORAYA

London, 2015

She scratched on Oliver's door, catlike, so he'd know it was her, despite the fact that they were the only two people living in the flat. It had been their tradition since they lived together in student halls, a signal to indicate that the person behind the door wasn't the weird girl who frequently requested hugs from them.

"Come in!"

Soraya pushed the door open. She knew without saying anything that he'd know what had happened. Her tearstained face communicated it all. Although she'd tried to wipe her face clean on the walk from the bus stop to their flat, tears rematerialized.

"You saw it?" he asked.

"Yes."

She sat down on the armchair opposite his bed, her usual spot, while he lay down. In these positions, she should have been the therapist and he the patient, but they never did things the right way around. They never stuck to convention.

"We shouldn't jump to conclusions," he said.

"But you would, wouldn't you?"

He threw a roll of toilet paper at her, which she caught. She blew her nose, multiple times, surprised by how much snot one could produce when devastated.

"God, why did he have to be such a . . . such a *cunt*."

Oliver whistled. "Oh, you are mad."

She threw her arms up in the air. "It's not even an insult, is it?

It just means vagina. I never get why people dislike the word so much."

He watched her carefully, as he always did. "I'm just saying, we don't know for sure what the post means yet. You need to unfriend him from Facebook for your own sanity, though."

She didn't want to say the words, aware of how doing so would make her seem, even to Oliver. *But then all ties will be broken.* She felt ridiculous comparing her relationship with Magnus to other people's breakups because they had only dated briefly, and it hadn't even been real.

"I'll think about it," she said instead.

Soon afterwards, she downloaded Tinder. "You need to be here while I do it. It's scary," she said.

"I thought you didn't like Tinder. Didn't you say it was only for superficial people?" He raised a judgmental eyebrow at her.

"You're allowed to change your opinion."

Tinder was downloading.

"Sure, whatever," Oliver said, monotone as always.

"You're cranky."

He exhaled, puffing out his lips, before slowly looking up at Soraya. "I don't want to complain about my life right now, not when you're . . . you know."

His comment stung. She picked up one of the nail varnishes from the vanity next to her and lifted it to the light to distract herself from the hurt that was no doubt showing on her face. The varnish was a coppery color, but in the strong light she could see flecks of lilac and pink. Oliver owned the nicest nail colors in the varnish he sporadically wore.

"It's all relative. What's up?" she asked.

"Nothing massive, you know, apart from my love life being a hot mess, as usual. And work—I don't know . . . I always wanted to work in publishing and I thought once I got in, it would be a certain way, you know? But I don't fit in at all."

This surprised her because Oliver fitted in everywhere; everyone loved him.

"What do you mean?"

"I can't really be myself at work. Everyone is so posh and, I guess, white. Which is fine, but I feel like I'm expected to be like them, and if I disagree with them, I'm the difficult one, the loud one."

She understood. Wasn't this the problem they'd both had while growing up, in varying degrees? Wasn't this precisely why they wanted to create their own publication, so their otherness could be at the forefront, celebrated, instead of something to be ashamed of and hidden away?

"I just feel like the token black guy in the room. Whenever they talk about diversity they automatically look at me, as though because I'm black I can speak for every ethnic minority." He paused. "And you know what? It's not my job to make their company more 'diverse,' it's their mess." He sighed. "Take it from me, having your dream job isn't all it's cracked up to be."

"Focus your energies on our lit journal," she said. "It's our thing. And change *will* happen, it'll get better, it has to. You just have to be patient."

"Right back at you."

One thing Soraya could safely say she'd gained from dating Magnus was the new sense of confidence he'd instilled in her—when it came to her looks anyway. He had made her feel unique, with her large dark eyes, high cheekbones, and petite frame. So when she uploaded photos to Tinder she was confident they would be taken seriously, whereas pre-Magnus no one from the opposite sex, apart from Oliver, had ever complimented her on her appearance.

With this thought running through her mind, she swiped right to a plethora of guys she was aware she was never going to talk to, and felt satisfaction when "It's a match!" appeared on the screen.

These small highs were fleeting.

Days after her talk with Oliver, when she was sitting in bed, coffee cup in one hand, Tinder open on her phone, she found the first guy she had seen on the app that she actually considered attractive. And he looked nothing like Magnus. His black hair was cut short and he had a full fringe. He was slender, well dressed in muted colors.

He had also been at Goldsmiths while she was there, and she thought she might have seen him in the library.

She swiped right.

It's a match!

Her eyes widened. She locked her phone and tucked it under her duvet. Contemplating why she felt so excited, but also terrified, she took a long sip of her now lukewarm drink.

Oliver was at work so she couldn't run to his room to discuss it with him. Not being able to do so made her feel as though she was matching with this guy secretly. The compulsion to tell someone, anyone, was enormous.

Her phone pinged.

Jacob has sent you a message.

Chapter 54

SORAYA

London, 2015

Soraya sat opposite Jacob in a quaint Italian restaurant in Peckham. When she had suggested going for a drink, he'd said he didn't drink alcohol. At this, she felt embarrassed. As the Muslim surely she should be the one to say that. Except, if she followed the rules, she wouldn't be on Tinder talking to, and subsequently meeting, a boy.

"How come you're on Tinder then?" he asked once the customary small talk had passed.

"You know, to meet new people." As soon as she said the words, she wished she could swallow them. Did "people" make it sound like she was dating multiple men? And if that's what it sounded like, was that a good or a bad thing? "What about you?" she asked.

He smiled, his teeth almost too white and straight, the candlelight casting shadows on his face.

"Honestly? I want to meet someone, for something serious." He shrugged. "I know that's not really what you're meant to say, but whatever."

Her mouth was suddenly dry. With soft music, dim lights, and traditional gingham tablecloths, the restaurant was a perfect date spot. Perfect perhaps for the characters in the books she read. They would have swooned.

She pinched her thigh under the table, squeezed the flesh hard. Her nails over the past weeks had become so soft and stumpy from being bitten that she was giving them a break today. Had to because she was scared about what was happening to them.

"I mean it's good to be honest," she said. "I feel like there's this weird stigma around just saying you want a relationship."

"Exactly," he said, his blue eyes glittering. "That said, I'm more than happy to have fun in the meantime."

The waitress brought them their drinks and he took a sip of his sparkling water.

"How come you don't drink alcohol anyway?"

"I like to keep a clear head."

"How come?"

He laughed. "You say that like wanting to keep a clear head isn't normal."

"It's just you seem like you'd want to drink." As the words came out of her mouth she regretted them, again. "I mean you're a . . . young man." More regret. "You know what I mean."

"Please expand." He folded his small but well-defined arms and looked at her. He had freckles all the way down to his wrists. She had never seen anyone with that many before. They gave him a boyish quality.

"I don't want to." Soraya was smiling, despite herself.

He leant forward. "Why not?"

"I was stereotyping. It's something I do a lot, I've realized."

"And what would you stereotype me as?"

She couldn't quite meet his eyes.

"A bit of a hipster, I guess."

He laughed loudly. "What was that?"

"Never mind. I think I'm talking rubbish to be honest." She chuckled again.

"Come on." He reached over, touched the inside of one of her wrists, ever so lightly. It caused a shiver to run through her. She stopped laughing and her mouth openly slightly.

At that moment their food arrived. She had ordered four-cheese gnocchi and he had chosen chicken breast with aubergine tomato sauce.

When he cut into it, she watched the flesh part. Somewhere along the way she had become more militant in her vegetarianism. She wasn't even sure when or how she had grown so sensitive to other people's eating habits, but watching him eat meat made her feel nauseous. The smell was pungent. He ate it with relish, clueless as to what she was thinking.

"So, what have you been doing since we graduated?" he asked.

"I'm working in a shop while I apply for jobs," she said eventually. She had nothing more to offer. Had she always been this boring? "How about you?"

"I work in film production, which sounds way cooler than it is." He laughed.

For a long time they spoke about their favorite films. He, too, was a Studio Ghibli fan, had even been to the museum in Tokyo. She had always wanted to go to Japan, and decided she'd make it her goal to visit the country in the next five years. Her reservations about Jacob gradually eased. It was comfortable talking to him, like talking to a friend you hadn't seen in years.

He told her about his parents' relationship. How they had lived next door to each other in their twenties. One time his mum knocked on his dad's door at 3:00 A.M. to complain about the noise he was making, and then their eyes met. The rest was history.

Soraya couldn't help but feel slightly resentful towards him for that. For his parents having a meet-cute story that ended in a happy marriage.

"Do you want to come back to mine?" he asked later as they walked towards the bus stop.

Soraya hesitated. She wanted to make out with him, yes, but anything more she wasn't sure of. She was under no illusions; she was using him to erase thoughts of Magnus. But she certainly didn't want to have sex with him, to lose her virginity to him.

"Completely up to you," he added quickly.

Her hands were shoved into her pockets for warmth. London in January was brutal.

"Why not? We could watch a film or something."

He gave her a sidelong smile.

Once they arrived at his surprisingly clean house, they went up to his loft room.

His bedroom was huge, with a sofa at one end and a large TV opposite. Everything was in order, which made her wonder if that was why he didn't drink alcohol—because he relished control over every aspect of his life, which was no bad thing.

After a fifteen-minute debate about what to watch on Netflix, they decided on a comedy. And within thirty seconds of it being on, he leant in to kiss her. Time slowed then. She seemed to have forgotten how to kiss. But soon his lips were on hers, and then his hands were on her breasts. She shut her eyes tight, pushed out of her mind any thought of who this was. It was in this moment that she sincerely wished he drank alcohol, or that she'd had something at dinner.

Jacob was a surprisingly good kisser. His lips were soft, and when his tongue touched hers she felt a shiver of desire. And then somehow his T-shirt was removed, and she touched his chest, his neck, his back. His body was the complete opposite of Magnus's, his chest covered in dark hair, which she hadn't expected.

He pinned her to the bed and hastily removed her jumper.

"I thought we were watching a film," she said, wrapping her legs around his waist.

"You want it back on?" He looked briefly to her discarded jumper, then back at her.

Soraya kissed him, silencing him. She didn't want to answer that, to talk anymore.

And then the familiar feeling of guilt washed through her. Stronger than before because he wasn't Magnus. And she wished he was.

She stopped kissing him, slackened her legs, sank lower on the bed. At first he didn't seem to notice. He pushed her bra away. She raised a hand. "No, stop."

His brows knitted together. "What?" he said, almost sharply.

"I—I need to go home." Soraya scrambled off the bed, put her jumper back on, and looked around for her bag and coat.

"You were totally into it." Jacob's tone was accusatory, as though she was implying something.

"I know and I'm sorry, I just don't feel comfortable—"

"You act like you're really innocent, but what did you think was going to happen when we went back to mine?"

She sighed and put more space between them. How could she explain the unexplainable?

"It doesn't make sense to me either. I just don't feel comfortable right now."

"Why? You were with that guy for months, and there were rumors going round that you . . ."

Soraya's heart skipped a beat. The words acted like a heavy weight deep inside her stomach. "What?"

"Oh, come on. He's a man slut." Jacob laughed. "You guys were fuck buddies or something, right? What, you'll fuck him but not me?"

She couldn't believe the words that were coming out of his mouth.

"Stop acting like a child."

"Tell me, did you drop to your knees on the first date with him? Or were you frigid with him too? Was alcohol a must to loosen you up?"

She was speechless. There was a long silence. When she felt steady enough she picked up her bag and went to walk down the stairs.

"Listen, I'm sorry, I didn't mean to . . . I don't know, forget it," Jacob mumbled.

She was halfway down the stairs when rage fired up inside her. She stomped back up to his room and looked him in the eye. "What the fuck? 'Forget it'? I'm so sick of men like you treating me like dirt. So fucking sick of it. I changed my mind and I didn't want to have sex with you—it's not hard to understand." She ran back down the stairs.

It was only when she was outside his house, in the quiet street, that she realized she was crying.

The next day she didn't go into detail with Oliver about why the date was bad. She felt ashamed on too many levels and wanted to forget the whole evening. It seemed she was losing her faith piece by piece, and didn't know how to get it back. The only thing she was doing right, she felt, was to believe in God. Everything else she did was wrong, so wrong.

If she tried to talk about her guilt in being a nonpracticing

Muslim to Oliver, he'd say she was the most moral person he knew, and that it didn't matter she wasn't practicing, so long as she was a good person. That point of view comforted her but also gave her nothing. If the person she was talking to was an atheist, of course to them it wouldn't seem a big deal.

If she tried to talk about it to her mum, her mother would encourage her to pray, marry a nice Muslim man, wear a hijab, and insinuate, because she pretended not to know, that Soraya should stop drinking and wearing revealing clothes. And Soraya didn't want to do that. She wanted a middle ground that didn't exist, would never exist. She wanted to feel connected to God, be reassured that everything was happening for a reason, and be given guidance on how to be a better person. But did that mean she had to be told how to dress? And who did her romantic relationships affect, other than herself? Perhaps, she realized, that was the point. Perhaps she needed to acknowledge that she mattered and didn't deserve any more pain. She needed to protect herself because no one else could.

Soraya deleted Tinder.

Chapter 55

NEDA

Brighton, 2015

Without Hossein the house was clean, homey even, though Neda felt bad for thinking that. The cushions on the sofa were in place and the floor was clear of pistachio shells. The house smelt of nothing in particular, a pleasant change from the BO that followed her husband around.

While her children seemed to cope with his absence, Tyzer appeared to struggle the most without him. He sat by the patio door, waiting for hours at a time, until hunger or tiredness took over and he momentarily forgot who his owner was at the lure of a sachet of Whiskas or a warm bed.

Now that the secret was out in the open Neda reached out to Laleh and suggested she come to the house for the first time in over fifteen years.

I'd love it if you came, she had written.

I'll think about it, Laleh replied.

Neda couldn't blame her daughter for her reluctance to come back to the family who had rejected her when she needed them the most, but how else was she meant to make it up to her daughter? Her optimistic nature meant she couldn't believe it was too late. She had to try, even if she knew she didn't deserve a second chance.

"What's really wrong, Soraya?" she asked her youngest daughter.

They were at the M&S café. It was that time of year when the excitement of Christmas was over and everyone was waiting for the arrival of spring and sunlight.

Despite Soraya being bundled up in multiple layers and a faux-fur coat, her teeth chattered as they walked from the car park to the store. It worried Neda—it was cold, but it wasn't *that* cold. She noticed how gaunt her daughter's face had become, how her stomach had flattened out, how thin and frail her wrists looked.

So after an hour of browsing she suggested going to the café, where she bought Soraya a large hot chocolate, insisting on adding whipped cream.

"You look unwell," she told her daughter. "Is it because of what happened with your dad and Laleh?"

"No, it's nothing, I'm fine," Soraya said, eating some of the whipped cream with her forefinger. Neda wished she would use the teaspoon instead, but thought better of saying so.

Neda's gaze was steely. "Oh, come on. You're so skinny now—what's going on?"

Around them were various groups of elderly people. No one Soraya's age. Neda saw the way she looked around, noted this fact, the way her face looked ever-more sad. Something in her daughter's expression reminded her of Hossein's when they first moved to England, when he first told her he felt he didn't belong, that he felt like a loser.

"It's nothing to do with Dad or Laleh."

Neda sighed. She searched for something to say, something to help, but struggled. She always seemed to struggle to help her family and she was sick of it.

"He is sorry, you know," she said finally.

Soraya's head shot up. "What?"

"I know I always talk badly about him and . . ." Here Neda paused, the word stuck in her throat. "I'm sorry."

"What do you mean?" Soraya's brows were furrowed.

Neda noticed the nail of her daughter's forefinger digging into her thumb, and the raw pink skin there. She almost grabbed Soraya's hand, wanting to force her to stop, but that kind of parenting hadn't helped her children in the past.

She made herself lean back in her chair.

"I've been going to counseling," Neda said. "And I've held on to a lot. I've always thought it's better to keep things in, but secrets are no good. They just wear you down. And when I spoke about you . . . about how much you dislike your dad, how anxious you are, how you think no one notices when you pull at the skin around your nails . . . well, I realized I needed to say to you, I'm sorry."

"I don't understand." Soraya put her hands between her legs and squeezed them together.

"I've always come to you children to complain about your father. Amir and Parvin always ignore me. But you're my little girl. You're the only one who listens to me." Her face softened. "I didn't think what that would do to you."

She noticed Soraya becoming tearful then, avoiding eye contact.

"Your dad loves you. I know you don't believe it, but he does. He does bad things, but he . . . he doesn't even recognize what he's doing. The day after he hit us those months ago, I heard him crying in the living room. He thought no one could hear."

"But he still hit us! He's not—"

"He's not perfect, and I don't *like* him. But it's not that simple. He's depressed, he always has been. I just ignored it."

"Everyone always forgets things, always pretends bad behavior is OK if it's in the past. But it's not. It's not." Soraya wiped her tears away quickly. The elderly white people around them probably considered them highly dysfunctional, Neda thought, crying in the M&S café in the middle of the afternoon. Maybe they were.

"In Islam we're taught to forgive. That's something I struggle with, but I'm working on it."

"What about Laleh?"

"We have to make things right, not focus on the past. I feel sick when I think of all the lost time, how much she must have needed us . . ." Neda took a deep breath. "Laleh has agreed to visit us, whilst your dad's away, with her boyfriend and Zara." Neda tried to keep her face neutral when she said the last word, but her nose wrinkled almost reflexively.

"You're OK with meeting her boyfriend?"

"What can I do? I've tried but you children do whatever you want." She shrugged. "Maybe they'll get married. They have been together fifteen years, it's about time."

"Maybe," Soraya said quietly.

"I wish you and Parvin would make up."

"We've not fallen out."

"She's always had it hard with your dad too."

"Why does he like her more then?"

"To be honest, she sucks up to him, and he likes that. You and Laleh never did, you both pointed out his faults, which he hates. He's a stubborn man, but that doesn't mean he doesn't love you."

"But I don't get why she sucks up to him," Soraya persisted.

"It's her way of coping, Soraya dear. Don't be so hard on her." There was a short silence. "What's going on with this boy then?"

Soraya picked up her hot chocolate; she took a sip. Neda watched, a small smile on her face.

"What boy?" Soraya asked.

"The one who took the picture of you."

"You told me not to see him anymore, so I don't."

Neda's smile didn't falter, if anything it widened.

"I know you, azizam, you didn't stop seeing him."

"Well, I haven't seen him in months so . . ."

"What happened?"

Soraya pursed her lips, no doubt wondering if this was a trap. And perhaps years ago it might have been. It wasn't that Neda wanted her daughters to talk to boys, but she knew she needed to accept it as inevitable. She had brought them up in England, they were adults, and she had to respect their decisions.

"Why are you asking these questions?"

"You're grown up now. I'm trying not to make the same mistakes. I don't want secrets between us. I want you to trust me."

"We aren't talking anymore."

Neda nodded slowly.

"And you're sad about that?"

"I guess."

"He's not worth it. No man is." At this, Soraya rolled her eyes. Her mother continued, "Ey, I mean it. Look what happened to me, look what happened to Laleh. The reason I've been so strict with you isn't just because of Islam, it's also because I've *seen* what picking the wrong man can do. Men can ruin your life, and I don't want that for you. I want you to have the best of everything.

"So, focus on yourself first. Get a job you enjoy, create a life for yourself, and then you can think about boys."

"I can think about boys? Since when?"

Neda laughed. "You think I think you listen to me? I know what young people get up to. I was young once. But you're a good Muslim inside, you're a good person, and that's all that matters."

"But I don't practice it at all . . . I'm bad."

"Oh, azizam, you're a good girl. The most moral in the family. That's all Islam is really—being a good, caring person. You're finding yourself. Just make sure you've found yourself before you get involved with men. And find a good husband."

Neda couldn't help but add the last part, she was human after all.

"Tell me about him."

"Who?"

"The boy. I'm curious."

"But it's over . . ."

She saw the tears well in Soraya's eyes, and her heart broke for her. She had so much pent up inside. This time it was Neda's turn to listen to her daughter, and she would make sure she was a good listener, as Soraya had been for her.

"Tell me."

And so, Soraya told her about Magnus. About the confidence he gave her, how he sympathized about Hossein because he was in a similar situation with his dad, his writing, his positivity.

"Poor boy," Neda said about his dad.

"I mean yes, but he's still a bastard," Soraya said with a small smile on her face.

Neda laughed.

"I've taught you well, darling. Shall we go to Waterstones after this? My treat."

Chapter 56

SORAYA

Brighton, 2015

Soraya knocked on Parvin's door. Her mum's words were fresh in her mind.

"Come in," she called.

Soraya opened the door tentatively. When Parvin saw who it was, her face hardened and her lip jutted out. She was sitting on the floor painting her toenails.

"Hi," Soraya said.

Parvin continued painting her nails.

"Can we not fight anymore?" Soraya said quietly.

"I never wanted to. You're the one with the attitude."

Parvin saw Soraya's facial expression, pained, drawn from lack of sleep, angular from lack of appetite. "Oh, God, who even cares? Let's just forget about it," she said, patting the floor next to her. Soraya sat cross-legged while her sister took hold of her hand and began buffing her nonexistent nails.

"What's happened?"

Soraya poured her heart out for the second time that day. It was freeing, letting it all out.

"He'll come back," Parvin said confidently.

"Did you just hear what I said? Our relationship was all fake, and now he lives in Paris and has a new girlfriend."

"You broke up because you never speak about your feelings and he's rebounding. Trust me."

Soraya rolled her eyes. "It's not that simple."

"If it will be it'll be. Put your faith in higher beings and let it go."

Soraya nodded slowly, considering her sister's words.

"I'm sorry I was a bit of a bitch before," Parvin said.

Soraya had never heard her sister apologize to her.

"When I found out about Laleh, I freaked out a bit. I'm meant to be your big sister and I'd always told you to go after boys, but then to find out that she'd gotten herself pregnant, and Dad's reaction to it . . . My mind was a bit messed up after that."

Soraya had been so absorbed in her own problems she hadn't considered how the weight of holding Laleh's secret would have affected Parvin. They all had different ways of coping.

"It's OK. God, I can't believe they actually disowned her."

"I know. When we joked that we'd be disowned if we did something wrong, I don't think I ever truly believed it. Yes, they would shout and scream, but how could they abandon her when she was pregnant? It's mad."

A silence fell between them.

"I think, though, they've changed since then," Parvin said thoughtfully.

"What do you mean?"

"Our parents. Laleh was their firstborn. They were superstrict and overprotective with her—even more so than with us. Mum and Dad were arguing more than ever back then. I think if the same thing happened now they'd react differently."

"I bloody hope so."

"I guess we all make mistakes, some bigger than others."

Soraya sighed. She partly agreed, but their parents had had so many years to rectify their mistake, and they hadn't. Were they too ashamed, embarrassed? Of themselves, or of Laleh? Perhaps both.

"Laleh is thinking of coming to see us all in a few months, you know," Parvin said.

"I heard. I really hope she does."

Parvin continued to fix Soraya's nails in contented silence. For the first time in a long time Soraya's life felt like it was on its way to being whole again.

It was true what her mum said. Soraya needed to find herself, before she found anyone else.

Chapter 57

SORAYA

London, 2015

Weeks ticked by, and became months, until it was almost spring. Soraya had been offered a marketing and design internship, three days a week, at a large theater company. She did this as well as working at the clothes shop part-time. When she rose to go to work it was no longer dark. It was these things that gave her hope. Not that she was short on that. Hope was the reason so many of her expectations had been systematically dashed.

One by one.

But she was trying to change her outlook.

She used her love of searching the Internet to work on her excessive nail-biting. She downloaded a mindfulness app and practiced it every morning for ten minutes. She also began going to a nail salon in an attempt to prevent her from shredding the skin around her nails. Paying twenty-five pounds every three weeks for gel nails became a good reason not to ruin her fingers.

She adopted a new approach, borrowed from Oliver, in her attempts to get over Magnus: pretend he was dead. And no, she wasn't joking. She allowed herself to cherish their memories, but because he was dead there was no hope that they could ever be together. Nothing particularly heinous had happened, but it finally made sense to block him on *all* social media.

She was at her job in the shop, standing by the till, watching the world go by. The store was empty. She was alone with her thoughts and the store playlist that repeated the same ten songs all day long. So in her cruel solitary confinement, also known as working in retail, she thought about how Magnus had so quickly forgotten about their messed-up relationship, and how she couldn't. She decided to change her own narrative.

The launch day for their journal, *Millennials*—a semi-ironic title—was steadily approaching. As well as working her two jobs, Soraya busied herself with designing the cover and layout. She took her laptop everywhere and in the hours between her two jobs she would find a Pret, order a filter coffee, and design. It was cathartic, and held her together. It made her recognize what she was passionate about, after having spent so long worrying that she wasn't passionate about anything. She also learnt that it was pointless to compare herself to everyone else. Once they left university everyone's journey was completely different. Focusing on those around her made no sense anymore. She needed to focus on what made her happy, and she finally found those things in the little acts that brought her joy in the day, like buying herself a nice coffee every so often, or reading in the nearby park on her lunch break on sunnier days.

They found an independent venue, which acted as a café by day and bar by night, to host the journal's launch party for free. The party was the highlight of Soraya's year. All other events before were pre–launch party, and anything after was post–launch party. Whereas, up until recently, life had been pre-Magnus and post-Magnus.

Collectively they decided on which pieces would be included in the journal, and she provided illustrations for each of them. The whole experience cemented what she already knew: she wanted to work in design. And with her internship it seemed Soraya was finally moving in the right direction.

She had also written a piece featured in *Millennials*, but that was something she was desperately trying to forget about.

"You *need* to—you have so much baggage that should be let out," Oliver had said to her in the kitchen one day.

"Are you sure we just haven't had that many good submissions?"

He pursed his lips, let out a breath. "Well, there's that too, but that's not why I'm saying this."

"It feels very personal . . ."

There was an awkward silence. "You're right, I shouldn't push you. It's just . . . never mind."

"What?"

"Nothing." He busied himself with picking up the plate in front of him and walking over to the sink to clean it.

"Come on! What is it? What were you going to say?" She could barely hear herself over the sound of hot water and the clatter of plates in their very full sink.

He turned the water off and looked at her.

"I was just going to say, a couple of months ago you were talking about your dad. Now it seems you've closed up again."

"I'll think about it," she muttered.

Soraya found that it was surprisingly easy to write; it came almost too naturally. But when she read the first draft, before agreeing to do it officially, she realized how superficially she was writing about her experience. It was as though she was an onlooker in her own life. So when she brought the lens closer, and talked about how these things affected her mentally and physically, it triggered waves of vulnerability. Just having the words written down stripped her bare. And that was before anyone had even looked at it. Her face was tearstained, her whole body tense from writing up her experience.

It was in that moment she knew she needed to tell her story. Even if just one person read it and could relate, that would be enough. It felt selfish of her not at least to try to make one person feel less alone.

The day of the launch arrived. The venue was in Deptford; the café-bar was on the ground floor and the basement was a larger room with plain white walls. The copies were laid out on a table at the back of the basement, and every time she looked at them Soraya felt a rush of pride. She finally had something tangible that she could produce to show she had achieved something, that she was good at something other than selling overpriced dresses to stuck-up customers.

The cover was simple; she had played with typography and contrasting colors to make it stand out. She'd also drawn some illustrations of small birds, which were printed in foil; they shimmered in the light.

A couple of hours in and the bar was busy, faces Soraya recognized merging with others she didn't know.

When it was time for the readings, the basement fell quiet. Soraya's palms were clammy, and she would have preferred less engagement from the audience.

All eyes were on Priya, Oliver, and Soraya as they stood at the front of the room.

"Thank you all so much for coming to the *Millennials* launch party!" Oliver said, breaking into a grin. She had never seen him so happy. There were claps and cheers from the audience. Oliver's new boyfriend, Kiran, wolf-whistled from the back row. Soraya had met him a few times and finally felt that Oliver had met someone worthy of him. "*Millennials* is a journal celebrating stories from people whose voices aren't ordinarily heard. We're so excited to show you something we've been working really hard on. We're going to start off with some of the contributors reading excerpts from their pieces, and then you can buy a copy, have a drink, mingle . . ."

"And get smashed," Priya added, sticking her tongue out. Soraya cringed, but the crowd seemed to enjoy it.

Soraya had rehearsed what she would say, but with all eyes, those of both strangers and friends, on her, she clammed up. She looked to Oliver, and he gave her the slightest nod. *Fuck it*, she thought.

"And the theme for this issue is breaking free. It's a theme so many of us can relate to. Whether you're breaking free from toxic relationships—involving others or yourself. Graduating from university and finding yourself. Breaking free from societal expectations, from supposed norms. The list goes on. And Issue One is just a snapshot of us breaking free. I hope you all enjoy it."

Priya jumped on the spot. "And leading with that . . . the beautiful Soraya Nazari will begin with her piece, 'A Prison of Silence.'"

Oliver and Priya sat down. The piece of paper shook in Soraya's hands.

She had practiced this over and over. She had it memorized; the printed copy was just insurance. Earlier in the day when they had run through it together, she'd been told she needed to speak louder and slower. At the time she was aware she was speaking too quickly, but fear of being truly heard held her back. Again, *Fuck it* rang loud and clear in her head. Once it was over, she could hide away and be embarrassed.

"Hi, I'm Soraya," she said, and then cleared her throat. "Obviously," she added. Oliver gave her a supportive smile. She focused on him. Settled on him, and only him. " 'The first time I told someone my dad is a drug addict, I burst into tears. The first time I told someone, my best friend, my dad is a drug addict, I was twenty years old. All my life until then I stayed silent, as though I had done something wrong, as though I were to blame. It took meeting my best friend, my confidant, to change that.

" 'My dad is selfish, cowardly, and often a bully. What saddens me most about all of this is that I'll never know if that's his personality, or the drugs. I never knew my dad before he became addicted to opium, and then methadone, courtesy of the NHS. I will never know him sober because he doesn't want to quit. Or maybe he simply can't.

" 'It's taken me a while to realize the effect his drug taking has had on me, physically and mentally. When I have a moment to think, I peel the skin by my nails. It often bleeds. It hurts. But I can't stop. It's compulsive. I grew up in a disrupted house. Life was never smooth sailing with a drug-addicted dad, so in adulthood I can't see my life being smooth. Therefore, when it ticks along, and there's no immediate threat, I peel the skin by my fingers, and wonder: what horrible thing is going to happen next?' "

Her vision of Oliver was blurry by now, but she continued speaking, needing to finish her piece before she cried.

" 'So, I'm learning to forgive, to understand my dad better, to change my future. I made a decision to break myself free. Free from the shackles of my dad, from my anxiety, from his addiction. I'm allowing myself to soar, unrestrained by the weight of my dad's mistakes. I am his daughter, yes, but I am not my dad.' "

The clapping in contrast to the silence before made Soraya jump. She put up one hand to cover her smile, and to wipe away her tears. Oliver stood up, clapping loudly. She heard a familiar yelp above the clapping. It took her all the way back to graduation day. She wiped away any lingering tears and looked out over the seated crowd.

Magnus.

Just as she had at graduation, despite her grand speech about change, she moved out of the spotlight and sat down in the front row, next to Priya, while Oliver introduced the next speaker. All the while her head was pounding. Was she going mad? Or had she seen Magnus Evans, who was supposed to be in Paris, listening to her read? Convinced it couldn't have been him, she turned in her seat to peer at the back row. Sure enough, there he was, looking right at her. He smiled. She turned back to the front again. Her brain couldn't compute what was going on. *This isn't supposed to happen,* her mind moaned, *he's meant to be dead to you.* The technique didn't quite work when the subject was in the same room. And very much alive. A minor flaw.

Another contributor finished reading her piece, and there was more clapping. Soraya rose and hurried out to the upstairs bar. Her legs were shaking.

"Can I get a vodka cranberry?" she asked the barman, her voice wobbly. *Hold yourself together.* The main bar was empty apart from the staff. She could hear the next contributor speaking downstairs and felt a pang of guilt.

It was still only just light out, the in-between phase at which in the blink of an eye the sky would turn gray and then night would arrive.

She handed the barman the money while taking a sip, and experienced the familiar warmth of alcohol.

Predictably, she felt a presence behind her.

She shut her eyes, counting to ten, wishing what she knew to be wrong.

On six he spoke. "Soraya," Magnus said. She'd forgotten his accent, forgotten how real it made him. In her head his voice was neutral, without flaw. Out loud she was reminded of how he always pronounced her name with the emphasis on the wrong letters.

Somewhere she was aware of the noise from downstairs, and probably the barman looking at her like she was a psycho, but she couldn't open her eyes. This was her way of burying her head in the sand. Her attempt to escape. Cornered and with no way out, she chose simply no longer to see. But it was no good. There was no escaping Magnus's presence; even his scent seemed to overwhelm her.

"Soraya," he said again, his hand ever so lightly placed on her shoulder. She recoiled, snapping her eyes open in the process.

When she turned and saw him she felt the familiar tingle of embarrassment. *Why can't I behave normally?*

His hair was longer, collar-length and wavy, and he had let his stubble grow. Her gaze traveled to his arms, which were still defined under his top. This only annoyed her further, because unlike before he wasn't pursuing her, he wasn't *hers* anymore. He was just a stranger coming at the worst time, distracting her from an important event.

"Oh, hi," she said.

He, too, seemed speechless. His hand was still raised in front of him and he lowered it slowly, as though in a daze. As though he hadn't quite expected her to turn around. This pushed her over the edge. She walked around him and hovered by the door. She couldn't leave, it was her event, but she longed to be out of this room. How could she go downstairs and sit quietly when her mind was racing, her heart pounding?

"Your piece was really beautiful—" she heard him say.

She didn't let him finish.

"Why are you here?" she asked.

He sighed, his brown eyes soft, imploring her to understand. But understand what?

"You deleted me," he said.

"And?" she replied. It came out more sharply than she intended.

He gave her a wounded look. She wanted to walk away from

him, make him feel how he had made her feel all those months ago. But her curiosity was piqued. Her hopes were raised. And it was better to dash them quickly.

"Why?" he said. It was almost a whisper, and she couldn't believe it had come from him. She looked at his face closely, trying to gauge what exactly it was he was thinking.

"It seemed unnecessary to have each other on Facebook," she said. "Besides, you live in Paris now—why are you even here?"

"I'm not just talking about Facebook. You also blocked me on Instagram, Twitter, and even my number . . . there was no way for me to contact you. I hoped at least we could be friends."

Soraya rolled her eyes. He still hadn't answered her question. "Magnus, we didn't end things well. Our whole relationship was a sham. *Why* would we be friends?"

He looked wounded for a moment. "It wasn't a sham. I thought maybe once the dust settled . . ."

"Well, I don't want to talk to you. I haven't forgiven you." The words stuck in her mouth, were a struggle to let out, but she knew she needed to say them.

He shut his eyes briefly and pinched the bridge of his nose. He breathed deeply. It was unnerving. "I fucked up, OK, I fucked up, and I want . . ."

"You want what?" She kicked herself for asking.

"I don't . . . I don't know."

"Well, I need to go back downstairs." Soraya moved towards the stairs, her back to him.

"Can we talk after?"

"I suppose."

"Soraya, please."

She turned again, gritting her teeth. "We can talk next week." She had no intention of meeting up with him.

"You're only saying that," Magnus said.

"I said I would, why would I lie?"

"I know you, Soraya. I know you like to think I don't, but I do." Again, the soft voice. "Please, have a drink with me after the launch, or let me walk you to the bus stop. I just want to talk."

"Fine, whatever, OK. I have to go now."

She went downstairs, drink in hand, sneaking back to her seat in the front row. She felt embarrassed to be coming in during a reading. Priya and Oliver gave her questioning looks and she shook her head, her face still flushed from the surprise of her past coming back to haunt her.

Chapter 58

SORAYA

London, 2015

The evening was a blur of congratulations. Strangers and friends came over to Soraya, Priya, and Oliver, asking questions, telling them which piece resonated with them the most, and they felt high from every interaction. They had actually pulled it off. They took turns standing behind the table selling copies of the journal. When it was Soraya's turn a girl walked over to her. She looked at the girl, blond, slim, and beautiful, and felt misgivings. When did she become so jaded?

"I wanted to say I loved your piece," the girl said, her voice only just audible over the R&B music and chatter. "My mum is in a similar situation and it was nice to be able to hear someone else talk about what it's like. Well, I don't mean 'nice,' but you know what I mean."

The words washed over Soraya and her posture softened. "I'm sorry to hear that," she said, awkwardly. She still didn't know what to say to people who said they were in a similar position to her; she didn't yet have the vocabulary down. The girl clenched her fists and held them slightly behind herself. That too Soraya could relate to. "It's shit, isn't it?" she said, finding the words she would want someone to say to her. And perhaps that's what she needed to do—not give apologies for someone else's behavior or say dismissive things such as "I'm sorry." It's shit that people get addicted to substances, and there's not always a great deal more to say about it.

"I'd like to buy one," the girl said, handing Soraya the money.

"Yeah, sure." She took the money in exchange for a copy. "Thank you."

A brunette came up behind the girl, placed her hands around her waist, and gave her a smile. "Great publication," she said to Soraya. The blond girl seemed visibly to relax and smiled at the new arrival.

"You made me jump," she said, her voice breathless but happy all the same. To see that this girl had someone in her life made Soraya smile.

"If you ever want to talk about what you said, send me an email. It's on the first page," Soraya said.

"I will. My name is Kate, by the way."

"I'm Soraya. I hope you enjoy reading the journal."

When Kate left Soraya exhaled, but also felt a weight on her shoulders in the familiar form of Magnus Evans, looming in one corner of the room. Seeing that she was on her own, he walked over to her.

"Hi," he said.

"Hi," she said back.

"Can I buy a copy?"

"Of course. That'll be six pounds." He handed her a ten-pound note, and when she took it their hands brushed against each other. She was careful to hand him his change by dropping the pound coins into his palm, to prevent any further touching.

"Can you sign it for me?" He opened it up to her piece, and she couldn't tell if he was joking.

She laughed.

"I'm serious," he said, pulling a pen out of his backpack.

"You know I'm not a writer . . ."

"I think you'll find you are. A published writer in fact." He gave her a smile.

She scribbled her name onto the page and handed it back to him.

She hated the effect he still had on her.

Someone stood behind him, wanting to buy a copy. Magnus moved out of the way and wandered the room again. Soraya was trying her hardest to be present during the transaction, but her eyes kept straying over to him as he read the excerpts on the wall. Then he settled on a bench, opened the journal and, she assumed, began reading her piece. Watching him study it made her skin crawl.

Oliver came over, with his catlike strut, a frown on his face. "What is *he* doing here?" His gaze settled on Magnus.

Soraya rolled her eyes. "Your guess is as good as mine."

"Well, what did he say to you?"

She glanced over; he was still reading. "He said he wants to talk later."

Oliver made a sound of disapproval. "He's a piece of trash," he muttered.

She nodded, not truly agreeing. "That he is."

The rest of the evening passed quickly. Her launch party persona was similar to her retail work persona: overenthusiastic and full of faux confidence. That said, with the praise and good vibes of the party, she felt her self-esteem boosted. It was the first time since she'd graduated that she felt empowered by something she had done intellectually, as though what they said at the graduation ceremony was feasible: you can achieve anything you set your hopes on.

And all too soon, the night was over. There were only a handful of people left, and the music had quietened down.

"We're going to the pub now, you sure you can't come, Soraya?" Priya asked, putting on her mini backpack.

"Ah, I can't, I have work early tomorrow." That was true.

"Not even for one drink?" Oliver said.

She looked over at Magnus, who was still there, saying goodbye to someone he had met during the party. Soraya had kept a close eye on him throughout the night and admired the way he effortlessly made friends.

"I just want to hear what he has to say . . ."

"He's a player, Soraya," Priya said, emphasizing each letter of "player." "He's just messing with your head."

Soraya eyed Oliver, and he looked grim. "I mean, you know how I feel about him. He's no good."

She wanted desperately to agree with them. But unfortunately hope had already begun to blossom.

"Doesn't he have a French girlfriend anyway?" Priya asked what Oliver would not.

Soraya was outnumbered. She knew what she was doing was stupid, but she didn't care. In that moment, feminist or not, she wanted to hear him out.

"It's not a big deal," she muttered, packing one of the suitcases they had brought with the remaining copies. "I'll finish up here and take what I can."

"We'll get the rest tomorrow, don't carry too much," Oliver said, before giving her a pat on the back. "Good luck," he called over his shoulder. They walked past Magnus, and she saw how he almost greeted them both, before seeing that they were giving him dirty looks. She felt embarrassed for him, until she remembered his new girlfriend. *He doesn't deserve my pity.*

"Or my time, for that matter," she whispered to herself, feeling a change of heart coming. But it was too late; only Magnus and Soraya were left in the basement now.

Across the room Magnus smiled at her. His new friend had gone. Soraya gave him a grimace in return.

"So," she said, unable to endure an awkward silence.

"So," he said in return.

She had finished packing the journals into the case and zipped it up. She stretched her back, rolling her shoulders in an attempt to get rid of a knot in them. She was *tired*. There had been months of work leading up to this point and now it was over she was fatigued. But instead of going home to sleep, here she was in front of Magnus, when she'd thought she'd never see him again. Had resigned herself to that fact.

He walked towards her, an anxious look on his face. She had forgotten how big he was. In her memory he had been smaller. His eyes intently searched hers.

"How have you been?" he asked, softly.

"Fine."

Silence.

"Look—" he said, at the same moment Soraya said, "Why are you back?"

"I was in the area?" He smiled. She didn't. He scratched the inside of his arm nervously, looking down. "I fucked things up with us and . . ." His hand seemed to be reaching for something—the right words perhaps?

"And?" she said, impatient for him to say what she had wished he would say for months. But it was too late now, wasn't it?

He closed the space between them, and somehow within the blink of an eye his hands were cupping her face. Despite her better judgment, she closed her eyes and allowed it. Just the touch of his fingertips against her cheeks sent sparks through her.

"I need you to know something: I really wasn't involved in that bet. I hate that you think I would do something like that, to *you*."

She could hear the pain in his voice, knew instantly that he wasn't lying. But did it even matter anymore whether he had lied? Did any of it matter now?

"I've missed you," he whispered, quietly. So quietly, she wasn't sure if she had imagined it.

"I've missed you too," she replied, despite her gut telling her not to.

His lips grazed hers gently. She wrapped her arms around his neck and he lifted her up, setting her down on the table. He grabbed her legs and she wrapped them around his waist. He suddenly deepened the kiss, each movement deeper and more desperate than the last. His mouth was hot, his tongue expertly caressing hers, and his hands held her waist like she was made of glass.

It was Soraya who broke the kiss first. "Wait," she said, putting a hand on his chest, imposing a much-needed barrier. "You can't just . . ." She shook her head. "You can't just come back, after all this time, and kiss me, and expect me to fall at your feet." He gave her a small smile. His lips were a deep shade of pink, a reminder that she'd done just that.

He raised his hand to her cheek again. She was very conscious that her legs were still wrapped around him, and felt too scared to let go—in that moment she didn't want to draw attention to herself, she just wanted to understand what he was thinking, what he was doing.

"I've missed you, Soraya."

"You said that already."

"Are you seeing someone?" he asked, his eyes suddenly anxious.

"I'd be worried if I was." She laughed, untangling herself from him. "I mean, you are, aren't you?" She had forgotten that for a moment and felt ashamed. No one wanted to be the other woman.

"What do you mean?" He was still standing close to her, her legs either side of him. Her eyes briefly flickered downwards.

He was everywhere, his scent too close, his body too close, and she needed to regain her senses. "You have a girlfriend, right?" She closed her eyes as he lifted up her chin.

"Open your eyes."

She shook her head.

"Open your eyes."

"I can't right now," she said.

"Soraya," he breathed.

She opened them tentatively and was met with the sight of his large brown eyes focusing on her.

"It's only ever been you."

She shook her head again. "Lies," she breathed.

"Soraya, I love you."

A punch to the gut. Her head was shaking uncontrollably. "No, you don't."

He frowned, stepped back, turned away from her. His broad shoulders were hunched, hands shoved into his jeans pockets. He didn't say anything.

She jumped off the table, her legs wobbly. As she stepped towards him her movements were slow and careful. She didn't have anything to say, but the distance between them felt wrong.

"What are you thinking?" she asked.

"That I just told you I love you," he said, almost angrily. All she could see was the tension in his back, and she was sure if she touched it, it would be rock-hard. She tested her theory. Her palm lightly grazed his shoulder, and she was rewarded with a shiver. "Don't," he said quietly. She tugged at him so he'd turn to her.

"You're seeing someone," she stated.

He breathed heavily. "I *was*."

"What happened?"

He made a dismissive noise. "I don't want to talk about that, Soraya. I just—I want you to know how much I care about you. I don't want to talk about girls from my past."

"*I'm* a girl from your past! I came before her; she's more recent than me!" The words came out almost in a shout.

"I only dated her to forget about you, and it didn't work. It just made me miss you more." Soraya stared at the balloons they'd decorated the space with, unable to meet his gaze. "Soraya, look at me."

Her teeth were chattering, her whole body a knot of nerves. "How do I know I'm not just another rebound from some other girl you've dated?"

There, she thought. At least she had said it, what she had feared all along.

Magnus didn't seem to comprehend. "She knew what she was to me. I was clear about my intentions."

"I went on a date with a guy a couple of months ago. He knew you from uni. Said you'd basically slept with everyone. Is that true?"

Magnus furrowed his brow, pushed his hands deeper into his pockets. "What? Who was it?"

"That's not the point. I worry that I'm just . . ." She couldn't quite finish her sentence. Thinking that Magnus only wanted her for sex was one thing, but having him there in front of her, reminding her of their past, how gentle he'd always been, she couldn't say the words. She didn't believe them anymore.

"None of the girls I've been with before meant anything to me, they were always short flings or . . . I don't know, I don't really want to talk about it. I want to talk about us. Whether there could still be an *us*. Or have I got this wrong? Was what you said in your diary how you really felt? Am I being a total idiot here?"

"No, you're not being an idiot," she said quietly. "Nothing has changed. I'm still not sure I'm ready to have sex. I need to find myself, I guess. And if or when I do want to do it, it'll take me a while. I want to take it at my own pace, and I know that annoyed you—"

"It didn't annoy me—"

"Oh, come on, it annoyed you. So much so that you lied to your friends about it."

He took his hands out of his pockets and ran his fingers through his hair in frustration. "Soraya, these past months without you have been awful. I went to Paris to escape, thinking if I wasn't in London anymore, if I had a new adventure, I could forget you, forget about my family, but I can't. I know I've been shit, but I'm asking you to let me show you that I won't be this time, that what we have is real, it just started off a bit weird. I'll show you all that if you give me another chance."

"Come on, if we still haven't had sex in a year, you're saying you'd be OK with it?" She laughed. "Be realistic."

Both his hands were on her face, his lips inches from hers. "I just want you. However much you can give, I'll be happy with."

"I want to believe you—"

"Then do," he breathed.

"You said I don't talk about my feelings," she said tentatively. She didn't want him to jump on this flaw of hers, but it had to be said. "That you don't even know me. And maybe you don't. How has that changed?"

"I was projecting on you, I realize that now."

"What do you mean?"

He sighed. "I've always been annoyed with myself for bottling up my feelings about my parents, for quite literally running away from them, leaving home as soon as I could and only going back at Christmas. I think I projected that onto you. All the things I said to you, I guess I was saying to myself. But we're all different in how we deal with these things, and I shouldn't have said what I did. You should be able to tell me things in your own time. I'm sorry."

"But some of what you said was true, and I'm working on it," she said. "And I'm sorry. For the things I said in my diary. I didn't mean them."

He didn't say anything.

"I guess it's a good job I didn't write about how much I fell for you," she said, laughing nervously. "That would have been embarrassing."

He smiled. "I think I would have liked that actually."

"Wait, aren't you living in Paris?" she asked.

He gave a laugh, his breath mingling with hers, making her dizzy.

"Barely. I could quite easily move back. I *want* to come back."

"Why?" she asked, in a small voice.

"Soraya"—he put his forehead against hers—"you're so special to me. You know that, don't you?"

She shook her head.

"Well, that's my fault. I should have made it clear how important you are." He paused for a moment and frowned. "Of course, if you're not interested, if you've moved on, that's fine. Obviously it's fine," he said quickly. "I'll leave you alone. Although I'd like to be friends eventually, if you would."

She smiled; couldn't help it. Normally she was the one to ramble. She stood on her tiptoes and pressed her lips to his.

"I'd like to try again," she said finally. "But I know I also need to work at finding myself, whatever that means. I'd still like to take things slow."

"You don't know how happy you've just made me," Magnus said, grinning.

"I was wrong about you, you know. We're not that different after all."

"I guess we were wrong about each other." He smiled down at her and linked his fingers with hers. She looked down at their hands together, hers small and tan, his large and white. He squeezed her fingers, and in that moment she felt safe, loved. More than that, it felt something like coming home or letting out a long-held breath.

"By the way"—she looked into his eyes, and for the first time said exactly what she was feeling—"I love you too."

EPILOGUE

Brighton, 2015

It was the time of new beginnings, forgiveness, fresh starts. Ahead of Nowruz, Iranian New Year, Neda spring-cleaned the entire house. She dusted the tops of the wardrobes, flipped mattresses, and cleaned windows.

In the weeks that followed, she set to work redecorating Laleh's bedroom, removing Hossein's belongings from the room. Neda placed her daughter's old things in boxes, opened the windows, and let the room breathe. She painted the walls a soft pink. It was the first time she had ever painted anything. She could have found a decorator but it felt right for her to do it. She needed this. More than that, she wanted it.

She had purchased furniture from Habitat, all white and sleek. Soraya helped her assemble the different pieces. The bedroom would no longer be stuck in the nineties. It was now inviting and neutral. Unrecognizable. When choosing a new bedspread, Neda wondered what her grandchild would like, and such thoughts gave her hope.

She spoke to Hossein every day. He seemed to be thriving in Tehran, had even agreed to go to a rehabilitation center. It was the longest he had been sober. The future ahead of them was unknown; part of her still resented him, but at least she now understood him. She knew better than to pin too many hopes on his recovery; for the moment she thanked Allah that things were changing, and remained patient.

She knew Soraya had gotten back together with the English boy. They did not speak openly about it, but she noticed a change in her daughter. She appeared lighter, happier. She was not sure if it was because of the boy, or because he was no longer a secret she was keeping from her mother. Neda knew the weight of secrets all too well.

Neda, too, remembered Soraya's surprise when she first discovered Laleh had stayed with her boyfriend all this time.

"But it's been ages," Soraya had marveled. "And they were so young when they first met. I never imagined that they'd still be together."

She had replied at the time that while he was not Muslim, he seemed like a good, caring man, and ultimately that was all that mattered. Neda had changed a lot over the past year; this was not something she would have said to her daughter openly before. She would have worried it would give Soraya ideas that she could also make a relationship work with a non-Muslim man. She still worried, but needed to let her children live their own lives. There was a lot of unlearning to be done.

Of course, Neda too was surprised that Laleh and her boyfriend had stayed together. It was not what she expected from an English man. She had always thought English people switched romantic partners like it was nothing. Admittedly, she was proven wrong, in this instance at least. It was one of the few times Neda was overjoyed to be mistaken.

And then the day finally arrived.

Neda wore her finest hijab: blue silk with a subtle floral pattern, bought from Liberty London ten years ago.

"This is weird," Soraya said.

Amir and Parvin were dressed conservatively, Amir in a button-up shirt and trousers, and Parvin in a long flowing dress. As ever, Soraya did not get the dress-code memo and wore a minidress with thick tights and an oversize jumper. Neda was thinking about telling her to change when there was a knock on the door.

They all froze for a second. Neda made her way towards the door, but before that she hissed, "Amir, be nice to the boy."

Of course, Neda didn't like that Laleh and Matthew were still unmarried, but she'd lost the right to have an opinion on the matter when she allowed her child to be disowned. She knew that, at least.

Amir grumbled something in response. His tone reminded her of Hossein's.

"You've had girlfriends, you can't talk, remember that," she shot back. There was a definite change in the family dynamics. Amir's misdeeds, which formerly had been let slide, she now called him out on. She was reconsidering what had been ingrained in her thinking: that exceptions were always to be made for men. She'd always known it was wrong, the way she treated her daughters differently from her son, but had ignored her own misgivings, too caught up in Hossein to check herself.

But that was changing now.

It was a start.

Through the stained glass in the front door Neda could make out three figures. Sixteen years had led to this point. So much lost time, so many missed firsts. Would her daughter hate her? Would her granddaughter be scared, resentful even, of the family that disowned her mother because of her? It was different talking on the telephone, the small talk during those strained conversations. It was nothing like now. You can't hide how you're really feeling in person, Neda thought.

Neda wrung her hands three times, needing to release her nerves.

With her eyes closed, she turned the handle and opened the door.

Standing before her was her long-lost daughter. Laleh. She was taller now, perhaps after a growth spurt in her later teenage years. Next to her stood an even taller man and behind them a young woman. Matthew was slender, with thick circular glasses and curly hair. His skin was almost translucent, mirrored in their daughter, who was pale with black curly hair. Her eyes were large. She stood nervously behind her father, despite him trying to push her in front.

"Hello, Mum." Laleh's voice cracked.

"Darling," Neda said.

Neda saw so much of herself in Laleh, but her daughter was her own woman now. There were small lines by Laleh's eyes, Neda hoped from laughing. It was one thing to see her daughter grown up in pictures, but to see her standing before her left Neda almost speechless.

Zara was her mother's daughter. In fact, Neda was sure if she'd seen her in the street she would have known instinctively that this was her granddaughter. Zara had Laleh's strong jaw and soft hazel eyes, but she also had her father's solid, straight nose.

Neda's heart hurt from wanting to know everything about the women before her, understanding she should have done this much, much sooner. She blinked past the tears and turned her gaze to the man.

"Hi, I'm Matthew," Laleh's partner said, his voice polite and measured. He gave her a small wave, while simultaneously attempting an equally small bow. She imagined Laleh had briefed him on the fact that Muslim women couldn't shake hands with men.

"Hi," Zara said quietly, her Scottish accent audible, shifting her weight nervously from leg to leg.

"Do you know who I am?" Neda asked Zara in the tone she adopted whenever she addressed anyone under the age of sixteen.

They had spoken on the phone several times, usually on Zara's birthday, but their conversations were always short. They didn't know each other well enough to have a rapport.

Neda had to raise her head to look Zara in the eye while she spoke. The girl was tall for a recently turned fifteen-year-old.

She nodded. "Yeah, you're my grandma?" She looked to her mother as she spoke.

Neda smiled and then covered her mouth, eyes brimming with yet more tears. It was not the hesitation in her granddaughter's voice that made her tearful, but rather the possibility of redemption the child's visit represented. Neda understood she was being given another chance at a relationship with her granddaughter and daughter. This time she would be assertive, fair, an ally to all her family. She would be everything she had wanted Maman to be to her, instead of letting history repeat itself.

"Come in, come in, everyone!" Neda said, not meeting their gaze for fear she would start crying in earnest.

As they removed their shoes by the front door, she offered them plastic slippers to wear inside. Laleh accepted but Matthew and Zara declined.

"It's part of Iranian culture to wear slippers inside the house," Laleh explained to Zara.

"Yes, it's a lot more hygienic and comfortable," Neda chimed in, proud of her daughter for remembering. "Have you had a long journey to get here?"

"We came to London on Friday and did some sightseeing yesterday," Matthew said. "And then got the train to Brighton this morning. It gave us an excuse to go to London as a family at least!" Neda detected a slight lisp in his speech and wondered if it came out more with nerves. He had an air of softness about him, quite unlike the men she had grown up around.

"Ah, that sounds lovely," she said.

While other families might have gathered to greet their guests at the door, Neda's children were socially awkward and sat waiting in the living room. She imagined them grimacing together. She would scold them about this later.

When they walked into the living room, Parvin, Amir, and Soraya stood up, eyes ranging in every direction—towards the sister they hadn't seen for sixteen years, her boyfriend, and the niece they hadn't known about.

Neda noticed Soraya, in particular, observing the couple before her, who had managed to stick together despite all the odds that were stacked against them. Soraya and Neda had both always thought love prevailing over all was just the stuff of fiction. Until now.

Eventually there were tears—Laleh and Parvin couldn't hold them back when they first saw each other, and because Neda was already on the brink she let her own tears flow. They embraced in a three-way hug, with Neda muttering, "I'm so sorry," while Parvin said, "I've missed you," and Laleh repeated, "It's OK." Holding her daughters together felt right, and for the first time in sixteen years Neda was whole again. She hadn't realized how big a part of her was missing without her eldest child and granddaughter, until now. A piece of her had finally returned.

Soraya, Amir, Zara, and Matthew watched the three women hold each other as they sobbed.

Despite having been told not to, Amir began sizing Matthew up.

"You're all so big," Laleh said, taking in her siblings.

Zara looked to the doorway, where their heights over their childhood were marked. Neda followed her gaze.

She power walked to the kitchen and returned with a marker pen.

It seemed even Amir, despite resenting the way Matthew had not yet married Laleh, had thawed towards him when he learnt his sister's partner was a fellow accountant. They had begun an in-depth conversation about the merits of setting up your own business.

"Look here." Neda pointed to the doorway. "When your mum was your age she was this tall." She indicated a point on the door-frame.

Zara tentatively walked over. She ran her fingertips along the frame. She grinned, exposing her small teeth, which reminded Neda so much of Hossein's.

"Ha! Look, I'm way taller than you were at my age, Mum," Zara said after a moment of observing. She looked at Laleh triumphantly.

"You get it from your dad." Laleh laughed.

"Can I . . . do you want to put your height here?" Neda asked.

"Why not?" Zara said.

Hope.

"Brilliant," Neda told her granddaughter. She handed Parvin the marker and watched as Soraya laughed with her niece, and Parvin marked Zara's height on the frame.

Neda looked at Laleh, her eyes reflecting years of regret and apologies.

"Welcome home, azizam."

ACKNOWLEDGMENTS

This book would not exist without the help of many wonderful people who encouraged and guided me along the way—and to whom I am forever grateful.

First, thank you to my agent, Niki Chang. I knew from our first phone call that you immediately got *The Mismatch,* and believed in Soraya's and Neda's stories. Since then you've continued to champion this book, giving invaluable editorial guidance, and *The Mismatch* truly wouldn't be what it is today without you. I feel very lucky to have such a brilliant agent, who always has my back.

Thank you to the whole team at The Good Literary Agency: Salma, Nikesh, Arzu, and Julia.

Thank you to the Arrow team. Cassandra Di'Bello for acquiring *The Mismatch.* Although we didn't work together for long before you returned to Australia, I'll never forget our first meeting and how infectious your excitement for *The Mismatch* was. A big thank-you to Jennie Rothwell and Emily Griffith for tirelessly whipping the story into shape. And Isabelle Ralphs and Roisin O'Shea for doing the brilliant marketing and PR work for this book.

Thank you to Hilary Teeman and Caroline Weishuhn at Ballantine for your insightful editorial feedback and guidance towards the later stages that really brought the story together even more.

Thank you to everyone at Spread the Word for all the support you've given me over the years. It was through being part of the Flight 1000 scheme in 2016 that I realized people may actually want to read my stories, even if I hadn't seen stories like mine in the books I was reading, and that getting my writing published wasn't as beyond my reach as I had once thought. Then in being part of the London Writers Award scheme in 2018 I met some amazing, insightful people, with whom I formed a writing group and who really gave me the tools to look at my work more critically. So thank you, Ruth, Eva, and Bobby from Spread the Word—and my LWA pals Riley, Kira, Tice, Jarred, Koyer, and Sofia.

Thank you to my Faber Academy writing group. Having such an honest, motivating group when I wrote the first draft of *The Mismatch* was an invaluable experience. I had written one novel before, in my teens, but I didn't think I'd be able to write another one, and it was through this course and being surrounded by such inspiring people that I managed it.

Thank you to MT, who over the many years it took to write and edit this book remained my own personal cheerleader, always believing in my writing and in me. I am very lucky to know you.

Thank you to my close friends who dealt with the many semi-breakdowns that I had whilst writing this book. (I am a very dramatic person, it was never really that deep.) You're all great.

And of course, thank you to my wonderful family for all the support you have given me. I'm lucky to have a close-knit family and I'm proud of where we are today. Thank you, Mum, Dad, Ali, and Azadeh.

A special mention, too, to my beloved cats Tyzer and Tyson, who passed away during the editing of this book. They both were so special and important to me, so as you may have noticed I featured them in this book!

Finally, a big thank-you to *you*, the reader, for choosing to read *The Mismatch*. It means the world to me, and I hope you enjoyed it.

the
MISMATCH

SARA JAFARI

A BOOK CLUB GUIDE

Questions and Topics for Discussion

1. Soraya embarks on her plan to get her first kiss from Magnus because she feels that she is behind her peers in terms of life experience. Has there ever been a time where you felt pressured to "catch up" to peers in one way or another?

2. Soraya thinks she could never have feelings for Magnus, someone with whom she believes she has little in common, although she soon realizes that that's not quite the case. Have you ever judged someone prematurely, only to find out that you have much more in common with them than you would have guessed?

3. A large part of Soraya's struggle to find her footing as a young woman has to do with the fact that she has been raised with a set of values from her Muslim parents that often clashes with the values of the British culture around her. Have you ever faced a similar dilemma, in which you had to decide what your values were? Was it difficult for you to decide how you felt? Why or why not?

4. Soraya and Oliver are best friends because they can empathize with each other's complex family relationships. Have you ever bonded with a friend

in a similar way, through a shared, though separate, experience?

5. Although Soraya often seems to feel that she is unable to understand her mother and some of the choices her mother has made, we can see that Soraya's and Neda's stories are much more similar than they might seem to be on the surface. Do you think that this makes it easier for them to relate to and understand each other? Or does it make it more difficult? Why?

6. Soraya understandably has a very difficult relationship with her father, as a result of both his adherence to patriarchal values and his failings as an individual. How do you think this affected her relationship with her family, with Magnus, and with herself? Have you ever found yourself similarly disappointed in a family member's choices? If so, how did you react in that situation?

7. When Soraya finds out that Magnus has discussed their sex life with his friends and hears that a bet has taken place, she is upset by the idea that he has been using her. Magnus quickly points out, however, that Soraya herself (in her diary) admitted to using him in a similar way. Do you think that Soraya was right to be upset with Magnus? Was Magnus right to be upset with Soraya? Why or why not?

8. For much of Soraya's life, her sister Laleh has been an enigma. How do you think Soraya felt when she learned the real reason Laleh left? How do you think the news that Laleh created a good life for herself affects the way Soraya thinks about her relationship with Magnus?

ABOUT THE AUTHOR

SARA JAFARI is a London-based British Iranian writer whose work has been longlisted for Spread the Word's Life Writing Prize and published in *gal-dem* and *The Good Journal*. She is a contributor to *I Will Not Be Erased* and the romance anthology *Who's Loving You*. Jafari works as an editor and runs *TOKEN* magazine, which showcases writing and artwork by underrepresented writers and artists. *The Mismatch* is her debut novel.

ABOUT THE TYPE

This book was set in Photina, a typeface designed by José Mendoza in 1971. It is a very elegant design with high legibility, and its close character fit has made it a popular choice for use in quality magazines and art gallery publications.

RANDOM HOUSE BOOK CLUB

Because Stories Are Better Shared

Discover
Exciting new books that spark conversation every week.

Connect
With authors on tour—or in your living room. (Request an Author Chat for your book club!)

Discuss
Stories that move you with fellow book lovers on Facebook, on Goodreads, or at in-person meet-ups.

Enhance
Your reading experience with discussion prompts, digital book club kits, and more, available on our website.

Join our online book club community!

f ⑨ randomhousebookclub.com

Random House Book Club ™

Because Stories Are Better Shared

RANDOM HOUSE